Joan Jonke[…] is a
tireless can[…]tion
Victims of […] with
her son. Sh[…]he is
the author […]vious
Liverpool […]dline:
When One Door Closes, *Man Of The* […] *Home Is Where The Heart Is*, *Stay In Your Own Back Yard* and *Last Tram To Lime Street*.

Also by Joan Jonker

Try a Little Tenderness
Walking My Baby Back Home
The Pride of Polly Perkins
Sadie Was a Lady
When One Door Closes
Man Of The House
Home Is Where The Heart Is
Stay In Your Own Back Yard
Last Tram To Lime Street

Victims Of Violence

Sweet Rosie O'Grady

Joan Jonker

headline

First published in 1996
by HEADLINE BOOK PUBLISHING

First published in paperback in 1996
by HEADLINE BOOK PUBLISHING

20 19 18 17 16

ISBN 0 7472 5374 9

Typeset by Palimpsest Book Production Limited,
Polmont, Stirlingshire

Printed and bound in Great Britain by
Clays Ltd, St Ives plc

HEADLINE BOOK PUBLISHING
A division of Hodder Headline
338 Euston Road
London NW1 3BH

To my many friends for all their support.

And to the people of Merseyside whose humour has helped me write my books.

Chapter One

Nellie McDonough laced her chubby fingers together, then laid her hands flat on the table. 'D'yer know what, girl? If I could get me hands on that Hitler feller, I'd wring his ruddy neck! I was sayin' that to George last night, when we were havin' a quiet talk before we went to bed.' She shook her head in indignation, sending her layers of chins swinging from side to side. 'One man causin' all that trouble, it fair makes me blood boil.'

'I agree with yer, Nellie,' said her friend Molly Bennett. 'I can't understand why someone hasn't bumped him off before now!'

'Put a gun in me hand, point me in the right direction, an' I'll bump him off willingly!' Once again Nellie's chins did a dance. 'Mind you, someone would 'ave to show me how to use the ruddy thing first, otherwise I'd be shootin' me own toes off.'

A smile played around Molly's mouth as she eyed her friend with affection. 'Nellie, isn't it a pity Chamberlain doesn't know about you? 'Cos if he did, all his troubles would be over. All he'd have to do would be to lock yer in an empty room with Hitler just for five minutes, an' there wouldn't be no flamin' war.'

When Nellie grinned, the fat on her cheeks moved upwards to cover her eyes. 'Ye're right there, girl! There wouldn't be no Hitler, either, 'cos I'd pulverize him!'

'Pulverize or marmalize, Nellie, I wouldn't be fussy how

yer did it, as long as yer put him out of action for ever. A flamin' madman, he is! Did yer read in the *Echo* that some mothers are sendin' their kids away to places in the country? It's not natural that, it would break my heart to send our Ruthie away.'

'So even if a war does start, an' evacuatin' becomes compulsory, yer wouldn't let her go?'

'Would I heckers like! I'd never know a minute's peace if I let her go to strangers!' Ruthie was the baby of the family, and because she'd come along seven years after Tommy, the only boy, Molly was inclined to spoil her. 'I mean, how would I know if they were good to her, if she was gettin' enough to eat and if her clothes were being aired off properly?' The very idea sent a shiver down Molly's spine. 'Takin' a child away from her family an' stickin' her in with strangers, it doesn't bear thinkin' about, does it?'

'Don't let's think about it then.' Nellie gazed around the room, a knowing look on her face. 'But before we stop talkin' about it, can I say how jammy yer were, gettin' all this new furniture when yer did? With most of the factories on war work, pretty soon yer won't be able to get furniture for love nor money.'

'I've thought about that meself, Nellie! Jack winning that twenty pounds on the pools was a godsend.' Molly noticed the time and jumped to her feet. 'I've got a few bits of washin' to peg out, so d'yer want to hang on an' we can go up to the shops together? It'll only take me five minutes at the most.'

'No, I'll nip home and peel the spuds.' Nellie spread her hands on the table and pushed herself up. 'I've got me dinner cookin' on a low light. It's ham shank tonight, with onions, vegetables and barley.' She rubbed her tummy and licked her lips. 'Me mouth's waterin' just thinkin' about it.'

Molly gazed with affection at the eighteen-stone woman who lived three doors away. They'd been neighbours for over twenty years, since the day they'd both moved into the street of two-up two-down terraced houses as newly-weds. But over the years they'd become more than just neighbours . . . they were best mates. True, they'd had their fights when the kids were little, but their scraps had always ended up in laughter. They'd always been there for each other, sharing the good times and the bad times. And when the kids were little there were plenty of bad times . . . with not enough money coming in to make ends meet. Molly remembered now the day they'd sat at her table and emptied their purses. Ninepence ha'penny they had between them, and that was to feed two husbands, six children and themselves. Molly was in despair, but Nellie refused to be downhearted. With her basket resting in the crook of her arm, she'd marched down to the shops and come back with the makings of a huge pan of scouse which they shared between the two houses. Admittedly the meat was conspicuous by its absence, but there were no complaints. And for the rest of the week they'd lived on tick from the corner shop. But through it all there had been happiness, laughter and affection. And the bond between the two women had been strengthened a few months ago when Steve, Nellie's eighteen-year-old son, had become engaged to Molly's eldest daughter, seventeen-year-old Jill.

'In the name of God, Nellie, what's wrong with yer stocking? It's all wrinkled round yer ankle like a concertina!'

Nellie tutted. 'It's me flamin' garter, girl, the elastic's gone.' Gripping the back of a chair for support, she lifted her leg. 'I can't see that far down, these get in the way.' She patted her mountainous bosom with the other hand. 'It's years since I saw me feet . . . in fact if it weren't for me corns givin' me gyp, I wouldn't know they were there.'

'Ah, yer poor thing, me heart bleeds for yer.' Molly grinned as she stood up. 'Do somethin' with yer stocking before we next go to the shops, I'd be ashamed to be seen out with yer like that.'

'I'll walk behind yer if yer like.' Nellie drew herself up to her full height, pretending her feelings had been hurt. 'I mean, the last thing in the world I'd want to do is shame yer.'

'Will yer go home, missus, an' let me put me washing out? If we don't get a move on, the shops will be closed for dinner.'

'I'm goin', I'm goin'.' Nellie dropped her eyes to Molly's legs. 'Did yer know yer've got a dirty big ladder in yer stocking?'

Molly lifted her skirt and twisted her leg. 'I can't see a . . .' She glanced up to see the sly smile on Nellie's face. 'Why you . . . you!'

Nellie's chubby face was the picture of innocence. 'I could have sworn I saw a ladder . . . must 'ave been a trick of the light.' She waddled to the door and turned. 'Ever been had, girl?'

'One of these days I'll get me own back on you,' Molly called after her. 'Just you wait an' see if I don't.'

Standing by the front door, Nellie chuckled. 'Yer know, girl, after tryin' for twenty years I think yer deserve to catch me out. Otherwise yer'll be gettin' one of those in . . . infer . . .' She dropped her hand from the latch and walked back along the hall. 'What is it yer get when ye're always losin'?'

Trying to keep a straight face, Molly said, 'Yer mean an inferiority complex?'

Nellie fluttered her eyelashes. 'Aren't I lucky to 'ave an edicated mate? Anyway, we can't have yer gettin' one of them inferiority things 'cos it could be painful.'

Molly picked up a cushion. 'If ye're not out of that door in two ticks, missus, yer'll get this in yer physog.'

When Tony Reynolds caught sight of Molly and Nellie passing the window of his butcher's shop, a huge grin covered his face. Turning to his assistant, Ellen Clarke, he said, 'Ay out, here comes trouble.'

'I heard that!' Molly laughed. 'If ye're not careful, me an' Nellie will take our custom elsewhere.'

'Yeah!' Nellie's chins rippled like waves. 'We'll get the tram into town and get our half of mince from one of the stalls in St John's Market. The fellers down there are always pleasant an' accommodatin', yer wouldn't hear one of them insultin' their customers . . . especially when they're paying cash on the nail.'

Tony slapped an open palm on his forehead, nearly knocking his straw hat off. Feigning horror, he pleaded, 'Don't do that, ladies, please! I'd have to close the shop if you two took yer custom elsewhere.'

'Ay, well, we'll forgive yer this once,' Molly said before smiling at his assistant. 'How's it goin', Ellen?'

'Fine thanks, Molly.' Ellen was Molly's next-door neighbour and had good reason to be eternally grateful to her and Nellie. Married to Nobby Clarke, Ellen's life had been hell. He was a drunkard, gambler and wife beater. She had four children and none of them had known what it was to have a full tummy, decent clothes on their backs, or a fire in the grate. They all lived in fear of the violent man who lashed out with his hands or feet whenever the mood took him. But in the end he'd been his own worst enemy. One day he'd drunk himself into such a stupor he'd walked straight into the path of an oncoming tram. His legs had been so badly mangled they had to be amputated. He was in Walton Hospital for months, and although Ellen knew his violence towards everyone was part and parcel of his make-up, the staff at the hospital put it down to the trauma he'd suffered. Eventually though, he'd been diagnosed as being mentally insane and was now in Winwick Hospital.

They had been dark days for Ellen. With no money and nothing of value to sell, it would have meant the poorhouse for her and the children if these two neighbours hadn't stepped in to help. They'd cadged clothes for her, set her hair, made her face up, then found her two part-time jobs. One had been with Tony, and he'd been so impressed with her work he'd taken her on full-time. It was still hard making ends meet, but at least she had something she'd never had during her years of marriage . . . an easy mind, pride in herself, happy children and laughter in a house that was now a home.

'I think I'll have a tin of corned beef, Tony,' Molly said, pointing to the tins stacked in a pyramid. 'We can have corned beef hash tomorrow night . . . a nice easy meal.'

'I was sayin' to Ellen just before you came in, you ladies would be wise to start buying extra tins of food, getting a little stock in,' Tony said. 'There's bound to be a shortage of food.'

'Oh, ay, moneybags! Who can afford to be buying extra?' Molly turned the tin upside down to make sure the key was attached. The tins were awkward enough to open with the key, but without one they were impossible. If she had a penny for every time she'd cut her hand on the jagged edge of a corned beef tin, she'd be a rich woman.

'It's a good idea, though, isn't it?' Nellie puckered her lips, deep in thought for a few seconds. 'I know a way we could make a few bob . . . we could try our luck down Lime Street!'

'Wishful thinkin', Nellie!' Molly's head fell back and she roared with laughter. 'We'd have to pay the blokes!'

Once again Nellie pondered. Then a smile curved her lips. 'I know . . . we could take Ellen! She's younger than us, an' she doesn't look bad when she's all dolled up.' The big woman's tummy rumbled as a laugh made its way up to her mouth. 'Anyway, we could always find a dark entry, then they wouldn't be able to see what she looks like.'

Ellen's face was the colour of beetroot. Fancy them talking like that in front of her boss! It was enough to make a saint blush! Mind you, it was funny . . . but she'd wait till she got home to laugh about it. 'Don't you two be draggin' me into any of yer crazy schemes.'

'She's an ungrateful bugger, that one,' Nellie huffed. 'Here we are, out of the goodness of our hearts, tryin' to help her make a few bob, and look at the thanks we get! I mean, it's not as though we were expectin' her to go on her own! Me an' Molly would have gone along to help her carry the money, wouldn't we, girl?'

'Shut up, Nellie, ye're makin' the girl blush.' Molly was searching the compartments in her purse. 'I could have sworn I had a shilling, but it's disappeared. Ah, no, here it is.' She held the coin aloft. 'I'll have another tin of that corned beef, Tony. It won't go to waste if there's no war.'

'Oh, there'll be a war, Molly, yer can bank on it.'

Molly was reminded of Tony's words when, three days later, on the first of September, German troops invaded Poland. And two days after that, Britain and France declared war on Germany. Newspaper headlines screamed the news, and solemn-sounding commentators on the wireless issued bulletins throughout each day. Everywhere you went it was the topic of conversation, but because people's lives weren't being affected, they didn't feel as though there was a war on.

But on the eighteenth of September, everyone in the country was jolted out of their complacency when the aircraft carrier HMS *Courageous* was sunk with the loss of five hundred men.

'They didn't stand a chance, blown to smithereens,' Jack snarled through clenched teeth. 'We're supposed to have the best navy in the world – how the bloody hell did it happen?'

'I don't know, love.' Molly could sense Jack's anger. 'Don't get yerself all het up, yer'll make yerself ill.'

'Don't get meself all het up! Molly, five hundred men, the backbone of this country, have been killed . . . or murdered would be more like it.' Jack gave vent to his rage by banging his clenched fists on the arms of his chair. 'And every one of those men has left a family behind, don't forget! A wife, children, mother, girl . . . can yer imagine what they're goin' through right now?'

'They must be goin' through hell,' Molly said softly. 'I don't think I could bear it if it happened to one of mine.'

'By God, that bastard Hitler must think he's hit the jackpot! I bet he's struttin' up and down rubbing his hands in glee.' Jack ran a hand through his mop of dark hair. 'D'yer know, if I was a few years younger I'd join up meself.'

'Over my dead body yer would! I've been thankin' me lucky stars all day that you're too old to be called up, and our Tommy's too young! He's only fifteen, the war will be well over before he's old enough to be conscripted.'

Jack studied his wife's face. This wasn't going to be an easy war, Hitler had been building up his forces for years while the rest of the world looked on and did nothing. And he was a madman, you only had to look at his face to see that. He wouldn't think twice about using gas or germs, anything to achieve the power he craved. But it was no good troubling Molly with his thoughts. He needed a man to talk to, someone he could open up to and use the bad words that came into his head whenever he thought of the goose-stepping maniac. 'Would yer mind if I went out for a pint, love?'

'Why don't yer give George a knock?' Molly understood his mood and Nellie's husband was just the man to meet his needs. 'I'm sure he'd be glad to get out for an hour.'

'I will, if ye're sure yer don't mind.'

'Of course I don't,' Molly smiled, 'as long as yer don't make a habit of it and yer don't stay till chucking-out time.'

Jack was a fine-looking man. Tall, well built, strong face, thick dark hair and melting brown eyes that could make Molly's tummy do somersaults. 'Are yer all right for money?'

Jack grinned. 'As long as George buys his own pint.'

'Hang on a minute.' Molly opened the drawer of the

sideboard and brought out her well-worn purse. 'Here's a tanner . . . pay me back at the end of the week.'

Jack pocketed the sixpence before cupping his wife's face. Gazing into the vivid blue eyes, he said, 'Ye're as pretty as the day I married yer, Molly Bennett. Blonde hair, blue eyes, smashin' figure . . . who could ask for anythin' more?'

Molly grinned into his face. 'They say love is blind. The blonde hair is streaked with grey and the smashing figure went out the door after the children were born. Havin' three babies in three years doesn't do much for a girl's shape, yer know.'

'Are you blaming me for that?'

'Well, it wasn't the feller next door, that's for sure! Mind you, I have to admit I played a part in it. The trouble is, we both liked playin' games too much . . . especially mothers an' fathers.'

'I did give yer a long break between Tommy an' Ruthie though, didn't I? Yer've got to give credit where it's due.'

'Uh-uh, Jack Bennett, don't you be gettin' ideas! I know you, an' if yer don't push off, it won't be up to the pub, it'll be up to bed!'

Jack kissed her full on the lips before dropping his hands. 'You should be happy that yer still have that effect on me after all these years.'

'In case yer've never noticed, I'm not exactly an ice-maiden meself! Me heart's goin' fifteen to the dozen.' Molly gazed at him, loving every bone in his body and every hair on his head. 'But there's a time an' place for everything, and it isn't here and now . . . not with three grown-up children likely to walk in any minute.'

'We'll discuss that later, upstairs.' With a broad wink, Jack made for the door. 'Ta-ra for now.'

'Ask Nellie to come down for half an hour,' Molly called after him, 'she can keep me company.'

'Blimey! Yer've seen her half a dozen times today!' Jack's

head appeared round the door. 'What the heck can the pair of yer find to talk about all the time?'

'Everythin' and everyone.' Molly straightened the chenille cloth covering the table. 'This afternoon we got as far as how many blankets the woman in number two has on her bed.'

Jack raised his brows, feigning astonishment. 'Women! Well, they do say small things amuse small minds.'

'Ay, Mrs Waterman will have your life! Her blankets aren't small, they're all double-sized.'

A deep chuckle came from Jack. 'You've got an answer for everythin', haven't yer?'

'I've also got a ruddy big rolling pin that will be makin' contact with your head if yer don't move.' Molly shook a fist. 'Now skedaddle!'

Jack had only been gone a few minutes when Molly heard the yard door close and looked through the window to see Nellie swaying up the yard.

'My God, you've been quick! Did yer have yer shoes on, ready?'

'I'm not sittin' in the house on me own like one of Lewis's.' Nellie eyed the couch enviously. It looked so comfortable and inviting she almost succumbed to temptation. Then she pursed her lips and told herself that although it looked comfortable and inviting, in reality it was like a flaming mousetrap. Once she got herself down there, they'd have to prise her out. 'The three kids are out and your feller is leading my feller astray down the pub. So when Jack suggested I come down, I didn't need askin' twice.'

'I'll stick the kettle on an' we'll have a nice quiet hour on our own, eh?' Molly ruffled Nellie's already untidy thin, straggly, mouse-coloured hair. 'I hid a packet of custard creams at the back of the larder, where Ruthie couldn't find them, so we'll spoil ourselves.'

'Ay, isn't it lovely an' peaceful?' Nellie reached across to the plate of biscuits. 'It's always so noisy in our 'ouse, yer can't hear yerself think.'

'Jack was askin' me what we found to talk about all the time!'

'Nosy, isn't he?' Nellie dunked the biscuit in her tea. 'What did yer tell him?'

Molly repeated the part of the conversation that wasn't private, ending with the number of blankets on Mrs Waterman's bed.

Nellie tittered as she picked a crumb from her pinny and popped it in her mouth. 'Just out of curiosity, girl, in case someone should ask, like – how many blankets '*as* she got on her bed?'

'Go on, yer daft ha'p'orth! Jack says we're both crazy, an' he's not far off the mark.'

For once Nellie was serious. 'No, girl, we're not crazy. Just because we laugh a lot doesn't mean we haven't got anythin' between our ears. If yer think back to the years when we were so poor we didn't know where the next meal was comin' from, would we ever have made it through those days if we hadn't been able to see the funny side of everythin'?' She lifted her huge bosom and rested it on the table. 'Your feller an' mine have just walked down the road talkin' about the war . . . the terrible things that might happen. An' they're probably right, 'cos it's terrible those poor sailors gettin' blown up.' Nellie made the sign of the cross and sighed deeply. 'I'll lie awake tonight thinkin' of those poor souls an' their families, an' I'll be prayin' for them. An' when yer see me laughin' tomorrow, an' acting the goat, it won't mean I don't care! But if yer can't laugh, girl, or see the happy things in life, then life wouldn't be worth living, would it?'

'Helen Theresa McDonough, yer've got me crying.' Molly wiped a tear with the back of her hand. 'It's not often ye're serious, but when yer are then ye're worth listening to. And you're right, we've got a lot to be thankful for an' we should be counting our blessings.'

'That's the spirit, girl! Now can I have another biscuit because I was that busy talkin', I don't remember eatin' the others.'

Tommy was the first home. At fifteen, he was as tall as his dad and the spitting image of him. Fifteen is an awkward age for a boy . . . too old to play footie or kick the can in the street, and too young for going to dances or taking a girl to the pictures. Not that Tommy wanted to take a girl out: he'd had enough of females with his two elder sisters. Proper nuisances they were, always hogging the sink first so he had to wait to get washed, then preening themselves in front of the mirror so he couldn't even see if his parting was straight when he'd combed his hair. And they were bossy and talked too much. But, having said all that, they were his sisters, and if push came to shove, woe betide anyone who tried to hurt them.

'Been playin' cards at yer mate's, Tommy?' Nellie asked.

'Nah! We're fed up playin' cards, Auntie Nellie, so me an' Ginger went for a walk.' She wasn't really his auntie, but she'd been part of their lives for so long, all the children regarded her as a favourite member of the family. He gave her a wide grin. 'As per usual, we're skint an' happy until pay day.'

'Join the club, son,' Nellie laughed. 'I can't remember a day when I wasn't boracic lint.'

'You shouldn't be so badly off, Nellie!' Molly said. 'You've got all yours working.'

'Huh, hark at her! You've got three workin' as well!'

'Yeah, but I've got Ruthie to feed an' clothe, don't forget.'

'Ay, that's your lookout, girl! Don't be blamin' me for gettin' yer in the family way when yer mind should have been on other things.'

Molly's face flamed and her eyes shot daggers at her friend. Fancy saying that in front of Tommy! But she wasn't the only one embarrassed because Tommy decided it was his bedtime and bade them goodnight.

'Why don't you watch what ye're saying, Nellie McDonough! Fancy sayin' that in front of a fifteen-year-old boy.'

'Oh, ye gods!' Nellie huffed. 'If he doesn't know what it's for at fifteen, then he never will!' She leaned across the table and whispered, 'I bet he knows it's not to stir his tea with.'

Molly tried to look stern but it didn't work and she ended up laughing her head off. 'I don't know what I'm goin' to do with you, Nellie, you're past redemption.'

'What does that mean, girl? I know what past the post means, but yer keep bringin' in these big words an' I don't know whether to feel pleased or insulted.'

They were laughing so much they didn't hear the door open. It was Steve's deep voice that brought them upright. 'Has me mam been at the milk stout again, Mrs B.?'

'Oh, God, yer gave me the fright of me life! I didn't hear yez comin' in.' Molly smiled up at Nellie's son. He was a handsome lad, over six feet tall, dark hair, eyes that changed from hazel to green, a strong square jaw and deep dimples in his cheeks. He had his arm around the waist of her eldest daughter Jill, and Molly thought for the umpteenth time what a lovely couple they made. Next to Jill stood Doreen, the next-to-eldest. The two girls had their mother's colouring, long blonde hair and vivid blue eyes. They were both very attractive with slim figures and long shapely legs. But they had different natures. Jill was gentle and caring, and wouldn't argue if she could avoid it. But Doreen was a different kettle of fish. More outgoing, sure of herself and quick to say what she thought even if it meant a telling-off. Many's the time when she was younger she'd earned herself a cuff round the ear for giving cheek.

'Where's me dad?' Jill asked.

'He's gone boozing with Mr McDonough. An' if he's

not in soon I'm goin' to bolt the front door, the dirty stop-out.'

'Mam.' Doreen's eyes were shining, her face alive and eager. 'Have you heard Glenn Miller on the wireless playing "In the Mood"?'

'Not that I know of.'

'I've heard it,' Steve said, 'it's a crackin' tune.'

'It's all the rage.' Doreen's pretty face was animated. 'Maureen bought the record and we've been listenin' to it on her gramophone. And we've been practising jiving, like we've seen them doin' it at the Grafton.'

'Give us a demonstration,' Jill begged. She couldn't dance herself but admired the poise and grace of her sister. 'Go on, be a sport.'

'No chance!' Doreen blew out a sharp breath. 'I haven't got the hang of it yet 'cos it's not half hard to do. And anyway, yer need a partner for it.'

'Don't look at me!' Steve shook his head. 'Yer know me with me two left feet.'

'What did yer say this song's called?' Nellie asked, her folded arms resting on the ledge made by her tummy.

'"In the Mood".' Doreen started to hum the tune. 'It's great.'

'Funny name for a song . . . "In the Mood". Could mean all sorts of things.' Nellie's eyes slid to the clock on the mantelpiece. 'I mean, our fellers have been out long enough to have supped enough ale to make them in the mood . . . what d'yer say, girl?'

Steve bit his lip to keep himself from laughing, Jill blushed, Doreen raised her brows questioningly, and Molly jumped to her feet.

'That's it, now, everyone . . . time for bed.' She gave Doreen a push in the direction of the stairs, then nodded to Jill. 'See Steve out, sunshine, then turn in.'

'Ah, ray, Mam!' Doreen protested. 'What's the hurry?'

'There's a hurry because I say there's a hurry . . . OK?' The look on her mother's face warned Doreen not to argue and she quickly climbed the stairs.

Molly closed the door and faced Nellie with her hands on her hips.

'Nellie McDonough, yer'll be the death of me yet! Yer've no right to make suggestive remarks in front of the children.'

'Make suggestive remarks! Me!' Nellie put a hand on her heart as she struggled to bring a hurt expression to her face. 'When 'ave I ever said anythin' suggestive in front of the children? Me, what goes to church every Sunday . . . I'd never do a thing like that.'

'You just did!'

'Why, what did I say? Now, come on, what did I say?'

Molly blew her breath out. 'Yer know ruddy well what yer said! That the men might be in the mood when they come in. It doesn't take a brain-box to figure out what yer were insinuating.'

Nellie looked around her as though seeking support from the furniture. 'Molly Bennett, yer've got a bad mind or yer wouldn't 'ave miscon . . . mistru . . . oh, yer wouldn't have taken what I said the wrong way. Only people with bad minds think bad things.'

'The word yer were lookin' for is misconstrued . . . an' I haven't got a bad mind, either! Sometimes I don't know where to put meself, the things you come out with.' But Molly was running out of steam. When it came to acting, her friend could out-act Greta Garbo any day. 'We both know damn well what yer meant when yer said the men might be "in the mood".'

With a look of angelic innocence on her face Nellie said, 'I only meant they might be in the mood for a cup of tea, girl, or a jam butty. What's the harm in that?'

Molly was beaten and she knew it. She couldn't hold out much longer anyway – the laughter was bubbling in her tummy, ready to explode any second. Throwing her hands in the air she said, 'I give up! It's like floggin' a dead horse.'

Nellie preened, and a smile was spreading across her chubby face when they heard the key turn in the lock. She leaned towards Molly and whispered hurriedly, 'You carry on bein' a good, clean-livin' girl, Molly, it'll definitely earn yer a place in heaven. But me, I'm doomed for damnation anyway, so I've nothin' to lose. I'm hopin' my feller's in the mood for more than a ruddy jam butty.'

Jack pushed the front door open and was greeted by peals of laughter. 'Just listen to them,' he said over his shoulder as he slipped the key out of the lock, 'have yer ever known any like that pair in yer life?'

'No, thank God,' George chuckled. 'I don't think the world is big enough for another two like them.'

Chapter Two

'Six more goes, then that's me lot,' Molly muttered through clenched teeth as she plunged the dolly peg up and down on the clothes in the tub. 'If they're not clean by now after bein' in steep all night, they never will be.'

Her muscles aching, she rested her hand on top of the dolly peg and sighed as she watched the heavy rain hitting the window-panes so hard it sounded like small stones. 'The weather's enough to give yer a pain in the backside.' Molly gave voice to her thoughts as she always did when she was alone in the house. Not that she would have cared if anyone was there to hear her because she enjoyed talking to herself. Her reply to anyone who said she was going doolally was that if you wanted an intelligent conversation, then the best person to have it with was yourself. That way there was no argument so you won every time. 'It's me own fault for not takin' notice of Jack. He told me this mornin' when he was goin' out to work that the heavens were goin' to open, an' he was right. But did I take any notice? Did I heckers like! Now I'm lumbered with this lot.'

Molly dallied for a while, thinking that if everything had gone to plan, the washing would be pegged out by now and she'd be scrubbing the front step. It just went to show you should never make plans because nothing was certain in this life . . . especially the flaming weather!

Lifting the dolly peg from the water, Molly held it over the tub for a few seconds until the excess water had dripped off, then she placed it on the floor. 'I'll rinse them out and put them through the mangle, then with a bit of luck the rain might 'ave cleared.' She pulled a face as she put the plug in the sink and turned the tap on. 'Ay, an' pigs might fly.'

The folded washing was piled neatly on the draining board when Molly heard the latch drop on the yard door. 'This'll be Nellie.' She had the door open ready for her friend to dash in out of the rain. 'Wouldn't the weather give yer the flamin' willies?'

'Yer ain't kiddin', girl! It's cats and dogs out there!' The raindrops were trickling from Nellie's hair, down her face, over each of her chins, then disappearing down the neck of her dress to form a pool in the valley between her breasts. 'Me coat an' dress are soppin' wet and me shoes are squelchin'.'

'Give us yer coat an' I'll put it in front of the fire.' Molly couldn't help smiling at the sorry state of her friend. 'I'd ask yer to take yer dress off, but I don't think I could stand the sight of yer nearly naked . . . it might put me off me dinner.'

'Well sod you, Molly Bennett! I'm drenched through to me bones an' now I'm gettin' insults thrown in!' Nellie reached for the towel hanging on a nail behind the kitchen door and rubbed it briskly over her fine hair. 'If ye're hopin' to get yer washin' out, girl, yer can forget it. By the look of those dark clouds there's a lot more rain to come.'

'I could swear.' Molly draped the wet coat over the fireguard and pulled it nearer the fire. 'I was goin' to starch a couple of Jack's shirts and collars, but they'll have to wait . . . see what sort of a day it is tomorrow.'

'Put the kettle on, girl, an' make us a cuppa to warm me up. I'm frozen right through to the marrow.' Nellie watched the steam rising from the coat and tutted. 'If that coat shrinks, it won't go near me! The ruddy thing only fitted where it touched before.'

Molly was standing by the stove, willing the kettle to boil. 'Haven't yer got another one yer can wear?'

'Ooh, listen to moneybags! Who d'yer think I am, girl, a ruddy moneylender?' Nellie hitched up her bosom. 'That coat, which is shrinkin' before me very eyes, is the only one I've got to me name. If it's gone for a burton, I'll have to stay in until the summer comes.'

'Serves yer right!' Molly poured the boiling water into the brown teapot then covered it with a knitted tea cosy. 'I'm fed up tellin' yer to buy an umbrella.'

'Bah!' Nellie growled. 'Nothin' but a flamin' nuisance they are! I've poked more people's eyes out with an umbrella than soft Joe.'

'I've often wondered why there's so many one-eyed people in Liverpool – now I know.' Molly set down two mugs of hot tea. 'Get that down yer, sunshine, it'll warm the cockles of yer heart.'

Nellie sipped gingerly on the piping-hot tea. 'A drop of whisky in this would go down a treat.'

'Ye're in the Bennetts' house, sunshine, not the ruddy Adelphi!' Molly leaned her elbows on the table and curled her hands around the mug to savour the warmth. 'Are yer goin' to the shops?'

'I was goin', 'cos I've got nothin' in for the dinner.' There was a look of dejection on the chubby face that was usually not far from a smile. 'But I can't go now, I've nowt to wear. You'll have to get me shoppin' for me.'

Molly was thoughtful for a while, then she asked, 'Has George still got that black oilskin cape?'

Nellie's brows shot up in surprise. 'What the 'ell made yer think of that?'

'Well, yer could wear it to go to the shops! Don't say it won't fit yer, 'cos a cape will fit anyone.'

'Have yer lost the run of yer senses, girl?' Nellie asked with some spirit. 'I'd be the talk of the neighbourhood if I went out in that thing . . . a right bloody laughing-stock!' Her head went one way, her chins the other. 'I'd look like a pregnant penguin!'

Molly put the cup down before she roared with laughter. In her mind's eye she could see Nellie waddling down the street in the black cape, and, yes, she did look like a pregnant penguin. But she wasn't going to tell her mate that. 'Since when have you worried what yer look like just to go to the shops? Gettin' fussy in yer old age, aren't yer?'

'Say what yer like, girl, but I ain't walking out with that thing flappin' round me ankles.'

'Have yer ever tried it on?'

'Not ruddy likely!'

'Then how d'yer know what yer'll look like? An' no one is goin' to take a blind bit of notice of yer anyway; they'll be too busy dashin' to get home out of the rain.'

'Why can't you get me shoppin' for me? I'd do it for you willingly if yer were in the state I'm in.'

'Ah, ray, Nellie! Miss Clegg will probably want a few things, I've got me own shoppin' to get, an' I've only got one pair of hands.' Molly lowered her voice and coaxed, 'Go an' get the oilskin and try it on. I promise I'll tell yer if yer look a nit in it.'

Nellie glanced at the window. 'It's still teemin' down.'

'Yer can put me coat over yer shoulders an' I'll lend yer me umbrella. One of the spokes is broken but it'll keep the rain off yer.'

While Nellie was away, Molly searched under the chair cushions until she found an old newspaper. Then she picked out a few pieces of coal from the coal scuttle, placed them carefully on top of the glowing embers, pulled the damper out and held a sheet of the newspaper in front to try and coax some life into the fire. Holding the piece of paper with one hand, she felt her friend's coat with the other. 'Oh, lord, it's soppin' wet! It'll take a month of Sundays to dry out over the fireguard. It needs hangin' up to dry out proper.'

Molly peeped over the top of the paper and was gratified to see a few flames licking around the new pieces of coal. 'I'll give it another few minutes, then I'll nip up and get a coat hanger.'

When Nellie came back she was holding the black oilskin cape at arm's length, a look of disgust on her screwed-up face. 'If yer think I'm goin' out in this, yer've got another think comin'. I'd be the talk of every ruddy wash-house from here to the Pier Head.'

'Let's just wait and see, eh?' Molly pointed to the door leading to the lobby. 'Look, I've hung yer coat up, it'll dry out quicker like that. When we go out we'll close all the doors to keep the room warm, then tonight yer can leave it hanging in your livin' room. It should be well dried out by the mornin'.'

When Nellie didn't answer, Molly took the cape from her. 'Let's see what it looks like on me.' She shivered as the cold material fell about her shoulders. 'By the stripes, it's cold enough to freeze the you-know-what off a brass monkey.' After fastening the studs down the front, she did a little twirl. 'Well, how do I look?'

'Only half as stupid as I'd look in it.'

'Oh, don't be so miserable, Nellie McDonough! Yer've got nowt else, so it's any port in a storm.' Molly slipped the cape off and handed it to her friend. 'Go 'ed, have a try.'

But Nellie's efforts were so half-hearted Molly got exasperated. 'Move yer hands out of the way an' let me do it. We'll be here all day at this rate.'

Molly stood back to inspect the end result, wishing the words pregnant penguin wouldn't keep coming into her head. But the description fitted Nellie better than any she could come up with. Her friend looked so woebegone, though, Molly wasn't about to say anything to upset her. 'There yer are, what's wrong with that? An' look, it's got slits for the arms . . . I didn't notice them before.'

'Molly, I'd slit me ruddy throat before I'd go out in it.' Nellie ground her teeth. 'If you don't think it looks ridiculous, then you wear it an' I'll wear your coat loose across me shoulders.'

'OK, you win!' Molly threw up her hands in surrender. 'I'll get yer shoppin' in! It'll mean two journeys, mind, 'cos I'll never carry everythin' in one go on account of holdin' me umbrella.'

Her face set in childlike innocence, Nellie asked, 'What d'yer need yer umbrella for, girl?'

'What the hell d'yer think I need me umbrella for, yer daft article? To keep the flamin' rain off me, that's what!'

'Oh, has it started to rain again? It wasn't rainin' when I went home before.'

Molly was stunned into silence. Her eyes slid to the window then back to her friend. 'You rotten thing! Yer've been havin' me on all this time?'

'Oh, not all the time, girl! I mean, I didn't ask the woman next door to aim her hosepipe at yer window so yer'd think it was rainin'. An' much as I like a laugh, I didn't throw a bucket of water over meself so I'd be soaked to the skin.' Nellie laid the oilskin cape over the back of a chair before hitching up her mountainous bosom. 'No, I'll not take credit I haven't earned. I'm an honest woman, as yer know, an' I won't tell no lies. I've only been pullin' yer leg since I went back home for that ruddy cape.' Laughter rumbled in her chest but she managed to keep it at bay. She could read Molly like a book, and knew that right now her friend was searching her mind for a way to save her face and also wreak revenge. Her pride wouldn't let Nellie get away scot-free.

'I'm not gettin' yer shoppin' for yer, so there!' Even as the words left her mouth Molly realized how pathetic and childish they sounded. But they were the best she could think of at such short notice. 'Ye're so flamin' clever, get it yerself.'

'I don't blame yer one little bit, girl! If I was in your shoes I'd say the same thing! It was a lousy trick, pullin' yer leg like that.' Nellie brushed an imaginary speck off her brown, hand-knitted cardigan. 'I know it's not your fault, girl, 'cos none of us can help the way God made us. But it's a great pity He didn't see fit to give yer a sense of humour. 'Cos if He had, yer'd have died laughin' if yer'd seen the look on yer face when yer were tellin' me that ruddy cape looked OK on me. Yer make a rotten liar, girl.'

'I don't know how I can be a rotten liar when I've been mates with you for twenty years, 'cos you're the biggest liar on God's earth!' Molly pinched her bottom lip and turned her head slightly so Nellie couldn't see her weakening. 'Yer'd think in all that time I'd have picked up some of your bad habits.'

Nellie slapped her forehead with an open palm. 'Now yer mention habits, it's reminded me of what yer looked like in that ruddy cape! Yer looked like a nun!'

Molly blessed herself as her eyes rolled to the ceiling. 'She doesn't mean no harm, God, so don't take no notice of her.'

'Listen, girl, if anyone's got a sense of humour, it's Him up there. Where d'yer think I get all me tricks from?'

'Nellie McDonough, I don't know what I'm goin' to do with you!' Molly glanced at the clock and got a shock when she saw it was nearly twelve. 'Ay, I'll have to get a move on, missus, or the shops will be closed for dinner.' She opened a drawer in the sideboard and rooted until she found one of Ruthie's pencils and a scrap of paper. 'While I'm combing me hair an' puttin' me coat on, write what messages yer want down on that. An' I hope yer've got some money with yer 'cos I've only got a few bob.'

Nellie's tongue flicked out to lick the end of the pencil,

while she patted the pocket in her cardigan. 'I've never forgot what I learned in the scouts . . . always be prepared.'

Molly opened her mouth to say only boys could be scouts, but shut it quickly when she realized that that was just what Nellie was expecting her to say. Feeling pleased with herself, she hummed softly as she combed her hair in front of the mirror. She was learning . . . that was one trap she hadn't fallen into.

Victoria Clegg was peeping through her net curtains when Molly and Nellie came out of the house opposite. They were arguing in a good-natured way, and the old lady couldn't help smiling when Molly gave Nellie a playful push. It must be nice to have such a close friend, Victoria thought wistfully. She'd never had a real friend in her life. There had been a boy once . . . oh, she must have been in her early twenties if her memory served her right. But being an only child she'd put her duty to her parents first and the romance fizzled out through lack of commitment on her part. She'd loved her parents very much and had devoted her life to them until they died. It was only when she was left alone that she realized she had no one in the world . . . no kith nor kin, or any friends. But she hadn't minded living on her own: she had plenty to occupy her time, what with the housework and the shopping. And for company she had her beloved wireless.

Nellie's bawdy laughter brought Victoria away from her memories. Anyone who didn't know the two friends would think they spent their time laughing and joking, without a care in the world. But Victoria had reason to know that behind all the smiles and jokes were two kind and caring people . . . the salt of the earth, her father would have called them.

Last year, at the age of eighty-six, she'd had a stroke and really thought she was going to die. In fact she probably would have if Molly, Nellie and her next-door neighbour, Mary Watson, hadn't stepped in to care for her. The stroke had left her paralysed in her right arm and she'd been afraid she'd end up lying in hospital until the good Lord took her. Instead, her life had become more full than it had ever been. Every day one of the three women would call and get her shopping in, help with the housework and bring her a hot dinner. They took it in turns, and today was Molly's day.

Victoria let the curtain fall when she heard the friends shouting 'ta-ra' to each other. She didn't need to open the door because Molly had a key to let herself in.

'Mornin', sunshine!' Molly came in bright and breezy. 'Did yer notice I didn't say "Good morning", 'cos it's ruddy well not!'

Victoria smiled. Molly's presence was like a breath of fresh air in the room. 'It's not very pleasant, is it?'

'Nah, it's lousy! But Nellie cheered me up, she's had me in stitches.' Molly giggled. 'I don't know why I'm laughin' 'cos the joke was on me, as per usual, but honest to God she is so funny.'

'What was she on about this time?'

'Can I tell yer later, sunshine? I want to get to the shops before they close. Have yer got yer list ready?'

'I only want a small tin loaf and a quarter of butter.' Victoria couldn't let Molly go without asking the question that was uppermost in her mind. 'Has Doreen had a letter from Phil?'

Molly shook her head. 'None came through the letter-box. But she sometimes meets the postman on her way to the tram, so she might have got one off him.'

'He's coming home next Monday on two weeks' leave.' The old lady's eyes were bright with excitement. 'Isn't that good news?'

'It sure is, kiddo! Our Doreen will be like a dog with two tails.' Molly noticed one of the buttons was loose on her navy-blue stroller coat and made a mental note to get the needle and cotton out when she got home. If she lost the button she'd never get one exactly the same, so she'd either have to sew an odd one on or fork out for a set of four.

'I won't be long, Victoria.' Molly smiled fondly at the old lady. She was the oldest resident in the street and everyone respected her. She was a real lady, was Miss Victoria Clegg. Never been known to raise her voice or have cross words with a living soul, and in all the time she'd known her, Molly had never heard her use a swear-word, not even a mild one. 'I'll have a quick cup of tea with yer when I've done the shopping, and we'll have a little natter. How about that, eh?'

Victoria followed her to the door. 'I'll put the kettle on the hob, then it won't take long to boil when yer get back.' She put her hand on Molly's arm. 'Phil came into our lives in a strange way, but I thank God every night that he did. He writes every day as he promised and I don't half look forward to his letters. Makes getting out of bed worth while.'

'They say truth is stranger than fiction, sunshine.' Molly could see the old lady wanted to talk, but if she didn't put a move on she'd miss the shops. She bent to kiss the wrinkled face. 'We'll talk about it when I get back, eh?'

Armed with her shopping list, Molly set off at a brisk rate. The Maypole first, then Waterworth's and the butcher's last. With her basket tucked in the crook of her arm and her routine mapped out in her mind, Molly's thoughts went to what Victoria had said about it being strange the way Phil Bradley had come into their lives. It was strange all right, but it had turned out to be a blessing to both families. And particularly to Miss Clegg, who, in offering him a bed for the night when he was in need, had gained the family she'd never had. She and the young man had become devoted to each other and he'd made her home his home.

And as for our Doreen, Molly thought as she pushed open the door of the Maypole, well, she thinks Phil is Clark Gable, Alan Ladd, Spencer Tracy and Gary Cooper all rolled into one. And she wasn't far wrong, either, Molly decided as she felt in her pocket for the shopping list. He was a cracker of a lad, and she could see why her daughter had fallen for him.

'Hello, Molly.' Peggy, the young assistant, approached. 'What can I do yer for?'

'I'll get Nellie's first, then I won't get mixed up with the money. She wants a half of marge, a quarter of brawn and a quarter of loose tea. An' will yer be a pal, Peggy, an' write the prices on everythin'?'

Molly leaned on the counter, and as she watched the assistant pouring the tea from a scoop into a cone-shaped bag, she wondered what to get for the family's dinner. It was a worry every day trying to think of something they all liked. She made up her mind quickly: sausage, egg and mashed potato were a safe bet, the whole family were partial to that. Even Ruthie, who was more fussy about her food than the other children had ever been. Mind you, Molly had to admit, it was her fault for spoiling her youngest child. Times were harder when the others were her age; they had to eat what they were given and like it . . . it was that or go hungry.

'The brawn was a bit over, Molly.' Peggy pushed Nellie's groceries across the counter. 'That comes to one and tuppence.'

'I'm sure my mate's pulled a fast one on me.' Molly was scrutinizing Nellie's list. 'She's a right bloody crafty Clara! Three shillings and sixpence she gave me, saying it was plenty. An' look at her flamin' list! Apart from what she's got down from Waterworth's, she wants five mutton chops and a pound of suet! I'll never get all that on the two shillings and fourpence I'll have left.' The hand holding the list started to shake as she let out a throaty chuckle. 'Just look what she's written on the bottom, Peggy! "Yer can have a penny for yerself for going".'

Peggy let out a high-pitched laugh. 'She's a real case is Mrs McDonough.'

She glanced down the counter to where the manager was

serving a customer. 'She even had old misery-guts laughin' the last time she came in, an' that takes some doin', believe me! Even the Three Stooges can't make him crack his face.'

'That's nothin'! D'yer know Father O'Connor from the church down the road?' Molly waited for a nod, then continued. 'Well yer know how surly he is, always in a bad temper. Yer never see people sittin' in the pews outside his confessional box . . . they're all terrified of him. Apart from gettin' a lecture off him about the doors of hell bein' open to yer if yer don't mend the error of yer ways, he gives yer six times more Hail Marys and Our Fathers for penance than any of the other priests.

'Anyway, I went to confession with Nellie the other week and when she saw all the people waitin' for Father Kelly, she said she hadn't got all night so she'd go to Father O'Connor. An' I had to go with her, there was nothin' else I could do. But I made her go in first . . . I thought if she came out in a huff, I'd move down to the next confessional box even if she wouldn't wait for me an' I had to walk home on me own in the dark.

'The church was deadly quiet, yer know what it's like, yer can hear a pin drop. The only sound I could hear was me heart pounding with fear. Then suddenly I heard Nellie's chuckle, followed by a loud cackle from Father O'Connor! Every head in the church turned – there was such a look of amazement on all the faces yer'd have thought we'd witnessed a miracle. An' d'yer know what, Peggy? To this day I've never been able to get out of Nellie what she'd said to make him laugh.'

'Go 'way!' Peggy shook her head. 'As I said, she's a case.'

'She's more than that, she's the one who puts the sunshine in my life. I don't know what I'd do without her.' Molly pushed the slip of paper into her pocket – she'd show it to Jack later to give him a laugh. 'Now, Peggy, I want a quarter of butter for Miss Clegg. And don't let me talk any more, or I'll miss the shops.'

Chapter Three

From the upstairs front bedroom window, Victoria had watched for her neighbour's return. When she'd seen Molly turn into the street laden down with shopping, the old lady had descended the narrow stairs as quickly as she could to lift the kettle from the hob and pour the boiling water into the teapot. Now they were sitting at the table enjoying a refreshing brew out of china cups which had belonged to Victoria's mother and which she treasured. 'Molly, d'you think Doreen could do something with my hair?' Her eyes were shy as they peered above the rim of the cup. 'I can only manage to comb it myself and it always looks a mess. I do so want to look my best for Phil coming home.'

Molly placed the delicate cup carefully in the saucer then smiled at the old lady. 'Yer know, sunshine, if I didn't know better, I'd think yer were settin' yer cap at young Phil.'

Victoria returned her smile. 'I'll be honest with you . . . if I was seventy years younger I'd be trying to push your Doreen's nose out of joint.'

Her head tilted to one side, Molly gazed at the fine white hair. 'What d'yer want doin' to it? Our Doreen's not a hairdresser, yer know.'

'She's so clever with her own, though, isn't she? Every time I see her she's got it in a different style.'

Molly chuckled. 'That's because she changes it every time she goes to the pictures! Sometimes when she walks in I think it's a stranger come to the wrong house! It could be Veronica

Lake with her hair combed forward to cover one eye, Joan Crawford with a page-boy, or even Mae West with all her hair piled up on top in curls! But she's got the hair to do it with, sunshine, an' for the life of me I can't see you gettin' away with any of them styles.'

'Oh, I wasn't thinking of anything so ambitious, Molly, I know I haven't got the hair for it. I thought perhaps if it was parted down the middle and combed away from my face, it could be pinned into a bun at the back of my neck.'

Molly leaned her elbows on the table and cupped her face in her hands. For a few seconds she stared at the head of hair in question, then she closed her eyes and let her imagination take over. 'Yeah, it would probably suit yer!' Carried away now, she asked eagerly, 'I don't suppose yer've got a pair of earrings, have yer?'

'I've got about a dozen pairs, but they're very old. Some of them belonged to my mother and the rest I bought when I was working. But it's years since I've even looked at them, never mind worn them.'

Molly rubbed her hands in excitement. 'I'll get our Doreen to do yer up like a dog's dinner. Ooh, I can't wait! It'll be the first time yer see Phil in his soldier's uniform, an' the first time he's seen how glamorous you can be.'

Victoria looked apprehensive. 'I don't want to look like mutton dressed as lamb, Molly!'

'Don't be daft!' Molly patted her hand. 'Just you get yer bits of jewellery out an' leave the rest to me an' our Doreen.' She scraped back her chair. 'I'll have to go, sunshine, it's my turn to pick Ruthie an' Bella up from school an' I've got stacks to do before then.' Bella was the daughter of Mary Watson, Victoria's next-door neighbour, and the two girls were inseparable. 'I'll send our Doreen over tonight and yer can have a chin-wag with her.' Reaching the door Molly turned, a huge grin on her bonny face. 'If she's had a letter from Phil, she'll be that thrilled she'll leg it over here without being asked.'

'Oh dear,' Victoria put a hand to her mouth, 'I didn't pay you for my shopping! Will you wait till I get my purse?'

'No, leave it an' pay me tomorrow.' Molly stepped into the street as the door to the Watsons' opened and Mary appeared. 'Hiya, Mary!'

'I knew yer were in there, an' I've been listening for sounds of yer leaving.' Mary Watson was in her mid-thirties, a nice-looking woman with a slim figure, auburn-coloured hair, hazel eyes and a ready smile. 'I want to ask yer a big favour.'

'If it's a loan ye're after, I charge half a crown in the pound interest,' Molly joked. 'An' that's only for a week – me charges go up after that.'

'It's a bigger favour than that.' Mary played nervously with the bow at the neck of her blouse. 'I wondered if yer'd have Bella for a couple of hours? I'd like to slip down to me mam's to see how she is . . . she hasn't been too well lately.'

'Good God, is that all! Considerin' our Ruthie practically lives in your 'ouse, I can hardly refuse, can I? Of course I'll have Bella.'

'I know I've got a cheek, but would yer keep her straight from school an' give her some dinner? Harry's workin' overtime, he won't be in until after eight, so if I go now it'll give me a few hours to do a bit of housework for me mam.'

'Bella will be all right with us, so don't be worryin',' Molly told her while mentally counting how many sausages she'd got in her basket. Then she decided it wasn't worth troubling herself about. None of them would starve if they got half a sausage less on their plate. 'An' there's no need to hurry back, either.'

'Oh, I won't be that late, I've got to get home to see to a meal for Harry. He only takes a few sarnies for his carry-out, so he'll need something substantial after workin' twelve hours.'

The wind was cold and Molly pulled up the collar of her coat to cover her ears. 'Yer can go with an easy mind over

Bella, she'll be fine with us.' Molly noticed Victoria was still standing at the front door and she shook a finger at her. 'Get in by the fire or yer'll be catchin' ruddy pneumonia.'

'Ta-ra, Molly.'

'Ta-ra, sunshine.' Molly began to cross the cobbled street. 'Ta-ra Mary, an' don't forget what I've told yer . . . don't worry!'

But she knew Mary would worry. Bella was her only child and she was frightened of the wind blowing on her. Still, I suppose I'd be the same if I only had one, Molly told herself as she slipped the key in the lock.

She carried the basket through to the kitchen and started to transfer the groceries on to the draining board. She couldn't imagine only having one child. 'I call my four fit to burn, sometimes,' she told the bag of sugar, 'but I wouldn't part with one of them.' To the packet of margarine she said, 'I love them so much I could eat them.'

When she picked the packet of sausages out of the basket, she gave a loud chuckle. 'Now if you'd been a nice cream cake, or a quarter of lean boiled ham, I might have told yer how much I love my husband . . . but even I'm not daft enough to discuss my personal life with a pound and a half of ruddy sausages! So there!'

Ruthie and her friend were sitting at the table playing a game of snakes and ladders. They'd been playing peacefully but Bella's quick eyes noticed a wrong move. 'You only threw a four, but yer've moved five places.' She gave Ruthie such a dig in the ribs she nearly sent her flying off the chair. 'Ye're a cheat, that's what yer are, Ruthie Bennett!'

'I didn't move five, I only moved four!' Ruthie's pixie face, beneath the thick fringe, was set in stubborn lines. 'Yer weren't watchin' proper.'

'I was too!' Bella poked a finger at the board. 'Yer should

have gone down that snake, but yer cheated an' went up that ladder.'

In the kitchen Molly was mashing the potatoes, a smile on her face. Not for one second did she doubt that her daughter had cheated. But Bella was just as bad when it came to cheating: it was a case of who got caught out first. They'd been pals since they were babies and their quarrels were never carried over to the next day. Bella with the dark features of Mary, and Ruthie with the fairness of her mother and two sisters, were destined to be lifelong friends.

Molly went back to her mashing with an ear cocked. If things started to get out of hand she'd soon put a stop to it.

'Put that counter back where it should be,' Bella insisted. 'Go on, down the ladder an' down the snake.'

'I won't!' Ruthie's mouth was set.

'Yer will too, or I won't play with yer any more.' Bella was equally firm.

'Don't then! See if I care.'

Bella moved away from the table and sat back in the chair. 'I don't care either, 'cos ye're a cheat.'

'An' you're a cry-baby.'

In the kitchen Molly speared a sausage with the prongs of a fork and turned it over in the frying pan. Was it time to intervene, or should she wait and see if they kept to their usual pattern? She decided to leave it a while longer.

Ruthie gazed at the offending red counter on a square at the top of a ladder. Silently, her pink tongue sticking out of the side of her mouth, she considered the options open to her. She couldn't play on her own, that option was out. And she wasn't going to admit she cheated, so that was out too! Pretending to scratch her head, Ruthie's eyes slid sideways to where her friend was sitting, looking miserable but still determined. 'I'll tell yer what.'

Bella's face lit up and she sat forward and leant on the table. 'What?'

'You can 'ave two throws of the dice.'

'Yeah, OK!' Satisfied that justice had been done, Bella picked up the eggcup and shook it. 'An' next time I cheat, I'll let you 'ave two throws.'

'Mam, there's someone at the door.'

'Open it for us, sunshine, I've got me hands full. It'll only be Auntie Ellen.'

Molly came from the kitchen wiping her hands on the corner of her pinny. 'D'yer know, Ellen, it's been one of those days where I haven't sat down but don't seem to have done a damn thing! It was the flamin' weather this mornin', put a jinx on the whole day.'

Ellen called in every night on her way home from work. She only ever stayed a few minutes because her four children would be waiting for their dinner. Her eldest, Phoebe, was twelve now, and well able to take care of the others until she got home. She was a sensible girl, didn't have to be told what to do, just got on with it. Right now, the pan of scouse Ellen had made last night would be heating slowly on the stove ready for her to dish out. 'Molly, have yer thought about the blackout curtains we've all got to have?'

'Thought about it, yes, but haven't done anythin' about it. I think it's ruddy diabolical . . . black curtains, gas masks, and no street lights! I don't know what the world's coming to.'

'It's goin' to be compulsory in a few weeks.' Ellen always looked nervous, as though she was ready to bolt any minute. It was a legacy her husband had left her with. She had improved a lot since he'd been away, but old habits die hard. 'Anyone without them will be fined.'

'I know, me an' Nellie were talkin' about it the other day. I'll get Jack to measure all the windows an' see how much material we'll need.'

'How much d'yer think it'll cost?' Ellen had to count every penny and this was an expense she could ill afford.

'I haven't a clue.' Molly felt deeply for Ellen, but pity was the last thing her neighbour wanted, so Molly didn't give it. 'You'll need the same as me an' Nellie, so we'll get yours if yer like. We'll look around for the cheapest – T. J. Hughes or Blackler's will probably be the best bet. An' our Doreen will run them up for yer on the machine when she's doin' ours.'

Ellen rubbed a hand across her tired eyes. 'I'll have to miss the rent one week to pay for it.'

'Mr Henry won't mind, yer can pay an extra shillin' a week until yer make it up.'

Ruthie had been listening with interest. 'Why 'ave we got to have black curtains, Mam? They'll look 'orrible.'

'Because a lot of men who should know better are playin' silly beggars, that's why. But it won't be for long, sunshine, so don't worry yer head about it. Get back to yer snakes an' ladders and finish the game before I need to set the table.'

'I'll get home.' Ellen wrapped her coat closer around her thin body. 'Yer won't forget, will yer, Molly?'

'I couldn't even if I wanted to – Jack's at me about it every night. No, I won't forget, Ellen, I promise. An' I'll get our Doreen to run them up while she's doin' mine and Nellie's.'

'Did I hear my name mentioned?' Doreen came through the door bringing the cold air in with her. 'What have yer got me doin' now, Mam?'

'Makin' blackout curtains for us. I told Ellen yer wouldn't mind doin' hers as well.' Molly's eyes dared her daughter to refuse. 'Yer will do them, won't yer, sunshine?'

'Yeah, they won't take long.' Doreen had learned to use a sewing machine at Johnson's Dye Works, where she'd been employed since leaving school. She made all her own clothes, and Molly hadn't had to buy dresses for herself or Ruthie for a couple of years.

'Thanks, Doreen.' When Ellen smiled her whole face was transformed. 'I'll see yer tomorrow, Molly . . . ta-ra.'

Doreen waited until she heard the front door close, then turned to her mother. 'Guess what, Mam?'

'Phil's coming home on Monday, on two weeks' leave.'

'Oh, I suppose Miss Clegg told yer? She's taken the wind out of me sails, I wanted to surprise yer.'

'She couldn't keep that news to herself, she's too excited.' Molly patted Ruthie on the head. 'Time to clear the table, dinner's ready.' She motioned for Doreen to follow her into the kitchen, saying softly, 'Little pigs have big ears.'

While setting the plates out, Molly told her daughter about the old lady's wish to change her hairstyle for when Phil came home. 'I told her yer'd go over tonight, so will yer?'

'Yeah, 'course I will!' Doreen nodded, setting her long blonde hair bouncing about her shoulders. 'I promised Phil I'd keep an eye on her. An' Maureen's coming about eight o'clock, so she'll have the two of us to keep her company.'

Molly looked pleased. 'Oh, she'll like that! She must get lonely, on her own all the time now that Phil's away, so she'll be glad of someone to talk to.' Spooning some mashed potato on to a plate, Molly winked broadly at her daughter. 'D'yer know what she told me? If she was seventy years younger, she'd give yer a run for yer money.'

Doreen's wink was just as broad. 'If that's the way she feels I'd better make a mess of her hair, then, hadn't I? I don't want no competition.'

The dinner was over and the dishes washed when Mary came to collect Bella. 'Has she behaved herself?'

Molly glanced at the two upturned faces, waiting wide-eyed for what she had to say. They looked as though butter wouldn't melt in their mouths: nobody would have dreamed that just five minutes earlier they'd been going at it ding-dong over who was higher in the class at sums. Jack was settled in his easy chair smoking a Woodbine, and she grinned at him before answering Mary. 'They've been as good as gold, the pair of them . . . haven't they, Jack?'

Jack thought that if Molly could stretch the truth, he'd stretch it even further. 'They've been that quiet I'd forgotten they were here.'

'Then our Bella must be sickening for something.' Mary gave a knowing smile. 'Anyway, sweetheart, let's get yer home, washed and in bed before yer dad comes in from work.'

'Aw, Mam, can I just stay for another five minutes?' After the glowing reference her friend's parents had given her, Bella thought she was in with a chance. 'Please?'

'Uh-uh! Get yer coat on – pronto!'

'Come on, sunshine,' Molly urged, 'Ruthie's goin' to bed now.'

When Mary had left, dragging her daughter behind her, Tommy emerged from the kitchen where he'd been getting washed. 'Mam, yer can't half tell 'em! They're little horrors, the pair of them!'

'We are not!' Ruthie pulled out her tongue at him. 'Me mam and dad said we'd been good, so there!'

Molly pinched the bridge of her nose. 'Don't start! It hasn't been the best of days an' I'd like a bit of peace an' quiet . . . it's not too much to ask, is it? You, Tommy, are old enough, big enough an' ugly enough to know better. So get yerself out an' up to Ginger's.'

She turned to her daughter just in time to see the little pink tongue flick out in the direction of her brother. 'Right, that does it! In the kitchen, yer cheeky madam, an' get stripped. I'll be out in a minute to wash yer down, an' if yer give me any lip I'll be using the scrubbing brush on yer.'

As meek as a lamb, Ruthie left the table. But on her way to the kitchen she had to pass her brother and she couldn't resist the temptation to kick him in the shin.

'Ow, ow, ow!' Tommy lifted his leg and rubbed vigorously. 'Mam, did yer see what she did?'

Her hands on her hips, her face red, Molly leaned towards her husband. 'Jack, will yer put yer foot down with these two? An' don't tell me yer've been workin' hard, 'cos I haven't exactly been sitting on me backside all day, either!'

One look from his dad and Tommy was out of the door before you could say Jack Robinson. 'D'yer want me to see to Ruthie?'

'No, I'll give her a quick rub-down. She'll be in bed in five minutes, then I can sit down an' put me feet up.'

'The girls are takin' long enough to get ready.' Jack took a last puff before throwing his cigarette stump in the fire. 'They've been up there for half an hour.'

'They're no different to other girls,' Molly said wearily. 'I was the same meself at their age.' There was a droop in her shoulders as she walked to the kitchen. 'It's been a day an' a half, all right. I'm that tired, I feel as though I've scrubbed every inch of the Empire Theatre all by meself.'

'Don't tackle a job like that on yer own,' Jack chuckled, 'take Nellie with yer next time.'

Molly popped her head round thc door. 'I'll tell yer later about the stunt Nellie pulled on me today . . . yer'll laugh yer socks off.'

Jack reached for the unopened *Echo*, then sat back in his chair feeling relieved. Once his wife started talking about Nellie, she'd be smiling again. And that's the way it should be . . . she didn't seem properly dressed without a smile on her still pretty face.

'Hello, Mrs Bennett . . . Mr Bennett!' Maureen Shepherd laid her bag on the table and rubbed her arms briskly. 'It's freezin' out.'

'Come an' stand by the fire, Mo, an' yer'll soon get warm.' Molly pushed her chair back to make room for Doreen's friend. They'd both started work on the same day at Johnson's and had been firm friends since. This had pleased Molly because Maureen was a sensible girl and a good influence on Doreen, who was inclined to be outspoken and impulsive.

Maureen stood with her back to the fire and lifted her coat, feeling the warmth travel up her legs. She was an attractive girl with dark chestnut-coloured hair cut in a short bob around her face, large brown eyes set beneath perfectly arched brows, flashing white teeth and a bubbly personality. 'Isn't Doreen ready?'

'Yeah, she won't be a minute, she's just gone down the yard.' Molly looked down at Mo's high-heeled shoes and shook her head. 'It's no wonder ye're freezin' in them things! Ye're just like our Doreen . . . it's a miracle yez don't catch yer death of cold. Haven't yer got a sturdy pair of shoes?'

'Molly, will yer leave the girl alone?' Jack peered over the top of the paper. 'Yer'll be tellin' her what to eat next.'

'I don't mind, Mr Bennett.' Maureen flashed a brilliant smile. 'I had a lecture off me mam before I came out.'

'Ay, an' I bet yer took as much notice of her as my daughter does of me,' Molly said. 'It's like talkin' to the flamin' wall.'

There was a rustling of paper as Jack laid the *Echo* on his knees. 'I remember your mam saying the same thing about you, oh, it must have been all of twenty years ago.'

'Oh, here he goes, got to get his twopenny's-worth in.' Molly's tone was light-hearted because she too was remembering. 'He's determined to pick a nark with me tonight.'

Just then the kitchen door banged and Doreen came in, her arms wrapped tightly about her body. 'I wish we had an inside lavvy.' She was shivering from head to toe, her nose and cheeks glowing pink. 'It's ridiculous havin' to go down the yard in this weather.'

'They say if yer wish for somethin' hard enough, then yer wish comes true.' Molly pulled her chair back to let Doreen near the fire. 'But I don't think yer stand much chance of yours comin' true . . . it's either a quick run down the yard or a chamber-pot under the bed.'

'Mam!' Doreen was mortified. 'Fancy sayin' that!'

'I know, I'm as common as muck.' Molly grinned. 'I wasn't brought up, yer see girl, I was dragged up.'

'I wonder what your mother would have to say about that?' Jack folded the paper and threw it on the couch. Every page you turned was full of war news, and in the end it made you feel down in the dumps. 'I'll mention it to her next time I see her.'

'You needn't bother, I'm goin' round there when I've rested me legs for ten minutes, so I'll tell her meself.'

Jack looked surprised. 'Yer didn't say yer were going out.'

'I've only just made up me mind.' Molly pinched Doreen's backside. 'Come on, you've had a warm, get yerselves over to Miss Clegg's.'

While she was putting her coat on and wrapping a muffler round her neck, Doreen told her friend what the old lady wanted her for.

'That's great!' Maureen's face lit up. 'I'll help yer do her hair – we can try a few styles, see what suits her best.'

Chattering away, they walked down the lobby and Molly smiled across at Jack. 'Those two are goin' to be like me an' Nellie . . . mates for life.'

'Yer were goin' to tell me somethin' about Nellie; what was it?'

Molly stared into the flames, her lips curling into a smile as in her mind she quickly relived the scene. 'Have yer ever seen that black oilskin cape of George's?' When Jack nodded, she said, 'Well I'll start at the beginning. Yer know what a mornin' it was, the flamin' rain was lashin' down . . .'

Ten minutes later Jack was holding his tummy, doubled up with laughter. He didn't have the quick wit or humour of Molly and her friend, but he did have a good imagination. And Molly was a good storyteller. She described the scene so well, he could see the expression on Nellie's face when she asked, *What d'yer want yer umbrella for, girl?*

'Oh dear, I feel sick with laughin'.' Jack fell back in the chair, still holding his tummy. 'Me ribs are aching.'

Molly pulled a piece of paper out of the pocket in her pinny and passed it over to him. 'Read that.'

Jack looked puzzled. 'It's a shoppin' list.'

'Read the very bottom,' Molly spluttered, 'she's told me to keep a penny for meself for goin'.'

Pressing hard on his ribs Jack managed to say, 'Don't tell me any more, love, or I'll burst.'

'Oh, there's a bit more to come! Just listen without takin' it in, then yer can have a good laugh when yer pain goes.' Molly leaned forward, her eyes wet with tears. 'She gave me three and six to get her messages, said it would be plenty. But it came to four and twopence . . . an' d'yer know what she had the nerve to say? All straight-faced, like, she told me she wouldn't send me on her messages again because I was too extravagant!'

Jack rubbed the heels of his palms into his eyes. 'She must be the funniest thing walkin' round on two legs.'

Molly was thoughtful for a while, her mind ticking over. 'I don't know about her bein' the funniest thing on two legs . . . that parrot of Mrs Foster's is very funny. The only thing is, he swears like a ruddy trooper.'

Jack aimed a cushion and it landed on Molly's knee. 'Will yer shut up, missus, before I'm in agony.'

'Yeah, OK love, I'll leave yer in peace. I want to go round to me ma's for an hour, anyway.'

'Why this sudden decision to go to yer ma's? Yer didn't mention it earlier.'

'Because I didn't think I'd have the energy, that's why. But Ellen was askin' me about the material for blackout curtains, an' I'm goin' to have to buy it soon. If I leave it too late, it means our Doreen havin' to do the curtains for six houses all in a rush. She wouldn't be very happy about that.'

Jack ran his fingers through his hair. 'Six houses?'

Molly nodded. 'There's me, me ma, Nellie, Ellen, Miss Clegg and Mary Watson.'

'That's a lot of curtains for her to sew, love.' Jack did a bit of mental arithmetic. 'It's about sixty curtains . . . minimum.'

'I know!' Molly stood up and stretched. 'For heaven's sake don't sympathize with our Doreen, or she'll have a right gob on 'er. I'll just get her to do one lot at a time, then it won't be so bad.'

'D'yer know how much material yer'll need?'

'That's your job, sunshine! I want yer to measure all our windows, see how much I'll need, then we can multiply by six, 'cos all the houses are exactly the same.' She went into the hallway for her coat. Slipping her arms in the sleeves, she shivered as her skin came into contact with the cold lining. 'We've only got the two bedroom windows, these two in here, an' the kitchen.'

'And the fanlight, don't forget.'

'Oh ay, I wouldn't have thought of that.' She bent to kiss him. 'Aren't I lucky havin' a husband who's not only handsome, but clever into the bargain!'

Jack pulled her back for a longer kiss. 'Yes, there's not many like me around,' he whispered, 'so yer better look after me. Treat me well . . . d'yer know what I mean?'

'I know what yer mean all right.' Molly laughed into the face she held so dear. 'It means ye're a dirty old man.'

'But yer love me?'

'To death.' Molly waved from the doorway. 'I won't be late, love, ten at the most.'

Chapter Four

Molly rapped briskly on the brass door knocker before sliding her hand back inside the sleeve of her coat. 'Come on, Ma, it's freezin' standin' here.' She saw the light go on in the hallway and lifted a foot, poised in readiness to dash in when the door opened. But before she knew what was happening, her arm was gripped and she was pulled unceremoniously over the front step. Staggering to regain her balance, she asked, 'What the hell's up, Ma? I nearly tripped an' broke me flamin' neck!'

Without releasing her hold, Bridie Jackson kicked her foot backwards and closed the front door with a bang. 'I'm glad to see yer, me darlin', so I am.' She pushed her daughter towards the living room. 'It was getting so late, hadn't I almost given you up?'

'I've been runnin' late all day because of the flamin' weather,' Molly said before smiling at the man sitting in the comfortable armchair at the side of the hearth. 'You look nice an' cosy, Da, as snug as a bug in a rug. And believe me, the fireside is the best place to be on a lousy night like tonight.'

'I know that, lass, that's why I'm staying put.' Bob Jackson's white hair was well brushed, his white shirt spotless and the navy-blue cardigan, hand-knitted by his wife, was neatly turned up at the cuffs. Although he was still a fine-looking man, he was only a shadow of the man he had been two years ago, before he had a heart attack. He'd had to leave work and was warned by the doctor to take life very easy.

But being idle didn't sit well on the shoulders of a man who was used to going out to work every day and bringing a wage packet home at the end of the week. He never complained, but Molly knew what his enforced retirement had cost him in loss of pride and dignity.

'Here, give me yer coat or yer'll not be feeling the benefit of it when yer go out.' As Bridie bustled out to the hall-stand, Molly's eyes followed. There's something up here, she thought, me ma's got herself worked up into a real lather.

'What's goin' on, Ma? Yer look like the cat that got the cream.'

'Better than that, me darlin'.' Bridie pulled a chair from under the table and turned it towards the grate. 'Sit yerself by the fire an' get a warm while I make us a cup of cocoa.'

'Hang on a minute, Ma! Don't keep me in suspense, spit it out!'

'It's the most marvellous news, and yerself will be as excited as I am, so yer will.' Bridie clasped and unclasped her hands. 'But I don't want to rush tellin' yer, so I'll make our drink first.'

'She's a proper little bossy-boots, isn't she, Da?'

'She bosses me around something shocking, lass, I don't know why I put up with it.'

'Oh, is that right now?' Bridie called from the kitchen. 'An' wouldn't yer be altogether lost without me?'

Bridie had lived in Liverpool for over forty years, and although her lilting Irish brogue was tempered with a touch of the Liverpool accent, it was sweet and musical. She was turned sixty now, but carried her age well. Her figure was slim, her back ramrod straight. And even spidery lines on her handsome face didn't detract from the beauty of her finely chiselled features.

Molly winked broadly at her father. 'She's not goin' to tell me she's pregnant, is she Da?'

Bob chuckled behind his hand, thinking if his wife had

heard that, she'd be making the sign of the cross and, with her eyes heavenward, begging God to forgive her daughter.

Glad to see the smile on her father's face Molly went on, 'If she is, I'll get Maisie from the corner shop to ring the *News of the World.* Yer'll be the talk of the wash-house, Da, but I wouldn't worry yer head about that because yer'll be sittin' pretty with a few bob in yer pocket.'

'Tut, tut, tut! Can yer not be makin' that tongue of yours behave itself?' Bridie asked, coming through with a laden tray. Even though there was very little money coming in, she never lowered her standards. She kept her little house sparkling, never allowing a speck of dust to settle longer than it took her to fetch a duster. Everything had a place and was kept in it, all neat and tidy like the tray she carried in. A hand-embroidered cloth covered it, and the china cups and saucers set out gleamed as though she'd polished them. 'There's only arrowroot biscuits, lass.'

'That's all right, Ma, I'm not hungry.' Molly lifted a cup of cocoa from the tray and placed it on the table in front of her. 'Well, what's this news yer have for me? I hope it's good news, 'cos I could do with cheering up.'

'Sure it's the grandest news, so it is.' Bridie opened a drawer in the sideboard and took out an envelope. 'I got this letter from home two weeks ago.' Even after forty years, Bridie still thought of Ireland as home. She was sixteen when she left her family in County Wicklow and set sail for Liverpool, full of hope that she would find work and send money back to help her family who were struggling through difficult times. But it didn't work out as she'd hoped, and she never had a penny to spare to send home. The only job she could get was as a live-in maid-of-all-work with a rich family in Princes Avenue in Toxteth. Treated like a skivvy, she was paid the princely sum of four shillings a month and her keep. Out of this she was expected to buy her own clothing.

Bridie had been desperately lonely, missing her family and

the lush green hills of her native land. Once a month she was given a Sunday off, and with no friends to go out with or visit, she used to go down to the Pier Head to feed the birds with stale bread given to her by the cook. It was on one of these days that she'd met Bob, and it was love at first sight. They were married when she was eighteen and had been blissfully happy ever since. But never a day went by when she didn't think of home, and regret she'd never been able to afford to go back to see her parents before they died. Now the only contact she had with the old country was a niece, Eileen, whose welcome letters brightened her heart. Bridie pulled out a chair and sat down, facing her daughter, her hands covering the envelope. 'I didn't mention it at the time, me darlin', in case nothing came of it.'

Molly looked into the bright eyes and wondered what on earth it could be that had pleased her mother so much. Usually Eileen's letters were friendly and chatty, but had never before contained anything that had produced this effect. 'Go on, Ma, yer've got me curious now.'

'Yer've heard me talk about Eileen's husband, Martin O'Donnell, have yer not?'

Molly nodded patiently. 'Yes Ma, many times.'

'And d'yer know that Martin has a sister named Monica, an' she has four children?'

Molly grinned. 'I hope she's got a husband as well.'

Bridie, missing the humour, continued. 'Monica's husband, Mick O'Grady, works on a farm near Glendalough. Sure 'tis a beautiful place, the nearest thing to heaven you're likely to find anywhere in the whole world. But beauty doesn't put food into mouths, so it doesn't, and don't I remember that from when I was a young girl? The O'Gradys, God bless them, are having a struggle to keep body an' soul together. Two of their children, a girl an' a boy, are old enough to work, but sure there's no jobs to be had when ye're livin' miles from anywhere. The boy can earn a few bob workin' on the farms, but for the girl there's nothing.'

When Bridie fell silent, Molly gazed at her through lowered lids. 'If Eileen's letter was full of woe, Ma, what are yer so happy about?'

This was the question Bridie was waiting for. Her smile wide, her eyes brimming with happiness, the words tumbled from her mouth. 'Monica asked Eileen if she would write an' ask me and Bob if we'd take the girl in if she came to Liverpool to find a job.'

Molly gasped. 'Yer couldn't do that, Ma! Yer don't know what she's like, an' you and Da are too old now to have the worry of a young girl! Especially me da, he needs peace and quiet, an' he wouldn't get it if there was a noisy youngster in the house.'

'Oh Molly, me darlin', that's where you are wrong! Sure wouldn't yer da an' meself be over the moon to have someone to talk to besides ourselves? It would be like a new lease of life for us both, don't you see?' Bridie gripped her daughter's arm. 'That's why I didn't tell yer, 'cos I knew yer'd try to stop us.'

Molly appealed to her father. 'It's a big thing yer know, Da, takin' in a young girl, particularly a stranger. Yer know nothin' about her an' yer might live to regret it.'

Bob gave a gentle shake of his head. 'I don't think so, lass. I know ye're only thinkin' of our welfare, but don't fret, me an' Ma have talked it through carefully before making up our minds. We would welcome having some company, and according to Eileen's letter she's a bonny lass, well behaved and a good worker.'

'We're not that old, me darlin',' Bridie said softly, 'and if she's everything that Eileen says she is, then sure won't she be bringing a lot of pleasure into our lives?'

'I'm not sure, Ma, I'm really not!' Molly found the whole thing disquieting. Her mother had her hands full looking after her father, never mind a boisterous teenager. And if it didn't work out, they could hardly send the girl packing. 'It needs a lot of thinkin' about.'

'We've already agreed to have her, Molly; she's coming over on the night boat next Monday.' Bridie sighed. 'I'm sorry we kept it from yer, it wasn't that we wanted to be underhand. But yer see, I knew fine well you'd not see it our way.'

Molly let out a deep sigh. 'Well, if that's what yez want, who am I to argue?' She could see her doubts had taken some of the pleasure from her mother's face, so she made an effort to sound enthusiastic. 'What did yer say her name is? And how old is she?'

Bridie was visibly relieved. 'Her name's Rosemary an' she's just turned fifteen.' As she took the letter from the envelope, a photograph fell on to the table. 'Look, this is her when she was four years of age. Eileen said they didn't have a more recent one, an' I can understand that 'cos when there's no money for food, the last thing yer'd be thinkin' about is havin' yer picture took.'

Molly picked up the faded black and white photograph and at once a smile crossed her face. Looking up at her was a child with black curls tumbling over her forehead and cheeks, a chubby face lit up in a wide grin which revealed two missing front teeth, and eyes that were full of mischief. 'She was certainly a bonny baby.'

'Sure an' she's got a look of the Irish about her, so she has.' Bridie took the photograph from Molly's hand and studied it. 'I've got a feelin' in me bones that she's goin' to bring a lot of happiness to this house . . . and to me an' Bob.'

'So there's no going back?' Molly asked. 'No second thoughts?'

'No second thoughts or doubts.' Bridie folded the letter and tucked the photograph inside. Then she looked Molly straight in the eyes. 'An' Molly me darling, I hope when Rosemary gets here yer'll make her welcome. 'Tis a big step for a young girl, leavin' her friends and family behind, and who would be knowin' that better than meself? I remember as though it was yesterday how afraid I was when I landed in Liverpool. It was so noisy with trams bringing people to the Pier Head, and there were more people than I'd ever seen at any time in me life before. Sure, it was a far cry from the countryside I'd left behind. If I'd had the money I'd have turned tail an' boarded the boat again.'

'I'm glad you didn't, sweetheart,' Bob said, giving her that special look. 'What would my life have been like without you?'

'An' mine without you, me darlin'?'

'Oh, don't start that, you two! Pair of soppy beggars, an' at your age, too!' Molly gave them each a smile before saying, 'Of course we'll make her welcome, Ma . . . we all will! Yer don't think for one moment we'd give the kid the cold shoulder, do yer?' She put on a pained expression. 'My only concern now is, if her accent is as thick as yours was when I was a toddler, I won't understand a word she's got to say for herself.' She rested her chin on her hand. 'Ma, I hope she's got a sense of humour.'

'Now did yer ever in yer life know an Irish person that didn't have a sense of humour?' Bridie was light-hearted now that her daughter had come around. 'Isn't it a fact that we've all kissed the blarney stone and have little leprechauns at the bottom of our gardens?'

Molly smiled, remembering the stories her mother told her when she was little. How the mischievous leprechauns used to play tricks on them and sometimes made magical things happen. If this young girl was like her mother, she would bring nothing but happiness into *all* their lives. 'D'yer know, Ma, I'm startin' to get excited meself now! I'll be there to welcome her when her boat docks next Tuesday.'

Bridie put a hand over Molly's. 'Thank you, me darlin'.

I don't want her to feel as lost and lonely as I did when I first stepped ashore in Liverpool. First impressions are important.'

'No fear of that, Ma! We'll all make her welcome.' Molly gently squeezed her mother's hand. 'She'll feel at home in no time.'

Bob had sat quietly listening. He had expected Molly to object because she was very protective of Bridie and himself. Since he'd had the heart attack, she watched them like a hawk. So it was good to hear her and Bridie making plans for the girl. His wife would rest easy now, and anything that made her happy made him happy.

Molly glanced at the clock and pulled a face. 'I told Jack I'd only be half an hour – he'll wonder what's keepin' me. But how the 'ell did I know yez were goin' to spring such a surprise on me? I dunno,' she huffed, 'I only came round to tell yer not to worry about blackout curtains, I'll get yours when I get me own.'

'Oh, that would be grand . . . save me the journey into town.' Bridie stood up, returned the letter to the drawer and took out her purse. 'Have yer any idea at all how much it'll be?'

'Not a clue, Ma! Don't give me any money yet, I'll let yer know when me an' Nellie are goin' in for it.'

Bridie's eyes ran down the length of the curtains on the front window. 'I'd say yer'd need two and a half yards for each curtain, 'cos there's hems top an' bottom. That's four curtains for these two windows, an' the same for upstairs. Then there's the kitchen, but that's only half the length.'

Molly scratched her head as she mentally reckoned up. 'It's over twenty yards! Bloody hell, they'll cost a fortune! We'll be livin' on fresh air that week!'

'Twenty-three yards to be exact,' Bob muttered softly, while Bridie bristled. 'Will yer not be using bad language in my house, Molly Bennett?'

'Ay, ay, sir!' Molly pushed back her chair, stood to attention and saluted smartly. 'Permission to leave, sir?'

'Away with yer, yer big daft ha'p'orth.' Bridie was smiling as she opened her purse. 'I'll give yer a pound, then it's off me mind. I'll settle up with yer if it's any more.'

Molly took the pound note, because to refuse would dent her mother's pride. 'It won't be any more than that, Mam! I'm goin' to leave it to Nellie . . . she's the one who gets the best bargains. If she hasn't lost her touch, yer'll be gettin' change out of this.' She bent to kiss her father. 'Goodnight an' God bless, Da, I'll see yer tomorrow. I'll get me coat on the way out.'

Molly's brain was running round and round as she made her way home. What with Phil coming home on Monday, and now Rosemary arriving on Tuesday . . . it was going to be a busy week! She just hoped her ma and da weren't taking on more than they could cope with. They'd been right about one thing – she would have tried to talk them out of it if she'd been told earlier. In fact, she'd stop it now if she could. They were too old to be taking on something like this. Still, they weren't on their own; the whole family would give a hand. And her ma wasn't daft, not by a long chalk – she wouldn't agree to anything she wasn't sure about. She was so wrapped up in her thoughts, Molly didn't see the figures standing outside her front door until she was upon them. 'Good God, yez frightened the life out of me!'

Jill and Steve had been too busy kissing and cuddling to notice Molly's approach and they broke apart, embarrassed to have been caught out. 'Doin' a bit of courtin', are yez?' Molly grinned as she put the key in the lock. 'It's a pity we haven't got a parlour, then yer could do it in comfort and privacy.'

'Ye're right there, Mrs B.!' Steve was glad of the darkness, it hid his blushes. 'I keep tellin' me mam the same thing, but she won't budge from here because of her best mate.'

'I wonder who that can be?' Molly chuckled as she stepped into the hall. 'If yez stand there much longer, yer'll be catching yer death of cold. Why don't yez stand in the hall? I promise I won't peek.'

'No, I'll be coming in now,' Jill said. 'It's getting near bedtime.'

As soon as the door closed, Steve took her in his arms. 'It would be nice to have a bit of privacy, wouldn't it? The nearest we get to bein' on our own is on the back row at the pictures.'

'Never mind.' Jill rumpled his hair. 'We'll be married in a couple of years with a little house of our own.'

'I can't wait!' Steve held her close. There'd never been anyone else for him: he'd loved Jill since she was a baby, before he even knew what love meant. 'When the time comes, Mr Henry might get us a house around here, near our families.'

'Yeah, I wouldn't want to be far away from them.' Jill gave a soft sigh. 'I hope the war's over soon, before they call you up.'

Although he didn't think so, Steve kept his thoughts to himself. 'It will be, don't you worry yer pretty little head about that! Our lads will soon sort Hitler out when they get goin', you mark my words.'

'I hope so! I don't know what I'd do if you went away.'

'I wouldn't leave yer, I'd put yer in me pocket an' take yer with me.'

Steve bent his head to cover her lips in a gentle kiss. He didn't want to talk about the possibility of being parted from the girl he adored. It didn't bear thinking about.

Chapter Five

Molly sat back on her heels and pushed a strand of hair out of her eyes. Putting a bit of elbow grease into the scrubbing certainly warmed you up. She'd been freezing when she came out to whiten the front step but now she was sweating so much her dress felt soaked. It was a good job she'd done the outside of Victoria's house yesterday, she wouldn't have the energy to do it now.

Molly glanced at the red-raddled window-sill which had been given a good polish and looked a treat. Then her eyes dropped to the step. It was nice and white now, but wait until the gang came home and stepped all over it. She'd once asked them to learn to walk on their hands, but they weren't having any. A very uncooperative lot were her family, she thought with a chuckle.

'Ah, well, I'd better move.' Molly struggled to her feet. 'I want the place lookin' nice for Phil today, and Rosemary comes tomorrow. An' we've got to be at the dock first thing in the morning, so if I don't get it all done today, I've had it.'

'Talkin' to yerself again, eh, Molly Bennett? Haven't I warned yer time an' again about it? Yer'll be gettin' carted off to the loony-bin one of these fine days.'

'Hiya, Nellie!' Molly pressed her hands into the small of her back and let out a groan. 'I've never stopped since I got out of bed, I'm worn to a frazzle.'

'Serves yer right!' Nellie swayed towards her. 'The way ye're carryin' on, anyone would think the Queen was comin'!'

'You're a fine one to talk! Who was up at the crack of dawn, eh? An' whose ruddy step was as white as snow by eight o'clock?'

'Mine needed doin', yours didn't.' Nellie pushed her arms through the front of her floral wraparound pinny. 'I'm not a glutton for punishment like you are . . . you spend yer time lookin' for work while I spend me time lookin' for ways of avoiding it.'

Molly stooped down to pick up the donkey stone and threw it in the bucket. 'Yer know, Nellie, anyone listenin' to you would think yer house was filthy.'

'I couldn't give a monkey's uncle what they think, girl! They've no right to be listenin' in to me private conversation anyway!'

'Have yer been over to Miss Clegg's this mornin'?' Molly asked. 'She'll be a nervous wreck if yer haven't 'cos she wants everythin' to be just right.'

'It's all under control, so don't be gettin' yer knickers in a twist. Her place is like a palace an' she's done up like a dog's dinner. But she's so nervous it rubs off on yer! Every time she looked at the clock, which was every second, I looked at the ruddy clock. Every time she plumped a cushion, I plumped a cushion that didn't need plumpin' in the first place! I'm tellin' yer girl, if she doesn't calm 'erself down she'll be good for nothin' by the time Phil arrives.'

'Well I'm goin' to tidy meself up, then go an' see Mrs Corkhill.' Molly placed the bucket inside the hallway and ran her wet hands down the sides of her pinny. 'We haven't been up since Friday, an' we did promise Corker we'd keep an eye on her.'

'OK, OK, I get the message!' Nellie backed away. 'I'll give yer fifteen minutes, then give yer a knock.'

Molly moved the curtain in Mrs Corkhill's living room to

study a house on the opposite side of the street. 'What are the new people like in Bradley's old house?'

'They seem a nice family and they keep the outside of the house spotless. The woman is out every day either cleaning the windows or swilling the pavement. She's not the size of sixpence-worth of copper, but she's wiry, always on the go.' Mrs Corkhill gave a half-smile. 'A definite improvement on the Bradleys; they didn't believe in cleaning anything. The lowest of the low they were, biggest gang of ruffians I ever had the misfortune to meet. I don't think there was one house this end of the street that didn't have something pinched by them. If they hadn't moved when they did there'd have been a riot, 'cos everyone was up in arms over them.'

Molly let the curtain fall and moved towards a chair by the fire. 'If it hadn't been for Phil Bradley, they'd still be there.'

'When yer come to think about it, it was that swine of a stepbrother of his that brought things to a head.' Nellie nodded her head knowingly. 'If Phil hadn't caught 'im red-handed tryin' to break into Miss Clegg's house an' given him a good goin'-over, they'd still be here makin' life hell for the neighbours.'

'Yeah, that sly, thievin' little bugger did everyone a good turn,' Molly agreed. 'When Victoria offered to let Phil sleep there that night because he couldn't very well go 'ome after beatin' his stepbrother up, it was the best thing she ever did. He started off as a lodger but he's more like a son to her now . . . she idolizes him. An' it gave Phil the opportunity of finally breakin' away from the Bradleys.'

Mrs Corkhill looked from Molly to Nellie. 'I still can't believe he lived there all that time an' nobody knew he even existed. I mean, I live right opposite an' I never laid eyes on him.'

'That's because he didn't want yer to.' Molly stretched her legs towards the glowing fire. 'He used the back door all the time. He was ashamed of them, yer see. Of course yer know that Tom Bradley wasn't his real father, his mam was pregnant when she married him. From all accounts the boy she was courtin' was a fine man, honest as the day is long. He got killed in an accident at work just weeks before they were to get married, and never even knew she was in the family way. So when Tom Bradley offered to marry her, she must 'ave jumped at the chance.'

Deep in thought for a moment, Molly pinched her bottom lip. Then she gave a deep sigh. 'Who knows that we might not have done the same thing? When ye're in trouble, it's any port in a storm.'

'Blimey! She'd 'ave been better off out in a ruddy storm!' Nellie huffed. 'I'd 'ave put up with all the waggin' tongues an' the shame rather than marry a thieving swine like Bradley! Scum of the earth, he is!'

'Phil's mother doesn't think so, she thinks the sun shines out of his backside!' Molly leaned forward. 'When push came to shove, she took his side against Phil, her own son, didn't she?'

'Some mother she is to do that!' Nellie was getting herself all worked up. 'Fancy goin' against yer own flesh an' blood! If I ever come face to face with 'er, she'll not half get a piece of my mind, I can tell yer!'

Molly gave a throaty chuckle. 'Don't give her too much, sunshine, ye're short on top as it is.'

'Ho, ho, very funny.' Nellie looked fierce, but the creaking of the chair told her friend laughter was on its way. 'I'd be just about on a level with you then, girl, wouldn't I? We'd both be as thick as two short planks.'

Lizzie Corkhill was really enjoying the exchange as her eyes swivelled from one woman to the other. They were real comics these two, just the tonic to brighten a miserable day. 'If you two are goin' to come to blows, will yer go out in the yard? I don't want blood all over me carpet.'

'There's no fear of that, Mrs Corkhill, I'm not as green

as I'm cabbage-lookin'.' Molly pursed her lips and made blubbering noises as she blew out sharply. 'One go-along from Nellie an' me feet wouldn't touch the ground until I ended up on the landin' stage at the Pier Head! She packs a powerful punch, does Nellie Theresa McDonough.'

'Ay, an' yer'd do well to remember that in future before yer start givin' me any of yer lip.' Nellie turned her head to wink at Mrs Corkhill. 'D'yer know she's makin' me get up at six in the mornin' to go and meet the Irish boat? I must be barmy!'

'I didn't ask yer to come!' Molly said, rising to the bait. 'You insisted on coming, and d'yer know why? 'Cos ye're terrified of missing anything.'

Nellie grinned. 'If a seagull is goin' to spend a penny on your head, girl, then I want to be there to see it.'

'Mind yer bring a piece of paper with yer, so yer can wipe its bottom when it's finished.'

Laughing softly, Mrs Corkhill stood up. 'I'll make a pot of tea.'

'Have yer heard when Corker will be home?' Molly called. 'He should be due any day now.'

'I had a letter last week, but he didn't say where he'd been or when he'd be home.' The gas popped as the old lady held a match under the kettle. 'Mind you, with the war bein' on I don't suppose they're allowed to say much.'

Molly opened her mouth to say that Ellen Clarke had had a letter, too, but a warning voice in her head told her to keep quiet. She wasn't sure if Corker's mother knew how close he was to her neighbour, so least said, soonest mended. The last time Corker was home on leave he'd persuaded Ellen to go and see a solicitor about getting a divorce from Nobby, but chances were he hadn't told his mother. 'He'll walk in on yer one day soon, sunshine, an' yer can spoil him with yer apple pies.'

'I hope he rings Maisie at the corner shop when his ship

docks, like he usually does, so I can get a decent meal ready for him. I like everything to be just right for him when he gets home.' Mrs Corkhill walked through with the teapot and stood it on the hob at the side of the fire. 'I'll get the cups.' She was reaching up to where the cups were hanging from hooks screwed into the edge of a shelf, when she heard Molly's voice.

'Nellie McDonough, I can see right up yer clothes! Cover yerself up an' try to be respectable.'

Nellie lifted the skirt of her dress to reveal pink fleecy-lined knickers. Stretching her leg out, she tucked her stocking top firmly into her garter. 'Even though I say it meself, girl, it's not a bad bit of leg, eh? I have to keep them well covered, otherwise I'd drive all the men wild with desire for me body.'

'Wishful thinking, sunshine,' Molly tutted. 'It's enough to put anyone off their dinner.'

'Green with envy, yer are, girl, just 'cos I can get any man I set me sights on . . . includin' your feller.'

Molly left her chair to stand in front of her friend. Cupping the chubby face in her hands, she said, 'Nellie McDonough, yer can have all the men yer want, but if I ever catch yer givin' my Jack the glad eye, I'll flatten yer.'

'Mrs Corkhill!' Nellie cried. 'Come an' help me, she's batterin' the livin' daylights out of me.'

But the only sound that came back from the kitchen was the sound of the old lady's laughter. If she'd paid ninepence to sit in the best seats at the Astoria picture house, she couldn't have enjoyed herself more. They were a proper caution, were Molly and Nellie. She'd have to remember all the tricks they'd been up to while Corker had been away: he was bound to ask.

A tiny hand clutched in each of hers, Molly walked up the street between Ruthie and Bella. 'There's yer mam at the door waitin' for yer, Bella.' She let go of Bella's hand expecting her to run ahead, but when she looked down she saw the little girl nodding her head vigorously at Ruthie and mouthing, 'Go 'ed, ask her.'

'Oh ay, what yer after now?' Molly pulled on her daughter's hand. 'Come on, out with it.'

'Can me an' Bella go round to Patsy Dickinson's before tea, Mam? Remember I told yer her dog had had babies? Well we couldn't see them before 'cos they were too little, but she said we can go round tonight and have a little hold of them.'

Molly smiled. 'You can go, but I can't speak for Mrs Watson. Bella will have to ask for 'erself.'

Bella took to her heels, a wide grin on her face. If Ruthie could go, then her mam was bound to let her go. But it wasn't that easy. Mary was very protective of her only child, didn't like her out of her sight, and when Molly walked up there was a look of doubt on her neighbour's face.

'I'm not happy about her goin', Molly, I don't know the Dickinson family.'

'Of course yer do! They only live in the next street an' yer must have seen Mrs Dickinson in the corner shop hundreds of times.' Molly got a little impatient with Mary for the way she mollycoddled Bella. She often wondered what would happen when her daughter grew up and started going out with boys. The poor lads would probably get the third degree and have to have references and a doctor's note before Bella was allowed out with them. 'She's a nice woman, about your height with mousy-coloured hair. Yer've probably stood next to her without knowin' who she was. That comes from not bein' nosy, like me.'

'Has she got a little girl of about three?' Mary asked. 'A pretty little thing with blonde curly hair?'

'That's the one! An' if yer don't make up yer mind quick, the ruddy pups will be fully grown dogs.'

Mary capitulated. 'OK, yer can go. But you be back here in half an hour, d'yer hear? It'll be dark soon.'

The two women watched as the girls ran hell for leather up

the street, chattering excitedly, swinging their joined hands between them.

'She thinks I'm doin' her a favour,' Molly said with a smile, 'but it's meself I'm thinkin' of. I'll have the dinner on the go in no time without her under me feet pestering the life out of me.'

'I'd rather Bella was somewhere where I could keep me eye on her.' Mary knew she fussed too much but couldn't help it. 'I worry when I don't know where she is.'

'For cryin' out loud, Mary, will yer give the kid a break? Yer'll stunt her growth if yer keep her tied to yer apron strings.'

'I know, Harry keeps on at me about it.' Mary moved away from the door and straightened up. 'But I can't change the way I am, can I?'

'Yer goin' to have to if yer want Bella to be a normal, happy child.' Molly started to undo the buttons on her coat as she turned away. 'I'd better get a move on or they'll be back before we know it.'

Molly was halfway across the cobbled street when she turned. 'I gather there's no sign of Phil?'

'No, not yet. Miss Clegg was lookin' pale and tired, so I've settled her on her chair in front of the fire with her feet up on a pouffe. She's goin' to try and have forty winks, otherwise she'll be good for nothing.'

'Good idea.' Molly crossed to the pavement opposite. 'I'll see yer later, Mary. Ta-ra.'

Molly cut around the pastry overlapping the basin and let it fall on to the scrubbed draining board. Spinning the basin with one hand, she used two fingers of her other hand to pinch the edge of the pastry, making a pattern. Then she reached for a knife and cut two slits in the top of the steak and kidney pie.

'There yer go!' Molly slipped the dish on to the top shelf

of the preheated oven. 'There'll be no moans tonight because they all like steak and kidney.' She gave a low chuckle. 'Just as well, seein' as there's nowt else. As they say, hunger's good sauce.'

As she gathered up the pieces of left-over pastry, a smile crossed Molly's face. If Ruthie had been here, she'd have been covered in flour, shaping the pastry into tarts and asking for them to be put in the oven. Nobody ever ate the tarts because they came out as hard as a rock, but Molly didn't discourage her daughter as she thought it was good practice for when she was older.

Molly was scraping some stubborn bits of flour from the draining board when it suddenly struck her that Ruthie should be well home by now. She poked her head round the kitchen door to see the time. It was a quarter to five! 'I bet the little monkey's over in Mary's! I'll finish cleanin' up here, then I'll go and get her.'

But when Mary opened the front door, she shook her head. 'They haven't come back yet. I knew I shouldn't have let her go.'

'Oh stop yer worryin', missus, they're probably havin' a whale of a time playin' with the pups.' Molly tutted. 'Was your mother the same with you when yer were Bella's age? Frightened of lettin' yer out of her sight, terrified in case the wind blew on yer?'

Mary gave a half-smile. 'No, she wasn't as bad as me.'

'There yer are then! A little freedom didn't do you no harm, did it?' But mentally Molly was threatening to give Ruthie a clout for not being home at the time she was told to be.

'But it's nearly five o'clock, Molly.'

'I know, I'm keepin' track.' Molly bit on her bottom lip. 'I'll nip home, lower the gas, then I'll go around to the Dickinsons'. An' it's woe betide that little tinker of mine when I get me hands on her. She'll not pull a trick like this again in a hurry.'

Molly waved to Mary, then pushed open the door she'd left ajar. Halfway down the hall she stopped when she heard the sound of childish laughter. 'Well, I'll be blowed!' Molly growled, thinking of Mary worrying herself sick while the two little beggars were in here all the time, and enjoying themselves by the sound of it. They must have come in the back way! Throwing the living-room door open, Molly barged in. 'You better get yerself home, Bella Watson, 'cos ye're in deep trouble. And as for you, Ruthie Bennett, you're about to get yer ears boxed and sent to bed without any dinner.'

Molly knew she was talking through her hat, making threats that weren't going to be carried out, but they couldn't get away with being naughty without at least having the fear of God put into them.

'What . . .' Molly didn't get any further. There's something not right here, she thought. The two girls were sitting on the couch leaning towards each other, and the smiles that were on their faces when she'd entered the room had dropped, to be replaced by a look of fear . . . or was it guilt?

'What's goin' on here?' Molly bent down, her eyes narrowed. She could have sworn Ruthie's gymslip moved then, but the girl was sitting perfectly still, so she must have been mistaken. 'Come on, what 'ave yez been—' Well she wasn't mistaken this time, the skirt of the gymslip had moved again and was still moving. 'What 'ave yer got under yer gymslip?'

'Nothin', Mam, honest!'

Molly bent closer and lifted the hem of the dress, to gaze into the blinking eyes of a tiny black and white pup. 'In the name of God what are yer doin' with that?'

'Mrs Dickinson said we could 'ave it, Mam!'

'She did, Mrs Bennett!' Bella came to her friend's aid. 'She said we could have it for nothing.'

'Oh, I'm sure she did!' Molly didn't know whether to laugh or cry. 'If I 'ad a litter of puppies to get rid of, I'd be delighted to give them away for nothing.'

Ruthie brought the pup from its hiding place and held it to her cheek.

'We can keep it, can't we, Mam?'

'Can yer heck keep it! Don't yer think I've got enough mouths to feed without a ruddy pup?' Molly was having dark thoughts about Mrs Dickinson. Fancy giving a pup to a seven-year-old child without first asking the parents! Flaming cheek, that's what she had. 'An' get it off me couch before it piddles all over it. The whole house'll smell in no time.'

Scratching her head, Molly closed her eyes to block out the sight of tear-filled eyes begging her to change her mind. That Mrs Dickinson's pulled a fast one, dropped me right in it. If I say they can't keep it I'll be the worst in the world, but if I give in I'll be lumbered with a ruddy pup that isn't even house-trained! And who's the one who'll have to clean the mess up after it? Me of course, who else?

Molly breathed deeply a few times to settle her nerves, then she opened her eyes. 'Who exactly did Mrs Dickinson give the pup to?'

'Both of us,' Ruthie said, while Bella added, 'It's between us.'

'Then I think we'll see what Mrs Watson has to say about it.' Molly pointed a threatening finger at her daughter. 'Keep it off that couch, d'yer hear? Ye're in enough trouble as it is.'

Mary was standing on her step, her worried eyes searching both ends of the street. When she saw Molly she cried, 'Have yer been to see if they're round there?'

'There was no need,' Molly bawled, 'they're in here. I think yer'd better come an' meet the latest addition to yer family.'

'What's goin' on, girl?' Three doors up, Nellie stepped on to the pavement. 'Mary was nearly sendin' for the police.'

'Oh, ye're there, are yer?' Molly didn't really feel like grinning, but the sight of her mate always brought out the best in her. 'Wouldn't be a show without Punch, would it?'

'Yer know I like to keep me eye on things in the street.'

Nellie swung towards her. 'Make sure the wheels of life are oiled an' running smoothly.'

'Well I'd hate yer to miss out, so if yer've got yer oil can handy, yer'd better come in with Mary.' Molly stepped into the hall, turned and whispered, 'Nellie McDonough, if yer laugh I'll break yer neck.'

'Girl, I won't even crack me face, I promise.'

But Nellie was hard-pushed to keep her promise when she saw the look of horror on Mary's face as Molly quickly explained the situation and showed her what their daughters had brought home with them. Mary's reaction was fast and definite. 'I am not havin' a pup!'

'It's better than havin' a duck egg, girl, far less painful.' Nellie thought the whole thing was hilarious and even the daggers being sent her way by Molly couldn't shut her up. 'I don't know what all the fuss is about, it's a lovely little pup, all cuddly like.'

Ruthie and Bella fastened their eyes on Nellie, seeing her as their salvation. 'He's lovely, isn't he, Auntie Nellie?'

'He certainly is, sweetheart, a real little beauty.'

Molly gave Mary a sly dig before saying, 'There yer are, Ruthie, there's yer answer! Let Auntie Nellie have the pup an' you an' Bella can call an' see him every night. Yez can tuck him up in the lovely dog basket Auntie Nellie is goin' to get for him, and when he's older yez can take him for a walk on the posh lead Auntie Nellie's goin' to buy.' With her hands on her hips Molly glared at Nellie. 'Now get out of that!' But Nellie was laughing so much she couldn't speak. Her whole body was shaking: her tummy and bosom were in unison, but her chins were wobbling in all directions. Gripping hold of the back of a chair for support, she laughed and wheezed as the tears rolled down her cheeks.

'What's wrong with her?' Mary asked. 'Is she all right?'

'Don't ask me what's wrong with her, 'cos it would take too long to tell yer.' Molly was eyeing her friend with suspicion.

Nothing had happened in the last ten minutes to bring on such a bout of laughter, so there was something behind it all. 'Nellie, will yer stop that racket an' tell us what yer find so funny?'

Gulping for air, Nellie waved a hand. 'Give me a chance.'

They watched in silence as she fought to control her breathing. Then she turned to face them, her chubby cheeks wet. 'Don't say anythin' to start me off again, all right?'

'Seein' as we didn't say anything to start yer off in the first place, I don't know what ye're on about,' Molly said resignedly. 'Anyhow, go 'ed.'

'I was comin' down here when I saw Mary standin' at the door.' Nellie screwed her eyes tight, sending the fat on her cheeks moving upward to meet her eyebrows. She took a deep breath and let it out slowly. 'Yez know that Mrs Dickinson lives at the back of us, her entry door is facin' ours.' Another deep breath as laughter gurgled. 'She came up our yard before an' asked me to tell yer to make the girls take the pup back because it's only four weeks old and shouldn't be taken from its mother. She was quite upset about it.'

'What!' Molly transferred her gaze from Nellie to the two upturned, frightened faces of the children. She was lost for words, wondering who to shout at first. In fact, and she was ready to admit it, she was more angry with herself than anyone else. Why was she always stupid enough to let her friend get one over on her? As soon as Nellie had appeared on the scene she should have known that mischief was brewing.

Ruthie found her mother's silence unnerving. She'd rather have had her bawling and shouting, getting it over with. In the end she could stand it no longer. 'Mam, Patsy said we could have the puppy, honest!'

'If you've got any sense yer'll keep yer mouth closed,' Molly snapped. 'Just wait until yer dad gets home.'

'Now there's no need to tell Jack, or Harry,' Nellie said. 'It's not the girls' fault that I've got a warped sense of humour.'

'That doesn't alter the fact that they shouldn't have taken the puppy,' Mary said. 'It was very naughty of them.'

'Weren't you ever naughty at their age? If yer weren't, then there was somethin' wrong with yer, yer weren't natural.' Nellie moved to lift the sleeping pup from Bella's lap. She laid it gently in the crook of her arm and stroked its tiny forehead. 'I can remember wantin' a kitten when I was about six, but me ma wouldn't let me have one. I cried meself to sleep for a week.' She walked towards the door, still stroking the fine silky fur. 'I'll take the little feller back, but Mrs Dickinson told me to tell yez that yez can go round any time an' see him.'

'I'll see yer to the door.' Molly followed her friend down the hall and when she reached the door, tapped her on the shoulder. 'Nellie?'

Nellie turned her head. 'What, girl?'

Molly kissed the chubby cheek. 'Ye're an old softie, Nellie McDonough, but I love yer.'

Mary was standing behind with Bella's hand gripped tightly in hers. There was a catch in her voice when she said, 'An' there's two little girls I know who'll be yer slaves for life.'

'Ruthie was very quiet tonight.' Jack lowered the paper. 'No shouting match to stay up a bit longer.'

Molly grinned as she straightened the runner on the sideboard. If Ruthie had had her way, she'd have gone to bed before Jack came in from work in case the puppy was mentioned. A quiet lecture off her dad was far worse than her mother ranting and raving. 'She was probably tired. Anyway, she's up early tomorrow so I can get her ready before I go out. Jill's taking her across to Mary's for me when she leaves for work.'

'What time are you goin'?'

'Same time as you. Me an' Nellie are meeting me ma at the tram stop at a quarter past seven.' A loud clattering on the stairs had Molly jumping from her chair. 'Listen to the noise our Doreen's makin', the stupid nit! If she wakes Ruthie, I'll flatten her.'

Doreen's face appeared round the door, flushed with excitement. She'd been sitting upstairs for the last hour, keeping watch through the bedroom window. 'Phil's just coming up the street.'

'Hang on a minute.' Molly gripped her arm. 'Give him five minutes alone with Miss Clegg before yer go barging in.' When she was convinced her daughter wasn't going to make a break, she released her grip. 'I'll swill me face, comb me hair, then give Nellie a knock. We promised we'd go over just for half an hour, to say hello and have a piece of his welcome home cake.'

Doreen's mouth drooped at the corners and her eyes clouded over. Fancy having your style cramped by your mother and her friend on your boyfriend's first night home on leave! And once the pair of them got talking there'd be no stopping them – they'd be at it until it was time to go to bed. She wouldn't get to spend any time alone with Phil, wouldn't get a look-in.

Molly could read her daughter like a book, and the look of dejection didn't go unnoticed. 'Don't worry, sunshine, we won't stay long. And Miss Clegg will be in bed early 'cos she's been up since the crack of dawn. So you and Phil will have an hour to yerselves to hold hands and whisper sweet nothings in each other's ears.'

Jack was watching with interest, thinking how different in personality his two eldest daughters were. If Molly had spoken those words to Jill, the shy girl would have blushed to the roots of her hair and lowered her eyes. But not Doreen. She held her mother's gaze with a grin covering her face. 'Any tips, Mam? Can yer remember any of the sweet nothings yer used to whisper in me dad's ear while yer were holding hands?'

'What d'yer mean, used to? I'll have you know I still whisper sweet nothings in yer dad's ear, an' we still hold hands. But words between two sweethearts are secret. So yer'll have to think of some of yer own. Yer won't have no trouble; it comes natural.' Molly waved her hand. 'Now off yer go, sunshine, he'll have had time to take his coat off.'

Phil opened the door to Doreen's knock and the sight of her sent his pulses racing and his heart thudding. 'God,' he said softly, 'yer'll never know how much I've been looking forward to seeing you.'

He was more handsome than Doreen remembered. Taller and broader, his blue eyes more vivid and his hair more blond. She wanted to rush into his arms, to be held close, but she was suddenly overcome with shyness. Her feet refused to move and for once in her life she was tongue-tied. Phil opened the door wide and held his hand out. 'Don't stand on the step, love, come inside.'

The closing of the door and the touch of his hand restored Doreen's power of speech. 'Yer look smashin' in yer uniform.'

'And you're a sight for sore eyes.' Phil wrapped his arms around her and held her slim body close. 'Yer've been in me thoughts day and night, an' I've longed to hold yer like this.' He ran his fingers through her long hair while kissing her gently on the cheek. 'I've got it bad, Doreen.'

She pulled away to smile up into his face. 'Me too.'

Reluctantly he let her go. 'We'd better go in to Aunt Vicky, I don't want to neglect her on me first night home.' He held her hand as they walked down the hall and into the living room, where a cheerful fire burned in the grate. 'Here's the other woman in me life, Aunt Vicky.'

'Hello, Doreen.' Victoria was so happy she couldn't have dropped the smile from her face if she'd wanted to. 'Doesn't he look handsome in his uniform?'

'He certainly does.' Doreen's eyes ran down the length of

him until she came to his boots. 'They won't half weigh yer down for a slow foxtrot.'

'I've got me dancin' shoes upstairs.' He put an arm across her shoulders and squeezed. 'Just think, two whole weeks in civvies.'

Doreen blushed at the show of affection in front of Miss Clegg. 'Can we go to Barlow's Lane tomorrow night?'

'I'm looking forward to it.' Phil gazed at his adopted aunt. 'You don't mind if I go out, do yer, Aunt Vicky?'

'Of course not! You go out and enjoy yourselves.' Victoria winked at Doreen. 'I'll have him during the day and you can have his undivided attention every night.'

Phil was beside himself with happiness. 'Aren't I lucky to have two lovely women fighting over me?'

There was a loud rat-tat on the knocker and Doreen pulled a face. 'Here they come, the terrible twins.'

Molly, first through the door, flung her arms around Phil and kissed him soundly on both cheeks. 'It's good to see yer, sunshine.'

'It's good to be home, Mrs Bennett.' As he smiled down into the upturned face, Phil saw where Doreen got her good looks from. The resemblance between mother and daughter was very strong.

Nellie thumped Molly on the back. 'Shove over, missus, an' give someone else a chance! Honest to God, it's man-mad yer are. Anything in trousers an' ye're flutterin' yer ruddy eyelashes like Bette Davis.'

Phil chuckled as Nellie pulled his head down and pursed her lips for a kiss. 'Now I know I'm home.'

'Ay, that's enough!' Molly tried to look severe. 'Ye're not supposed to kiss a young man on the mouth, ye're supposed to offer yer cheek.'

Nellie's huge body was shaking as she released Phil. 'Seein' as ye're so clever with manners, girl, an' just in case I'm in the same situation in the future, can I ask yer which one of me four cheeks I should offer? Yer see, I have trouble bendin' down, an' whoever it was would have a lot of trouble trying to kiss me backside.'

Phil roared, Doreen grinned from ear to ear, and Miss Clegg covered her mouth to hide her smile. Only Molly kept a straight face. 'Nellie McDonough, I can't take yer anywhere! Yer'd shame the flamin' devil, yer would.'

'Tut, tut!' Nellie clicked her tongue on the roof of her mouth. 'What have I done wrong now, girl? Ye're tryin' to teach me manners, an' I'm doing me level best to learn! But if I'm not allowed to ask a question, 'ow the hell am I supposed to learn? I think it was a perfectly reasonable question. I mean, after all, a cheek is a cheek whether it's on yer face or yer backside!'

'Oh, I give up!' Molly threw her hands in the air and winked at Miss Clegg. 'Where's that flamin' welcome home cake? Stick a piece of that in her gob an' shut her up.'

Phil reached for Doreen's hand. They'd never know how happy it made him to be part of these families. After nineteen years of living with the Bradleys, nineteen years of shame, he was now at peace with himself. He had Aunt Vicky who'd been so good to him and whom he adored, and he had Doreen, the girl of his dreams. And the icing on the cake were Molly and Nellie and their families. He was indeed blessed.

Chapter Six

The passengers disembarking at the Prince's Dock from the overnight boat from Ireland all wore the same weary expression on their faces. Many were shivering with the cold as they walked down the gangplanks positioned at each end of the boat, clutching one of the side ropes to steady themselves as the boat bobbed up and down in the water. The decks were crowded with people eager to feel their feet on terra firma, but progress was slow as passengers struggled with cases and bags. Occasionally a hand would be lifted in greeting when a familiar face was spotted amongst the small group waiting behind a barrier to meet friends or family, or a voice raised asking those in front to put a move on. But for the most part the passengers were silent, too tired for conversation or smiles.

'They don't look very happy, do they, Ma?' Molly was standing between her mother and Nellie. They'd been there for over an hour and she stamped her feet to get the circulation going while wondering how they would recognize Rosemary out of all those people . . . there must be hundreds of them!

'It's happy yer'd have them, is it?' Bridie shook her head. 'After spending ten hours on an open deck, with nothing to protect yer from the bitter wind, I don't think yerself would be full of the joys of spring, either!'

'It wouldn't do for me.' Nellie tightened the knot in the fleecy muffler around her neck. 'I'm perishin' just standing here.'

'Quiet now an' let's keep our eyes open for her.' Bridie was scanning the passengers as they stepped off the gangplanks. 'She'll be wearing a black skirt and shawl and a black hat.'

Thirty minutes later the crowds had thinned out and they still hadn't spotted anyone they thought could be the young Irish girl. 'There's plenty more people on the boat,' Molly said when she noticed her mother's brow creased with worry. 'Happen she'll be one of the last off.'

'Oh, look, I wonder if that's her?' Bridie pointed to a lone figure standing sideways on, a short distance from them. 'Sure, she's all in black so she is, and she looks as though she's waitin' for someone.'

'Ma, yer need yer eyes testing!' Molly grinned. 'That's never a fifteen-year-old girl! I can see her middle-age spread from here!'

Bridie went back to scanning the stragglers leaving the boat, but her eyes kept straying to the lone figure. 'I'm going over to ask. If it's not Rosemary, then there's no harm done.' Without further ado, Bridie rounded the barrier.

'She's wasting her time,' Molly said. 'If that's a fifteen-year-old girl, I'll eat me ruddy hat.'

'Have yer got a hat, girl?' Nellie asked, innocently.

Molly tutted. 'Now yer know I haven't . . . what would I be wantin' a hat for?'

Nellie screwed her face up, causing her eyes to disappear from view for a second. 'Yer'd be wantin' to eat it, girl. Turn around an' see for yerself.'

Molly gasped in surprise when she saw her mother standing with her arms around the 'middle-aged woman'. 'Oh, my God, come on!' She tugged on Nellie's arm. 'Fancy dressin' a young girl in old-fashioned clothes like that!' Oblivious to Nellie's panting as she pulled her along behind, she hissed, 'Remember what yer've got to say, it means a hundred thousand welcomes.'

When Bridie heard them come up behind her she stepped back from the girl. 'This is me daughter, Mrs Bennett.'

'Hello, Rosemary.' The breath caught in Molly's throat when she stared into the most beautiful eyes she'd ever seen. Deep blue, fanned by long black lashes, they were a mirror to the girl's soul. All her emotions were there, naked for all to see. Fear at starting a new life, sadness at leaving behind all she loved, and shyness at meeting the people whose lives she was going to share. From that moment, Molly took the frightened young girl into her heart. She knew instinctively that here was someone who would never lie to you or do you a bad turn. She held her arms wide. '*Cead mile failte*, sunshine.'

Like a trusting child, Rosemary walked into her embrace. 'I thank yer kindly, Mrs Bennett.'

'Hey! What's with the Mrs Bennett? I'm yer auntie Molly, sunshine, an' there's another auntie waitin' to meet yer. Here she is, my best mate and your auntie Nellie.'

Nellie's lips were moving silently, repeating the phrase over and over. Then she grinned at Molly. 'Yer've been that long I've nearly forgot what I'm supposed to say.' She turned her smile on Rosemary. 'I mightn't be able to get me tongue around it, girl, 'cos I can't even speak proper English, but I'll do me best. *Cead mile failte* . . . a hundred thousand welcomes to dear old Liverpool.'

Rosemary's huge blue eyes filled with tears and her lips trembled. 'Thank yer, Auntie Nellie.'

'Come on,' Bridie bustled. 'She's cold, tired and hungry, so let's get her home. You carry her bags, will yer, Molly me darlin'?'

Outside the dock and walking towards the tram stop, Rosemary's eyes were wide with wonder. 'Sure yer've foine big buildings here, so yer have. I've never seen anythin' so grand in all me life, an' that's the truth of it.'

There was a tram waiting at the stop and Bridie stepped

aboard, but Molly held on briefly to Rosemary's arm. 'That's the Liver Buildings with the two birds on top. Known all over the world, those birds are. An' one day I'll bring yer down an' show yer all the other beautiful buildings we have in Liverpool. An' we'll go on a ferry trip across the Mersey to New Brighton where there's a big fairground.'

'Is that right now, Auntie Molly?'

'It is, sunshine.' Molly gazed at the round, chubby face with cheeks as rosy as a polished apple. She was a bonny girl all right, plump in all the right places. But the clothes she was wearing didn't help. She looked comical in them, as though she was dressed for a role in a stage play set in the twenties. Especially the battered black hat with its two imitation cherries hanging down the side . . . that was more suitable for a woman of seventy than a seventeen-year-old.

'Come on, let's get on the tram before it goes without us.' She let Rosemary get on, then waited for Nellie. 'Come on, me old mate, I'll give yer a push up.'

Nellie pouted her lips and said in a childish voice, 'Only if yer promise to take me on the ferry to New Brighton an' let me have a go on the ferris wheel.'

'Shut up, yer daft ha'p'orth, an' get yer backside on that tram before the pair of us are left behind.'

Molly lowered the gas under the pan and, bending her head, she sniffed appreciatively. 'Mmm, that smells bloody lovely! I don't care what anyone says, yer can't beat neck of lamb for making a tasty pan of stew. Bags of potatoes, vegetables, onions and barley, with light fluffy suet dumplings. All that goodness is bound to put a lining on their tummies.' Replacing the lid she grinned. 'I remind meself of that poster of the Bisto Kids.' She rinsed her hands under the tap then reached behind the door for the piece of towelling. From where she stood she could see Ruthie sitting on the couch cradling her doll in the crook of her arm. The doll was called Shirley, after Shirley

Temple, and at one time had resembled the child film star, with bright blue eyes and long ringlets. But after two years of rough combing the hair was now tatty, the pink cheeks had been scrubbed white, half of her eyelashes were missing and she had a definite squint in her left eye.

Molly gave a low chuckle as she recalled the day Nellie had picked up the doll and laughingly said it looked like a woman of ill repute after a heavy night down on Lime Street. Fortunately Ruthie hadn't heard the remark, otherwise it would have taken all of Molly's gift for storytelling to explain what a woman of ill repute was, and what she was doing down Lime Street.

Molly finished drying her hands and looked towards the basin where the six round, floury dumplings were ready to drop in the pan twenty minutes before the stew was ready. The kitchen was spick and span, no dirty dishes or clothes hanging around, and Molly was feeling pleased with herself when she walked through to the living room. She paused near the sideboard to watch Ruthie, who had the doll over her shoulder and was patting its back saying, 'Come on, me darlin', get that nasty wind up for yer mam. If yer don't, yer'll get pains in yer little tum-tum.'

God bless her cotton socks, Molly thought, it doesn't take much to amuse her. 'I'm just nippin' up to the corner shop, sunshine, I won't be a minute.'

The doll quickly ceased to be Ruthie's little darling and was flung unceremoniously on the floor. 'Ah ray, Mam, I wanna come with yer.'

'No sunshine, you stay right where yer are.' Molly bustled to the door, keeping her head averted so she wouldn't be swayed by the pleading eyes. 'I'm only goin' for a packet of tea an' I'll be back even before yer know I've gone.'

Molly stepped into the street and pulled the door to behind her. She was turning left to go up to the shop when she happened to glance down the street just as a man turned the corner. Even though it was dusk and there were no lamps lit, there was no mistaking that figure. After all, how many men were there who were six-foot-five tall and built like a battleship?

'Corker!' Her message forgotten, Molly waved frantically as she hastened towards the giant of a man who had his seaman's bag slung over his shoulder and his peaked cap set at a jaunty angle. 'Corker, when did yer dock?'

'Hello, Molly me darlin'.' Apart from his height, Jimmy Corkhill would stand out in any crowd. A colourful character with a big bushy beard and thick moustache, he was well liked by everyone and a local hero to the kids in the neighbourhood who had named him Sinbad. 'It's good to see yer, Molly, an' ye're still as pretty as ever.' Corker lowered his bag to the ground and two hands the size of ham shanks circled Molly's waist and lifted her off her feet. He planted a prickly kiss on her cheek before setting her down. 'Jack and the kids all right, I hope?'

'Yeah, they're fine.' Molly smiled at the gentle giant she counted as one of her best friends. 'I can't get over seein' you! Yesterday Phil came home on two weeks' leave, this mornin' I was up with the larks to meet a young Irish girl who's come to Liverpool to find work an' is staying with me ma and da, and now you turn up!' She shook her head as though she couldn't keep track of events. 'When did yer dock?'

'This afternoon.'

'Does yer ma an' Ellen know ye're home?'

'I've just called into the shop to see Ellen.' Corker grinned and his white teeth shone through the mass of hair around his mouth. 'I'll get a tickin' off when I get home, though, me ma will have me guts for garters. I rang the corner shop to ask Maisie to let the old girl know I was on me way, but that was three hours ago.'

'Ooh ay, Corker, she'll be worried to death! Where've yer been all this time?'

'Don't you start, Molly, 'cos I'm in for an ear-bashin' when I get home.' Corker's chuckle was like the roar of a lion. 'I let the lads talk me into goin' for a pint and that was definitely a mistake. I've told yer about the pub where all the seamen meet, the White Star off Mathew Street? Well Alfie, who runs the place, gave us all a round of drinks on the house. Now we couldn't leave without buyin' him one back.' His head thrown back, the big man roared with laughter. 'The trouble was, there were five of us.'

Molly gasped. 'Yer mean yer've had five pints?'

'Six, including the one Alfie mugged us to.'

'My God, it's a wonder yer can walk straight!'

'Molly, me darlin', it's a sailor ye're talking to! Any seaman who can't drink six pints and still walk a straight line is not worth his salt.'

'I hope yer ma's in a forgiving mood, 'cos she probably had a dinner ready for yer hours ago.' Molly began to titter. 'Corker, me imagination is runnin' riot! I can just picture yer ma standin' on a chair to box yer ears.'

'No need for a chair, I'll lift her up.' Corker bent down and lifted his bag by the drawstrings. 'I'd better get home before she has the police out lookin' for me.' He swung the bag effortlessly over his shoulder and grinned down at Molly. 'What are you doin' out without a coat on? Waitin' for yer fancy man?'

'I was on me way up to the shop, we're a bit low on tea.'

Corker fell into step beside her. 'I'll be down later to take Ellen for a drink, so I'll call in and see Jack an' the kids. I'd like to see young Phil, too!'

'Him and Doreen are back together.' Molly rubbed her arms briskly, sorry now she hadn't thrown a coat over her shoulders. 'Talk about love's young dream, they can't take their eyes off each other.'

They stopped outside the shop. 'He's a good lad, Molly,' Corker said, 'Doreen could do a lot worse.'

'I know.' Molly wagged a finger into his face. 'Now go home, Corker, an' face the music. We'll see yer tonight.'

As she returned his wave, Molly's mind was on her pan of stew. Please God, don't let it have boiled dry.

The family sat around the table, silent as Molly told of Rosemary's arrival. 'Me heart went out to the kid, she looked so lonely and miserable. She's got a pretty face with rosy red cheeks and the most beautiful eyes I've ever seen. But the clothes she had on made her look like an old woman, and I was feeling really sorry for her. That is until we got back to me ma's and she pulled two ruddy long pins out of the shabby old hat and took it off. Then I was green with envy when a mass of black curls came cascading down around her shoulders. I swear I've never seen a head of hair like it in me life.'

'It's a big step for a kid of that age,' Jack said, munching slowly on a piece of liver that was a bit on the tough side. 'D'yer think she'll settle down?'

'Oh, I think so, given time. She looked a bit sad and was very quiet, but I think the busy streets with all the traffic frightened her at first. As me ma said, where she comes from is right in the middle of the country and they're lucky if they see another living soul for days on end. No shops handy if yer run out of anythin', an' no trams or cars. If yer want to get anywhere yer have to use shanks's pony, or go in the trap.'

'What's a trap?' Tommy asked, his mouth half full. 'I thought a trap was somethin' yer caught mice in.'

'Oh, very funny,' Molly said. 'What is it the dairy man uses to deliver his milk? The thing his horse pulls?'

'Oh, that kind of trap! With seats around the side?'

'Correct,' said Molly. 'See, if yer keep yer ears open, son, yer can learn somethin' every day.'

Doreen gave her brother a dig. 'Learn somethin' every day until ye're about ninety, our kid, an' yer could end up a doctor or a solicitor.'

Ruthie's interest had been roused. 'Mam, has she brought her pony an' trap with her?'

Molly laughed as she leaned over and chucked her youngest daughter under the chin. 'No, sunshine, ye're not allowed to bring a pony over on the boat.'

'Is she nice, Mam?' Jill asked. 'I mean, is she a happy person? Will she get along with Nanna and Granda?'

'Get along with them! They're goin' to spoil her soft!' Molly smiled. 'Yer can't help but like her, she a lovable lass. An' dead funny too, some of the things she comes out with are hilarious. Her accent is very thick, but it's attractive, like me ma's. She shouldn't have any trouble gettin' a job, especially with all the women goin' in the munitions factories, but she'll need some decent clothes. I'm hoping you girls will help her out in that department. Doreen, you could run her a couple of dresses up, that would make a difference.'

'Don't ask me to do anythin' this week, Mam,' Doreen warned. 'Not while Phil's home.'

'I'll lend her a dress to be going on with,' Jill offered. 'There's that blue one, I haven't worn it for ages.'

Molly chuckled. 'She'd make two of you, sunshine! I've told yer, she's a bonny lass!' Holding up a hand for silence, she cocked her head and listened. 'I asked Ma to walk her round so yez can all meet her, and this is probably them at the door now.'

Jack dropped his knife and fork and jumped to his feet when Bridie came in, followed by Bob and a very nervous-looking Rosemary. 'Hello, love,' he held out his hand, 'I'm very pleased to meet yer.'

'Thank you.' The hand Rosemary held out was shaking but her eyes held his. 'An' it's pleased I am to meet you.' She saw Molly standing behind Jack and a smile lit up her face. 'Hello, Auntie Molly, it's meself, so it is.'

Tommy raised his head and sniggered. 'An' here's me thinkin' it was the woman next door.'

'I'm surprised at yer, Tommy Bennett!' Bridie said. 'Sure there was no call at all to say such a thing.'

'It was only a joke, Auntie Bridget,' Rosemary said, smiling at Tommy's bowed head. 'An' I thought it was funny, so I did.'

Bob had taken his overcoat off and he handed it to Jack to hang on the hall-stand. 'Well you know who Tommy is now, so let me introduce you to the rest of the family. Jill is the eldest, then there's Doreen, and this little lady is the baby of the family, Ruthie.'

'Sit down an' make yerselves at home,' Molly said. 'I'll just clear the dishes away and make the place look a bit tidy.'

Tommy pushed his chair back and picked up his plate. 'I'll take this out an' then I'm goin' up to Ginger's.'

'Oh, no you're not!' Molly shot him daggers before stacking the plates. 'Yer'll sit down with our visitors for a while.'

'I'll take the dishes out, Mam.' Jill took them from her mother. 'You sit yourself down.'

'And I'll shake the cloth in the yard.' Doreen leaned over to take the cloth by the four corners. 'Phil's pickin' me up in about half an hour, we're going to Barlow's Lane.'

'He'll not mind waiting,' Molly said, flopping into her chair. 'You can spare a few minutes.'

Rosemary had been watching with wonder. She'd only ever been to the pictures a few times in her life because the nearest picture house was forty miles away from where she lived, but she thought Jill and Doreen looked like film stars with their slim figures, long blonde hair and pretty faces. And the dresses they had on, sure she'd never seen anything like them. ''Tis a foine-looking family yer have, Auntie Molly, an' no mistake. An' I'd not be tellin' lies, so I wouldn't, if I said I've never seen a finer.'

Tommy folded his arms and rolled his eyes to the ceiling. How long was his mother going to make him sit and listen to this rubbish? He didn't like girls at the best of times, but this one was more of a pain in the neck than the rest of them put together.

'Looks are not everythin', Rosemary,' Bridie said. 'It's what is inside that counts.'

'Wasn't me mammy an' me dadda always tellin' me the same thing?' With her mass of thick curly hair swirling about her shoulders and her deep blue eyes alive with interest, Rosemary smiled. 'But isn't it nice when the eyes have somethin' beautiful to look at? Sure the good Lord put a lot of beautiful things on this earth an' He wouldn't like it altogether if we didn't appreciate them.'

Jill and Doreen had come back to sit by the table and found themselves drawn to the lovely, lilting Irish brogue, and the warmth of the smile on Rosemary's face. 'Yer have three lovely daughters, Auntie Molly, so yer have. And Tommy's as foine a figure of a man as yer'll meet in many a long day.'

While the rest of the family spluttered with laughter, Tommy appealed to his mother. 'Mam, will yer shut her up?'

'Sure being handsome isn't somethin' to be ashamed of, Tommy, not at all.' Rosemary wasn't about to be shut up. 'There's nothing but truth in me words . . . you're a foine figure of a man.' She leaned back in her chair, smiling. 'As me mammy would say, you're "beef to the heel, like a Mullingar heifer".'

Molly had her head in her hands, weak with laughter, so she missed the dark look on Tommy's face. But when she heard his chair scraping back, she looked up just in time to see the withering look of disgust he threw Rosemary's way before fleeing the room.

But even though she could hear him running up the stairs, Rosemary wasn't finished with the poor lad. 'D'yer have a girlfriend, Tommy?' The room erupted. Jack had his head thrown back, banging his fists on the arm of his chair, while Bob leaned his elbows on his knees and covered his face with his hands. Bridie was wiping her eyes with a wisp of a handkerchief and Jill and Doreen had their faces down on the table, their bodies shaking with laughter. Ruthie came to sit on Molly's knee, and although she couldn't make head nor tail of it, the laughter was infectious and she rocked with her mother.

Rosemary had a wide grin on her bonny face. She didn't think she'd said anything funny, but was glad that whatever it was had caused so much happiness. She'd ask Auntie Bridget when they got home. After all, she only asked if Tommy had a girlfriend, because if he hadn't she'd like to fill the post. She was fifteen, and in Ireland you could go courting at fifteen.

Molly wiped her eyes with the back of her hand. She looked across at Rosemary and told herself this girl was going to bring laughter with her wherever she went. She'll do for me, she thought, but I can't speak for our Tommy.

Upstairs Tommy stood by the window in the bedroom that had a partition running down the middle. His father had put it up when he got too big to sleep in the same room as his sisters.

Girls! He hated girls! And that one downstairs, she was the worst of the lot! He'd make sure he was out when she came round, in future. But the trouble was, he loved his nanna and granda, and now *she* was living with them! It meant he couldn't go there any more, and that was a further black mark against her. Why couldn't she have stayed in Ireland where she belonged? Anyway, she wasn't going to spoil his night. He'd creep down the stairs and make his way up to his mate Ginger's. You knew where you were with a bloke.

Steve and Phil came out of their houses at the same time and met up outside the Bennetts' house. 'Aren't we lucky having girlfriends who live on our doorstep?' Steve laughed. 'Saves a lot of money on tram fares.'

'On shoe leather too,' Phil nodded. 'You can walk yerself home at the same time yer walk them home.'

'Don't let on, though,' Steve said with a wink as they waited for the door to be opened. 'They might think that's all we chose them for.'

The sight of the two tall handsome young men, one dark and one blond, took away Rosemary's power of speech. Her head was whirling as she thought of all the things she had to write home about. How all the people in Liverpool lived in grand houses with electric lights, and when you went to the privy you just had to pull on the handle of a chain. And how all the people were beautiful to look at, wore nice clothes and laughed a lot.

She was shy when she shook hands with the two men, and when they said they were pleased to meet her and hoped she'd settle down in Liverpool, she thanked them before lapsing into silence. No, she wouldn't tell her mammy about the nice clothes, it wouldn't be fair. Hadn't all the family had to go without to scrape the fare together to send her to England? But when Jill and Doreen were leaving with their boyfriends, she couldn't help comparing their clothes to the ones she was wearing. The long black skirt and knitted shawl looked fine back home, but here she felt out of place in them. Still, never mind, she'd try and get herself a job as soon as she could and save up hard, so she could send money home to help the family, and buy herself a nice dress.

'Rosemary.' Bob had wriggled to the end of the couch. The lass looked worn out, it was time they went home. 'Rosemary!'

But the girl was miles away, lost in thought.

Bridie touched her arm. 'Uncle Bob's been calling you, sweetheart, didn't you hear him?'

'No, I didn't, Auntie Bridget, I'm very sorry.' She put a hand over her mouth to stifle a yawn. 'I'm not used to getting me full title, yer see. Back home everyone calls me Rosie.'

'Oh sweetheart, why didn't you say? We were told in the letter your name was Rosemary, so we just took it for granted!' Bridie patted her hand. 'From now on, you'll be Rosie to all of us an' that'll make yer feel more at home.'

'You must be tired out, lass,' Bob said, 'let's get you home to bed.'

'Ye're not goin' out of my house without havin' a cup of tea! What would the neighbours say!' Molly sprang to her feet and pushed Ruthie towards Jack. 'It's way past her bedtime, love, will yer take her up for us while I put the kettle on?'

Molly was carrying a tray through when the knocker went. 'Oh God, who can it be now?'

'I'll get it,' Jack called, jumping down the last three stairs. 'It's probably yer mate, Nellie.'

But it was Corker, and he had a merry glint in his eye. 'I've called in to see the pretty Irish colleen.'

Rosie was telling herself she'd seen some grand sights today, but when she saw Corker bending his head to get through the doorway she had to rub her eyes to make sure she wasn't dreaming. Grand houses, beautiful people . . . but giants?

'Hello, me darlin'.' Corker lifted her bodily out of the chair and held her just above the ground. 'Are yer goin' to give yer uncle Corker a kiss?'

Looking down into the weather-beaten, hairy face and seeing the merry twinkle in his eyes, she gave a hearty laugh, the sound clear as a bell. 'Sure now, me mammy said I hadn't to speak to any strange men, so she did, but I didn't hear her mention anythin' about giants. Mind you, perhaps she doesn't know that yer have giants in Liverpool.' She pulled a face when her lips came into contact with his moustache. 'Ooh, it tickles.'

Corker set her down. 'Pretty as a picture you are, me darlin'. With that hair an' those eyes, yer'll have all the fellers in Liverpool after yer.'

Molly was pulling on Corker's arm. 'Have yer been to

Ellen's?' The big man shook his head as he rubbed the side of his nose. 'I met Tommy goin' up to Ginger's an' he told me about Rosemary. He was so full of it, I thought I'd call an' see her for meself.'

'There's a little story behind that, but I'll tell yer next time I see yer.' Molly turned to Rosie and winked before looking back at Corker. 'When ye're belting out "Sweet Rosie O'Grady" in the pub on Saturday night, don't be surprised if our Rosie comes a running 'cos she'll think ye're callin' her.'

Chapter Seven

Molly pulled the door shut behind her, feeling well pleased with herself. It was only ten o'clock and she'd done all her work. Beds made, washing on the line, everywhere dusted and polished until you could see your face in it, spuds peeled and a bacon shank in steep to get some of the salt out. 'Up in the mornin's the game,' she said cheerfully as she walked to Nellie's door and hammered on the knocker. 'Get nowt done sittin' on yer backside with yer feet up.'

She grinned when Nellie opened the door in all her glory. Her turban was skew-whiff, covering only one side of her head; streaks of coal dust covered her face and arms; a length of string was tied around her waist to keep her wraparound pinny in place; and one of her scruffy carpet slippers had a hole in the toe and was missing its red bobble. 'My God Nellie, yer wouldn't win any fashion contests looking like that.' Molly eyed her from head to toe. 'Yer look like Cinderella waitin' for her fairy godmother to appear with her magic wand. And it would have to be a bloody good magic wand to turn you into a princess.'

Nellie folded her arms and leaned against the door jamb. 'Is that all yer've come for, girl, to insult me? If someone's rubbed yer up the wrong way an' yer've got a cob on, why didn't yer just kick the cat? Would 'ave saved yer gettin' yerself all dolled up to walk the few yards to my house.'

'I thought about kickin' the cat, then remembered we didn't have one,' Molly grinned. 'No, I haven't got a cob on, sunshine, in fact I'm feeling on top of the world! An' when I'm in a happy mood, who do I want to share it with but me best mate.'

'If it was a slab of Cadbury's yer wanted to share, girl, I'd invite yer in. But unless yer feel like gettin' down on yer hands and knees and scrubbin' me kitchen floor, then sharing yer happy mood will have to wait until later, when I've got all me work done.' Nellie drew herself up to her full height. 'Come back in an hour an' yer won't know me. I'll look like one of them mannequin dummies yer see in the windows of those posh shops down Bold Street.'

'You don't need fancy clothes, sunshine, ye're beautiful enough without them.' Molly shivered suddenly. 'The winter hasn't half settled in, it's quite nippy out.'

'Then why the 'ell didn't yer stay in by the fire?'

'I want to go round to me ma's to see how they're gettin' on. I just hope the extra work isn't too much for her and me da.'

'My impression of Rosemary was that she'll be more help than hindrance. I really took to the kid.' A slow smile crossed Nellie's face. 'Mind you, I'm not much good at judging characters, am I? Look who I picked for me mate!'

'Cheeky article!' Molly grinned. 'Anyway, she doesn't like her full name, so it's Rosie from now on. Rosie O'Grady.'

'Go 'way! That's not her name, is it?'

'It is, sunshine, an' if yer make any cracks in her presence, I'll flatten yer.'

'I won't make any cracks, girl, 'cos I think she suits it. I mean, it wouldn't suit you or me, but she looks the part.'

'Anyway, the real reason I called is to talk about the black-out curtains. I lay in bed last night working it out. Mr Henry is due to collect the rent today, so how about asking if we can miss him this week and you an' me go for the material?'

'Yer mean none of us pay?' Nellie pulled a face. 'He wouldn't be very happy about that!'

'Me ma will be paying, an' I imagine Miss Clegg and Mary will. It's only you, me and Ellen that are the poor relations.'

'I'll do whatever you say, girl.' Nellie thought about it, then nodded. 'It probably would be a good idea to get it now 'cos if we leave it till the last minute they might be sold out.'

'Right, that settles it, we'll go for it tomorrow.' Molly turned to walk away. 'I'll see yer later, but if Mr Henry calls before I get back, tell him we're not paying.'

'Ay, ay!' Nellie stepped into the street. 'Come back here, you! Don't yer be leavin' me to do yer dirty work.'

'I can't stop now,' Molly called over her shoulder as she hurried up the street. 'Yer've kept me talkin' long enough.'

She reached the corner where she would turn to get to her parents' house, then looked back. Nellie was still standing on the pavement with her hands on her hips. When she saw Molly glance back, she clenched one of her fists and punched the air.

'Oh dear,' Molly chuckled, rounding the corner. 'I'll be in for it when I come home: there'll be blue murder. She'll be scrubbin' hell out of the kitchen floor right now, pretending it's my face.'

'Are yer all right, Molly?' one of the neighbours asked, giving Molly a strange look. 'Feelin' OK, are yer?'

'I'm fine, Mrs Gibson, just havin' a conversation with meself. Yer want to try it sometime . . . it's the gear! D'yer know, I haven't lost an argument with meself for donkey's years.'

Molly could hear the laughter as she lifted the knocker. 'Well, it sounds as though I've been worrying for nothing.'

Bob opened the door with a huge grin on his face and the signs of recent laughter tears. 'You're early, lass! Did yer smell the tea?'

The scene that met Molly was warm and welcoming. Smiling faces and a bright, cheering fire. It did her heart good to see her mother and father looking so content and happy.

'Hello, Auntie Molly!' Rosie's bonny face beamed. 'It's grand to see yer, so it is.'

Molly slipped out of her coat and laid it on the arm of the couch. 'Don't I get a kiss?'

The girl was over like a shot to throw her arms around her. 'It was in me mind, so it was, but I didn't know if I'd be doin' the right thing.'

'Sure I enjoy a kiss as well as the next man, so I do.' Molly's Irish accent sent Rosie into peals of laughter. 'Especially if it's from the man next door.'

'Hello, lass.' Bridie lifted her face for a kiss. 'Sit yerself down and get a warm.'

Molly sat on one of the straight wooden dining chairs and nodded her head at the tray on the table. 'I could murder a cup of tea.'

'I'll get it, lass.' Bob was halfway out of his chair when Rosie took him gently by the shoulders and sat him down again.

'It's meself that'll be pouring Auntie Molly a cup of tea.' The kiss that Rosie planted on his cheek brought a smile to Bob's face and a tear to Molly's eye. She didn't have to worry – her ma and da were in good hands with this young girl. Her presence had already added something to the house, and Molly sought a word to describe it. She gazed at the familiar room and it looked as neat and tidy as it always did. There was always a decent fire in the grate, so it wasn't that. No, she couldn't explain it even to herself, but there was definitely something. 'Here yer go, Auntie Molly.'

Molly looked up into Rosie's smiling face and the word she'd been seeking hit her between the eyes. It was youth! Her ma had been right! Having a youngster in the house, full of vitality, made you feel younger yourself. And she could see it in the faces of her parents. Oh, how selfish she'd been to try and stop them adding this extra happiness to their lives! She above all should have known better, because what would her life be without her own children?

'Did yer sleep well, Rosie?'

'Oh, Auntie Molly, didn't I sleep like an angel! Sure the bed was so soft it was like floating on a cloud in the heavens.' The dark blue eyes clouded over for a second. 'Sure I missed me mammy tuckin' me into bed, so I did, but Auntie Bridget came in to kiss me goodnight an' I was soon fast asleep.'

She's so innocent, Molly thought, so young in the head for her age. But that was no bad thing. Some girls of today were old women before they were out of their teens.

Bridie had been watching Molly's face and knew what her daughter was thinking. 'Living on a farm miles from anywhere isn't the same as living in a city, me darlin'. Working with animals can make yer very outspoken and worldly in the ways of nature, but it doesn't always prepare yer for the pace or the social graces of life in a city.'

Bob chuckled. 'Our Rosie can be very outspoken, Molly! She's had yer ma's hair standing on end a few times this morning.'

'Oh ay, what's she been saying?'

Bridie blushed with embarrassment. 'For the life of me I can't remember offhand.'

'Oh, I can remember, Auntie Bridget!' Rosie, her cheeks glowing and her beautiful eyes sparkling, was happy to oblige. 'Sure wasn't it about Farmer Murphy's bull I was tellin' yer? How it—'

'That's enough, Rosie me darlin'.' Bridie's face reddened. 'Didn't I warn yer to think about what yer were saying? Sure, people in the city know nothing about the behaviour of animals, an' they'd not take kindly to hearing it from the lips of a young girl.'

Molly felt sorry for Rosie. It must be hard coming to a strange country and having to adjust to a new way of life. But looking at the bonny face, Molly knew she didn't need to feel sorry. The smile and the look of innocence were still there. 'Sure I'll try and remember what yer told me, Auntie Bridget.' Rosie's lips parted and she stuck her tongue out. 'This is the divil, an' I'll be keeping me eye on it in future, yer have me word on that.'

'Don't do that, sunshine,' Molly laughed, 'or yer'll end up cross-eyed and we wouldn't want that.'

Rosie's laugh was music to the ears and her face a feast to the eyes. 'Sure yer have a fine sense of humour, Auntie Molly, are yer sure ye're not Irish?'

'Ay, sunshine, don't push yer luck! We Liverpudlians can match the Irish for humour any day.'

'I'll let yer off then, seein' as ye're half Irish.' Rosie leaned her elbows on the table and cupped her face in her hands. 'It's good to laugh, isn't it, Auntie Molly? Me mammy always says, "If ye're wearing a smile, then ye're always welcome, but if yer wear a frown nobody wants yer."'

'If yer like a laugh, sunshine, then Auntie Nellie's the one.' Molly hid a smile as a picture of Nellie shaking a fist at her flashed through her mind. 'She's been makin' me laugh for over twenty years now.'

'And does Auntie Nellie have to think before she says anything that might offend?'

From his seat on the couch, Bob let out a roar. 'If Nellie had to think before she spoke, she'd never open her mouth!'

When Rosie looked puzzled, Molly touched her hand. 'It's like this, sunshine, it's Auntie Nellie's looks and her actions that make her so funny. Like just now, when I gave her a knock.' Molly pushed her chair back. 'I'll show yer.' First she described how Nellie looked, right down to her big toe sticking out of the old slipper. Then she related the conversation, changing voices as she changed characters. 'An' the last I heard was Nellie shoutin', "Hey, come back here, you!"'

The loudest laughter came from Rosie. 'Oh, wasn't that the funniest thing altogether, Auntie Bridget?'

'There's plenty more me daughter could tell yer about Mrs McDonough,' Bridie said. 'Some of them not to be repeated in front of young girls. But I have to admit that Nellie, and Molly, have been blessed with a rare sense of humour. And with something much more precious, a true and lasting friendship.'

'Oh ay, Ma! Don't be goin' all poetic on me!'

'Now that was a nice thing Auntie Bridget said.' Rosie looked very impressed. 'And isn't it the truth, though? As me mammy always says, "A friend in need is a friend indeed."'

'Your mammy has a lot of sayings, doesn't she, sunshine?'

'She has that, Auntie Molly.' Rosie wagged a finger to invite Molly to lean closer. Then she said in a loud whisper, 'But I think most of them would be included in the things I'm not supposed to say.' She tapped her forehead. 'I'll have to be doing a lot of thinkin' before I open me mouth, so I will.'

'Rosie O'Grady, ye're a girl after me own heart.' Molly stood up to plant a kiss on the rosy cheek. 'An' I think you and me mate are goin' to get on famously.' She reached for her coat. 'I'll have to be makin' tracks, Ma, but I'll see yer soon. It might not be tomorrow, 'cos me and Nellie are goin' for the blackout material.'

'We're all right, me darlin', yer've no need to worry about us. Give our love to Jack an' the children.'

'Tell Tommy I was askin' after him, Auntie Molly,' Rosie said, 'an' I'll be round to see him soon.'

Molly was chuckling as she followed her father down the hall. If her son knew she was coming he'd be up and out like a shot.

Bob opened the door and stood aside to let her pass. 'She's everythin' they said, isn't she, lass?'

'And more,' Molly agreed. 'You won't go far wrong with Rosie.' She put her foot out to step into the street, then drew it back. 'By the way, what about Farmer Murphy's bull, just in case Nellie asks?'

Bob shook his head. 'Ask yer ma, but make sure ye're alone when yer do.'

Molly was curious as she walked down the stairs after seeing Ruthie to bed. There'd been two knocks on the door while she'd been up there and although she'd strained her ears, she couldn't recognize any voices. She stepped off the bottom stair, turned into the living room and froze with surprise. The room was jam-packed! Every chair was taken, the couch was full and, horror of horrors, the arms of the couch were being used as seats. 'Ye gods, where have yez all come from? Are we havin' a party an' someone forgot to tell me?'

'It's you who forgot to tell anyone, an' yer forgot on purpose.' Nellie folded her arms and hitched up her bosom. She was seated by the table, oblivious to the fact that her legs were wide apart and everyone could see her stockings which were rolled down to her chubby knees and twisted around her elastic garters. 'I said to George, she thinks we won't find out. That's what I said, didn't I George?' Without waiting for a reply from her long-suffering husband, Nellie went on, 'Fancy a mate doin' a thing like that! I've a good mind not to go to her party! Weren't those my very words, George?' To everyone's amusement she banged on the table and glared at her husband. 'George, will yer sit up straight when I'm talkin' to yer an' listen to what I've got to say?'

With the room ringing with laughter, Molly gazed around the happy faces and her heart swelled with pride. Doreen and Phil were sitting at the table holding hands, Jill and Steve sat opposite, their arms around each other's waists, George was seated in Jack's chair, Corker and Ellen were on the couch and Jack and Tommy were perched on its arms. But for once, Molly told herself to hell with the furniture. People were more important than ruddy pieces of wood. After all, a table wouldn't listen to yer troubles, a chair wouldn't tell you a joke and make you laugh, and the couch wouldn't lend you a couple of bob when you were skint.

'Aren't you goin' out, Doreen?'

Doreen shook her head. 'We were goin' to the dance, but we've changed our minds, haven't we Phil?'

'I wanted to see Mr Corkhill,' Phil answered. 'He went away so soon after the trouble, I didn't get a chance to talk to him properly.'

'What about you, Jill?' Molly was mentally counting the number of cups and saucers she had that matched. Certainly not enough to go round this lot! 'Are you an' Steve goin' out?'

It was Steve who answered. His dimples deepening in his handsome face, he smiled at Molly. 'Ye're on a loser, Mrs B., 'cos we're staying in, too!'

Molly turned hopefully to Tommy. 'You're goin' up to Ginger's, aren't yer, son?'

'Nah, not tonight Mam, I'm havin' a night in.'

Molly heard the loud creaking of a chair and she spun round to see Nellie shaking with laughter. 'If you break that chair, Nellie McDonough, I'll break yer ruddy neck!'

But once Nellie had a fit of the giggles there was no stopping her. 'Ye're stuck with the lot of us, girl,' she wheezed, her chins moving in the opposite direction to her head. 'Yer'd best give in gracefully and get the whisky an' port out, an' start making a pile of sarnies. Corned beef if yer've got any in – they're me favourite.'

'I'll give yer a hand with the sandwiches, Molly,' Ellen said quietly and in all seriousness. 'I don't mind, honest.'

'What flamin' sandwiches?' Molly stood in the middle of the room with her hands on her hips. 'I've got nowt in to feed this ruddy lot!'

'Molly, girl, I don't want to put yer to no trouble,' Nellie said, her face the picture of innocence. 'Yer know I'm not a fussy person, so if yer've no corned beef in, don't worry, I'm not too proud to eat meat paste.'

Molly bent forward until their noses were nearly touching. 'Yer know what you can do with yerself, don't yer, Nellie McDonough? Yer can—' Molly was silenced when Nellie put a hand across her mouth.

'Now girl, just remember what ye're always telling me. Don't say anythin' naughty in front of the children. An' what you were about to tell me to do was not only naughty, it would have been physically impossible an' ruddy painful!'

The floorboards and chairs creaked and the room shook with laughter. Corker was rocking as the tears rolled down his face to be soaked up by his thick, wide moustache. 'D'yer know, I don't half miss you two when I'm away. A good belly laugh is the best tonic yer can get.'

Jack caught George's eye and winked. 'Corker, me an' George have been waitin' for yer to come home to ask yer a question. Do they still have press gangs? You know, where men used to get knocked over the head and carted off to sea?'

Corker was quick to get the drift of where Jack's question was leading. 'Yeah, they still have them. Not like they used to, of course, but it isn't unheard of. Why d'yer ask?'

'We were just wonderin', like, if there was any chance of gettin' rid of our better halves for a couple of months.'

'Ooh, ay! Wouldn't that be the gear!' Nellie leaned so far forward she almost toppled off the chair. But, undeterred and gripping the edge of the table for support, she went on, 'They'd have no need to knock me over the 'ead, I'd go willingly! In fact, if Corker could see 'is way clear to get me a seaman's outfit I'd go as a feller an' nobody would know the difference.'

All eyes fastened on Nellie's mountainous bosom. It was a while before Corker could trust himself to speak. 'Nellie me darlin', yer'd never get away with it. Yer see, yer've got a problem.'

'No, Corker,' Jack said, 'she's got two big problems.'

George, always so quiet, couldn't resist. 'And they're only the ones yer can see.'

'That's enough now,' Molly said, worried the conversation was getting out of hand in front of the young ones. 'Let's be serious for a minute. I don't possess enough decent cups to go round an' I haven't a thing in to make sandwiches. So now yez know.'

'Don't be worryin' yer pretty head, Molly,' Corker said. 'Me and the lads will go down to the pub and bring some bottles back. An' while we're doing that, the girls can run to the chippy for half a crown's worth of chips with plenty of salt and vinegar on. So all you've got to do is butter some bread.'

Molly looked doubtful, remembering Corker's capacity for beer. 'And how many pints will yez have before yer come back? Don't forget, some folk have to go to work tomorrow.'

Corker let out a loud guffaw. 'Yer don't trust me, do yer, Molly? Yer think I'm goin' to lead them all astray.'

'The thought had crossed me mind,' Molly admitted. 'Jack and George are old enough to know better, but I don't want yer leading Steve an' Phil into bad habits.'

'Yer don't need Phil to go with yer, do yer?' Doreen didn't want to lose a minute of their time together. 'Or Steve?'

'I want to go with them,' Phil said, showing he had a mind of his own. 'We'll just have the one pint, then come straight back.'

Corker glanced sideways at Ellen. 'Do I have your permission, love?'

Blushing furiously at the public endearment, Ellen answered quietly, 'Yer don't need my permission . . . ye're big an' ugly enough to look after yerself.'

'The same goes for my feller.' Nellie nodded her head

emphatically. 'An' I'm sure Jill has no objections to letting Steve out of her sight for half an hour . . . do him good to be in the company of men for a change.'

'Of course I've no objections.' Jill gave Steve that special look as she squeezed his waist. 'As long as he doesn't come rolling home.'

Corker raised a quizzical brow at Doreen, who, finding herself in a minority of one, and being afraid that Phil would go no matter what she said, gave in. She nodded her head and smiled at the big man they'd all called Uncle for as long as she could remember. 'If he comes home drunk I'll take the rollin' pin to yer, Uncle Corker.'

Reaching for his peaked cap which was on the floor at his feet, Corker grinned. 'Come on, lads, let's get away from these nagging tongues for a bit of peace and some intelligent conversation.' He looked up at Molly who was still standing in the middle of the room. 'When we come back I want to hear all about the antics you an' Nellie have been up to.' The men were all standing now, except for Tommy, who was sitting on the arm of the couch looking dejected. Corker noted his glum face and after donning his cap he punched the boy lightly on the shoulder. 'Sorry, son, but in another couple of years yer'll be able to join us.' Then the big man had an idea which brought a smile to Tommy's face. 'I'll bring back a bottle of lemonade an' yer can have a shandy. How about that?'

'Yeah, great, Uncle Corker . . . thanks.'

Ah, he's a good scout is Corker, Nellie thought. He thinks of everything, never leaves anyone out. 'I'll have some tales for yer when yer come back, Corker! I tell 'em better than me mate.'

Jack and George were halfway down the hall when Corker paused at the door, turned and pointed a finger at Nellie. 'What was this me ma was tellin' me about you an' yer pink fleecy-lined knickers?'

'Right, that does it!' Molly pushed Corker into the hall.

'Out yer go, an' take yer bad mind with yer. An' you, Steve McDonough, an' you an' all, Phil Bradley – yez can wipe those smiles off yer faces.' She shooed them down the passage and into the street. 'Be back in half an hour, d'yez hear? An' if one of yer mentions the word "knickers", I'll flatten yer.'

Back in the living room Nellie looked from Jill to Doreen, her head shaking slowly and sending her chins rolling like ocean waves. 'I'll get the blame for this, yer know. I haven't said a word, not a thing out of place, not a dickie bird! But I'll bet yez a pound to a pinch of snuff I'll get the blame.'

Molly came back into the room just as Doreen leaned across the table, her eyes alive with mischief. 'Have yer got yer pink ones on tonight, Auntie Nellie?'

It was past midnight when Molly was standing at the door bidding goodnight to Corker and Ellen and Nellie and George. They'd spent two hours laughing and joking – mostly at the expense of Nellie. They were still boisterous and Molly, fearful for her neighbours, put a finger to her lips. 'Be quiet, ye're makin' enough noise to waken the dead!'

'Yesh, mishus.' Corker hiccupped loudly, pretending to be drunk. 'Don't forget we've got a date for Saturday night, an' bring Bridie an' Bob along.'

'I won't forget.' Molly moved a step back into the hall. 'Now scarper an' let decent people get to bed. Goodnight and God bless.' She closed the door quickly and quietly, thinking she'd never get Jack and Tommy up in the morning. Still, it was worth it, they'd had a smashing night.

'Me dad and Tommy have gone up.' Doreen was still sitting at the table holding hands with Phil, while opposite sat Jill and Steve.

'It's about time you two went to bed – it's work for you in the morning. You too, Steve!'

'I'm goin' now, Mrs B.'

Every bone in Molly's body was aching and she knew that as

soon as her head hit the pillow she'd be asleep. But she wasn't too tired to miss the pleading in Steve's eyes when he looked at Jill. Poor beggar, she thought, he's got nowhere to give her a goodnight kiss. That was the worst of living in a two-up two-down when your children were growing up. There was nowhere for them to do their courting, no privacy.

'I'm goin' to bed now because I'm dead beat. But before I do, can I make a suggestion? Instead of sitting lookin' at each other like stuffed ducks, each hoping the other will make a move, why don't yez work it out between yer? Toss a penny in the air an' heads gets a goodnight kiss in the hall, tails gets it in here. OK?'

Steve, blessed with the same sense of humour as his mother, grinned. 'Can yer lend us a penny, Mrs B.?'

'Sod off, Steve McDonough! Just be quick about it, 'cos yer'll be gettin' up for work in a few hours.' Molly smiled, ruffled his hair, then turned to Phil. 'The same goes for you, 'cos milady here can't afford to miss a day's pay.'

But something was nagging at the back of Molly's mind, and she was reluctant to go to bed until she'd got it off her chest. Her brain was seeking a way of saying it without causing embarrassment, when her problem was solved by Jill saying she'd walk Steve to the door. After Nellie's son had kissed her goodnight, Molly waited until she heard the front door open, and knew that the couple would be too busy kissing and whispering sweet nothings to hear anything she was saying.

'Phil, I don't want yer to take this wrong, but I've got to say it. Our Doreen might be sixty in the head, but she's only sixteen years of age. Yer'll bear that in mind, won't yer?'

Doreen was mortified. 'Mam! I bet yer've never said that to Steve an' our Jill was only sixteen when they started courting.'

'Jill isn't as headstrong or as impulsive as you, sunshine.'

When Doreen looked ready to protest, Phil covered her hand with his. 'It's all right, Mrs Bennett, I understand. You don't need to worry about Doreen, not where I'm concerned anyway.'

'I know that, son,' Molly gave a tired smile, 'but I had to say it. Yer see, I love the bones of her an' would lay me life down for her, or any of me kids, but I can still see their faults. And Doreen is very headstrong and too quick off the mark for her own good. But she's crazy about you an' I'm hopin' yer'll have a stabilizing effect on her.' She turned her gaze on her daughter who was wearing a mutinous expression. 'Don't think I'm pickin' on you, sunshine, 'cos our Tommy will get the same lecture when he's old enough to go courtin', and our Ruthie as well, when the time comes.'

They were quiet as they listened to Molly's weary tread on the stairs, then Phil put his arm around Doreen and held her tight. 'Come on, it's not the end of the world!'

'She had no right!' Doreen was choked. 'Fancy showin' me up like that!'

'Doreen, she had every right! It shows she's a good mother, wanting the best for you.' Phil lifted a length of the long blonde hair and let it slip slowly through his fingers. 'You don't know how lucky you are with your mother and your whole family! I've never known the love that you take for granted.'

Remembering his family, and the way she herself had turned her back on him at first when she found out who he was, Doreen was immediately contrite. 'You can be like one of the family, as Steve is. They all like you.'

'And I want them to carry on liking me.' Phil gave her a quick kiss then pushed his chair back and stood up. 'I've just heard Jill going up the stairs so it's safe to go out now.'

'Stay for just another five minutes,' Doreen coaxed. 'Me mam won't know, she'll be fast asleep.'

'No, it's late an' you've got work to go to.'

'I wish I could take a day off, but they dock yer pay an' I can't afford to lose pay.'

'You only work a half-day Saturday so I'll meet you outside work and we can go straight into town.' Phil pulled her to her feet. 'We'll go somewhere nice.'

'Where's somewhere nice? Go on, tell us.'

'No, it's going to be a surprise. But put yer best bib and tucker on 'cos yer don't know where we'll end up.'

Their arms around each other's waists, they walked down the hall. 'I've really enjoyed meself tonight,' Phil said. 'Your family and the McDonoughs have a lot of fun, don't yer? I've never laughed so much in all me life as I have tonight. And Corker, well, he's great . . . a fine man if ever there was one.' He lifted Doreen's arms to circle his neck and held her close. 'Is he courtin' Mrs Clarke?'

'That's a long story, but I think they'll end up gettin' married. Her husband's in a mental hospital and they say he'll never get better, so Uncle Corker has been to see a solicitor to see if Mrs Clarke can get a divorce.'

'Yer can tell me all about it tomorrow night when we go to the pictures.' Phil bent his head and kissed her full on the mouth, sending shivers down her spine. 'Every time I kiss yer me heart turns over.'

'Mmm, mine too,' Doreen said dreamily. 'It's like goin' down that big slide thing at New Brighton fairground.'

'I'm crazy about yer, Doreen.'

'An' I'm double crazy about you.'

He unlocked her arms from his neck and held her from him. 'Tomorrow night we'll carry on where we left off. But right now it's goodnight, my darling.'

Doreen was in a daze as she walked up the stairs. She'd never sleep . . . not after he'd called her darling for the very first time! Oh, wasn't being in love just the best thing in the whole world?

Chapter Eight

Molly's head was pounding as she walked along the hall to answer the knock at the door. She didn't normally suffer from headaches, so she put it down to the late night they'd had. The last thing she needed right now was visitors.

'Ma! I didn't expect to see you!' Molly squinted, wishing she had a couple of matchsticks to keep her eyes open. 'Hello Rosie, come on in, sunshine, it's nice to see yer.'

'We're off to town to buy Rosie a dress,' Bridie said. 'Sure she'll need something decent if she gets an interview for a job.'

After her visitors were seated, Molly pulled a chair out from the table. She looked at the young girl and groaned. The long black skirt and shawl were bad enough, but that ruddy hat looked ridiculous on her. 'Why have yer got yer beautiful hair hidden under that hat? If I had hair like yours, sunshine, I'd be showin' it off, not keepin' it covered up.'

'I'm wearin' me hat to look respectable goin' into the big city, isn't that the truth of it, Auntie Bridget?'

In her mind, Bridie had the same feelings about the dreadful hat as Molly did. But she couldn't think of a way of telling the girl without upsetting her. 'I told you to wear what yer wanted to, sweetheart.'

Molly rubbed her knuckles hard over her forehead. Should she mind her own business, or do what she thought was in the girl's best interests? 'Come here, sunshine.' Molly lumbered to her feet. 'Stand in front of that mirror.'

Rosie stood in front of the fireplace, and as she looked in the mirror she saw Molly's reflection appear behind her.

'Take a real good look at yerself, Rosie.' Molly waited a while, then said, 'Now take yer hat off.'

The long hatpins were drawn out and handed to Bridie for safe keeping before the hat was removed and the rich abundance of hair cascaded down to form ringlets around the girl's shoulders. 'And you want to keep this covered up,' Molly said, her fingers lifting the dark, luxuriant tresses. 'Yer must be crazy, sunshine.'

Rosie's bonny face with its permanent smile turned to Bridie. 'And does yerself think I'm crazy, Auntie Bridget?'

'Yes I do, sweetheart,' Bridie told her. 'If I had a head of hair like yours, sure wouldn't I be wanting everyone to admire it?'

'Then I'll not be wearing the hat.' Rosie nodded at her reflection in the mirror before meeting Molly's eyes. 'Will Tommy think I've got nice hair, Auntie Molly?'

'Tommy's still got a lot of growing up to do, sunshine, he's not interested in girls, or their hair.' Molly grimaced as a sharp pain hit her between the eyes. She stumbled to her chair. 'I'll have to sit down.'

Bridie's eyes narrowed. ''Tis pale yer are, Molly me darlin', are yer not feelin' too grand?'

'I'm all right, Ma, just a bit under the weather.' Molly quickly told of the impromptu party. 'So yer see, I'm paying the price for too many drinks and too late to bed.'

'Well now, just you sit there an' me and Rosie will make yer a nice cup of tea an' yer'll soon feel better.'

Molly grunted and closed her eyes. She just felt like dropping off to sleep. There'll be no more nights like last night, she vowed. Any parties in future would be on a Saturday night when everyone could have a lie-in the next day.

'Here yer are, me darling, drink that up.' Bridie placed the cup in front of her daughter. 'Hot and sweet, so it is.'

Molly took a sip and tried to collect her wits. 'I'm supposed to be callin' for Nellie soon, to go for the material. But right now I feel more like flying.' She had her hands curled around the cup when she remembered something. 'Oh, I forgot to tell yer, we're all goin' to the pub on Saturday an' Corker asked if you an' me da would come.'

'Well thank Corker kindly for me, but we won't be able to go on account of Rosie. We couldn't very well leave her on her own.' Bridie raised her finely arched brows and added, 'I've got to say, me darlin', ye're not a very good advert for hitting the bottle. A sorry sight yer are an' no mistake. One look at you an' most sane people would join the temperance movement.'

A grin finally appeared on Molly's face. 'I tried to join that club once, but they wouldn't accept me on account of me mate, Nellie. They thought she wasn't suitable, yer see. So I told them straight, Ma, wherever I go she goes. If yer won't let her join, then I'll just have to stay on the booze.'

Rosie's clear, sweet laughter filled the room. 'Oh, you are funny, Auntie Molly. Sure I've a lot to write an' tell me mammy, so I have.'

'While ye're at it, sunshine, ask if she's got a saying that will cure me of the demon drink.'

'Oh I'm sure she has, Auntie Molly! Hasn't me mammy got a saying about everything under the sun?'

Molly and Nellie stepped off the tram in London Road and linked arms as they crossed to T. J. Hughes's. 'I didn't see Ellen to get any money off her, so I've borrowed a pound off Mary till she calls tonight.'

'Waste of bloody money,' Nellie moaned, her hips brushing Molly's as she waddled from side to side. 'The flamin' government should pay for it, seein' as how it's them what's tellin' us we've got to have it.'

'I don't think we're goin' to be able to carry it all in one go,' Molly said. 'It comes to a hundred and thirty-odd yards for the six houses.'

'Gawd'strewth! We'll need a ruddy handcart for all that!' Nellie pushed the wide door open and sighed with pleasure as the warm air of the shop greeted them. 'How about a nice cup of tea while we're here, girl?'

'Uh-uh,' Molly grunted, pulling her friend towards the board which would tell them which floor the materials were on. 'We can't afford it. Remember we've got the wire runners to buy, as well.'

'What a bloody life! If I ever lay me hands on that Hitler, I'll kick him from here to eternity.'

The trade in blackout material was brisk, keeping the assistants on the run. Molly and Nellie waited patiently until Nellie saw an opening. 'Quick, there's an empty speck by the counter – get in before someone beats us to it.'

There were several types of material, ranging from ninepence a yard to half a crown. But Nellie told the assistant not to bother with the expensive stuff because, although they spoke posh and dressed like toffs, they lived in a two-up two-down terrace house, not Buckingham Palace. So it was down to either the ninepence a yard, or the elevenpence-halfpenny.

'I'll 'ave the ninepence a yard: it's enough to pay.' Nellie had made her decision.

'But it won't wash,' Molly told her. 'One wash an' yer'll be able to see through it.'

'Wash! Sod off, girl! Who the 'ell is goin' to wash black curtains?'

Nellie leaned on the counter after successfully elbowing two customers out of the way. For the umpteenth time she pushed back the scarf which was threatening to cover her eyes. It was tied in a knot under her layer of chins, and every movement of her head loosened the knot and allowed the scarf to fall at will. 'No one is goin' to know if they're dirty, are they? An' besides, the ruddy war could be over in no time!'

Molly dithered while the assistant waited patiently. If the truth were known, she was glad of the break – they could take all day to decide for all she cared. She'd been on the run since the shop opened and her shoes were pinching.

'Ooh, I don't know what to do.' Molly fingered a piece of cloth from each of the bales. 'I'd better get the elevenpence-ha'penny for me ma, she's so fussy.' She looked hopefully at the assistant. 'Would yer cut it to size for us?'

'Certainly, madam.'

Molly breathed a sigh of relief. 'Eight pieces at two an' a half yards, an' two at one an' a half.'

While the assistant was measuring and cutting, Molly whispered, 'We've only got six pounds, it's not nearly enough.'

'Well yer will go throwin' yer money around like a man with no hands,' Nellie grinned. 'If yer'd stuck to the ninepenny, we'd 'ave had enough.'

Molly moved down the counter to where the assistant was slicing through the material with a huge pair of scissors. 'Listen, love, would that cheap stuff be thick enough?'

The scissors stopped halfway across the fabric. 'People must think so because we've sold more of that than any other. Besides, if you leave your other curtains up, like my mother's doing, you'll have two thicknesses and that should be sufficient.'

'Thanks, love.' Molly had a smile on her face when she returned to Nellie. After repeating what she'd been told, she said, 'So, it's the cheap one for the rest of us.'

'We're not tryin' Blackler's then?'

'It's not goin' to be cheaper than here, is it? We could be traipsin' around all day an' end up back where we started.'

'Here you are, madam.' The assistant passed the wrapped material over. 'That's one pound, two shillings and a ha'penny.'

Molly had the six pound notes in a separate compartment in her purse so she wouldn't get mixed up, and she passed two of the notes over. While she waited for the change, she lifted the parcel. 'It's not too heavy, Nellie, try it. I think we could manage the lot between us if it was wrapped in four parcels, one for each hand.'

'Well for cryin' out loud, give her the measurements an' let's you an' me go for a cup of tea while she's gettin' it ready. Me blasted corns are givin' me gyp, the flamin' things.'

Nellie dropped on to a chair in T. J.'s café, and sighed with relief. 'Thank God for that! Yer don't know how lucky yer are, girl, havin' feet that don't give yer no trouble.'

'I'm fed up tellin' yer to buy shoes that fit yer properly! Yer need a wider fittin', anyone can see that! But will yer listen? No, not you, ye're too ruddy stubborn.'

'Oh, shut yer cakehole, missus.' Nellie eyed the scone on a plate in front of her and licked her lips in anticipation. 'I'm not half ready for this, me tummy thinks me throat's cut. Can yer hear it rumblin'?'

'Oh, is that what the noise is? I thought that bein' near Lime Street station it was the trains I could hear.'

'Ho, ho, very funny!' Nellie bit into the scone and left a smear of jam on her top lip. 'Mmmm . . . bloody lovely! Mind you, I'd need a dozen of these to satisfy me hunger.'

'I'm feelin' quite chuffed with meself,' Molly said, a smug smile of satisfaction on her face. 'With all the curtains cut to size, it means our Doreen's only got to put a hem top an' bottom. She'll have them done in no time.'

'You might be pleased with yerself, but did yer see the look on the face of the girl behind the counter?' When Nellie laughed, her tummy rose and lifted the table off the floor, rattling the cups and saucers. 'I thought she was goin' to have a duck egg when she saw yer list. An' you, cool as a ruddy cucumber, practically lookin' down yer nose at her, sayin' in yer posh voice that yer usually save for Sundays, "There's fifty curtains altogether, love, but would you be kind enough to wrap each lot separately, so I know where I'm up to? My friend an' I will pick them up when we've had a cup of tea."' Nellie raised her eyebrows, and lifting her cup, stuck her little finger out. 'All la-de-dah.'

'Sod off, Nellie, yer don't half exaggerate!' Molly grinned. 'Lookin' down me nose, usin' me posh voice . . . I don't know, yer tell bigger fibs than our Ruthie.'

'I should bloody well think I do, the size of me to her! If I couldn't tell bigger lies than a seven-year-old girl, I'd pack in.'

Nellie stood on the pavement looking up at Molly on the tram platform. 'How can I get on with these ruddy things? If I tried it, I'd end up arse over elbow.' She gazed down at the heavy parcels she had in each hand. They were tied with string and it was biting deep into her palms. 'It takes me all me time to get on meself, never mind carryin' these weights.'

Molly glanced down the tram for the conductor, but he must have been on top collecting fares. And she could see the driver looked impatient, wanting to be on his way. 'Hang on a minute.' She threw her parcels in the space under the stairs and reached out to relieve her friend. 'Here, give us them, an' get on before the driver goes without yer.'

Nellie pulled herself aboard, red in the face with the exertion. 'Next time yer want to go shoppin' for the whole ruddy street, yer can go on yer own. I don't mind doin' a good turn for anyone, but this is bloody ridiculous!'

The driver, tired of waiting and worried about keeping to his timetable, turned his head to ask, 'Can I go?'

Nellie glared. 'Yer should 'ave gone before yer left the 'ouse.'

The driver looked puzzled. 'Gone where?'

'To the lavvy of course! Yer just asked if yer could go! In

our 'ouse they put their hand up, but I suppose everyone 'as their own way.'

The driver's laugh was so hearty it even brought the glimmer of a smile to Nellie's woebegone face. He clanged his bell, turned the brake handle and set the tram in motion. 'Yer can leave that shoppin' under the stairs,' he grinned, 'I'll keep me eye on it for yer.'

Molly struggled down the aisle to an empty seat. 'I'll put these on the floor an' we can put our feet on them.' She threw the packages down before sliding along the seat and squashing herself up against the side of the tram to make room for her friend. 'Thank God for that!'

'Yer should 'ave put those with the others,' Nellie said, one cheek of her backside on the seat, the other hanging over the side. 'He said he'd keep 'is eye on them.'

'Just give over, Nellie!' Molly was all hot and bothered. 'Honest, yer'd cause trouble in an empty house, you would!'

'Oh, pardon me for breathing!' Nellie bent her head to look into Molly's face. 'Got a cob on, have yer, girl?'

'Me got a cob on? Well I like that! It was you who started it!'

'Yeah, I admit, I did 'ave a cob on,' Nellie and her chins agreed, 'but it's gone now. Shall I kiss yours better?'

Just then they heard the conductor's voice. 'Fares, please!'

'I'll get them . . . I've got change in me pocket.' Nellie leaned sideways to reach into her pocket and nearly pushed Molly through the window. 'Two twos, please.'

The conductor threw the coppers into his leather bag, pulled two tickets from a roll and punched them in his machine. Handing them to Nellie, he asked, 'Been spendin' your feller's hard-earned money, have yer?'

There was a wicked glint in Nellie's eyes. 'Yeah! I went to the pictures last night to see Jean Harlow, an' she was wearin' one of those lacy see-through negligée things. An' I said to meself, "Yer want to get yerself one of them, girl, yer'd look the gear in it! An' it would do your feller the power of good, too! He'd think it was 'is birthday."'

The conductor didn't know whether to blush or to laugh. The driver had told him the fat woman was a caution, and he was right. But from the look on the face of the woman sitting behind Nellie, she didn't appreciate the conversation one little bit. And she looked the prim and proper type, just the sort who would report him. So he contented himself with whispering in Nellie's ear, 'I hope he likes it.' Then he went on his way, clinking the arm of his punch machine and calling, 'Any more fares, please?'

'What would George say if he'd been here an' heard yer talkin' like that?' Molly asked.

'He'd pretend he wasn't with me.' Nellie's guffaw travelled the length of the tram. 'He'd have got off at the next stop.'

'I wouldn't blame him, I know the feeling,' Molly muttered. But as she gazed out of the window there was a smile on her face.

Doreen gaped when she saw the material piled high on the sideboard. 'Ah, ray, Mam! That's a bit much, isn't it?'

Molly had considered the possibility of some opposition and she had a sweetener ready. 'We'll each buy yer a pair of stockings if yer make them. That'll keep yer goin' in stockings for a few weeks.'

That cheered Doreen up somewhat. She could do with some decent stockings, especially this week with Phil being home. Every pair she possessed had ladders in, like the ones she was wearing now. They'd do her a turn for work: no one could see the blobs of red nail varnish she'd dabbed on to stem the runs, but she was desperate for new ones. 'When do I get the stockings?' There was a calculating gleam in her eyes. 'Next pancake Tuesday, I suppose?'

'Ye're a crafty article, you are,' Molly said, putting a plate down in front of her daughter. 'Yer'll get the stockings when yer've done the job.'

Doreen's mind ticked over. The curtains only needed a straight hem top and bottom, she'd have them done in no time. 'I'll get the machine out when the table's cleared, I can get some done before Phil calls for me.'

Molly grinned to herself. She was a cute one all right, was Doreen. 'Suit yerself! But if yer do, I'll make sure yer get yer stockings at the weekend. Me an' Nellie are goin' to Cazneau Street on Saturday to get the wire runners, so I'll get yer half a dozen pairs.'

That bit of news took the gilt off the gingerbread. 'Mam, I'd rather get me own stockings! You'll only get the wrong colour.'

Molly had also prepared herself for this eventuality. 'Give me a pair of yer old ones an' I'll get the exact same colour.' She was ready to argue with her daughter on this point. Stockings in the market could be had for sixpence a pair while they were elevenpence-halfpenny in the shops. 'An' don't knock it, sunshine, just count yerself lucky.'

'Mam!' Ruthie piped up. 'Can I come to the market with you an' Auntie Nellie on Saturday?'

Oh, why didn't I keep my big mouth shut, Molly asked herself as she gazed at the eager look on the pixie-like face. Dragging a child around a busy market was no joke. You needed eyes in the back of your head to keep them from wandering off and getting lost in the thousands who thronged to the market every Saturday in the hope of picking up a bargain. And you couldn't browse in peace with a little one hanging on to your coat, asking you to buy them everything that took their eye.

'Go on, Mam!' The rosebud mouth puckered. 'Please?'

Molly sighed. Her youngest child could be a holy terror at times, but right now she looked like a little angel. And how could you refuse an angel? 'We'll see what the weather's like, sunshine, OK?'

'The gear!' Ruthie went happily back to eating her dinner. With a mouth full of mashed potato, she gloated, 'Wait till I tell Bella, she won't half be jealous.'

'If you start braggin' and upsetting Bella, then I won't take yer. Do yer understand?' But Molly knew she was wasting her breath. The two friends were always looking to score points off each other and Ruthie wouldn't pass up an opportunity like this. And you couldn't blame her: she didn't get many outings.

Chapter Nine

'In the name of God, where do they all come from?' Nellie viewed with amazement the mass of people milling around all the stalls in the market. 'We'll never get through that lot!'

Molly was grinning as she gazed at the width of her friend. 'Tell yer what, Nellie, you go first an' me an' Ruthie will follow.'

Nellie puffed out her cheeks. 'Oh ay, soft girl! Don't worry about me getting bashed and bruised, will yer?'

'It was your idea to come, so don't be moanin'.' Molly clung tight to her daughter's hand. 'Just look for a stall sellin' stockings, and we want some wire for the blackout curtains.'

'An' I want to get meself a couple of pairs of knickers.' Nellie bent her elbows in readiness. 'Right, let's go.'

Following in the wake of her friend, Molly and Ruthie had an easy passage. But as Nellie marched forward regardless, Molly felt sorry for the people who got in the way. She could see them rubbing the parts of their bodies that had come into contact with her friend's elbows, and knew many of them would be sporting bruises when they got home. There were a few dark looks thrown Nellie's way, and several people muttered that she should look where she was going, but the size of her put them off a direct confrontation.

'Here yer are, girl!' Nellie came to a halt where she could see shovels and hammers hanging on display outside a stall. 'We can get the wire here.'

'I'll get it in one piece, save the man messing,' Molly said, as Nellie pushed her way through the crowd around the stall. 'Jack can cut it to size with a pair of pliers.'

When it was their turn to be served, Nellie haggled with the stallholder. 'Don't we get a discount for buyin' so much?'

'I'm sellin' it dirt cheap as it is . . . practically givin' it away!' The man had jet-black hair, a swarthy complexion and a set of pure white teeth which gleamed when he smiled. 'Would yer take the bread an' butter out of me kids' mouths?'

'Butter? What's butter?' Nellie opened her eyes as wide as they would go. 'My poor family haven't never 'ad no butter.'

'Go on, missus, get the violin out an' play on me heart-strings.' The man laughed as he began to measure out the wire. 'Yer'll be tellin' me next yer've got a chronic sick 'usband at home who 'asn't worked for years, and twelve children to feed.'

'Yer know, the minute I laid eyes on you I knew there was gypsy blood in yer.' Nellie's face was deadly serious. 'It's the dark colouring that did it, that's how I knew.'

'What are yer on about, missus? I'm no gypsy!'

'Oh, come off it, yer must be! Yer've just told me fortune and yer hit the nail right on the 'ead.'

The man looked at Molly to see if this was a joke, but Molly had turned her head away. She wasn't getting involved in this! 'Are you tellin' me that yer've got a sick 'usband at 'ome and twelve children?'

'No, love, I'm not goin' to lie to yer, that wouldn't be fair.' Nellie looked all contrite. 'I've only got ten children.'

Molly spluttered and backed into the crowd, taking Ruthie with her. The little girl's eyes were popping out of her head . . . she didn't know Auntie Nellie had ten children!

The man made the mistake of taking his mind and his hand off the wire. A point not missed by Nellie. He gazed at the people crowded around the stall, all deeply interested in the conversation, and with a feeling of dismay realized they believed he could tell fortunes. He glared at the big woman. 'Is this a wind-up?'

'Is what a wind-up, love?' Nellie peered over the counter. 'Have yer got a gramophone with a handle back there? I'm sorry I can't help yer, I'm no good with these mechanical thingumajigs. Now if me 'usband was here, he could help yer . . . his mother 'ad a wind-up gramophone.'

The man scratched his head. 'I give up!'

Nellie beamed. 'Does that mean yer'll give us a discount on the wire, seein' as how we're buyin' so much?'

He raised his brows. 'No sick husband? No ten children?'

Nelly's beam widened. 'Healthy husband, three kids . . . but skint.'

The crowd roared with laughter. This was as good as a pantomime. 'Go on,' shouted one man, 'knock a few coppers off for 'er, she deserves it.' His call was joined by others. 'Go 'ed, don't be so ruddy tight!' And, 'Give it 'er for nowt, yer skinny beggar!' It was all cheerful banter and the stallholder forgave Nellie for making him the butt of her joke.

'I'll knock thru'pence off an' no more, 'cos I've got more ruddy kids to feed than she has.' He looked down at the wire. 'I've lost track of where I was up to.'

'I was watchin' yer,' Nellie said, helpfully, 'yer'd counted ten yards out.'

Molly waited on the edge of the crowd, and when Nellie came pushing her way towards her, she shook her head. 'Nellie McDonough, do yer always 'ave to cause a scene?'

'Oh, don't be such a long string of misery, girl, it was all good, clean fun! We saved ourselves thru'pence and the man's got more customers now than he would 'ave had . . . so everyone's happy.' Nellie passed over the wire which was wrapped in a piece of newspaper. 'Stick that in yer basket, girl, an' let's find a stall that sells knickers.'

Ruthie pulled on Nellie's coat. 'I didn't know yer 'ad ten children, Auntie Nellie! Do they all live in your 'ouse?'

Nellie bent down to gaze into the questioning eyes. 'God love yer for yer innocence, sweetheart!' She took the child's face in her hands. 'No, I haven't got ten children, I was only pullin' the man's leg. It was a joke, just for a bit of fun.'

The child lowered her eyes as she thought things over. When she looked up she was smiling. 'I think it was funny, Auntie Nellie.'

'Well I'm glad somebody does,' Nellie huffed, ''cos yer mam's got a face on her as long as a fiddle.'

'Shall I let yer into a secret, Nellie?' Molly gripped Ruthie's hand ready to move off. 'Me an' Jack will laugh ourselves sick over this little escapade of yours. It's one of the best yer've pulled this week.'

'Aye, well, that's all right then!' Happy now, Nellie took the child's other hand. 'Let's look around for me knickers.'

They found a stall that sold women's underwear and Molly picked out the six pairs of stockings in the colour Doreen wanted, and Nellie chose two pairs of pink fleecy-lined knickers. 'I'll pay for these,' Molly said, 'you pay for yer own.'

Nellie was rooting through her purse when a hand appeared from nowhere and snatched it from her hand. She gaped as her eyes followed the disappearing figure of a young boy. 'The little bugger, he's pinched me purse!'

Molly chased after the boy, but he was small and fleet of foot, able to push his way through the crowd with ease. Puffing loudly, Molly told herself she was wasting her time, she'd never catch him. But she'd reckoned without Ruthie. With her tongue poked out of the side of her mouth and a determined expression on her face, the child was even quicker than the boy. She caught up with him and grabbed hold of the back of his jersey. No matter how hard he pulled and twisted, the little girl hung on like grim death with her two hands. No one was going to steal from her auntie Nellie!

Gasping for breath, Molly appeared and grabbed the boy by the scruff of his neck. 'Yer little thief!' She noticed a small crowd was gathering and explained, 'He's just pinched me mate's purse! Look, there it is!' She whipped the purse from the struggling boy's hand as the crowd muttered dire threats. 'Give 'im a belt,' one man shouted, while a woman went even further, 'He wants horsewhippin'.'

Nellie came on the scene looking distraught. Her chest heaving, she gasped, 'Thank God yer've caught 'im. Every penny I've got in the world is in that purse.'

Molly put her hands on the boy's shoulders and turned him round to face her. 'It's the police station for you, me lad.'

Nellie came to stand beside her friend, intending to give the boy a clip round the ear for frightening her like that. But all the fight went out of her when she took stock of the lad. Poor bugger looked as though he hadn't washed or eaten for a month. His face, neck and ears were filthy, and although it was a cold day, he had no shirt or vest on under the moth-eaten jersey. Her eyes travelled down past his torn and patched trousers over filthy legs to his bare feet. My God, in this day and age – a barefoot child! She thought that was a thing of the past!

Nellie sighed. How the hell could you be angry with a kid who looked as though a good feed would kill him, and was dressed in rags? He looked terrified, and the mutterings of the hostile crowd weren't helping. 'Let's take him outside, Molly, we're causin' an obstruction here.'

While Molly led the boy through the stalls to the street, Nellie smiled at the crowd who looked disappointed at not seeing the thief punished. 'Thanks for yer help, folks. We'll sort him out.'

'What's your name, son?' Molly looked at the boy. When she saw the fear in a face that looked far too old for its years, her heart turned over. 'I'm not goin' to hurt yer, so don't be frightened.' She turned her head when Nellie appeared with Ruthie. 'I was just sayin', we're not goin' to hurt him, are we?'

'Not if he tells us the truth,' Nellie said. Her motherly instincts were rising and she felt like taking the boy home, giving him a good wash, dressing him in decent clothes and putting a good feed in front of him. But he was a thief and it would be wrong to let him think you could steal and get away with it. 'What's yer name an' how old are yer?'

The boy looked down at his feet. 'Me name's Denis an' I'm ten.'

'Well, Denis, tell me why yer tried to pinch me purse?'

The shame and guilt disappeared from the boy's face, to be replaced with another emotion. ''Cos me mam's got no money an' she's cryin'.'

Molly and Nellie exchanged glances. 'Have yer got a dad, Denis?' Molly asked. 'Or any big brothers or sisters?'

'I haven't got no dad, he died.' Tears weren't far away and Denis swallowed at the lump in his throat before continuing. 'I've got two brothers and two sisters, but they're all younger than me. I'm the oldest an' I 'ave to try an' help me mam.'

'An' do yer often go out stealin'?' Nellie asked, her voice gentle.

'I haven't never done it before, an' me mam will go mad if the police come to our 'ouse.' A tear trickled down his cheek, and as he wiped it away he smeared the grime on his face. 'I wouldn't 'ave done it, but the baby was screamin' with hunger an' me mam's got no money . . . that's why she was cryin'.'

'Are you tellin' us the truth, son?' Molly asked. 'Or is it all a pack of lies to get yer off the hook?'

'I'm not tellin' lies, missus, honest I'm not! Yer can come to our 'ouse if yer like, and see for yerself.' Then fear flickered across his face. 'But yer wouldn't tell me mam what I did, would yer? She's always tellin' me not to bring trouble to 'er door.'

Nellie dug Molly in the side and jerked her head to indicate she wanted to whisper. 'D'yer believe 'im?'

Molly nodded. 'Yeah, poor little bugger. I mean, have yer

seen the state of him? Apart from the rags he's got on, he's far too thin for a boy his age, so he's definitely not gettin' enough to eat. But what's puzzlin' me is, what do they do for money other weeks?'

'I don't know, an' I ain't asking,' Nellie hissed. 'We'll help him out now, but then I'm goin' to forget he exists. With the best will in the world, we can't take everyone's troubles on board. Just leave it to me an' don't take it to heart or yer'll 'ave nightmares.'

Ruthie was standing with her feet apart, gazing at the boy who had tried to steal her auntie's purse. 'You're a naughty boy, you are.'

Denis Latimer looked at the small girl's warm coat and scarf, her sturdy shoes and the knitted gloves keeping the cold from her hands. She doesn't know how lucky she is, he thought. I bet she doesn't have to try and keep warm at night wrapped in old clothes. She won't ever be hungry and I bet there'll be a roaring fire in their house when she gets home.

He screwed his eyes up tight. They used to have all those things when his dad was alive. Now they had nothing. His mother had had to pawn everything they had, bit by bit, to keep the wolf from the door. Now there was nothing left to pawn.

Molly had been watching the boy's expression and it was almost as though she could read his mind. Here was a boy who wanted to help his family, who felt he should be the man of the house, but his tender years were against him. Nellie was right, of course, they couldn't take everyone's troubles on board, but it wouldn't be Christian to ignore their plight.

'How old is the baby, Denis?' Nellie was also weakening. 'Is she on solid food?'

'She's fourteen months.'

'Right! Come on, we'll go to the shops an' get yer somethin' to take home to feed the family.' Nellie put an arm across his thin shoulders. 'It won't be much, mind, but anythin' is better than nothing.'

'I haven't got that much money left,' Molly said as she took Ruthie's hand and followed her friend across the street. 'I've only got a bob or two.'

'That's all right, girl!' Nellie stopped outside the Co-op. 'I left the knickers on the stall so I'll use that money and get the knickers another day.'

A short time later, they were to see the difference in Denis's face when he smiled. Cradled in his arms he had two large tin loaves, a half of marge, half a pound of corned beef, a pound of sugar, a quarter of tea and a tin of conny-onny. And stuck in his pocket was a block of carbolic soap. He couldn't believe fate had been so kind to him. He'd never forget these two women, not as long as he lived. And never again would he try to steal something that didn't belong to him.

'Where can I tell me mam I got all this from?'

Nellie smiled at him. 'It's a sin to steal, son, an' a sin to tell lies. But sometimes God doesn't mind yer tellin' a little white lie if it's to help someone. So you tell yer mam that two big fat women with loads of rings on their fingers asked yer to run a lot of messages for them, an' they gave yer half a crown each for yer trouble.'

Molly's mind hadn't been idle. 'If yer come to the market at the same time next week, I might 'ave some cast-off clothes that'll fit yer brothers an' sisters. They won't be anythin' to get excited about, but they might do a turn.'

Denis was lost for words. He couldn't believe it was happening and thought if he pinched himself he'd wake up to find it was all a dream. But these two women in front of him were no dream. He wanted to tell them how grateful he was, and how he was dying to see his mother's face when she saw the food. But he was too young to know the right words. All he could say was, 'Thanks, missus.'

'Go on, off with yer.' The joy on his face was all the thanks Molly and Nellie needed. 'See yer next week.'

The two women watched as he walked away. They were silent until he turned a corner and disappeared from view, then they faced each other. Sniffing loudly, Molly wiped a tear away with the back of her hand. 'It could only happen to us two, yer know that, don't yer? Someone steals yer purse, we nearly kill ourselves chasin' 'im to get it back, then yer spend the flamin' money on him! Jack will never believe this, not in a ruddy month of Sundays.'

'Ay, hang on a minute!' Nellie rubbed the side of her nose. 'You're talking as though it's been all my doin' an' you only went along for the ride! You fell for 'is sob story just the same as me!'

'I know I did! I felt sorry for the poor bugger, an' I believed every word he said!' Molly glanced sideways to see if her friend knew she was being teased. 'But let's face it, Nellie, it was your ruddy purse he stole . . . if yer'd been more careful, none of this would 'ave happened!'

'I don't bloody believe I'm hearin' this!' Nellie exploded. 'Who's the one who's arranged to meet him again next week? An' where the 'ell are yer gettin' the clothes from that yer promised him?'

'Off meself, the girls, Mary an' you!'

'Yer can go an' take a running jump, girl!' Nellie looked down at herself and an impish grin appeared. 'It would 'ave to be some baby to wear this coat.'

'If the mother is any good, she'll be able to unpick the clothes and make use of the material.'

'Bloody hell! Yer don't half let yer imagination run away with yer, girl! The mother's a seamstress now!' Nellie took hold of one of Ruthie's hands and started walking. 'Anyway, yer ain't gettin' this coat, it's the only one I've got to me name. I'm lucky it still fits me after that drenchin' I got.'

'Another thing,' Molly said, 'you've got a flamin' cheek sayin' two fat women! I'm not fat, just cuddly.'

'If ye're goin' to be like that, girl, then I'm not fat either! I'm just pleasantly plump.'

Ruthie walked quietly between the two women. Their raised voices didn't alarm her because her mam and auntie Nellie were always arguing. In a few minutes they'd be laughing their heads off. But they should have punished that boy because it's wrong to steal. If her teacher had been there, he'd have got six strokes of the cane. She got three last week and that was just for pulling Sadie Moore's hair and making her cry! Where was the justice in that?

Chapter Ten

It was only eight o'clock, but the lounge bar and the snug were full to capacity. The corner pub did a roaring trade on a Saturday thanks to the regular singer, Joe Pennington, who performed there every week. The landlord of the pub kept him supplied with beer for the night and considered it a small price to pay for the extra custom the singer brought in. Joe was an insignificant man: small, thin, receding hairline and very few teeth in his head. But on a Saturday night he became a celebrity as he enthralled the people with his fine voice.

'It's a good job we came early,' Molly said, glancing around. 'The place is chock-a-block.'

'They've all got the same idea as us, Molly me darlin'.' Corker used the back of his hand to wipe the beer from his moustache. 'After eight and it's standing-room only.'

'I see Joe's by the bar enjoying his usual two pints.' Jack smiled as he took stock of the little man. 'Yer wouldn't think, just by looking at him, that he's got a belting voice, one of the best I've ever heard.'

'It goes to show yer can't go by looks,' Nellie said, nodding her head knowingly. 'Take me, for instance. I mean, look at me! Yer wouldn't think, judging by me appearance, that I've got the voice of a lark, now would yer?'

Her husband put his glass on the table, knowing that what he was going to say would earn him a dig in the ribs. 'I would if the lark was dying of a cold.'

Nellie glared at him. 'Oh, ye're there, are yer? An' who turned the little key to wind you up, might I ask?'

'Only passing a comment, dear,' said mild-mannered George. 'Just passing a comment.'

'Well keep yer comments to yerself in future.' Nellie was good at feigning anger. 'Otherwise I'll belt yer one.'

'Listen who's throwin' her weight around!' Molly grinned. 'Anyone would think she's tough, but she's really as soft as a marshmallow!'

'You're a fine one to talk!' Nellie vaguely remembered her and Molly making a pact not to tell the men about the events of the day. But two glasses of sherry had loosened her tongue and she threw caution to the wind. Not that Nellie needed two drinks to throw caution to the wind, but it would be handy as an excuse when Molly had a go at her. 'D'yer want to know what the pair of us got up to today? Honest to God, yer won't believe it.'

'Go on, Nellie, tell us.' Ellen's thin face was eager. 'What did yer get up to this time?'

'I'll believe it,' Corker roared, his weather-beaten face stretched in a smile. 'I wouldn't put anything past you two.'

Nellie was having second thoughts. After all, yer shouldn't break a promise to a mate. She looked at Molly. 'Shall I tell 'em, girl?'

'Ay, go on!' Molly knew there was no point in objecting because after another sherry, Nellie would tell it whether she liked it or not.

Jack raised his brows at George. 'D'you know anythin' about this?'

George shook his head. 'I'm as much in the dark as you. Nellie doesn't tell me half the things she gets up to.'

'Well, just get an earful of this.' Nellie pulled her dress down over her knees then leaned forward, an action which had the dress riding high again to expose her stocking tops. But she was into her stride now and not in the frame of mind to worry about showing her legs off. 'Me an' Molly went to the market today, an' we had young Ruthie with us.' With her hands and mouth going fifteen to the dozen and her chins doing a jig, Nellie started at the stall where they bought the wire, and finished with the boy disappearing round the corner, his arms full of groceries. Her face and actions were so animated, her recollection so colourful, she held her audience spellbound.

When the story ended, Nellie took a deep breath and folded her arms. 'An' me mate here has got the cheek to say I'm as soft as a marshmallow! Talk about the pot callin' the kettle black!'

The group was silent, wondering whether this was one of Nellie's jokes, when Molly started to clap. 'Yer can't half tell a good tale, Nellie! Honest, listenin' to yer was better than being there!'

Ellen's eyes swivelled from Nellie to Molly. 'Yer mean it didn't really happen as Nellie said?'

'Oh yeah, it happened all right,' Molly said, noting Jack and George shaking their heads. 'I admit I fell for the boy's sob story, an' I still believe he was tellin' the truth. But if I was daft, then Nellie was a damn sight dafter, 'cos it was her money that bought the groceries.'

'That was a nice story, that,' Corker said. 'It had everything from humour, anger and sadness to a happy ending. What yez did was a fine thing, and God will pay yer back for it.'

'Well I hope He hangs on for a while, 'cos we're not finished yet an' He may as well pay us back all in one go.' Nellie nodded across at Molly. 'Big-hearted Annie here has arranged to meet the boy again next Saturday in the market. She's promised to take him some clothes for the family, but heaven only knows where she's goin' to get them from.'

'I've already got some, so that's one in the eye for you.' Molly stuck her tongue out. 'I met Mary Watson when I went up to the corner shop, an' she said she's got some dresses that Bella's grown out of, and a coat. She said it was a good chance to have a clear-out and by the weekend she'll have a bit more stuff for me. An' our Ruthie's got clothes that don't fit any more, so they can go as well.'

'I've got no clothes to give yer,' Corker said. 'But I can let yer have a couple of bob for food for them.'

'I wish I could help.' Ellen knew only too well what it was like to be penniless. 'But I don't see how I can.'

Corker patted her knee. 'Don't you worry, love, I'll give Molly an extra couple of bob for her to buy something from you.'

Nellie chuckled. 'I've told her she can have me old coat. The whole family could fit into that.'

'You little liar!' Molly wagged a finger. 'Yer said I couldn't have yer coat . . . proper miser you are.'

'Right,' said Nellie, squaring her shoulders and thrusting her vast bosom forward, 'if that's all the thanks I get, I'm not goin' anywhere with yer in future. Ye're on yer own from now on, girl!'

Molly rubbed the side of her nose, thinking of the amount of clothing she'd have to carry on her own if her friend didn't come with her. 'So ye're not comin' to the market with me next Saturday?'

'Uh-uh! Like I said, girl, ye're on yer own from now on.' Nellie stuck her nose in the air. 'What I might do is follow yer down, just to see yer makin' a fool of yerself. But yer won't know I'm there 'cos I'll hide meself.'

Molly gazed at her friend, all eighteen stone of her. With laughter bubbling inside she spluttered, 'Nellie, King Kong would stand more chance of goin' unnoticed in the market than you would.'

Looking at the smiling faces around her, Nellie's mouth gaped with feigned surprise. 'Fancy you sayin' that, girl, when it was just runnin' through me mind! It just goes to show that great minds do think alike.' She put her arms across her tummy and laced her fingers. 'I'm goin' to hide behind King

Kong. He's a mate of mine . . . yer didn't know that, did yer? Oh aye, he's married to one of me cousins. You know our Sadie, the one with the moustache an' hairs on her chin? She tried to grow a beard so Kong wouldn't feel out of place, but it didn't work. Not enough hairs, yer see.'

While the others doubled up with laughter, Molly left her chair. She leaned across the table full of glasses, and it was only quick thinking on the part of Corker and Jack that prevented the whole lot ending up on the floor. She grasped Nellie's chubby face in her hands and planted a noisy kiss on her mouth. 'Nellie McDonough, ye're a cracker an' I love yer to pieces.'

'Yer can soft-soap me as much as yer like girl, but I'm not comin' with yer next Saturday.'

Molly sat back with a smile on her face, knowing her friend wouldn't miss it for the world . . . she was far too nosy.

'Ay out, here's the singer.' Corker started to collect the empty glasses. 'Let's get a round in before he starts. I hate makin' a noise when he's in the middle of a song, it's not polite.'

Jack jumped up. 'I'll give yer a hand, Corker.'

Joe Pennington walked to his usual spot at the end of the bar. For six days a week he was a five-feet-four nobody, but on a Saturday he was a star, he was somebody. He watched the barmen serve the customers, waited until they'd returned to their seats, then coughed before opening his mouth and letting out a sound that was deep and rich in quality.

> 'She's an old-fashioned lady, with old-fashioned ways,
> And a smile that says welcome to me . . .'

'Oh, God, I love this,' Nellie said. 'It always makes me want to weep buckets.'

George whispered to Jack, 'I know we've said this before,

Jack, but how can women say they love somethin' that makes them cry?'

'Beats me, George.' Jack scratched his head. 'But then we don't know how a woman's mind works.'

Corker leaned across Ellen to add his views. 'There's not a man been born who can understand women. So just enjoy them an' don't try.'

There was loud applause as the song came to an end. Nellie swivelled on her stool. 'Give us somethin' lively, Joe! How about "Swanee River"?'

Joe was so good, if you closed your eyes you would think you were listening to Al Jolson himself. But Nellie didn't want to close her eyes and listen, she wanted to stand up and sing. Punching the air, she belted it out: 'Swanee, how I love yer, how I love yer, my dear ol' Swanee.'

'She's a case,' Corker said.

While George answered, 'Is that what she is?'

Four happy young people stepped off the tram, laughing as they linked arms to walk abreast. 'It's been the best day of me life.' Doreen looked up at the sky and even the stars seemed to be winking at her. 'I wish we could do it all over again, don't you, our kid?'

'I've got another eight days' leave yet,' Phil said, smiling down at her and squeezing her arm. 'We'll think of something to outshine today, won't we, Steve?'

'Not if it's goin' to cost as much,' Steve laughed. 'I'm only a poor apprentice, yer know, I get paid in buttons.'

'Today was worth it, though, I really enjoyed meself,' Jill said. 'But Steve's right, we couldn't afford it often if we want to save up for our bottom drawer.'

'When are yer getting married?' Phil asked. 'When ye're twenty-one?'

'That's when I'll have served me time, but with things the way they are I'll probably be in the army by then.' Steve exchanged a loving glance with the girl he'd adored since she was small. 'We'd get married tomorrow if we could, wouldn't we, sweetheart?'

'Yes,' Jill nodded, 'but I'd like to have enough money for a nice wedding and a little house ready to move into, like me mam and dad did.'

They were nearing their street when the pub on the corner started to empty out. From the singing and the laughter it was obvious they'd had a good night and would still be in the pub if the landlord hadn't put the towels over the pumps.

'Just listen to them,' Phil laughed. 'They've certainly enjoyed themselves.'

One voice, completely out of tune, rose above the others.

> 'Somebody stole my gal, somebody stole my pal,
> Somebody came and took her away.
> She didn't even
> Say she was leaving . . . voh-doh-de-oh-doh.'

Steve doubled up. 'That's me mam! She sounds as though she's had a skinful.'

'Let's catch up with them.' Jill pulled on his arm. 'Finish off a perfect day with a good laugh.'

Molly was the first to spot them. 'Hiya, kids! Have yez had a good time?'

'Ooh, Mam, we've had a wonderful day.' Doreen didn't know where to start. A few weeks ago she was a sixteen-year-old kid; now suddenly she had a boyfriend and was grown-up. 'We went to Jerome's in London Road to have our photographs taken, then we walked around the shops before having something to eat in Reece's, and we ended up in the Odeon on Lime Street.'

'By golly, that sounds like a day an' a half!' Molly had laughed and sung until her voice was hoarse, and seeing her two pretty daughters with their nice, dependable, handsome boyfriends was an extra bonus. 'Yez can tell me all about it tomorrow when me head's a bit clearer.'

Nellie had spotted them and was pushing her way through the crowd that would linger until they ran out of conversation. 'Where's me lovely son an' me beautiful daughter-in-law to be? Come on, give us a kiss.'

'Mam, to put it mildly, you are drunk.' Steve was chuckling as he felt two arms go round his neck and his face was pulled down to receive a sloppy, noisy kiss. He thought the world of his mother. He loved her warmth, her generosity and her everlasting sense of humour. And he roared with laughter when she released him and whispered in his ear, 'The day you see yer mam really drunk, son, I want yer to promise me yer'll sign me up for the Salvation Army.'

Jill was next in line. 'Come on, girl, give yer ma-in-law a big kiss.'

Then came Doreen. 'I don't know what I'll be to you when me son marries yer sister, but I know yer'll find somethin' to call me that's fit for respectable ears.'

'Auntie Nellie!' Doreen felt as though she was being smothered by a large feather cushion. 'Yer'll still be me auntie Nellie and I'll still love yer.'

'God bless yer, girl!' Nellie moved on to Phil, who had been watching with a huge grin on his face. It rounded off the day for him when he was counted in with the family and received a smacker on his cheek.

'Now,' said Nellie, her greetings over, 'where's all our gang? Ay, Corker, come on lad, let's sing our way home.'

She grabbed Molly's arm and linked it through hers, then she spotted Ellen standing quietly minding her own business. 'Oh, ye're not gettin' out of it, Ellen Clarke, so don't be tryin' to hide behind Jack.'

With Molly one side of her and Ellen the other, Nellie turned to make sure the men and the youngsters were following. 'Are yez all ready, behind?'

'We're ready when you are, Nellie, me little ray of sunshine.' Corker had to raise his voice to be heard above the laughter. 'You start off an' we'll all join in.'

Molly twisted her neck to see a smiling Jack standing between Corker and George. 'It's a good job me ma and da didn't come. This one will wake the whole ruddy street an' we'll get called all the names in creation. I'll be ashamed to show me face.'

Nellie jerked her round. 'Anyone that's in bed this time on a Saturday night must be dead miserable, girl, so sod 'em! Now, everyone keep in tune, d'yer hear? Those what can't sing, just hum or whistle.' And with that, she started.

> 'Oh, we ain't got a barrel of money,
> Maybe we're ragged and funny
> But we'll travel along
> Singing a song
> Side by side.'

The friends and families ended a perfect day walking up the street with their arms around each other. Content and happy, they sang their heads off. They sounded quite harmonious really – the only one out of tune was Nellie.

Chapter Eleven

'Why don't you an' Steve go to Barlow's Lane with Doreen and Phil?' Molly asked Jill on the Tuesday night as the family were having their evening meal. 'Be a change for yer.'

The corners of Jill's mouth curved upwards and a smile spread across her pretty face. 'Mam, you know I can't dance! I'm like a baby elephant and Steve is just as bad, we'd be bumping into everyone.'

'Half the people that go there can't put one foot in front of the other!' Doreen laid down her fork. 'Yer wouldn't even be noticed, Sis, honest! An' yer'd enjoy yerselves 'cos Maureen an' Sammy are meeting us there.'

'I don't know.' Jill wasn't keen on the idea. She'd seen her sister and Maureen in action on the dance floor and knew how well they could move. In comparison, she was as stiff as a board. 'I'll ask Steve, see what he says.'

'Don't ask him, tell him!' Doreen picked up her fork and speared a carrot. 'Yer've got some say in where yez go, haven't yer?'

'Ay, clever clogs, that's enough!' Molly said, her eyes flashing. 'Sweet sixteen an' yer think yer know it all.'

'That's our Doreen all over.' Tommy rushed to Jill's defence. 'She's too big for her boots, thinks she knows better than everyone else.'

Jack was about to intervene, but Jill beat him to it. 'I don't need you to stick up for me, I'm quite capable of doing it for meself.' She turned to Doreen who was sitting beside her. 'I never make arrangements without asking Steve first, and the same applies to him. That's how it is and that's how it should be when you're courting someone. It's share and share alike. But I will ask Steve when he comes round.'

Ruthie had been listening with interest, weighing up who was in the right. As she mashed a potato, she reached her decision. 'I like Steve, he's nice.'

'Of course he is, sunshine!' Molly ruffled her hair. 'Yer'll go a long way to meet another as nice as him.' She rested her chin on her laced fingers and gazed at Doreen's bowed head. 'Just out of interest, did yer tell Phil he was goin' to the dance, or did yer ask him?'

Although Doreen's face was straight when she looked up, there was a twinkle in her eye. 'I told him he was going!' She tossed her head, sending her long blonde tresses swirling around her shoulders. 'Then, after he'd picked me up off the floor, I changed me order to a request.'

Molly felt a grudging admiration for her headstrong daughter. Her quick tongue would land her in trouble one of these days, but at least she was honest enough to admit when she was in the wrong. 'I should think so, too! Start throwin' yer weight around with Phil, an' he'll be waving yer bye-bye.'

'He will too!' Tommy growled. 'He could get any girl he liked. I saw him in his uniform an' he's a dead ringer for Randolph Scott.'

'Ay, you!' Doreen pointed her fork. 'He's better lookin' than Randolph Scott, an' a lot younger.'

'Mam?' Ruthie piped up. 'Who's Randolph Scott?'

'He's a film star, sunshine.'

'Ooh, er!' Ruthie pushed her plate away, having lost interest in her dinner. 'It's not fair, I haven't seen Phil in his uniform. When can I see him, Mam?'

'I'll tell yer what, sunshine.' Molly leaned towards her daughter and whispered loud enough for the others to hear.

'Why don't yer ask Doreen if yer can go to the dance with them?'

'There's never a dull moment,' Jack chuckled, wondering whether conversations taking place around tables in other houses in the street were as lively as theirs.

'This is the time of day I look forward to,' Molly said, sitting on one of the chairs by the table. 'Ruthie tucked up in bed and the others off gallivantin' for the night.' She stretched her arms high. 'Peace, perfect peace.'

'I'm glad Jill and Steve have gone to the dance,' Jack said from the depths of his favourite chair. 'It's nice to see the four of them gettin' on so well.'

'Yeah, it did me heart good to see them goin' out of here all laughin' and joking.' Molly's finger traced a pattern in the plush of the chenille cloth. 'Ay, Jack, d'yer think our Ruthie's old enough to go to school on her own, now? She's eight in a few weeks an' I was only six when I started goin' on me own.'

'I don't know, love, I haven't given it any thought.'

'Well yer wouldn't, would yer? You're not the one who has to traipse there an' back every other day. Apart from me and Mary, yer only see about two other mothers outside the gate, the rest of the kids go home on their own.' Molly curled a finger and took aim at a crumb that had been hiding in the deep pile. 'An' it's not only the walk that gets me down, it's being tied to time. No matter where I am or what I'm doing, I've got me eye on the clock ready to down tools and scarper. Me life's not me own.'

Jack's brow was furrowed in concentration. 'D'yer know, thinkin' back, I can only remember me mam takin' me to school on me first day! I don't think she ever took me after that.'

'Perhaps she didn't want anyone to know yer belonged to her,' Molly grinned. 'A little raggedy urchin, were yer?'

'I'll have you know my mother, God rest her soul, always sent me to school neat and tidy.' Jack returned her grin. 'Mind you, after playin' ollies in the gutter, or climbing walls, I wasn't neat and tidy by the time I got home.'

'I've always been sorry I never knew yer parents.' Molly's voice was wistful. 'It's sad they both died so young.'

Jack laid the *Echo* down and reached for his cigarettes. 'It's been a long time now, but I've often thought of them over the years.' He held a match to his cigarette and drew deeply before continuing. 'Particularly on the extra special days in me life when I've wished they'd been here to join in. Like the day we got married, when each of the children were born, and on the day our Jill got engaged.' He flicked the spent match into the fire. 'They'd have been so proud of their grandchildren.'

Tears glistened in Molly's eyes and she bit her lip. Thank God her ma and pa were still alive and enjoying the things Jack's parents had missed. 'I believe in heaven, Jack, an' I bet yer parents know everything that's happened in your life. They'll be sitting next to God feelin' very proud of you an' the kids.'

Jack wasn't as sure in his faith as Molly, but he didn't voice his doubts. 'I hope so, love, I hope so.'

'Ay, we haven't half covered some ground in the last few minutes, that's for sure.' Molly made an effort to shake off the gloom that seemed to have descended. Keeping her tone light, she said, 'From the outside of the school gates to the pearly gates of Heaven . . . not bad in the space of five minutes.'

'To get back to what we were talking about, love, why don't yer try Ruthie on her own for one day, just to see how she gets on?'

Molly pulled a face. 'Mary's the fly in the ointment. I broached the subject a few weeks ago but she wouldn't hear of it. Said Bella was far too young to cross the main road on her own . . . Oh, I don't need to tell you what she's like, 'cos yer've seen it for yerself.'

'Then let Mary take Bella to school if that's what she wants. It doesn't mean you've got to follow suit.'

'I keep tellin' meself that, an' I'm full of good intentions until I come to face Mary.' Molly cast her eyes down. 'Then I lose me nerve.'

'Well now I've heard everything! I've seen you an' Nellie floor hulking big men like Nobby Clarke, but ye're frightened of Mary Watson who wouldn't say boo to a goose!'

'I'm not frightened of her, yer daft article, I just don't like upsetting her! I mean, we are friends, after all.' Molly started to titter and when Jack raised his brows, she chortled, 'I'm not soft, I only take people on when I know I've got Nellie to protect me. I start the fight, then I hold her coat while she finishes the job.'

Jack's laugh filled the room. 'Why don't yer send her over to sort Mary out then?'

'Ooh ay, Jack, don't you breathe a word to Nellie, whatever yer do! She'd think nothin' of blurting it out, and then the fat would be in the fire. An' I don't want to upset Mary right now, 'cos she's been so good sortin' Bella's old clothes out for me to take to that poor family on Saturday. In fact, I said I'd nip over tonight an' see what she's got.'

Molly stood up and pushed the chair back under the table. 'I'll go now while ye're reading yer paper, and be back before yer've had time to miss me.'

Molly went into the hall for her coat. When she came back, Jack was shaking his head. 'D'yer know, Mrs Woman, yer started off with our Ruthie goin' to school on her own, went all around the world, and ye're back now to where yer first started?'

'Well, talkin' doesn't cost nothin', does it? An' it passes the time away.' Molly bent to kiss him. 'I love you, Jack Bennett.'

'In that case, hurry home while we've got the house to ourselves for a change. We could even have an early night in bed.'

Molly leaned on the table. 'You've got a flamin' cheek, Jack Bennett! Yer accuse me of goin' all around the world to say somethin', but you don't, do yer? Right to the point yer are, with yer one-track mind. It's all yer think about. But yer can sod off 'cos I'm not in the mood. I've got a headache with talkin' too much, so there!'

She was halfway down the hall when she called back, 'I think nine o'clock would be a perfectly respectable time to go to bed, don't you?'

She was still chuckling when Mary opened the door. 'You're looking happy with yerself,' her neighbour said. 'Jack hasn't won the pools again, has he?'

'No such luck.' Molly waited until Mary closed the door then followed her down the hall. 'No, I was just laughing at something Jack said . . . it tickled me fancy.'

'Hello, Molly.' Harry Watson drew his long legs in to make room for their visitor to get near the fire. 'Jack been tellin' yer a joke, has he?'

'Nah, my husband doesn't tell jokes, he leaves that to me. It wasn't what he said that made me laugh, it was the way he said it.'

Mary dug her husband in the shoulder. 'Put the kettle on an' make us a cup of tea, Harry, while I show Molly the clothes I've got for her.'

'I dunno,' Harry said, struggling to his feet, 'work all day, then she expects me to work when I come home. I think the men in this street should form a union to protect ourselves from the women.'

'Ah, God love yer.' Molly sniffed while wiping away an imaginary tear. 'Yer'll have me cryin' for yer in a minute.'

Harry gave her a broad wink. 'One sugar is it, Molly?'

'Yeah, I don't need any more, Harry, I'm sweet enough.'

Mary drew Molly to the couch. 'These are the things, Molly.'

Mary had had a good clear-out of Bella's clothes. There

were knickers, vests, socks, shoes, a couple of dresses and a warm winter coat. 'Yer can throw out the ones yer think are no good.'

'Throw them out! Not on your sweet life!' Molly was over the moon. 'In the old days, me an' Nellie bought clothes a damn sight more worn than these at Paddy's Market!' She squeezed Mary's arm. 'Ye're a pal, an' I'm very grateful to yer.'

Molly stayed to have a cup of tea but she kept her eye on the clock. And at a quarter to nine she was crossing the cobbled street with a smile on her face and a song on her lips.

'Will yer be home for Christmas, d'yer think?' Steve asked as he stood with Phil in the foyer of the dance hall waiting for Jill and Doreen to come back from the cloakroom. When the two lads had first met, they'd sized each other up, liked what they saw, and an easygoing but firm friendship had been cemented. 'Be nice if yer were, because me mam an' Mrs B. always have a big party at Christmas.'

'I couldn't tell yer what's happening, Steve, 'cos nobody tells us anything,' Phil said. 'They're moving troops out of our camp nearly every day, and rumour has it they're being shipped over to France. But everythin' is very hush-hush, so really it's only guesswork. Our unit still has a couple of weeks' training, but after that we'll probably be shipped abroad somewhere.'

'And how d'yer like army life?'

'I wouldn't want to make a career of it, but it's not bad. I signed up with the King's Regiment and all the lads are from Liverpool. They're a great crowd an' we have a good laugh. We've got a couple of right scallywags an' the tricks they get up to yer just wouldn't believe.' A smile lit up Phil's face when he saw Doreen and Jill walking towards them. They were pretty enough to turn any man's head, he thought with pride. 'Aren't they both lovely?'

Steve turned his head just as the sisters reached them. He held out his hand to Jill while answering Phil out of the side of his mouth. 'That's the understatement of the year.'

'What is?' Doreen asked as she slipped her hand through Phil's arm. 'What is the understatement of the year?'

'That it takes yer a long time just to put yer coat in the cloakroom.' Phil squeezed her arm. 'Yer've been gone ten minutes!'

'We had to change into our dancing shoes an' comb our hair.' Doreen was so excited she felt as though there were a hundred butterflies in her tummy. 'Yer want us to look nice, don't yer?'

'Yer look good enough to eat.'

The dance floor was crowded with couples turning to the strains of a waltz. The lights were low and there was romance in the air. Phil couldn't wait to get on the floor and hold Doreen in his arms. 'D'yer want to dance, love?'

Doreen shook her head. 'I told Mo I'd see her near the stage so we'd better go and find her. And I'll have to find a chair to put me handbag under.'

Maureen saw them before they saw her. She noticed heads turning as they made their way through the crowd. Even in the dim light you couldn't miss the two tall, handsome men and their lovely companions. She turned to Sammy, saying, 'I thought Phil would be in his uniform.'

'Give the lad a break, he's probably glad to get out of it.' Sammy now accepted that his friend Mike had never stood a chance with Doreen. Even before Phil came on the scene she wasn't interested in his friend in the romantic sense. It was the same with Maureen. Sammy was nuts about her, but the feeling wasn't mutual. She treated him like a brother.

Phil's pleasure at seeing Maureen was genuine as he pumped her hand up and down. 'Hiya, Mo, it's great to see yer.'

Maureen's heart skipped a beat. Apart from being the most

handsome lad she'd ever seen, he had a nice nature to go with it. She could really fall for him in a big way. An unexpected wave of jealousy consumed her. It wasn't a case of she *could* fall for him – she had fallen for him, hook, line and sinker! Oh, why hadn't he seen her before he set eyes on Doreen? 'You look terrific, army life must suit yer.'

'That's debatable.' Phil grinned before turning to Sammy with his hand outstretched. 'Good to see yer, Sammy.'

'Yeah, you too, Phil.' Sammy was puzzled and a little sad. He'd been watching Maureen's face as she gazed up at Phil, and the expression he'd seen there had set him thinking. Surely to God she hadn't fallen for the bloke? He shook his head to clear his mind, telling himself he was imagining things. Maureen was too level-headed to fall for her mate's boyfriend, knowing she didn't stand a snowball in hell's chance of getting anywhere with him.

After Jill and Steve had exchanged greetings, the six young people stood chatting until the band struck up with a slow foxtrot. This was the moment Phil had been waiting for. 'Shall we?'

'Oh yes, please!' Doreen took his hand. They were one of the first couples on the floor and Phil quickly took advantage of the space afforded them. Their bodies close, they moved in time to the music with an ease and grace that had onlookers gazing in appreciation. Many couples on their way to the dance floor stood to watch in admiration, for it wasn't often one got to see such perfection. The two bodies moved as one, rising and falling, spinning and twirling, and all the while there were smiles on the two faces that told of their pleasure in dancing and their happiness at being together.

Jill watched, wide-eyed. 'They are absolutely brilliant! Oh, how I wish me mam and dad could see them, they'd be so proud.'

'Well they've put me off for life!' Steve chuckled. 'I'm not getting on the floor to make an exhibition of meself.'

'Don't be daft!' Maureen said. 'Not everyone can dance like those two! I'll tell yer what, I'll take you and Sammy can take Jill. Once yer've been on the floor and got a bit of confidence, yer'll be all right.'

Jill didn't look too happy, but Sammy didn't give her a chance to refuse. He took her hand and pulled her towards the dance floor, followed by Maureen and a very reluctant Steve.

The music came to an end but Doreen and Phil stayed on the floor waiting for the band to strike up with the second slow foxtrot. 'Oh, look,' Doreen said, pointing, 'our kid's been dancing with Sammy an' Mo's got Steve up! Well, wonders will never cease!'

'Never mind them, let's talk about us.' Phil still had his arm around her waist. 'We didn't get much time to ourselves last night with Aunt Vicky staying up so late.'

The piano player struck a chord to lead the band into the next dance and Phil pulled Doreen to him. Waiting for the right beat, he looked down into her face. 'Are yer definitely my girl?'

'Of course I am! I wrote to yer every day while yer were away, didn't I?'

'I'm serious, Doreen! I want to know if I'm yer steady boyfriend.' Phil tapped a toe to feel the rhythm before moving forward with long strides. He negotiated a turn, then went on. 'What I'm really getting at is will yer be going out with other blokes while I'm away?'

'I've never been out with a bloke before you . . . not on a date, anyway. When me an' Maureen go out in a foursome with Mike an' Sammy, it isn't really a date.' Doreen lifted a hand from his shoulder to give Jill the thumbs-up sign. 'We always pay for ourselves and we meet them inside the hall.'

'That doesn't answer my question, Doreen. Are you as serious about me as I am about you?'

If he could hear my heart pounding he wouldn't have

to ask that question, Doreen thought. I'm so happy I feel light-headed, and no one else but him could do that to me. She would like to tell him these things but was too inexperienced to find the right words. Perhaps when they were alone together some time the right words would come naturally, like her mam said, but right now she didn't know how to express her emotions.

The long silence brought a touch of fear to Phil's heart. He waited until they reached a corner of the dance floor, out of the way of the other dancers, then stopped and held her away from him. 'I take it you're not serious about me, then?'

Doreen looked stunned. 'Oh, I am! I am! I want to be your girlfriend for ever.'

Phil sighed as he pulled her back into his arms, mindless of the curious stares coming their way. The cloud had lifted and he was happy again. 'I'm crazy about yer, Doreen, so don't frighten me like that again, please?'

When the dance was over they returned to the corner where Jill and Steve were sitting, feeling quite pleased with their progress. They were determined to get up for the next dance even if they only managed to shuffle along. Jill's pretty face was animated as she thanked Sammy for putting up with her. 'I'm sorry about your broken toes, Sammy, but I really enjoyed myself.'

Sammy's eyes travelled over each of the three girls' faces. Maureen's dark colouring was in sharp contrast to the fairness of the two sisters, but she was just as pretty. In fact, anyone would be hard put to choose which one of the three was the nicest-looking.

For the rest of the night Sammy and Steve swapped partners for every other dance, but Phil stuck like glue to Doreen. Even in an 'excuse-me', when someone tried to cut in, he refused to part. Doreen's face was the colour of beetroot as he explained to the young man that he hadn't seen his girlfriend in months because he was in the army, and he knew he would understand him wanting her all to himself.

It was a happy group that emerged from Barlow's Lane dance hall, and they laughed and joked as they waited for a tram. Sammy was happy to be included because it meant being paired off with Maureen, and who knew? One of these days she might start to see him in a different light. And he'd have her on her own for a short while tonight because they both lived down Scotland Road, several stops after the others got off. And of course he would walk her to her door, see that she got home safely. That was the least a bloke could do. And if the bloke could pluck up the courage, he might even try stealing a kiss. But when the tram shuddered to a halt and they all ran upstairs to claim the back seat, Sammy told himself not to push his luck.

Chapter Twelve

Corker waited until his mother was ready for her afternoon snooze in front of the fire before saying he'd nip down and see Miss Clegg, in case he didn't get another chance before he went away. And he wanted to see Phil, too: he hadn't seen much of the lad while they'd been home. 'I won't stay long, Ma, just half an hour or so.'

'Don't hurry back, yer needn't worry about me.'

'Of course I worry about yer! Aren't yer the best mother in the whole wide world?'

'Oh, away with yer, an' leave me in peace for a while.' Mrs Corkhill's eyes were filled with love for this gentle giant who was her adored son. 'I'll pop the apple pie in the oven about four o'clock, so don't be too late.'

'Mmm, me mouth's watering already.' Corker pulled his reefer jacket on, planted a kiss on the upturned face and went out of the door whistling a sea shanty.

It was Phil who answered his knock, and his smile was one of pleasure. 'Come on in, Mr Corkhill, it's nice to see yer.'

'Thought I'd show me face in case Miss Clegg thinks I've fallen out with her.' Corker took off his cap as he entered the room and ran a hand over his thick mop of hair. 'D'yer know, Victoria, I'll swear yer get younger every time I see yer.' He bent to kiss the lined face. 'I like yer hairstyle, and those earrings look a treat.'

'I've got Doreen to thank for the way I look – she keeps me

in trim.' The old lady smiled as she waved Corker to a chair. 'She'll have me wearing lipstick next.'

'More power to her elbow, 'cos yer look ten years younger.' Corker laid his cap between his feet. He was about to say the young ones had everything going for them these days, then he remembered there was a war on and it was the young ones who would have the most to lose. 'Or is it because me laddo's home that ye're looking so pleased with yerself?'

Victoria nodded. 'It's lovely to have Phil home, the place hasn't been the same without him.'

Phil blushed. 'Yer won't be saying that when I'm home for good. Yer'll be sick of the sight of me.'

Corker lit one of his Capstan Full Strength and stretched his long legs out. 'When d'yer go back, son?'

'I've got to report for duty on Monday morning, so I'll have to get the overnight train from Lime Street on Sunday.' Phil pulled a face. 'Two weeks seemed a long time when it started, but it's not half goin' over quick.'

'Well, with a bit of luck yer may get another furlough before yer posting comes through.'

Phil shrugged his shoulders. 'Who knows? I read in the paper that we've got over a hundred and fifty thousand troops in France, so I've got a feeling we'll be shipped out there when our training's finished.' He saw his aunt Vicky's brow crease in a frown and wished he could take the words back. She'd been so happy since he'd been home, and they'd talked for hours on end. She'd reminisced about the days when she was young and her parents had been alive, and he'd told her of his hopes of getting a decent job when he came out of the army. Now, without thinking, he'd given her something to worry about and it grieved him. So he put on a happy smile and said cheerfully, 'But then again, for all we know the war could be over any time.'

Corker read his thoughts and kept quiet. He had his own views on the war and in his opinion it wasn't going to be over soon – not by a long chalk it wasn't! You saw a lot when the ship you were on was carrying cargo to the small countries where Hitler had his troops massed at the borders. They didn't stand a chance, those places, not against the might of Germany, and he could foresee the time when Britain would be standing alone. No, it was going to be a long and bloody war, and young lads like Phil were going to be in the thick of it. They weren't considered men until they were twenty-one, when they could earn a decent wage and have a vote on who should run the country. But come a war, then they were seen to be old enough to take up arms and fight for their country.

Corker stroked his beard and sighed inwardly as he gazed at Phil. He was a nice lad, clean-cut with an open, honest face. And he had a sensible head on his shoulders, too! 'I've got to report back to me ship on Sunday, an' if the loading has gone according to plan, we'll be sailing with the early tide on Monday. But I should be home again in a couple of weeks, 'cos I've asked for short trips on compassionate grounds. Me ma's gettin' on in years an' each time I come home I can see a difference in her. She's slowing down, getting more frail. So I don't want to be away from home for too long.'

'Molly and Nellie keep their eye on her, so you've no need to worry on that score,' Victoria said, wanting to relieve his anxiety. 'They go up every day, hail, rain or shine to make sure she's all right and got enough food in.'

'I know, I'd be lost without them. And they do more than just see she's all right for food; they cheer her up. She said they do her more good than a dose of Andrews'.'

Victoria tittered. 'I know what she means! I used to love going to the pictures, and was miserable when I got too old to go out on me own. But when Molly and Nellie start acting the goat, I get more laughs out of them than I ever did out of Charlie Chaplin or Buster Keaton.'

'You should be with us when we go to the pub – Nellie has

the place up!' Corker's guffaw boomed. 'An' the funniest part about it is George! He sits there watchin' his wife, and while the whole pub is roaring at her antics, he quietly sips his beer without even crackin' his face! They say God makes them and matches them – well He matched those two perfectly.'

'Mr McDonough was singing along with everyone last Saturday night.' Phil smiled at the memory. He would never forget one minute of that day: it would always go down as one of the best in his life. 'By the way, did yer get any complaints from the neighbours? We made enough noise to wake the whole street.'

Corker pulled on an ear lobe, grinning. 'Not a dickie bird, son, not a dickie bird. Mind you, would you complain to Nellie?'

'I'd think twice about it,' Phil laughed. 'I suppose yer'll all be there again this Saturday?'

'On me last night? Most definitely! It's a pity yer can't come with us, 'cos yer'd enjoy it.'

'I'd love to come, but Doreen wouldn't be allowed in. It would have been great though, all getting together for a drink on our last night home.'

'Yeah, 'cos God knows when we'll see each other again.' Corker shivered as though someone had walked over his grave. When things started hotting up, and he was in no doubt that they would, it wouldn't be a case of saying *when* we see each other again, but *if* we ever see each other again. Bloody war!

Smiling at Phil, Corker made an effort to banish his dark thoughts. 'I'll tell yer what, son, we'll have that drink together, I promise yer. I'll try and sweet-talk Molly into having a party at her house again. That way we can all be together and have a real knees-up, jars out, on our last night. An' I'm sure Victoria here would like that, wouldn't yer, me darlin'?'

'I'd love it, but I don't think Molly would be too happy.'

'I'll turn me charm on her.' Once again Corker's loud

guffaw ricocheted off the walls. 'If that doesn't do the trick, I'll have to call up the reserves . . . Nellie.'

Molly held her tummy in as she slipped sideways through the half-door of the corner shop. 'Top of the morning, Mr and Mrs Porter!' She grinned when she saw Maisie and Alec doubled under the weight of a sack of potatoes they were carrying between them. 'Funny what some people will do to earn money.'

'Funny isn't the right word, Molly.' Alec gave his wife a nod and they swung the sack gently back and forth before dropping it on the floor behind the counter. 'It's ruddy hard work, an' believe me we earn every penny.'

Maisie nodded towards the door. 'Has yer mate got a cob on with yer?'

Molly turned to see Nellie standing in the street outside. 'What the hell are yer standin' there for, missus? Get yerself in here, quick. You nagged me into havin' this party, said yer'd help with all the runnin' around, so yer can flaming well have half the worry.'

Nellie spread her hands, a pained expression on her chubby face. 'Girl, I'm wantin' to come in, I'm ready to come in, an' if someone will undo the bolts on the other half of this ruddy door, I'll come in!'

'Oh, yer poor thing!' Molly stood on tiptoe to reach the top bolt on the hinged part of the door that Maisie always kept shut to keep the cold out. 'Get yerself inside.'

Nellie swept in majestically. 'Have that door seen to, will you, Alec?' A haughty look accompanied her exaggerated posh voice. 'Hit's han hinconvenience to your customers what help you hearn ha living.'

Maisie took a fit of the giggles. These two were a definite improvement on lugging spuds around. 'Nellie, you're the only one who ever complains about the door! I'm sure yer could get through if yer put yer mind to it and really tried.'

Nellie waited until Molly had shot the bolt back home, then pointed to the narrow space afforded by the half-door. 'Lookin' at the width of that, and then at the width of me, yer still think I should be able to get through it?'

Maisie nodded. 'It might be a bit of a squeeze, but yeah, I think yer should be able to get through it all right.'

'Nah, dopey-drawers, it's an . . . erm, an . . . erm.' Nellie tapped a podgy finger on the top layer of her chins, her eyes closed as though deep in concentration. Then she looked at Molly. 'What's the word I'm lookin' for, girl? You know, when yer think somethin' will fit but it won't?'

'D'yer mean an optical illusion?'

'That's it, girl!' Nellie beamed all round. 'On the tip of me tongue it was, but it wouldn't come out.' She raised her eyebrows at Maisie. 'If yer don't know what it means, 'cos yer haven't got a clever mate like mine, I'll tell yer. It means yer want yer eyes testin', 'cos yer must be ruddy cock-eyed!' She smiled sweetly at Molly. 'Isn't that a good explanation, girl?'

'Yeah, go to the top of the class,' Molly said drily as she picked her basket up off the floor and placed it on the counter. 'Now, can we get down to business, please? I owe yer a couple of bob for the things I sent our Ruthie up for last night, Maisie, an' I'll pay yer for them first so I'll know where I'm workin'.'

Maisie opened the well-thumbed exercise book she kept at the side of the till to keep a note of the stuff that went out on tick, and flicked through the pages. 'Here it is . . . one and eleven, it came to.' She grinned as she added, 'And a penny interest on top.'

'Yer can sod off, Maisie Porter,' Molly said, rummaging in her purse. 'It takes me all me time to keep our lot, never mind keepin' you two in the lap of luxury.'

Alec was leaning on the counter, an amused expression on his face. 'If we live in the lap of luxury, how come we can't afford a party every few weeks like some people I know?'

'Ah, well yer see,' Molly grinned as she placed a two-shilling piece in Maisie's outstretched hand, 'the party's in my house, but I'm not the one forking out for it.'

'No, we're all muckin' in to pay for it,' Nellie said, resting an elbow on the counter with an air of nonchalance. 'Me an' Molly are payin' for the eats, an' the men are seein' to the booze.'

'Is it a private party, or can anyone come?' Maisie asked with a twinkle in her eyes. 'I mean, if I knocked on yer door with a cake in one hand an' a bottle of sherry in the other, would I be let in?'

Molly pretended to frown. 'How big's the cake?'

'A *big* jam sandwich cake with sugar on the top.'

Molly pursed her lips and turned her head to hide a wink. 'What d'yer think, Nellie?'

'A cake an' a bottle of sherry are not to be sniffed at, girl, I'd let them come.' Nellie's quivering tummy was a sign that she'd thought of something funny. And when the laughter came it was so hearty her elbow slipped off the counter: but for Molly's quick action in grabbing hold of her, she would have overbalanced. 'We can take the goodies off them at the front door,' she wheezed, 'then lead them through to the backyard. It's the only place there'd be room for them.'

'She's right,' Molly chuckled. 'The house will be burstin' at the flamin' seams! But yez are very welcome to come. An' if it's any consolation, yez won't be the only ones sittin' on the yard wall.'

'I won't be one, though, will I girl?' Nellie shook her head and set her chins quivering. 'I'm a host, yer see.'

'Yer mean hostess,' Molly corrected her.

'What's the difference?' Nellie asked. 'Same thing!'

'No, it isn't!' Molly said with infinite patience. 'A host is a man, a hostess is a woman.'

Maisie and Alec were thoroughly enjoying the exchange and hoping it wouldn't be interrupted by a customer, when Nellie turned a beaming face on them. 'D'yer hear that? Got an answer for everythin', my mate has. If I'd been lucky enough to 'ave gone to the same school as her, I'd have known I'm an 'ostess, an' not an 'ost.'

Molly put a hand over her friend's mouth. 'Will yer shut it, sunshine, an' let me get on with me business? I've almost forgotten what I came here for in the first place!'

Nellie pushed her hand away. 'Oh, I can tell yer that, girl! Yer came to ask if yer can have some stuff on tick.'

Molly dropped her head into her hands. 'What would yer do with her? I was goin' to work me way up to it, but Tilly Flop here just plonks her big foot in it.'

'Yer don't need to go all round the houses, girl! Just tell Maisie what yer want an' stop wasting time.'

'Wasting time! I'm the one wasting time, am I?' Molly huffed. 'We've been here ten minutes and because you've been messin' about, we've done precisely nowt!'

'No we haven't! Yer've paid Maisie the one and eleven yer owed her!' Nellie's face did contortions as she tried to keep the laughter at bay. 'An' now ye're goin' to ask her for five bob's worth of stuff on the slate. I think that's a very fair rate of exchange . . . Maisie gets one and eleven in one hand, and gives out five bob with the other!'

'Nellie, if yer weren't so big I'd lift yer up, sit yer on the counter and stick a lollipop in yer gob to shut yer up!' Molly spread her hands and shrugged her shoulders at Maisie. 'Honest to God, I want me flamin' bumps feeling for bringin' her out with me! If I'd been on me own I'd 'ave been back home by now.' She felt a tug on her coat and spun round to face Nellie. 'What the 'ell d'yer want now?'

Her face the picture of innocence, Nellie stuck out her bottom lip. 'Can I have a pink one?'

'A pink what?'

'Lollipop.'

Alec pressed his knuckles into the stitch in his side as he made his way to the stock room. He stood for a while to get his breath back before reaching for a side of bacon hanging from an iron rod suspended from the ceiling. He hoped Maisie asked again about them going to the party on Saturday. You were guaranteed a good time when Molly had a shindig. Hearing his name called, Alec laid the side of bacon on the wooden chopping table and poked his head around the door.

'I hope yer don't snore, Alec,' Nellie wagged a finger at him, ''cos if me mate doesn't put a move on, yer'll have three women in yer bed tonight.'

Alec, a mild-mannered man, slim with thinning dark hair, shook his head slowly. 'Nellie, I couldn't stand it, and I'm flaming well sure the bed couldn't, either!'

'Knocked back again!' The corners of Nellie's mouth drooped. 'How come I can never get a click? I mean, I've got a pretty face an' yer'd go a long way to find someone with a figure like mine . . . so what more do they want?'

'I know what I want right now,' Molly told her, 'and that's silence. Will yer shut up an' let me get sorted out with Maisie?'

Nellie stood to attention, her body as straight as she could get it. Then, in a voice they'd never heard her use before, she barked, 'Nellie Fleming, go and stand in the corner with your back to the class, and you will stay there until the lesson is over.'

Her head bent low, Nellie walked to the corner of the shop, saying meekly, 'Yes Miss Cartwright.'

Molly screwed her eyes up tight, praying under her breath, 'Dear God, please don't make me laugh or we'll be here until the cows come home.'

She kept her eyes closed until she had her emotions under

control, then focused her gaze on Maisie. 'Don't look at her, Maisie, and don't say a word.'

'It's all right for you,' Maisie told her, 'you've got yer back to her!'

Molly pulled a crumpled piece of paper from her pocket. 'Just look into my eyes, sunshine, an' then yer won't have to see her.' Smoothing the paper out on the counter, she said, 'This is a list of the things I want for Saturday. I'm hoping to have enough to pay yer for them, but if I'm a bit short, will yer be an angel an' let me have them on tick until next week?'

'Of course I will, I don't know why ye're even botherin' to ask!' Maisie took the list and scanned it for a few seconds. 'I'll make it up on Saturday mornin' and Alec will carry it down, save yer the trouble.'

'Ye're an angel, Maisie, an' I'll make sure yer don't have to sit on the yard wall on Saturday. On the stairs, maybe, or even the mantelpiece, but definitely not the yard wall.'

'Are yer sure yer want us to come? We'd love to, but I'd understand if yer said yer had enough with yer family.'

Molly smiled at the woman who had helped her and Nellie out in the days when things were grim. Many's the time they'd have starved if it wasn't for the owners of the corner shop. And she felt sorry for Maisie and Alec because they had no family of their own. They would both have loved children, but fate had decreed otherwise. 'At the last count there were about twenty comin', so another two won't make any difference. If things get too bad, we'll strip the wallpaper off to make more room.'

Maisie grinned. 'It would help if we all held our breath.'

'Yeah, that's an idea!' Molly chuckled. 'Especially a certain person who is not a million miles from us right this moment.'

'Did I hear someone takin' my name in vain?' Nellie walked to the counter and peered into Molly's face. 'Talkin' about me behind me back are yer, girl?'

'Now as if I would!' Molly put a hand under her friend's chin and raised her face until their eyes met. 'Have yer got over yer funny half-hour now?'

Nellie nodded. 'I'm dyin' to go to the lavvy, girl, so yer'd better make it snappy.'

'Just two more minutes to ask Maisie how much I've got in me Christmas club. It's not that far off now, just a matter of weeks.'

Maisie took a red exercise book from under the counter and turned the pages. 'Here we are – yer've got thirty shillings and sixpence in.'

'Ooh,' Molly groaned, 'not much, is it?'

'Better than a kick in the teeth,' Nellie said, moving from one foot to the other. 'Yer've got some in the butcher's, same as me, and a few bob in Waterworth's.'

'An' I've got me club woman to fall back on, I don't owe her that much now.'

Nellie held Molly's arm in a vicelike grip. 'I ain't kiddin', girl – when I say if we don't move quick, I mean I'll be having a nasty accident.'

Maisie came from behind the counter on the run. Reaching on tiptoe to unbolt the door, she stood aside to let a red-faced Nellie through. 'Is that why yer were sent to stand in the corner at school, Nellie Fleming? Had yer wet yer knickers?'

'Don't make me laugh, Maisie,' Nellie shouted over her shoulder as she hurried away, 'otherwise yer'll have to be gettin' yer mop and bucket out an' then yer'd be laughing the other side of yer face.'

Molly waved as she ran after her friend. 'Not very ladylike, my mate, is she? But she's good really, all heart.'

Chapter Thirteen

'Mornin', girl!' Nellie sounded bright and breezy as she swept past Molly and waddled down the hall with a grin on her face. 'I've just come to ask what time we're goin' down the market. I don't want to be too late back on account of getting ready for the party.'

'Yer know the men don't get in until one, Nellie, but I'll get meself ready early so we can dash off as soon as I've got the dinner over. Anyroad, I told the lad we'd meet him at the same time, so there's no point in us gettin' there any earlier.' Molly grinned as she eyed her friend from top to toe. Nellie's turban had slipped sideways to reveal the dinky curlers in her hair; she had a streak of coal dust across her forehead, a safety pin was holding the front of her blouse together and her stockings were wrinkled around her ankles. 'You look as though yer've had one over the eight already.'

'It was no good gettin' meself all dolled up just to walk down here, now was it? I mean, there's only you here, an' being me mate you don't count.' Nellie caught sight of the pile of clothes on the couch and pushed Molly aside to have a better look. 'Oh, my God! Yer've got enough stuff there to open yer own ruddy market stall! Where on earth did yer get that lot from?'

Molly pointed to the first pile. 'These are off Mary; this next lot are Ruthie's old clothes and a few things off the girls, and the rest I got off Mrs Coleman from the top of the street. With her havin' the two boys, I asked if she could help out, and as yer can see she came up trumps.'

Nellie sought a place between the dinky curlers to scratch her head. 'I know it's a daft question before I ask, but who the hell's goin' to cart that lot?'

'Thee an' me, sunshine!' Molly tried to hide her own doubts. She hadn't expected such a good response, and there was a hell of a lot of clothes for the two of them to carry. And that was without the groceries she'd been able to cadge. 'Two strappin' women like us, we should manage.'

'In a pig's ear we will!' Nellie huffed as she lifted a handful of garments off the top of one of the piles. 'Yer'll need a ruddy handcart for that lot, girl!'

'We'll see how it goes. I've put all the groceries in that big shoppin' bag yer lent me, that's all ready. An' I thought if I split this lot into two and find a pair of old sheets, we could tie up the four corners of the sheets an' carry them like that, one lot each.'

'Two old sheets? Since when 'ave you been flush enough to have two old sheets?'

'I've got one, so I'm relyin' on you for the other.'

Nellie's face was a picture as she gazed at each of the four walls in turn as though seeking divine help. 'We've known each other a long time, haven't we, girl? Long enough, I'd say, to be able to speak our minds . . . right?'

'Of course we have,' Molly agreed. 'We tell each other everything!'

'Well can you just tell me, give me just one good reason, why I should let yer include me in these daft ideas yer get? I mean, I'd be the last one to turn me back on yer when yer were doin' a good turn for anyone. But when it comes to walkin' down the street with a ruddy bundle of clothes perched on me head like a Mary Ellen, then it's time to draw the line.' Nellie straightened her back and thrust out her bosom. 'After all, I do have me pride, yer know, girl.'

'I'll give yer a reason – in fact I'll give yer two for the price of one,' Molly said, pushing her face close to her friend's. 'First, ye're that ruddy nosy yer'd do yer nut if I left yer out of anythin', and secondly, because yer love me.'

Nellie's face was deadpan. 'Yer know, girl, them's two very good reasons an' I can't argue with yer.'

'Yer can if yer like, but it won't get yer anywhere.' Molly pinched one of the chubby cheeks. 'Now go home, Nellie McDonough, an' let me get on with me work.'

'What! No offer of a Saturday mornin' cup of tea with a nice cream slice from Sayer's?'

'Saturday mornin' tea and cake? My God, Nellie, yer sufferin' delusions of grandeur! Now on yer bike, missus!' Molly helped her friend along with some gentle pushing. 'I'll see yer later. Ta-ra for now.'

Nellie looked up from the pavement. Jerking her thumb over her shoulder, she said, 'There's your Ruthie playin' with Bella . . . we're not goin' to have to drag her with us, are we?'

'Not now, thank God! I did think I was goin' to be stuck with her because I haven't the nerve to keep asking Mary to mind her, an' all my lot are goin' out. Liverpool are playing at home and Jack an' Tommy are goin' to the match, Phil is meeting Doreen outside work and they're goin' straight into town to meet up with Jill an' Steve. So I really thought I was goin' to be lumbered with the little one. But as luck would have it, I was pickin' these clothes up off Mrs Coleman when their David asked if he could go to the matinée. So after I'd dropped a few gentle hints, he said Ruthie could go with him an' his mate as long as she behaved herself. He's a sensible lad, turned ten now, an' I know he'll look after her. And Ruthie, well, she's absolutely cock-a-hoop, so everyone is satisfied.'

'Haven't I always said your flamin' face would get yer the parish, girl?'

'An' haven't I always said yours would take it off me?' Molly grinned as she began to close the door. 'Hop it, missus, an' I'll see yer about half one.'

Nellie looked down at the bundle at her feet and gave it a sharp kick. 'Fancy luggin' this all the way down here an' the little blighter hasn't turned up! I could spit!'

'Keep yer hair on, Nellie, he'll come.' But despite her words, Molly was beginning to lose hope. They'd been waiting for twenty minutes now and there was no sign of the boy. 'He might be waitin' in the wrong speck, yer don't know.'

'Five minutes more, then that's it.' Nellie gave the bundle another kick. 'An' I ain't carryin' this lot home, either! It can go to one of the stalls what sells second-hand clothes.'

Molly felt a tug on her coat and she wheeled round. Her face lit up when she saw the boy and her first thought was that it had been a good idea of Nellie's last week to buy that block of carbolic soap: the young lad looked decidedly cleaner. Even his clothes, though tattered and torn, were at least clean. 'We'd just about given yer up,' Molly said. 'We thought yer weren't coming.'

'I've been here half an hour, missus, but I've been waitin' inside the market.' Denis looked down at the bundles and his eyes were full of curiosity and excitement. He'd told his mother about them coming and it was all he'd thought about all week. So when they hadn't put in an appearance, or so it seemed, he'd been making his way home with a heavy heart.

'Well, these are all for yer mam,' Molly said, pointing to the bundles. 'I don't know whether there's anythin' in there that'll be any good to her, but if not she can always get a few bob for them.'

Seeing the lad again brought forth Nellie's motherly instinct. He looked a nice kid, but painfully thin and obviously undernourished. 'We've brought a few groceries as well, so they'll help yer mam out.'

Molly lifted one of the bundles up by the knots in the

centre. 'I hope yer don't live far, Denis, 'cos these are heavy.'

'It's only a few streets away, an' I can carry one.' Three times he tried to lift the heavy bundle without success, his thin face red with the strain. He was about to try again when Nellie stepped in.

'Don't be takin' me job off me, son.' She smiled as she spoke so his feelings wouldn't be hurt. 'I've carried it this far, so I may as well see it through to the end.'

'You take the bag of food,' Molly told him, 'but be careful 'cos there's eggs in it. Lead the way an' we'll follow.'

They left the wide main road and turned into a narrow street of two-up, two-down houses. 'Some of them keep their houses nice, don't they, Nellie? Windows and steps nice and clean, a credit to them.'

Denis suddenly turned into a side entry and after making faces at each other, the two women followed until they came out into the next street. 'That's our 'ouse, over there.' The boy's eyes were gleaming and his whole face was agog. 'I'll hurry on an' tell me mam ye're here.'

'He's goin' to be a smashin'-looking lad when he grows up,' Molly said, changing the bundle to her other hand. 'He'll break a few hearts in his time.'

'I'll tell yer what,' Nellie grunted. 'I don't know about breakin' hearts, he's broken my ruddy back this afternoon. I just hope it doesn't stop me from dancin' tonight.'

'Stop yer flamin' moanin', will yer? Pity someone doesn't break yer jaw an' give us all a bit of peace.'

They stopped outside the house Denis had disappeared into and dropped their bundles. It looked neat and tidy, as well cared for as any of the neighbouring houses. Two young girls came running to the door and Molly smiled as she nodded at Nellie. 'Just about right, eh? A bit younger than Bella an' Ruthie, wouldn't yer say?'

Before Nellie could answer, a woman appeared behind the

girls. She was dark-haired, tall from what they could see, and the smile on her thin face was friendly. Standing with a hand on each of the girls' shoulders, she said, 'I'm Denis's mother, would you like to come in?'

As they walked along the bare boards of the hallway the house echoed with their footsteps, a hollow sound as though the house wasn't lived in. And when they entered the living room the first thing that struck them was the bareness of it. No pictures or mirrors on the walls, not an ornament in sight. The floor was covered with scuffed lino, there was no rug in front of the clean fireplace and no fire burned in the grate. All the room contained were the absolute bare necessities – a table, four wooden chairs and a couch.

Denis and his two brothers stood on one side of their mother and his two sisters on the other while a baby, wrapped in a blanket, lay on the couch punching the air and crying to be lifted up.

'My name is Monica Latimer.' The woman held her thin body erect. She had long straight dark hair, combed back and tied with a ribbon to hang down her back. Her eyes were very dark brown, appearing almost black in the colourless face. Like the clothes on the children standing either side of her, her drab brown dress was shabby and had been patched in several places. But despite the lack of finery, she still had the looks of an attractive woman.

She touched each of the boys' heads in turn. 'Denis, Peter and John, and over on this side we have Hannah and Grace. The baby, who is about to scream the place down any minute, is Deborah.'

She's not a bit like I expected her to be, Molly was thinking. She's got a very refined voice, as though she's been well educated. I wonder what brought her so far down in the world? 'I'm Molly Bennett, an' this here is me mate, Nellie McDonough.'

Mrs Latimer turned to her eldest son. 'Denis, would you put the baby in her pram so the ladies can sit down?'

'Ah, Mam!' Denis was gazing at the big bundles, intrigued to know what they contained. After waiting all week, was he to be denied the pleasure of finding out if they had brought some clothing for him, to put a stop to the taunts of his school-friends?

As though she could read his mind, his mother smiled before reaching down and lifting the baby into her arms. 'Sit down, please.'

Nellie hesitated, viewing the couch with trepidation. If she got stuck in that she'd make a laughing-stock of herself. 'D'yer mind if I sit on one of the wooden chairs? Once I got down on that,' she nodded at the horsehair couch, 'yer'd never get me off it.' Her smile took in the wide-eyed children. 'That's the worst of bein' thin, yer see, kids.'

Monica Latimer waited until they were settled, then said, 'I hope Denis wasn't a nuisance to you last week. I found it very hard to believe his story when he came home with all those groceries and told us how he'd come by them. Not that they weren't welcome, because I can assure you they were much appreciated. But I wouldn't like to think he'd been forward, or cheeky.'

'He wasn't a nuisance or cheeky!' Molly said. 'In fact me an' Nellie don't know how we'd have managed without him, do we, Nellie?'

The chair creaked and Nellie's chins did a dance. 'Proper little godsend he was, an' that's a fact.'

'He told us all about you, an' his brothers and sisters.' Molly was doing some quick thinking, expecting any minute to be asked why they'd come today bearing gifts of second-hand clothes. She didn't want to get the lad into trouble. 'It was when he mentioned them, an' after him being so good, like, that I thought yer might be grateful for some of the clothes our kids have grown out of.' Better tread carefully, she told herself.

This was a proud woman who wouldn't thank them for feeling pity for her. 'I know by me own that it's hard keeping kids in clothes, they grow out of them so quickly. But I don't want to offend yer, and me and Nellie won't take the huff if yer say yer don't want them.'

'Me mam won't say that, will yer, Mam?' There was such pleading in Denis's eyes, it tugged on Molly's heartstrings.

'Look, why don't you kids go out an' play while we have a little talk to yer mam?' Molly willed the lad to understand that what she was trying to do was for his own sake. 'Take the baby out in the pram for ten minutes.'

Nellie brought out her scruffy purse from her pocket. 'Here yez are, a threepenny joey to buy sweets with. But share them out between yer, d'yer hear? Get the baby a ha'p'orth of chocolate drops.'

The wide eyes and gaping mouths told Molly and Nellie that this was a rare treat indeed. Within a few minutes they were all hanging on to the sides of the dilapidated pram as Denis pushed it down the yard. He was the one with the threepenny joey, and they weren't going to let him out of their sight.

'You're very kind.' A tear glistened in the corner of Monica Latimer's eye. 'It's a long time since they had any money for sweets.'

'Can I call yer Monica?' Molly waited for a nod, then leaned forward. 'Look, me an' Nellie here, we don't believe in beatin' about the bush . . . no manners, yer see, sunshine. So yer don't mind if we explain why we've landed on yer doorstep like two Mary Ellens, do yer?'

'No, of course not.' Monica sat back in the wooden chair, surprised to find herself wanting to laugh, and that hadn't happened in a long time. After all, she'd had very little to laugh about. She hadn't believed the story Denis told her about the two fat women, but it couldn't have been all lies or they wouldn't be sitting in her room right now! And she found herself warming towards them . . . they looked a real pair of characters, typical Liverpudlians with a great sense of humour and hearts full to overflowing with kindness.

'Well, it's like this, yer see, Monica.' Molly squared her shoulders before getting into her stride. 'Me an' Nellie here, we took a real shine to your lad last week . . . didn't we, Nellie?'

'Ye're dead right there, girl!' Nellie had been wondering when she was going to get her twopenny's worth in. 'Yer've got a great little lad there, Monica.'

'All the children are good, considering what they've had to put up with in the last eighteen months. Their whole world has been turned upside down.' Monica lapsed into silence, afraid the women wouldn't want to be burdened with her troubles.

'He's a chatty little feller,' Molly said, picking her words carefully. 'An' me an' Nellie being nosy, like, we were interested and asked him questions. We weren't prying, it's just like I said, we took a liking to the lad.'

'And he told you all our troubles?' Monica lifted her hand when Molly went to protest. 'Oh, it's all right, I wouldn't blame him if he had. In fact, I'd be happy if he had someone to unburden himself to. The poor boy keeps his heartache to himself because he's the oldest and thinks he's the man of the house now his dad has gone. And I haven't been much help, crying my grief in front of the children, which was very wrong. I didn't realize the harm I was doing until Denis walked through that door last week with his arms full of groceries. He looked so proud and so happy that he was helping, I felt thoroughly ashamed of myself. It was then I made up my mind not to cry any more, at least not in front of the children, and to get off my backside and do something about the poverty we're in.' She laced her fingers together and laid them in her lap. 'I don't know how I'm going to do it, but if a ten-year-old boy can try, then so can I. It's up to me to keep this family together, happy, well fed and decently clothed.'

Nellie laid her chubby hand on Monica's shoulder. 'Yer husband must've been very young when he died, girl?'

'Thirty-two.' Monica's fingers were white as she pressed her hands together to keep the tears at bay. Then, slowly, she told them how her husband had always worked and provided for them. He loved his family and would have given them the moon if he could. He never took time off work, and when he came home one day coughing and sneezing he just shrugged it off as a heavy cold. For four days he went out to work looking dreadful, but still insisting it was just a cold. Then one night he was sweating so much in bed the sheets were wringing wet, and when Monica felt his brow he was burning with fever. He still tried to drag himself out of bed for work, but Monica, five months pregnant with Deborah, was so worried she made him stay in bed and sent for the doctor. He was rushed to hospital with pneumonia but died two days later.

Recalling that terrible time was too much for Monica, and the tears rolled down her face as her body shook with sobs. 'I'm sorry,' she said, 'I'll be all right in a minute.'

Nellie was the first to reach her. 'You go right ahead an' cry, girl, it'll do yer good.' Her arms around the woman's shoulders, she rocked her back and forth. 'There now, get it all out of yer system.'

'I'll put the kettle on.' Molly picked up the bag of groceries and made for the kitchen. There was tea and sugar in with the groceries, and a tin of conny-onny, and in no time at all Molly came through carrying a cup of piping hot tea. 'There yer are, sunshine, get that down yer an' dry yer eyes before the kids come back.'

'You're both very kind.' A weak smile crossed Monica's careworn face. 'Denis said you were. He thinks you're his fairy godmothers.'

'Kind, my foot!' Molly said gruffly as she began to untie the knots on one of the bundles. 'If yer can't help someone, then yer've no right to be living on this earth.' She began to shake the creases out of the clothes before laying them across the table. 'Yer can look through these an' throw out what yer don't want.' Suddenly she began to chuckle. 'Ay, Monica, can yer imagine me an' Nellie with magic wands in our hands? Some fairy godmothers we'd make, eh? We look more like Two-ton Tessie O'Shea!'

'Ay, you speak for yerself, missus!' Nellie was heartened to see Monica's face brighten as she eyed the clothes with interest. 'Insult yerself if yer like, but leave me out of it.'

Monica put down her cup and approached the table. She was shy at first, picking up one or two things. Then when she realized there was something there for everyone except the baby, she became animated. 'How did you know the sizes? There's something here for each of the boys and the girls! And look,' she picked up one of the dresses Jill had put in, 'this will fit me! Oh, you are kind, and I'm very grateful.'

'How have yer been managing?' Molly asked casually. 'For money, I mean.'

'I've pawned everything we had.' Monica lowered her eyes. 'You wouldn't have known this room two years ago; it was comfortable and warm . . . a real home.'

'Can't yer get any money off the Public Assistance?' Molly asked. 'They should help yez out.'

'I've been too proud to ask for help. But not any more. Seeing our Denis's face last Saturday was just the jolt I needed to make me realize what I was doing to my children. You see, I adored my husband, and when he died part of me died too. I've been wallowing in self-pity, forgetting that the children had lost the father they loved and needed me more than ever. So on Monday I went down to the Public Assistance and asked for help. They sent an inspector on Wednesday to make sure I didn't have anything I could sell, and he said if I go down next Monday they'll give me an allowance. It won't be much, certainly not enough for everything. But even if it's only enough to pay the rent, buy a bag of coal and put pennies in the gas meter, then it'll be a load off my mind. I asked the woman next door if she'd mind the baby if I got a part-time job, and she's agreed. So if I can get a job, then we'll have food on the table. And these,' she gestured to the piles of clothes, 'they'll keep us looking decent for a long time.'

Molly and Nellie exchanged glances. Both were thinking that if they'd taken young Denis to the police station last Saturday, what a different ending there'd have been to the story. Monica wouldn't be smiling as she was now: she'd have been heartbroken.

'Well, me an' Nellie wish yer all the luck in the world, sunshine.' Molly began to button her coat. 'Yer've got a lovely family and a lot to thank God for.'

'I've got you two to thank for bringing me to my senses. But won't you stay and see the children? They'll be disappointed if you don't.'

It was Nellie who answered as she pushed herself off the chair. 'Not today, Monica, we've got to do a bit of shoppin' at the market an' we don't want to be too late home, 'cos we've got a heavy date on tonight.'

'We will call in an' see yer again, though,' Molly said. 'That's if yer don't mind?'

'I'd love you to call in again.' The first genuine smile in eighteen months lit up Monica's face. The kindness of these two women had put her on the road to recovery, and she didn't want to lose track of them. 'I was going to ask, but was afraid you'd think I had a cheek after all you've done for us.'

'Oh, yer haven't seen the last of us, we'll call in an' see yer one Saturday afternoon in the next few weeks.' Nellie waddled to the door then turned, a wide grin covering her face. 'I've just thought on, I lent Molly me shoppin' bag to put yer groceries in 'cos it was bigger than hers. An' I need it to put me potatoes an' things in.'

'Oh, I'm sorry, I didn't know. I'll get it right away.'

'Hang on a minute.' Molly pulled on Monica's arm. 'Your

Denis will be in in a minute – send him up to the market with it. We'll be at the first fruit stall, near the entrance.'

Nellie was getting worried as it was nearly her turn to be served. 'I want spuds, carrots, onions an' a turnip, an' I've no ruddy bag to put them in! I'm not getting on the tram with all them wrapped in newspaper 'cos it would be just my luck for the paper to burst an' all me spuds go rollin' down the aisles.' She tutted. 'It's your fault, yer should have let her get me bag for me while we were there.'

'He'll be here in time, so stop yer moanin'.' Molly's eyes were scanning the crowd for sight of the slim lad who, she knew only too well, could dart in and out of the crowd as fast as a whippet. 'Here he is!' She slapped Nellie on the back. 'I told yer he'd get here.'

Nellie flashed Denis a smile, grabbed the bag and bawled, 'It's my turn, I've been waitin' ages.'

But there was someone there with a bigger mouth than Nellie's. 'Tough luck, missus, 'cos yer'll have to wait a bit longer. I was here before yer.' The owner of the voice was less than half Nellie's size, but she didn't see that until it was too late to argue. So she stood and waited patiently for the woman to be served. She watched the greengrocer fill the bag then hand it over the counter. 'It's heavy, love, I hope yer can manage.' The man winked. 'If I could leave me stall, love, I'd willingly carry it home for yer.'

'I'll manage.' The lady tried to lift the bag with one hand, then tried again with two. 'My God, it weighs a ruddy ton! Have yer given me bricks instead of spuds? I'll have no arms left if I 'ave to carry that all the way home.'

Nellie could hear Denis talking to Molly behind her and an idea formed in her mind. 'How far yer got to go, love?' she shouted across to the woman. 'D'yer live near?'

'Off Scottie Road . . . not that far really, but I don't know 'ow I'm goin' to make it with the weight of this.'

'Well, look, I might be able to help yer out.' Nellie jerked her thumb over her shoulder. 'I always bring a lad with me to carry me bags, I don't believe in killin' meself for the sake of tuppence. I'll let you 'ave him if yer like, 'cos I've got me mate with me today to give me a hand. It's up to you, I don't mind one way or the other, I'm just tryin' to be helpful.'

The woman's body was leaning sideways with the weight. 'How much did yer say he charges?'

'He doesn't charge, missus, but I give him tuppence for his trouble. It's worth the money, I can tell yer.' Nellie shrugged her shoulders. 'Don't bother if yer don't want to, it's no skin off my nose.'

'Ask him for me, will yer?'

Nellie smiled down at Denis. 'Yer didn't mind me offerin' yer services, did yer, son? Tuppence is better than a kick in the teeth, is it not?'

'Oh, yeah!' Denis was convinced now that these two were definitely his fairy godmothers. 'I can give it to me mam.'

'I've got a better idea.' Nellie cupped his face. 'I bet it's a long time since anyone gave yer mam a bar of chocolate. Why don't yer buy her a slab of Cadbury's? I'm sure she'd be over the moon.'

The lad's face was such a joy to behold, Nellie wanted to make sure he wasn't robbed of the thrill of presenting his mother with a slab of chocolate. She turned to the woman. 'He'll do it for yer, love, but I always pay him in advance, so can yer pay him now?' She held out her hand, leaving the poor woman with the option of paying up front or carting the heavy load down Scotland Road.

After rummaging in her purse, the woman handed the coppers over. Just wait until she got home, she'd give her husband a right earful. Sitting in front of a roaring fire he was, listening to the ruddy wireless while she was left to do the hard work! If he thinks he's getting away with it next week he's got another think coming. And I'll get me tuppence back with interest! I'll tell him I gave the lad threepence, he won't know any difference, and I'll mug meself to a penny's worth of mint imperials.

Chapter Fourteen

'We'll have to take the table out, love, otherwise we'll never fit them all in!' Jack stood scratching his head. 'This room's full with just our six, never mind twenty!'

'We can't take it out, where the 'ell would we put it?' Molly's face was flushed. She had spent the last hour making sandwiches with the help of Jill and Doreen, and Maureen who had come along to give a hand. While they'd been doing that, Jack and Tommy were supposed to be sorting out the seating arrangements. 'Next time Nellie McDonough mentions me havin' a party here I'll clock her one.'

'Oh, come on love, you can't blame Nellie! I'd have backed her up on it if I'd been asked. It might be ages before we can get everyone together again, so let's get stuck in an' make it a good night.' Jack rubbed his forehead, knowing that his next suggestion would bring the ceiling down on him. 'The only place we can put it is in the yard.'

'In the yard!' Molly looked horrified. The table, like the rest of the furniture in the small living room, was her pride and joy. It had been bought when Jack came up on the pools, and she treasured it. 'Some hopes you've got, Jack Bennett! The only way this table will go in the yard is over my dead body.'

'Molly, just calm down for a minute, will yer, and tell me how yer expect to get twenty people in here? With the table out of the way, we'd have a lot more room for the chairs yer said Nellie's lending us. But as it is now, everyone will be crushed in like sardines and no one will enjoy themselves.'

Molly stood with her hands on her hips, her temper frayed at the edges. In half an hour the guests would be arriving and she wasn't even washed yet! 'I'll sort somethin' out,' she said, 'you get yerself washed while I nip up to Nellie's.'

When Nellie opened her front door dressed in her best frock, her hair neat and tidy and wearing lipstick, it was like a red rag to a bull. 'Nellie, while you've been preening yerself in front of the mirror, I've been runnin' around like a blue-arsed fly. So don't answer back or ask any questions 'cos I'm not in the mood,' Molly warned. 'Just get George down to our house on the double to give Jack and Tommy a hand with bringin' me table up here.'

Nellie rolled her eyes. 'To bring yer table up here?'

'You heard what I said, yer haven't got cloth ears.' Molly glared. 'It's either your house or the yard, an' I can tell yer now that my table isn't goin' in no yard.'

'But where can I put it, girl?'

'Nellie, I can think of an answer to that but I'm too much of a lady to say it. Move yer own furniture around, for God's sake, use yer head! An' when the men have moved the table, give them the chairs to bring down.'

'Ooh er, ye're in a right temper, aren't yer, girl? Fair spittin' feathers, yer are.'

'Well if you get off yer backside and supervise the moving of the furniture, it'll give me a bit of time to titivate meself up. Then perhaps there'll be an improvement in me outlook on life.'

Nellie turned her head to bawl down the hall. 'George, yer body's wanted by some woman at the door. She said she used to knock around with yer twenty-odd years ago, before yer met me. Got a daughter of twenty-two she has, an' she's the spittin' image of you.'

If someone had paid Molly a hundred pounds she couldn't have kept her face straight. Here she was, looking as though she'd been dragged through a hedge backwards, while Nellie was dolled up to the nines. She had every right to feel aggrieved, and yet her friend still had the power to banish her foul temper and bring a smile to her face. 'Nellie McDonough, I'll deal with you tomorrow. Right now, you an' George get down to ours and give Jack a hand.' Molly began to move away. 'Table up, chairs down – not too difficult to remember, even for you.'

'Yer did say supervise, didn't yer, girl?' Nellie shouted after her. 'I mean, yer wouldn't expect me to get me hands dirty, not with all me glad rags on?'

Molly clamped her lips together as she spun round, a hot retort ready on her tongue. But at the sight of her eighteen-stone friend, standing with her arms folded and an angelic smile on her chubby face, the words never left Molly's mouth. Instead she bawled, 'If I'm not ready by the time me guests arrive, Nellie McDonough, I'll marmalize yer.'

With her foot on the top step, Molly heard Nellie's parting shot. 'Let me know when ye're goin' to do that, girl, so I can change me clothes. I don't want no jam on me best dress.'

'Damn and blast this stud.' Jack lowered his arms in disgust. 'It takes me longer to get me collar on than it does to get washed and dressed.'

'Come here, yer useless article.' Molly had the job done in no time and held her hand out for the tie hanging over her husband's arm. 'Let me put this on yer, I make a neater knot than you do.'

'The place looks a lot bigger without the table, doesn't it?' Jack peered in the mirror to satisfy himself that his hair was in place, then he grinned at Molly's reflection. 'I bet Nellie's room is crowded, though.'

'There'll be nobody in there tonight 'cos Lily and Peter are goin' out, so it won't be in anyone's way. I just hope she's got it covered up, 'cos if there's a mark on it I'll slaughter 'er.'

'Well you can relax now, everything's under control.' Jack

put his arm around her waist and pulled her towards him. 'Ruthie's settled in happily next door with Ellen's kids, tickled to death to be sleepin' there tonight. The three girls are upstairs putting the finishing touches to their faces and your son and heir has gone up for his mate. Corker and Phil have stacked the crates of ale in the yard and the glasses they borrowed from the pub are laid out ready. We've got four bottles of sherry, some lemonade, and all the eats are ready. All yer've got to do now, love, is relax and enjoy yerself.'

A knock on the door brought a sigh from Molly. 'Here's the first of them – we just made it on time. I'll open the door.' On her way down the hall she shouted up the stairs, 'Come on girls, get down and take the coats off people as they come in and put them in the bedroom.'

Molly was flabbergasted when she opened the door to see Ellen, dwarfed by Corker, smartly dressed in a new, light grey dress with a belted waist set off with a neat white collar and cuffs. And she'd been to the hairdresser's in the dinner hour and had her hair marcel-waved. All in all, she looked very attractive. 'Hey, what's all this?' Molly cried. 'Got yerself a new girlfriend, have yer, Corker?'

The big man looked as pleased as punch as he cradled Ellen's elbow. 'Looks a treat, doesn't she? Now yer know how stupid I was not to ask her to marry me when we were young. I had a hankering to go away to sea, and she dropped me and went an' fell for Nobby.'

'Lookin' at her now, Corker, I'd say yer were a bloody fool.' Molly stepped aside to let them in. 'Still, it'll all come right in the end, please God.'

Molly had just closed the door when there was another rat-tat. 'You go in while I see who this is.'

The smile dropped from Molly's face with shock when she saw Sammy on the pavement outside, and standing next to him, Mike. Oh, dear Lord, she thought, Phil's not going to be very happy about this! She quickly pulled herself together.

'Hi, fellers, come on in.' As she closed the door behind them, Molly told herself she'd strangle Doreen if she'd invited Mike without letting on. He was a nice lad, and she was fond of him, but surely her daughter should have had more sense?

As soon as she'd shown the lads into the room, Molly grabbed Doreen by the arm and dragged her into the kitchen. 'What the hell d'yer think you're playing at? I've a good mind to break yer neck for pulling a stunt like this!'

Doreen looked puzzled. 'What are yer on about, Mam?'

'Mike! That's who I'm on about! You might think it's funny, but I doubt whether Phil will see the joke.'

'Mam, it was Phil who told me to invite Mike.' Doreen spoke quietly. 'The first night I met Phil I told him about me and Mo goin' out in a foursome with Sammy and Mike. He knows we're only friends an' he said he'd like to meet him. I should have told yer, but it slipped me mind.'

Molly's eyes narrowed. 'Are yer tellin' me the truth?'

'Of course I am! Yer can ask Phil if yer don't believe me!'

Molly breathed a sigh of relief. 'It fair gave me a turn when I opened the door and saw him standing there. It's no ruddy wonder me hair's going grey.' She began to laugh. 'I had visions of them duelling at dawn in Walton Park . . . I could even see a man offering them the choice of pistols or swords.'

'Oh Mam, don't be so melodramatic!' Doreen began to shake with laughter. 'Yer should never have gone to see *The Three Musketeers*, yer take things too much to heart.'

Jack popped his head around the door. 'What are yer doin' out here? The flamin' room's bursting at the seams an' you're standing here nattering.'

'Keep yer hair on, sunshine, I'm coming now an' I'll sort them out.' She pulled the skirt of her dress down, straightened her shoulders and put on a wide smile. 'I'm determined to enjoy meself tonight, even if it kills me.'

But when Molly entered the fray it was to find that Nellie

had taken charge and was bossing everyone about. She had Miss Clegg sitting in Jack's armchair, Bridie and Bob on the couch, and the male members of the party were being told to sit on the straight dining chairs with their appropriate partners on their knees. 'An' make sure yer stick to yer own, I don't want no hanky-panky 'cos it's not that sort of a party.'

Molly stood behind Nellie with her hands on her hips. 'Excuse me, like, but who's the hostess here?'

Nellie gave her audience a broad wink before turning to face her friend. 'You're the number one hostess, 'cos it's your house an' that's only fair. But I'm number two hostess, so they'd better watch themselves. Any shenanigans an' they'll be turfed out on their ears. There'll be no drunkenness and no tellin' of dirty jokes unless they're first approved by me.' She beamed at Molly. 'That's tellin' 'em, isn't it, girl? Oh, an' while I'm at it, I may as well put you straight. If you don't give me the respect I deserve as an honer, er, honour . . . oh sod it, as yer sidekick, then I'll go home an' kick hell out of yer table.'

'Mam?' Steve shouted, his arm around Jill's waist as she perched on his knee. 'Is it all right if we enjoy ourselves?'

'Of course it is, light of my life! Eat, drink and be merry, that's my motto in life. But remember, it's six o'clock Mass in the morning an' Father Murphy gets his dander up if anyone reels down the aisle smellin' of drink.'

'If number two hostess will shut her gob for a minute, I might be able to say hello.' Molly's eyes swept over the happy smiling faces and came to a stop to feast themselves on one of the happiest faces Molly had ever seen. 'Rosie! I almost didn't recognize yer! Oh, stand up, sunshine, and let's have a good look at yer.'

With all eyes on her, Rosie stood up. Her bonny face, framed by a mass of dark curls, shone with pride. She was wearing a dress in a deep cherry red, a colour which enhanced her dark looks. It had long sleeves, narrowing to fit snugly around her wrists, a plain round neck and a dropped waistline. Her black patent-leather court shoes had inch and a half heels and were adorned with a silver buckle. And to complete the outfit, she was carrying a black patent-leather handbag.

'Oh, don't you look lovely!' Molly eyed her up and down, amazed at the transformation. 'Twirl around an' let's have a good look at yer.'

'Who is this lovely maiden?' Jack asked, standing back with a look of surprise on his face. 'Will someone introduce us?'

'Sure I'll introduce meself, so I will.' Rosie entered into the pretence, loving every minute of it. 'I'm Rosie O'Grady, kind sir, an' it's pleased I am to meet yer.'

'Rosie, you look beautiful.' Jill smiled her pleasure.

'Yeah, yer certainly do.' Doreen was thinking of the new dress pattern she'd bought, and how the style would suit Rosie down to the ground. She'd make her a dress when Phil had gone back off leave.

'Sure I've never had so fine a dress in all me life, an' that's the truth of it.' Rosie's manner was so natural, so unaffected as she ran a hand down the skirt of the dress, there wasn't a person in the room who didn't share in her pleasure. 'And see me shoes, Auntie Molly? I feel really grown-up now with me high heels.'

'It's a pity yer mammy can't see yer, she'd be so proud.'

'Oh, I know what me mammy would be saying to me, right enough. "Neither a borrower nor a lender be", that's what she'd be sayin' to me. But I'll pay Auntie Bridget back when I start work, that I will. Every week without fail, I'll be paying her.'

Molly saw the pride on her mother's face. She had good dress sense did Bridie, and she'd chosen well for her young guest. The dress was ideal, the colouring suited Rosie to perfection and the loose-fitting style was one which hid the ample proportions of a young girl who had yet to lose her puppy fat.

'I told yer, me darlin', didn't I?' Corker said. 'Yer'll have all the young lads after yer.'

As though on cue Rosie asked, 'Where's Tommy? Sure I'd like him to see how grand I look.'

'He's sitting on the stairs with his mate, Ginger.' Molly tried to warn her not to expect too much from Tommy. 'But he's only fifteen, yer know, sunshine, an' he doesn't have much time for girls.'

'I must have been old for me age, then,' Corker roared. ''Cos when I was fifteen I used to stand on the street corner givin' all the girls the glad eye!'

'Sure I'm only fifteen meself,' Rosie said, 'an' if a friend of mine had new clothes, wouldn't I be the first to say I liked them?' With that she marched into the hall, and with everyone in the room holding their breath, they heard her ask, 'Where's Tommy?'

'He, er, he's gone upstairs.' Ginger scratched his head. He couldn't make out why his friend had scrambled up the stairs as though the devil was after him when he'd heard his name mentioned. Ginger would agree that girls generally were a nuisance and not worth bothering with, but he didn't agree with Tommy that this one was worse than any he'd ever met. And she certainly didn't fit the description he'd been given. Big and fat and never stops talking, his friend had said. But as Ginger scratched his head again, he thought she looked all right to him. In fact, she was more than just all right.

'D'yer mind if I sit beside yer and wait for Tommy to come down?' Rosie asked. 'Sure he can't be up there much longer, an' he'd be disappointed if I didn't wait for him.'

Bridie looked up at Molly. 'If we weren't supposed to be having a party in here I'd suggest we all congregated in the hall, because there's goin' to be a pantomime out there when Tommy comes down. Our Rosie's not so easily put off.'

'Yer mean *if* he comes down, Ma,' Molly laughed. 'If I know our Tommy, he'll stay up there until the coast is clear.'

Jack clapped his hands. 'Come on, Corker's ship will be sailing before we get the party started. All hands to the pumps, men, and get the drinks poured out.'

When he was sure everyone had a drink, Jack sat down between Corker and George and soon they were joined by Alec. The conversation drifted on to the state of the war, and after listening for a few minutes, Maisie moved her chair to where Molly and Nellie were sitting, near Miss Clegg, Bridie and Bob. 'Get a couple of men together with a glass in their hand and all they can talk about is flamin' war!' Maisie sounded disgusted. 'Wouldn't yer think they'd forget it for one night?'

'Yeah,' Molly chuckled. 'Look at poor Ellen sat on Corker's knee – she looks bored stiff.'

Nellie turned her head. 'Hey, Ellen, get yer body over here and bring yer new hairstyle with yer.'

'Ay, you, shut up!' Molly said as she watched Ellen sit in the space next to Bob. 'Ye're only jealous.'

'I know I am, girl!' Nellie admitted. 'I've been looking at Miss Clegg here, an' your Doreen's done a real good job with her hair.'

Looking pleased, Victoria touched the bun at the back of her neck. 'She's very clever with her hands, is Doreen.'

Nellie, her legs wide apart as usual, gave Molly a sharp dig in the ribs. 'D'yer think she'd do somethin' with my hair?'

'Ay, Nellie, she's good but she's not that good!' Molly chuckled. 'It's a miracle worker yer want, to do anythin' with your tatty head.'

'Oh charming, that is!' Nellie drained her glass. 'Some hostess you are, insultin' yer guests and letting them sit with empty glasses in their hands.'

It was left to Steve, Phil, Sammy and Mike to make sure everyone's glasses were topped up. And Molly was heartened to see that Mike wasn't being left out and seemed to be enjoying himself. As the glasses were emptied and refilled, the conversations became noisier, the laughter louder, and Molly knew the party would soon be in full swing.

'Molly,' Bridie touched her daughter's knee. 'Would yer pop yer head out an' see how Rosie's getting on?'

Bob laughed. 'I don't think yer need worry about Rosie, but yer'd better see how poor Tommy and Ginger are getting on.'

Rosie was sitting on the bottom stair, Ginger on the second, and Tommy on the fourth. 'Are you all right out here?' Molly asked.

'Sure we're fine, Auntie Molly, so we are. An' Tommy likes me new dress fine, don't yer Tommy?'

Ginger felt uncomfortable when his friend didn't answer, so he said, 'I think it's nice.'

'Why don't yer come in and join the party?' Molly took pity on her son who looked so forlorn. 'You and Ginger can have a shandy.'

'Will yer ask Tilly Mint to move out of the way, then?' Tommy's voice was gruff.

'Come on, Rosie,' Molly pulled gently on her arm. 'Me ma's wondering where yer are.'

'I'll come then, Auntie Molly, 'cos I wouldn't be wantin' me auntie Bridget to be worried.' She stood up and looked back at Tommy. 'I'll see yer later, Tommy.'

'Not if I see yer first, yer won't.' It was said quietly, but Molly heard and smiled. Life was going to be very interesting with these two at loggerheads. Still, there was never a dull moment.

'Who's going to give us the first song?' Corker asked. 'Let's have one of the ladies first, eh? What about you, Bridie me darlin'?'

'I'll give yer a song later,' Bridie smiled, 'when yer've all had a few more drinks.'

'I'll sing for yer, Uncle Corker,' Rosie said. 'But I only know Irish songs.'

'As long as yer can sing, we don't care where the songs come from.'

Molly looked at her mother and mouthed, *Can she sing?*

Bridie shrugged to say she didn't know.

'Of course I can sing!' Rosie's head went back and her clear laughter filled the room. 'Sure can't everyone in the whole world sing?'

'I can't!' Steve said.

'Me neither,' Phil admitted.

George couldn't resist. 'My wife can't, either! Voice like a foghorn, she's got.'

Molly swiftly put a hand across Nellie's mouth. 'Don't take it to heart, sunshine, some of us like foghorns.'

Corker pulled Ellen from the couch and sat her on his knee. 'Right, Rosie O'Grady, let's be havin' yer.'

Without a trace of shyness, Rosie began. And as her clear, sweet voice filled the air, a silence descended.

> 'Come back Paddy Riley, to Ballyjamesduff,
> Come back Paddy Riley to me.
> The whole world's a garden of Eden they say,
> And I know the lie of it still . . .'

In the kitchen, a glass of shandy in his hand, Tommy pulled a face. 'I wish she'd go back to this Ballyjamesduff, wherever it is, an' give us a bit of peace.'

'Oh, go 'way, Tommy,' Ginger said. 'I think she's got a crackin' voice.'

'It's crackin' all right,' Tommy growled. 'Crackin' me flippin' head in two.'

As Bridie listened to the sweet voice singing a song she hadn't heard in years, memories came flooding back, bringing tears to her eyes. She felt her husband's hand cover hers and knew that, as always, he was conscious of her sadness. She turned to the man she'd loved for over forty years, and as she gazed at his dear face she knew that, if she had to choose between the land she loved or the man she loved, the man would be an easy winner.

When the song came to an end, there was complete silence. Everyone had been affected by the purity of the voice and the poignant words of a song most of them had never heard before. Then, as though they had collectively cleared their minds, they all started to clap.

Nellie, always a sucker for sentiment, sniffed. 'After that, I agree I do have a voice like a foghorn.'

'Well, Rosie O'Grady, ye're goin' to be a hard act to follow.' Corker gave her a broad wink. 'Yer voice is as bonny as yer face, me darlin'.'

'Mike can sing,' Sammy said. 'He'll give yer a song.'

'You can get lost!' Mike huffed. 'I can't sing!'

'Yes, yer can!' Sammy insisted. 'Don't be so miserable! If I had a voice like yours, I'd be glad to sing.'

'Come on, Mike,' Doreen coaxed. 'You start an' we'll all join in.'

'Oh, OK, but don't say I didn't warn yez.' Mike cleared his throat. 'What shall I sing?'

'D'yer know "Girl of My Dreams"?' Phil asked, pulling Doreen closer.

Mike nodded, his face flushed with embarrassment. 'Don't forget to help me out if I get stuck.' He cleared his throat again, then began.

> 'Girl of my dreams I love you, honest I do, you are so sweet,
> If I could just hold your charms, again in my arms
> Then life would be complete.'

Doreen and Mo stood with their eyes and mouths wide. They'd worked with this lad for two years, been out with him and Sammy dozens of times, and never knew he had such a fine voice! And to think all the girls at work called him 'shy Mike'! They'd get their eye wiped if they could hear him now.

'Shall we dance?' Phil whispered. 'We could try the hall.'

'Yeah, come on.' Doreen led him by the hand, saying to Mike, 'Sing it again, will yer Mike, so we can have a waltz?'

Mike got a very good reception when the song came to an end, and there were calls for an encore. He refused at first, but was talked into it. 'OK, just one more.'

'Hang on a minute Mike,' Molly said. 'Let's get some of these chairs into the kitchen and we can all have a dance.'

The men quickly cleared the room, then Corker said he had a request and whispered in Mike's ear. 'Sweet Rosie O'Grady, she's my little rose, And we will be married, that everyone knows.'

Molly went round pulling everyone to their feet. 'Come on, get in there and shake a leg.'

Everyone partnered off except Rosie, and she wasn't having any of that! So she marched into the kitchen where Tommy and Ginger were leaning against the draining board. 'Will yer dance with me, Tommy?'

'I can't dance.'

'Sure everyone can dance!' Rosie wasn't easily put off. 'All yer have to do is put one foot in front of the other.'

Tommy didn't even look up. 'I can't dance, an' I won't dance! So will yer leave me alone?'

Ginger and Tommy had been friends since the day they'd started school together, and they'd never had a falling-out. But right now Ginger felt like thumping his friend. 'I'll dance with yer, Rosie. Mind you, yer'll have to show me what to do.'

'That's kind of yer, Ginger, an' it's thankful I am to yer.' She took his hand like a child and together they edged their way into the room heaving with bodies. 'You put yer hand on me waist, Ginger, an' I put my hand on yer shoulder. Then we'll just watch what the others do an' follow suit.'

Corker had seen Rosie go into the kitchen and knew what her mission was. When he saw her emerge with Ginger, he couldn't help but chuckle. That Tommy was a stubborn bugger all right. Rosie would have her work cut out with him. But this song had been requested especially for her, and by golly, Corker was going to make sure she enjoyed it. He waited until Mike finished singing and the couples left the centre of the room, then he whispered in Ellen's ear before catching hold of Rosie. 'Let you an' me show them how it's done, my little Irish colleen.'

Singing at the top of his voice 'Sweet Rosie O'Grady', Corker swung her round and round, her laughter and obvious pleasure bringing a smile to all those who watched. Then they all joined in the singing until the rafters rang.

In the kitchen, Tommy stood alone, his empty glass in his hand. He was missing all the fun and it was his own fault. He knew he shouldn't have been so rude to Rosie, but she'd embarrassed him so much on the night they met, he was terrified of her. Not that he would admit it to anyone – they'd think he was a cissy. And now here he was, stuck in the kitchen while they were all enjoying themselves.

But Tommy was in the thoughts of both Bridie and Molly. Bridie loved her grandson dearly and was upset that he wasn't having a good time with the rest of them. Upset, too, that Rosie had caused the trouble. But there was no harm in the girl, she was still only a child in her ways. Tommy would get used to her eventually, but it was a shame he wasn't in here laughing and singing with everyone.

'Molly, me darlin'.' Bridie beckoned her daughter over. 'Will yer try an' get Tommy to come in?'

'I was just going to, Ma.' Molly clicked her tongue against the roof of her mouth. 'I feel sorry for him because he's a shy lad, an' I'd rather he was like that than be a ruffian. But sometimes he can be so stubborn he cuts his nose to spite his face! Anyway, I'll get him in here one way or the other.'

It was easier than she thought it would be. Acting as though there was nothing amiss, Molly sailed into the kitchen. 'Will yer do us a favour, sunshine? You see if any of the ladies want their glasses filling, an' I'll ask Ginger to see to the men. OK?'

'Yeah, OK, Mam.' Tommy put his glass on the draining board and followed her into the room, making for the woman who, after his mam, he loved most in the whole world. 'D'yer want another sherry, Nan?'

'Just half a glass, son, no more.' Bridie smiled up at him. 'Yer wouldn't like to see me drunk, would yer?'

Nellie had her ear cocked. 'Don't be givin' me no half glass, Tommy Bennett, or I'll clock yer one. Fill mine right up to the brim, d'yer hear?'

Nellie's appearance had deteriorated somewhat during the course of the evening. Even though she'd put up with the pain of sleeping in her dinky curlers all night, and worn them all day under her scarf, the curls she had arrived with were long gone, and her straggly hair was hanging limp around her face. And because she didn't believe in being uncomfortable if she didn't have to be, when her corns started giving her gyp she discarded her shoes and was in her stockinged feet.

Tommy grinned down at her as he took her empty glass. 'I heard yer, Auntie Nellie. In fact, I think the whole street heard yer.'

'Ay, don't get cocky with me, Tommy Bennett! You just remember, we've got your posh table in our 'ouse.'

Molly's head appeared over Tommy's shoulder. 'What's this about me posh table?'

'You haven't brought your kids up proper, yer know, girl! I've just been gettin' a load of old buck off your Tommy, an' I warned him that if there was any more of it, I'd accidentally on purpose stand me boiling kettle on yer posh table.'

Victoria Clegg and Bridie exchanged glances and grinned. It was a treat when Molly and Nellie started one of their slanging matches.

'You do that, Nellie McDonough, an' yer'll live to rue the day.' Molly managed to keep her face straight. 'You just mark my words.'

'Oh ay, an' whose army are yer callin' in to help yer, girl?' Nellie pushed her short sleeves higher up her arms before putting her hands on her hips in a fighting stance. 'Yer couldn't tackle me on yer own 'cos I'd only have to blow on yer an' yer'd end up on yer backside.' By now the room was quiet as everyone listened with grins on their faces.

'Oh, I'm not daft enough to come to fisticuffs with yer!' Molly bared her teeth. 'Oh, no, that's just not my style. All I'll do is tell everyone yer little secret an' yer'd never be able to show yer face in the street again.'

'Oh ay? An' what secret is that, pray?' Nellie pushed her face to within an inch of Molly's. 'I ain't got no secrets, yer see, so do yer damnedest, girl.'

'That's what you think! Now I'm not one to embarrass a friend in front of company, but yer are askin' for it, sunshine! What was it yer were buyin' at the market stall when yer got yer purse pinched?'

Nellie looked puzzled. 'Yer know what I was buying.'

'Yeah, an' yer didn't get them, did yer? Which means yer haven't got none!'

The penny dropped, and Nellie's tummy started to shake. She knew she'd be in trouble with George if she carried on, but what the hell, it was only in fun. 'Ay, girl, don't tell them that or they'll all be lookin' up me clothes when I bend down.'

It was Corker who asked, 'What was she buyin' at the market that she didn't get?'

Molly hesitated, looking first at her friend. 'Shall I?'

'Yeah, go on.'

'She was buyin' knickers, but ended up not getting them. So me mate, sittin' here in all her finery and givin' the pay-out, is absolutely knickerless!'

George's laugh was as loud as anyone's and Nellie breathed

a sigh of relief. Not that she was afraid of her husband, but he had no sense of humour did George, an' it was difficult to argue with someone who had no ruddy sense of humour.

It was two o'clock when they joined hands to form a circle around Molly and Jack to sing 'For They are Jolly Good Fellows'. And Tommy will never know how he came to be standing next to a very happy-looking Rosie, and holding her hand.

Chapter Fifteen

'Thanks, Mrs B., it's been a terrific night.' Maureen stood between Sammy and Mike, her arms linked through theirs. 'I've had the time of me life.'

'I don't think anyone could say they didn't enjoy it,' Mike said. 'It was the best party I've ever been to.'

'Yer can say that again.' Sammy's white teeth gleamed in the darkness. 'Thanks for havin' us, Mrs B.'

'Yer were more than welcome.' Molly smiled down at them. She was feeling dead tired but it was a pleasant tiredness. It really had been one hell of a party. 'We'll see yer again some time.'

Doreen and Phil were standing behind Molly, and Doreen leaned her chin on her mother's shoulder. 'You were a turn-up for the books, Mike! Wait till I tell the girls at work how good yer sing – they'll have yer serenading them in the dinner-break.'

Phil slipped past Molly to join the threesome on the pavement. He shook hands with each of them, saying, 'I'm relying on you three to keep an eye on Doreen for me, so don't let me down. We'll get together again next time I'm on leave, eh?'

'You take care of yerself, Phil, and come home soon.' Maureen swallowed the lump in her throat, knowing it was useless to wish for someone she could never have. Phil only had eyes for Doreen. 'We'd better be on our way: we've a long walk in front of us. It's a good job it's Sunday and we don't have to go to work.'

They'd only gone a few steps and Molly was giving a last wave when her parents came along the hall, followed by Rosie. 'We'll be on our way, lass,' Bob said, helping his wife down the step. 'I'm sorry we're leaving you with a right mess on yer hands, but there's not much we can do.'

'Don't worry about the mess, Da, it won't take long to clear up with all the gang to help.' She chuckled. 'Nellie McDonough ain't getting out of this door until me house is back to normal. She can have her first lesson in the hard part of being a hostess.'

Bridie kissed her cheek. 'Goodnight and God bless, me darlin', and thank you for a lovely party.'

'Yes, Auntie Molly, I'll be thankin' yer as well.' Rosie flung her arms around Molly's neck. 'Sure, wasn't it as good as any ceilidh we've ever had at home?'

'Thank you, sunshine, I'm glad you enjoyed it.' Molly kissed her cheek. 'I'll be around to see yer on Monday . . . if I've got over me hangover.'

'Well, now, I might not be in on Monday, Auntie Molly, 'cos Auntie Bridget is taking me down to the Labour Exchange to see about getting a job. It's time I was working, so it is.'

'Then you call here an' let me know how you get on.' Molly edged her way back to the step. 'I'll leave yer to say goodnight to Doreen an' Phil and get back to me guests before Jack thinks I've run off with the milkman.'

The men, including Tommy and Ginger, were standing in the middle of the room where Corker was giving them the benefit of his views on Hitler.

'My God,' Molly stood with her feet apart and her hands on her hips, 'will yez look at the state of this place an' you lot have got nothin' better to do than stand around talkin' about some little upstart with a stupid moustache, who walks around with his arm in the air and his feet doin' the goose-step! If yez don't move yerselves quick, I'll start a ruddy war of me own!'

'I told them, girl.' Nellie was perched on one of the straight chairs, positioned near Miss Clegg, Ellen and Maisie. 'I said to them, "Just wait until the 'ostess gets back, there'll be merry hell to pay." But would they listen? Would they hell's like . . . said they weren't frightened of you 'cos ye're all talk.'

Corker's laugh boomed. 'Nellie, yer'd start a fight in an empty house, you would!'

Nellie rested her chin on a hand, grimacing as she pretended to concentrate. After a while she said, 'Ye're wrong there, Corker, 'cos that would be an, er . . . an, er . . . oh what's the word I'm lookin' for, girl? You know, when something can't be done?'

'Yer mean an impossibility, do yer, Nellie?'

'That's the word!' When she grinned, Nellie's eyes sank into folds of flesh. 'Yer know, I should write all these big words down in case I ever need them again.'

Molly let her breath out slowly. 'Nellie, what is an impossibility?'

'What Corker said, of course!'

'Nellie, it's such a long time since Corker opened his mouth, we've all forgotten what he said.'

'He said I could start a fight in an empty house.' Nellie wagged a finger at the big man. 'That's what yer said, isn't it? Well that's an impossibility. 'Cos if I was in the house, it wouldn't be empty, would it?'

'Nellie,' Corker chuckled as he stroked his beard. 'I didn't think yer had the brains to figure that out.'

'Don't encourage her, Corker, for God's sake, or we'll be here until this time tomorrow. Let's start clearin' some of this mess up.' Molly's eyes lit on Tommy's friend. 'Ginger, you should be home in bed by now, yer mam will wonder what sort of a house I'm keeping. And Tommy, you may as well pop off to bed as well. If we can get rid of a few bodies, we might be able to see the floor.'

When Phil and Doreen came in, Victoria looked relieved. She'd had a lovely time, but she was feeling very tired now and her bed was calling. 'Will you take me across, Phil, I'm ready for bye-byes.'

'Mam, can I go across with them?' Doreen asked. 'I won't stay long.'

Molly could hear dishes being washed in the kitchen and knew that Jill and Steve were busy. She really should make Doreen stay and do her share but it would be a bit mean, seeing as it was Phil's last night. And she wasn't so old that she'd forgotten how it was when she and Jack were courting and seeking a bit of privacy. 'OK, but half an hour at the most.'

Nellie stood up when Miss Clegg had left with Phil and Doreen. Stretching her arms above her head, she yawned. 'I think I'll be on me way as well, girl, I'm dead beat.'

Without saying a word, Molly marched out to the kitchen and returned carrying a long-handled brush. 'Nellie, when all the glasses and dishes are washed, when all the beer bottles are standing in the crates in the yard, when all the chairs we borrowed from yer are stacked in the hall ready to take back in the morning, and when every crumb has been brushed from this floor – then, and only then, will any one of yer get through that door. So Ellen and Maisie, yer'd better hop to it.'

'Molly me darlin',' Corker grinned, 'ye're not half pretty when ye're in a paddy.'

'I don't want no flannel from you, Corker, just get crackin', 'cos right now I could sleep on a ruddy clothes line.'

'Come on George, Corker, and you Alec, let's get crackin',' Jack winked. 'I know my missus, an' she means business.'

Molly put her finger to her lips as she stood on the top step with Jack's arm around her waist. 'Don't make a noise for God's sake – it's turned three o'clock.'

'We'll be as quiet as church mice.' Corker's whisper echoed in the dark, deserted street. 'Thanks a million, it's been a great night. I don't know anyone who can throw a party like you and Jack.'

'Hear, hear!' Alec nodded his agreement. 'Marvellous night.'

'Ay, ay! Hang on a minute!' Nellie's face couldn't be seen but the sound of her voice told them she was wearing her indignant expression. 'D'yer know those sarnies yer had? Well I'm the one that scraped the margarine on them an' then scraped it off again, so how about a bit of praise for me, eh?'

'George, take her home, will yer? It'll be time to get up before we get to bed! Goodnight and God bless everyone.'

Molly and Jack stood with their arms around each other as their friends moved away. They heard Ellen saying 'Goodnight all', then Maisie asking, 'Are yer walking up with us, Corker?'

'No, I'll go in with Ellen, make sure the kids got to bed all right.'

Alec sat on the side of the bed and slipped one of his shoes off. He let it fall to the floor, chuckling as he did so. 'By, that was a party and a half, that was.' He let the other shoe fall, then turned to where Maisie was getting undressed. 'There's something about the Bennetts' house that gives yer a feeling of warmth and well-being. It always seems to be full of love and laughter. That party tonight wouldn't have been so much fun in anyone else's home.'

Maisie slipped her nightdress over her head. 'I know what yer mean. It's because they're a happy, contented family . . . Molly and Jack are good parents, they love their kids and the kids adore them. And each one of them has inherited Molly's sense of humour.'

'Ay, when her an' Nellie get together they're bloody hilarious, aren't they? I've never known anyone like them, they seem to bounce off each other.'

Maisie slid between the sheets and shivered. 'God, it's cold in here. Hurry up, Alec, an' let me put me cold feet on yer back.'

'I dunno,' Alec said. 'Is that all yer want me for, a ruddy hot-water bottle? I should have married someone like Nellie, she must be as good as having an extra eiderdown on yer in bed.'

'Corker, yer'd better go, look at the time.' Ellen pointed to the clock on the mantelpiece, then looked up into the big man's face. 'Yer'll only get a few hours' sleep.'

Corker reached for her and held her tight. 'Let's have a quiet few minutes together.' He picked her up and sat her next to him on the couch. 'I don't want to go away tomorrow, don't want to leave yer. I miss yer when I'm away, Ellen, and sometimes me body aches for yer.' He drew her closer, moaning softly. 'I wish we were married, love, an' I was going up those stairs with yer. I want yer, need yer, and I don't know how much longer I can hold out.'

Ellen put her hands on his chest and tried to push him away. She knew how he felt, because her longing was as great as his. It would have been easy to succumb, except for that little voice in her head reminding her that she was still married to Nobby Clarke. 'Corker, please!'

'Oh, don't worry, me darlin', I'm not going to do anything yer don't want me to. I respect yer too much for that. But I have to hold you, tell yer how I feel – I can't keep it bottled up inside me. I'm not made of stone, love, I'm a man with passion in me heart, a man with needs. But I can wait, sweetheart, I'll not do anythin' to hurt yer, because I love yer too much.'

'And I love you, Corker, very much.'

As he bent to claim her lips, Corker murmured, 'Next time me ship docks, we'll go and see that solicitor feller, see if he can't hurry the divorce through.'

* * *

Molly and Jack sat for a few moments with Jill and Steve, too tired even to climb the stairs. The room looked reasonably tidy: at least they wouldn't be coming down to a pigsty. And it would only take half an hour, when they got up, to get the chairs back to Nellie and bring their table down. Then the place would look like home.

'D'yer know, I'm that tired I could doss down on the floor here.' Molly was having trouble keeping her eyes open. 'I'm absolutely dead beat. Even me ruddy eyelashes are tired.'

'Here's yer mate.' Jack yawned. 'I feel as though I've done a twenty-four-hour shift.'

'It was worth it, though.' Steve grinned. 'It was a crackin' night.'

'Thank you, sunshine.' Molly gazed at him fondly. 'D'yer know, I'm glad ye're going to be me son-in-law.'

'Not half as glad as I am!' Steve laughed. 'I think I'm gettin' the best of the bargain.'

'Mam, why don't you and me dad go to bed?' Jill said. 'You've been on the go all day and you look worn out.'

'I'm waitin' for them to finish arguing.'

Jill frowned. 'Who's arguing?'

'Me feet,' Molly said. 'They're having a fight over which one is going to make the first step towards the stairs.'

'Come on, love.' Jack stood up and reached for her hand. 'I'll give yer a leg-up.'

'If our Doreen's not in by the time Steve's ready to go, give a knock on the window over there,' Molly said. 'I told her to be no longer than half an hour.'

'I'll do that, Mam, so go to bed and stop fussing.'

No sooner were her parents out of the room than Jill and Steve made for the couch. It wasn't often that they got any time alone together to do a bit of courting, so they made the most of the opportunity. His arm across her shoulders, Steve's face wore a look of bliss. 'I love you, Jill Bennett.'

'And I love you, Steve McDonough.' Jill gave a sigh of

contentment as her lips met his. 'I hope we're as happy as my mam and dad when we get married. But we will be, I know we will.'

'Yer can bet yer life on it.' Steve's tongue licked her ear. 'I'll treasure yer, take care of yer, and tell yer I love yer every day of me life.'

'When we get married and have our own house, we can have parties like the one tonight, can't we?'

Steve gave a throaty chuckle. 'Yer'll have to be sure to invite my mam and your mam. They're the only ingredients yer need to make a party go. Just put them in a room with our friends, give them a couple of glasses of sherry and you're away.'

'We're lucky with our families, aren't we, Steve?'

'We are that! And when we're married and have children, we'll have our own little family.'

Jill dropped her head to hide the blush. 'They'll be spoilt rotten by their two grandmothers.'

'If they take after their grandmothers, they won't go far wrong in the world.' Before their lips met again, he muttered, 'The next three years can't go quick enough for me.'

In a house on the opposite side of the street, Doreen and Phil were locked in an embrace.

'I've never known two weeks go so quick.' Phil ran his fingers through Doreen's long blonde hair. 'When yer want the time to go quick it always seems to drag, but when yer don't want it to, it flies over.'

'Yer might get another leave soon, perhaps for Christmas.' Doreen was misty-eyed. 'I'd love yer to be home for Christmas.'

'I'll have a word with our sergeant, see if I can wangle it.' A picture of the sergeant flashed through Phil's mind and he couldn't think of anyone less sympathetic than the man who barked orders at them when putting them through their paces. Tough as old rope he was, but then he'd have to be to make decent soldiers of them. He'd never been known to laugh, and Phil doubted if the antics of the aunties Molly and Nellie could even raise a titter from him.

'Will I come over 'ere tomorrow afternoon, or will you come to ours?' Doreen asked. 'I want to spend as much time with yer as I can.'

'You come over here, I don't want to leave Aunt Vicky on me last day.' Phil rubbed a thumb gently over the back of her hand. 'Will yer mam let yer come to the station to see me off? The train doesn't leave until about midnight.'

Doreen looked pleased with herself. 'I've already got that sorted out. Our Jill and Steve said they'd come so I don't have to come home on me own at that time of night, so me mam said it would be all right.'

'How old was your Jill when she got engaged to Steve?'

'Jill was seventeen, Steve was eighteen. Why?'

'If I asked yer to get engaged to me when ye're seventeen, what would yer say?'

Doreen leaned her head on his shoulder and gazed into eyes that were as blue as the sky on a summer's day. She sighed blissfully. 'Oh, yes, please.'

Molly turned to lie on her back. She thought she'd be out for the count as soon as her head hit the pillow, but no, it hadn't happened. Her maternal instincts wouldn't let her rest easy until all her offspring were safely tucked up in their beds. 'I'll strangle our Doreen when I get me hands on her.' She plucked at the sheet pulled up under her chin. 'An' I'm surprised at our Jill . . . I asked her to go over and knock for her.'

Jack rolled over. It was no good attempting to sleep with Molly tossing and turning and muttering aloud. 'Give them a break, love! I can remember when we used to sit in your house waiting for your parents to go to bed, so we could have a few minutes on our own. It didn't happen very often 'cos I don't think yer ma trusted me, and even when they did go to bed and leave us, she'd be banging on the bedroom floor with her shoe before I even had time to purse me lips for a kiss!' He put his arm across her tummy and tried to turn her towards him. 'Come on, love, give us a cuddle.'

'Yer know what you can do with yerself, Jack Bennett, yer can sod off!' Molly slapped his hand. 'Anyway, all the moanin' yer did about being so tired, how come yer've got the energy?'

The springs on the bed creaked as Jack laughed softly. 'I haven't, love! If yer'd have said yes, I'd have died of humiliation.'

The springs creaked louder as Molly's laughter joined his. And then they heard the front door open, Doreen's voice, then Steve's 'Goodnight'.

'Right, all me babies are in now so I can sleep easy.' Molly leaned across to kiss Jack, but he'd had the same idea and their heads collided, bringing a fresh outburst of laughter. 'Stay where yer are an' I won't miss yer this time.'

The kiss over, Molly said, 'I love yer, Jack Bennett, an' I suggest yer try yer luck tomorrow night.'

The house was silent, everyone asleep except for Tommy. He lay on his bed, wide awake. He'd handled it badly tonight. Like Ginger said, what he should have done was treat Rosie as if she was one of the lads. Yes, that's what he should have done. Next time she tormented him, he'd talk about football or train-spotting . . . she'd soon get fed up and leave him alone. The solution to his problem solved, Tommy turned on his side and was asleep in no time, a smile on his face. Rosie O'Grady wasn't going to get the better of him!

Chapter Sixteen

'Rosie, for heaven's sake will yer give yer mouth a rest?' Doreen looked up from her kneeling position where she was pinning a hem on the dress Rosie was trying on. The girl was standing on a dining chair, the seat of which had been covered with an old pillowslip for protection. 'I wouldn't mind if yer only talked with yer mouth, but yer flippin' hands are waving all over the place. If yer don't stand still, this hem's goin' to be all skew-whiff.'

Rosie threw her head back and her cheeks, as bright and shiny as two red apples, spread into a wide grin. 'Sure, isn't me mammy always saying it would be easier to stop the River Shannon from flowing than to stop my mouth going fifteen to the dozen?' Her clear laugh rang out. 'She said I was talking as I was being born an' have never stopped since.'

Doreen was smiling as she fell back on her heels. You couldn't be angry with Rosie for long because she wouldn't let you. You could insult her all ends up, but it made no impression. 'I can well believe it! There's times I feel like breathing for yer, 'cos yer don't even come up for air! But if yer want this dress to sit right, then please keep yer mouth shut and yer hands still for the next five minutes.'

'I'll do that right enough, Doreen, so I will. I'll be as good as gold.' From her great height, Rosie gazed down to where Molly was sitting on the couch patching a pair of Jack's working trousers. 'Now don't yer keep talkin' to me, Auntie Molly, because ye're gettin' me into trouble.'

Molly put her hand on the square of material to keep it in place before answering. 'Don't you be layin' the blame on me, Rosie O'Grady! In case yer hadn't noticed, I haven't opened me mouth for the last fifteen minutes.'

'Is that a fact, Auntie Molly?' Rosie shook her head from side to side. She was so childlike in many ways, unaffected and innocent, but some of her actions and sayings were those of an older person. 'Sure doesn't the time just fly over?'

'You'll be flyin' off that chair if yer don't behave yerself.' Doreen pulled some straight pins from a strip of paper. 'I don't care if yer go out looking a fool in a dress with a wavy hem, but I do mind when people know I'm the one who made the flippin' dress! My reputation is at stake here, so stand still and shut up.'

When Molly saw the impish grin on Rosie's bonny face she quickly lowered her eyes and went back to her patching. And as the needle wove in and out of the material, her thoughts strayed. It was hard to credit it was only four months since they'd first set eyes on the young Irish girl because she'd settled in so well, she was like one of the family. Molly knew there had been spells of homesickness at first, because Bridie had told her. Her mother, forever wise, never slept until she knew the young girl was asleep. And on the nights when the longing for her mammy and daddy brought on the tears, Bridie would slip into Rosie's bed and hold her in her arms until the sobbing ceased and sleep came.

Molly twisted the cotton around her finger several times, then broke it off with a sharp jerk. Reaching for the reel at her side, her mind travelled back over those four months. Such a lot had happened in that time: Rosie was working in a shoe shop on Walton Vale, Ruthie had had her eighth birthday and now went to school on her own, Phil had been home on a week's leave before being shipped off abroad, and Christmas had been and gone. They had food ration books now, and the days when she and Nellie used to wander round the shops choosing what they fancied for their families' meals were a thing of the past. The food allowance was very meagre . . . four ounces of bacon a week per head, four ounces of butter, twelve ounces of sugar, and the amount of meat they were allowed was pathetic. How they expected housewives to feed a grown-up family on the ration, God only knew.

But it wasn't just the food shortage that had put a damper on Molly's life, it was the signs of war all around them. The calling-up age for men for military service had gone up to twenty-seven, and men who were past that age were either joining the Home Guard or becoming air-raid wardens. And they didn't half throw their weight around, and all. One little chink of light showing through the blackout curtains and you'd have one of them banging on your door warning you to be more careful. And then there were the posters stuck up everywhere telling you Walls Have Ears, or Careless Talk Costs Lives, and others with instructions on how to get to your nearest air-raid shelter if the sirens started. Barrage balloons now dotted the skyline, and wherever you went you had to carry the gas masks that had been issued to everyone. They were a right nuisance to contend with, they were, especially if you had both hands full and the strap kept slipping off your shoulder.

'Mam!' Doreen was walking around the chair, her head on one side, her eyes narrowed. 'Does that hem look straight to you?'

Molly gave a cursory glance. 'It looks all right from where I'm sittin', sunshine!'

'Right, Tilly Mint!' Doreen slapped Rosie's bottom. 'Down yer get an' I'll start sewing it. It won't take me long, so yer can take it home with yer and get me nan to iron it.'

Molly lowered her head. Her train of thought had been interrupted and she wanted to get back to it before she lost the thread completely. Where was she up to? Oh yes, the signs of war. Well, if anyone was in any doubt about whether the powers that be were expecting the Germans to bomb the city, all they had to do was take a bus into Liverpool and get off at the Pier Head. Everywhere you looked there were sandbags piled up outside the entrances to the huge buildings facing the Mersey. She and Nellie had got the shock of their lives when they'd seen them. And it was the same in Dale Street, Castle Street, Church Street and all the other main thoroughfares of the city. They couldn't figure out what good sandbags would be if a bomb fell on one of the buildings, but they agreed someone must know what they were doing.

'Hey, Mam!' Doreen's nimble fingers were moving quickly along the hem of the dark blue dress. 'It's a quarter to nine: what time are me dad and Tommy working till?'

'Oh, my God!' Molly dropped her sewing. 'Here's me day-dreaming, forgettin' all about them, an' they'll be in any minute!' She pushed herself up hastily from the couch. 'I've left their dinners on the stove on top of pans of water and I bet yer any money the ruddy pans have boiled dry by now.'

'Ah, 'tis a terrible housewife yer are, Auntie Molly.' Rosie was settled in Jack's chair and had no intention of moving until she'd seen Tommy. All she'd get from him was a grunt, but she would be satisfied with that. She'd told Bridie and Molly that she intended marrying Tommy when they were older, but the two women had decided not to pass that bit of information on to Tommy, as he had no sense of humour where Rosie was concerned.

Molly threw her a smile as she made a dash for the kitchen. 'I suppose yer mammy has a saying for women like me, has she?'

'She has that, right enough, Auntie Molly. But I've been told to think very carefully before I speak, so I'm doing that.' Rosie was silent for a few seconds, then she said, 'I'll not be tellin' yer that one, Auntie Molly, 'cos I don't think Auntie Bridget would approve.'

Molly pulled the two pans away from the gas jets and with a

towel shielding her hands from the steam, she lifted one of the plates. 'Saved by the skin of me teeth. Another few minutes, and the pans would have had no backsides on them.'

'Here's me dad now, Mam!' Doreen called.

'OK, I hear yer! Be a good girl and get the knives and forks out for us while I bring their dinners through.'

Jack looked weary when he walked through the door, but he managed a smile for the girl sitting in his chair. 'Hello, Rosie, been gettin' tried on for the new dress, have yer?'

'I have that, Uncle Jack, and such a grand dress it is. I'll look a real lady when I walk out in that.' She smiled before letting her eyes stray to Tommy. 'Hello, Tommy.'

'Humph.'

'Ye're working too hard, an' that's the truth of it.' Rosie nodded knowingly. 'Sure, working until this time every night is too much, an' they shouldn't expect it of yer.'

Tommy threw her a dark look as he made his way to the kitchen to wash some of the grime off. 'There's a flippin' war on,' he growled in a voice now fully broken, 'or hadn't yer noticed?'

Jack, following closely on his heels, gave him a dig in the back. 'There's no need to be sarcastic, son.'

'Well, she gets on me wick.' Tommy turned on the tap and reached for the block of soap. 'Why doesn't she mind her own business an' leave me alone?'

'There's no call to be rude to her.' Jack nudged his son to one side and held out his hand for the soap. 'She's a nice girl, and I'm blowed if I can understand what yer've got against her.'

'I don't know what's nice about her.' Tommy's voice was muffled as he towelled his face. 'I just wish she'd go back to where she came from.'

Molly's mouth twitched as she carried the plates through. Little did Tommy know that the girl he was talking about had designs on becoming his wife. And she wouldn't be put off that easy, either! She was only fifteen and a half, but she was a very determined little lady. Look how she insisted on tagging the half-year on to the fifteen. Said she was nearer sixteen, and that was well old enough to go courting. The only way Tommy would escape her advances was by joining the Foreign Legion!

Rosie proved she wasn't easily upset when Tommy came back from the kitchen. 'That's better, Tommy! We can see yer handsome face now.'

'Mam!' Tommy's eyes were pleading. 'Will yer do somethin' with her? Can't yer shut her up?'

Doreen looked up from her sewing. 'Some hope you've got, our kid! I've been trying to shut her up for over an hour an' had no luck.'

'Hush, the lot of yer.' Molly pulled out a chair and sat down to study her husband's tired face. 'You look dead beat, love.'

'Then I look just how I feel.' Jack picked up his knife and fork and stared at the meal in front of him. 'I haven't even got the energy to eat this, an' I'm not hungry anyway.'

'You'll sit and eat every bit, Jack Bennett, even if I have to feed yer off a spoon like a baby! Yer need food inside yer to keep yer strength up.'

'I know that, love, but yer get past it. I've no appetite.'

'Just try,' Molly coaxed. 'Once yer start yer'll wake up yer taste buds.'

Jack glanced sideways to see Tommy tucking in with gusto. What it was to be young and able to work twelve-hour shifts without turning a hair. He felt more like flying than eating, but he knew Molly would sit there until the plate was clean, so he speared a carrot and began to eat.

'D'yer have to work late every night?' Molly asked. 'Surely yer could have a couple of early nights?'

'Molly, I'm not doin' it for pleasure! I don't want to be comin' home this time every night because life is all bed and work. But there's a war on and everyone's got to do their bit. Remember, there's lads of ours over in France, and they don't want to be there either!'

Molly sighed, thinking of Phil. 'I know that, love, but yer'll kill yerself if yer carry on like this. And our Tommy!'

'Tommy doesn't have to work overtime,' Jack said. 'At his age they can't make him. He does it to earn a few extra bob. Anyway, we've got somethin' to look forward to . . . we're off on Saturday and Sunday.'

Molly left her chair to round the table and wrap her arms around Jack's neck. 'Thank God for that!' She kissed him soundly. 'I'll have me husband to meself for two whole days.'

'Yer'll have no husband at all if yer don't leave go, ye're strangling me to death.'

Molly planted a kiss on the top of his head and was returning to her chair when she happened to glance at Rosie. The young girl was staring into space, a frown creasing her brow. 'What's up, sunshine? Yer look as though yer've got the cares of the world on yer shoulders.'

'I've been thinkin', Auntie Molly,' Rosie said, tapping a finger on her chin. 'That's what I've been doing.'

Tommy jerked his head to the ceiling. 'What's she been thinkin' with?'

Rosie glared, the smile she usually reserved for him notably absent. 'I'm not talking to you, Tommy Bennett, I'm talking to me auntie Molly. So I'll be thankin' yer to keep yer nose out of it.'

Jack nearly choked on a piece of potato, Doreen's mouth gaped, Molly chuckled and Tommy blushed to the roots of his hair.

'Anyway, as I was saying before I was so rudely interrupted,' Rosie went on, 'I've been thinking, because that's what God gave me brains for! But if He hadn't wanted me to tell anyone what I was thinking, then why did He give me a mouth?'

The room erupted with laughter. Even Tommy had to lower his head so they wouldn't see his mouth twitching. He had no intention of giving her the satisfaction of knowing he thought it was funny. Give her an inch and she'd take a yard, that one would. But he had to admit to himself that the way she said it, so serious, was dead funny.

'Rosie O'Grady, you're priceless,' Jack said, rubbing his eyes with the heel of his hand. 'When I came through that door I didn't think I had a laugh in me, but you've managed to raise one.'

Molly wiped the back of her hand across her nose. She was about to say that Rosie must come from a very warm, happy home, where there was always plenty of laughter. But she bit the words back just in time. To mention the family and home she'd left behind would only sadden the girl. But one day she'd ask her mother for Rosie's address in Ireland and she'd write and tell her parents what a delight their daughter was.

Rosie's face was wreathed in smiles. She liked nothing better than to see people happy. But she still wanted an answer to her question. 'It's true though, isn't it, Auntie Molly? God gave us everything for a purpose.'

'Of course He did, sunshine! Don't take any notice of this lot makin' fun of yer, 'cos they really don't mean no harm. Yer should hear them makin' fun of me when I talk to meself.'

Rosie leaned forward, her face eager. 'You talk to yerself, do yer, Auntie Molly?'

'All the time, sunshine! The best conversations I have are with meself. Especially on a Monday, wash day. I stand in the kitchen with me dolly peg and call everyone for everything . . . all except me mates, of course.'

'Here yer are – catch!' Doreen tossed the finished dress across the room. 'All finished, bar the ironing.'

'Ooh, thank yer, Doreen, I'm grateful to yer, so I am.' Rosie lifted the dress up for all to see. 'Isn't it posh? Sure if I was goin' to a ball wouldn't I be the belle of it?'

'You certainly would, sunshine.' Molly stood up. 'I don't want to throw you out, but it's time you went home. Me ma will be worried to death about yer being out in the blackout.'

Rosie carefully folded the dress while eyeing Tommy. 'Would yer like to walk me home, Tommy?'

Doreen saw her brother's face darken and jumped to her feet before he had time to throw any more insults at the girl she had grown fond of. 'Tommy must be tired after working all day, Rosie, so I'll walk yer home.'

'That's true, right enough.' Quite unconcerned about the daggers coming her way, Rosie smiled. 'Some other time then, Tommy, when ye're not so tired.'

Tommy waited until the front door closed before saying, 'She'll have to wait a bloody long time for that to happen!'

'Hey, watch yer language!' Molly warned. 'And d'yer know when God was givin' us these brains and mouths an' everythin'? Well you must have been behind the door when He was giving us a sense of humour, because you ain't got one.'

'Just because I don't think she's funny doesn't mean I haven't got a sense of humour!'

'I was only pulling yer leg, son.' Molly ruffled his hair. He was her only son, the apple of her eye, and for all he was as tall as his dad, he was still only a kid and didn't understand girls. 'She's taken a fancy to yer, that's all. Yer should be flattered, I suppose.'

'Well I'm not!'

Molly folded her arms and leaned her elbows on the table. 'Let's forget about Rosie an' tell us what ye're goin' to do with all this overtime money yer'll be picking up. D'yer want me to meet you and yer dad with a handcart?'

Now this was more to Tommy's liking. He'd been working overtime for a few weeks now, and had a little nest egg stored away upstairs. 'I'm puttin' me money away until I've got enough to buy meself a good pair of trousers, a proper man's jacket an' a pair of shoes.'

'That's sensible, son,' Jack said, smiling. 'At least yer'll see something for all yer hard work.'

Molly felt her heart bursting with pride. He was a handsome lad, tall and well built. A little rough around the edges, perhaps, a bit on the gawky side, but he'd grow out of that. After all, you couldn't put an old head on young shoulders. A year or two from now and he'd have plenty of girls running after him. There was no doubt in Molly's mind that Rosie would be leading the field. Right now she was a rank outsider, but didn't outsiders sometimes win a race . . . with good odds?

'Ooh, I enjoyed that laugh, girl, it did me a power of good.' Nellie wiped her eyes with the back of her hand. 'What did God give me a mouth for if it wasn't to speak . . . oh, I think that's the best I've heard yet. I was goin' to say I'd tell George, give him a laugh, but I've changed me mind.' Nellie was facing Molly across the dining table, and the creaking of the chair told her friend that laughter was once more on its way. 'Yer know what George is like, he'd probably look me in the eye, dead serious, an' say he didn't think God intended mouths to be used as much as mine is.'

Molly chuckled. 'Nellie, when it comes to talking, you're not in the meg specks. I never thought the day would come when I'd say it, an' I know it doesn't seem possible, but Rosie O'Grady can out-talk you any day.'

'Tell my feller that, girl! He won't take no notice of me, but he might believe it if you tell him.' Nellie stretched her hand towards the plate of biscuits in the middle of the table. 'These are all broken, girl, did yer drop them?'

'I know they're broken, yer daft article, that's how I bought them! And don't be so flamin' fussy! Anyone would think yer weren't used to buying broken biscuits.'

'Yeah, those were the days, weren't they? I was only thinkin' about it this mornin' after all the gang had gone to work. I sat meself down to enjoy a nice quiet cup of tea, but I didn't ruddy well enjoy it at all, just made meself miserable.' Nellie stretched again to the plate, but seeing there wasn't a piece big enough to be worth while taking on its own, she grabbed a handful. 'I was remembering the days when the kids were all little an' we only had the one wage coming in. Robbing Peter to pay Paul every week, weren't we, girl? Now when we should be sittin' pretty with enough money comin' in to be on easy street, they've gone and rationed the bloody lot on us! We've got the money, but there's nowt to spend it on!'

'I know, it's ironic, isn't it?'

Nellie's brow furrowed. 'What did yer say it was, girl?'

'Ironic! You know, er . . . what's another word for it now?' Molly searched her mind but couldn't find an appropriate word to explain ironic. 'Oh, I can't think . . . yer'll just have to guess.'

'Shall I help yer out, girl?' Nellie's face was the picture of innocence. 'Why don't yer say it's just our bloody luck?'

A knock on the front door took away the smile that was just about to form on Molly's face. 'I wonder who this can be?'

'I'm in no hurry, girl, me time's me own. So if yer want to sit an' have a guessing game, it's all right by me. Mind you, for most people the easiest way to find out who's knockin' on their door is to open the ruddy thing!'

Molly stuck her tongue out as she pushed herself up. 'Very funny, sunshine, very funny.' She made her way down the hall, saying, 'It's probably a rag-and-bone man.'

'Well if it is, don't let him in, for God's sake,' Nellie bawled. 'He might throw me on his cart.'

When Molly opened the door and saw a young policeman standing on the pavement outside, her heart lurched. Had one of the family had an accident at work? Was it something to do with Phil? Putting a shaking hand to her mouth, she croaked, 'What's wrong?'

'It's all right, missus, it's not you I'm after.' The officer pointed to the house next door. 'I'm looking for a Mrs Clarke, I believe she lives here?'

Molly breathed a sigh of relief that it wasn't bad news for her. But what was in store for Ellen? 'Mrs Clarke works in Tony Reynolds's butcher's shop on the main road. She won't be home until tonight, is it important?'

The officer pinched his bottom lip. 'Do you know Mrs Clarke well?'

'Yeah, we're good friends! Why, what's happened?'

'We were asked to contact her by Winwick Hospital. Apparently her husband is a patient there and they say it's urgent she gets there as soon as possible.'

'Oh, dear God, has something happened to Nobby? That's her husband.'

'I can't tell you any more, that's all the information I was given.' He went to move away. 'Thank you for your help, I'll go along to the shop to pass the message on.'

'Hang on a minute, Constable, please.' Molly's head was racing. 'Mrs Clarke's a very timid, nervous woman, and she's goin' to get a shock. I'll slip me coat on an' follow yer down, in case she needs someone with her.'

The officer smiled. Mrs Clarke was lucky to have such a good neighbour. 'I'll walk slowly and you can catch me up.'

Molly didn't bother closing the door. She raced down the hall, grabbing her coat from the hall-stand as she passed. 'Nellie, it was a policeman for Ellen. She's got to go to Winwick Hospital right away. It's somethin' to do with Nobby, an' it must be important for them to ring the police.' Molly buttoned her coat and reached into a bowl on the sideboard for her front door key. 'I'm goin' down to the shop . . . yer know what Ellen's like, she'll go to pieces.'

For all her eighteen stone, Nellie was out of the chair like a shot. 'I'm comin' with yer, girl.'

They caught up with the policeman just before he reached the shop. He raised his brows. 'D'you want to go in first?'

'I think it might be a good idea to warn her,' Molly said. 'If you go in an' ask for her, she'll die of fright.'

'Go on, then,' the constable nodded. 'But I can only wait a minute because I'm needed back at the station.'

Tony's face lit up when he saw the two women he called the terrible twins. 'If you two are after meat, I hope yer've got yer ration books with yer.' He suddenly realized the usual smiles and cheery greetings were missing. 'What's up?'

Ellen came through from the store room at that moment, carrying a tray of stewing meat. 'Hiya, Molly, Nellie!'

'Ellen, don't start panicking, but there's a policeman outside with a message for yer. He let us come in first because I told him what a worry-wart yer were. So put the tray down and stay calm.' Molly took a deep breath. 'He'll tell yer himself, but yer might take it better from me. It's somethin' to do with Nobby, and the hospital want yer to go there right away.'

Ellen stood like a statue, her face drained of colour. Tony took the tray from her, and as the policeman entered the shop Molly slipped behind the counter to put her arm around her neighbour's shoulder.

The officer took his helmet off. 'I can see your friend has told you, Mrs Clarke, but I have to make it official.'

Ellen didn't hear a word the man said; her head was in a whirl. Oh, where was Corker? Why wasn't he here to help her, tell her what to do? She could stand anything if the big man was by her side.

'Get yer coat on and go home, Ellen,' Tony said when the officer had left, his duty done. 'I'll be all right here, I can manage. You go with Molly and Nellie, they'll look after you.'

Ellen walked home between her two neighbours, her mind and body shaking with shock and fear. 'He must be ill,' she said softly. 'Either that or he's done somethin' bad an' they're going to move him.'

'Whatever it is, Nobby Clarke can't hurt yer no more, so just keep telling yerself that.' Molly held the thin arm tighter. 'We'll go back to my house, have a cup of tea to calm yer down, then think about what to do.'

But the tea didn't have the desired effect. Instead of calming down, Ellen became more agitated. 'I can't go 'cos it costs a few bob to get to Warrington an' I haven't got it.'

'We'll help yer out, Ellen,' Nellie said. 'Me an' Molly will lend yer the money.'

'I'm not goin'!' Ellen's body was jerking as though she was being operated by strings. 'Last time I was there, he went for me! He would have killed me if Corker hadn't come between us.' She looked pleadingly into Molly's eyes. 'I can't go, Molly, I just can't!'

Molly sighed as she rubbed her forehead. 'Yer'll have to go, Ellen, ye're still his wife an' yer have no choice! The hospital wouldn't have gone to the trouble of contactin' yer if it wasn't important, so whether yer like it or not, yer've got to go.'

'Then come with me, Molly, please? I couldn't go on me own, I'm absolutely terrified of him.'

Molly glanced at the clock. 'It's eleven o'clock. Would we be back before Ruthie gets home from school?'

'I don't know, Molly! I don't know what they want me for!' The tears were rolling unchecked down Ellen's face. 'All I know is I'm not goin' on me own. The place itself puts the fear of God into me, never mind havin' to face Nobby.' She doubled up, her thin arms clasped around her slim waist. 'Oh, if only Corker were here, he'd know what to do.'

'Well he ain't here, Ellen, so yer'd better buck yer ideas up.' Molly didn't like being sharp with her neighbour, but right now it was the only way. Left to herself, Ellen would go to pieces and do nothing. 'If Nellie will keep an eye out for Ruthie, in case we're not back in time, I'll come with yer.'

'Oh thanks, Molly! I don't know what I'd do without yer; a real friend yer are.'

'Right, take that bloody overall off and get in the kitchen and swill yer face. And stop yer cryin', for God's sake! I'm not sittin' on the bus with yer if ye're goin' to make a holy show of me.'

'Yer can do that yerself, without any help, can't yer, girl?' Nellie tried to lighten the situation. 'In fact I'd say yer were an expert at it.'

'Shut yer face, sunshine, or I'll shut it for yer.' Molly gave her a wink. 'It's about time someone put yer in yer place.'

'Lots of people have said that!' Nellie's chubby face creased. 'Nobody's ever done it though. And d'yer know why I think that is, girl? 'Cos they'd need a crane to do it, and yer don't see many of them round our way.'

There was an improvement in Ellen when she came back in from the kitchen. A rinse under the cold water tap had cleared her mind and she felt more in control of her emotions. But it was knowing Molly was coming with her that really bucked her up. 'What about money? I've only got about two shillings.'

'Let's empty our purses on the table and see how much we've got between us. If it's not enough, I'll ask Maisie to help out until pay day.' Molly pressed the clip on her well-worn purse. 'And you can dig deep in yer pockets, Nellie McDonough, 'cos I can tell by the way they sag that yer keep money in them.'

'You cheeky sod! What about the pocket in me knickers? D'yer want to have a feel to see if I'm hiding some loot in there?'

Molly wrinkled her nose. 'Touch your knickers? No thanks, I'll walk all the way to Warrington before I'll do that.'

Chapter Seventeen

Molly felt someone walk over her grave as she watched the man in the white coat lock the door behind them. The place was dreary enough to give you the willies without being locked in. Glancing down the corridors running either side of the massive door, she shivered again. It was certainly a bleak place, more like a prison than a hospital. She could understand now why Ellen was reluctant to come on her own. Molly wasn't easily scared, but right now she was feeling very apprehensive. She felt sorry for the people in there because, God knows, they couldn't help the way they were. As her mother would say, 'There but for the grace of God go I,' and it was true.

'I'll take you to the doctor, Mrs Clarke, he wants to have a word with you.' The man clipped the key on to the bunch hanging from a belt around his waist. 'Follow me, please.'

Molly linked her arm through Ellen's as they turned left and set off down the corridor. Her neighbour was as white as a sheet, her eyes staring straight ahead and her lips quivering. 'Don't worry, kid, it'll soon be over an' we'll be on our way home.' She lowered her voice. 'Is he a doctor?'

'I don't know!' Ellen had more worrying things on her mind than the man walking in front of them. Something really bad must have happened for them to send for her. Had Nobby attacked and hurt someone? She'd had plenty of experience over the years to know how violent her husband could be. Hadn't she been a punch-bag for him since the day they got married? And the way he'd gone for her the last time she was here had taught her that, even confined to a wheelchair, Nobby Clarke was a dangerous man. She turned to Molly and there was a catch in her voice as she begged, 'Yer won't leave me, will yer, Molly?'

'Of course I won't leave yer.'

They passed several closed doors before the man stopped outside one and motioned for them to wait. Then he knocked, opened the door, and they could hear the deference in his voice when he announced, 'Mrs Clarke is here to see you, sir.'

Ellen was rooted to the spot and Molly had to propel her forward and through the door. The man sitting behind the desk rose to his feet and extended a hand. 'I'm Dr Jefferson, Mrs Clarke.'

If Molly hadn't been there to push on her elbow, Ellen would never have shaken the man's hand. She was literally numb with fear.

'Sit down, please, Mrs Clarke.' He looked towards Molly. 'And Mrs . . . ?'

'I'm a neighbour of Ellen's – me name's Molly Bennett, Doctor.'

Wearing a dark grey suit with a white shirt and sombre grey tie, the doctor had the bearing of someone in authority. He was probably in his sixties, slim, with thinning white hair and blue eyes. 'How long is it since you saw your husband, Mrs Clarke?'

Looking down at her clasped hands, Ellen's voice was barely audible. 'It's a long time, probably four months.'

Molly groaned inwardly. He'd make mincemeat of Ellen because she wouldn't stick up for herself, wouldn't explain her side of it. I mean, on the face of it, it did sound bad that she hadn't been to visit her husband in months. But for anyone who knew the circumstances and the life Ellen had had to put up with, well that was a different kettle of fish altogether. 'Mrs

Clarke has a full time job, Doctor. She's got her work cut out with four children to keep, and she has to work.'

'I understand, Mrs Bennett. My question wasn't meant as a criticism.' His face softened when he smiled. 'I can appreciate that Mrs Clarke hasn't had an easy life. The only reason I asked was because over the last few months there has been a great deterioration in her husband's condition. He is now a very sick man and therefore we felt it was our duty to inform the next of kin.'

'Sick?' Ellen's eyes were wide in her thin face. 'I know Nobby's sick in his head, that's why he's here, but I don't think yer mean that, do yer?'

'No.' The doctor shook his head. 'Your husband's mental state has nothing to do with his illness. But what that illness is I can't tell you because it has my colleagues and myself baffled. We can find nothing wrong with Mr Clarke, no medical reason for his deterioration.'

'That's funny, isn't it, Doctor?' Molly said. 'There must be somethin' wrong with him.'

'Nothing that we can find, Mrs Bennett, and we've had specialists in to see him who are as baffled as ourselves. Mr Clarke simply refused to get out of bed one day and also refused food. Because he often had dark moods, the staff at that time weren't unduly worried. But when it carried on, day after day, he was taken along to the medical wing for tests. When the tests showed there was nothing wrong with him, I ordered him to be fed by the staff. This proved impossible because he simply pushed the food, and the staff, away. We then tried to drip-feed him, but as soon as he was connected to the drip, he pulled it out.' Dr Jefferson met Ellen's eyes. 'I don't need to tell you how strong your husband was when in one of his violent moods; he had the strength of ten men. Sedating him so he could be force-fed was out of the question because he wouldn't allow anyone near him.'

'Stubborn bugger!' Molly thought her voice was so low it

wouldn't travel to the other side of the wide desk, but when she saw a smile flicker across the man's face she knew he'd heard. 'Excuse me language, Doctor, but it just slipped out.'

'That's all right, Mrs Bennett, it's an expression that often slips out of my own mouth.' He looked almost boyish when he smiled. 'There's a lot of them around, aren't there?'

Molly smiled back. What a nice man he was! 'There certainly are,' she said, 'and accordin' to my husband, I'm the biggest one of them all.'

Ellen was impatient; couldn't understand how these two could smile when she was worried stiff. 'So how is he now, Doctor?'

'We are managing to get him to take liquids, but he steadfastly refuses solids and is getting weaker by the day.' Dr Jefferson was silent for a while, his eyes fixed on an ink blot on the desk. Then he gave a long sigh and looked up. 'This is only my opinion, Mrs Clarke, and I can't prove it, but I think your husband has just given up. He is tired of living and has made up his mind to opt out.'

Ellen gasped. 'Nobby wouldn't do that!'

The doctor shrugged his shoulders. 'I said it was only my opinion.'

'Oh, dear,' Ellen wailed, 'I feel bad now, not comin' to see him for such a long time.' She turned tearful eyes on Molly. 'I should 'ave come, Molly, he is still me husband.'

Molly knew words of sympathy were expected but she couldn't utter them. She couldn't be so hypocritical. 'He was yer husband when he was actin' the big man every night, standin' in the pub with his cronies. Spending money like water, knocking pints of ale back until he was pie-eyed, while his wife and kids huddled together to keep warm, their bellies empty. He was yer husband when he backed the gee-gees every day and came home to beat his wife up when his horse didn't win an' he was skint. And on the days when yer were too ashamed to leave the house because yer face was black and blue, wasn't it your husband who had done that?'

Molly closed her eyes and sighed. Perhaps it wasn't up to her to say those things, even if they were true. But someone had to remind Ellen of the reality of being married to Nobby Clarke, or she'd spend the rest of her life feeling guilty. 'He was a lousy husband and a lousy father, Ellen, and yer'd be lying if yer said otherwise.'

Ellen met Molly's eyes briefly before letting her head drop. 'Me friend's right, Doctor, he made my life hell. And the children, they were terrified of him.'

'Mrs Clarke, you have nothing to reproach yourself for,' the doctor told her kindly. 'Every staff member, myself included, found your husband to be a bullying, violent man. It was impossible to get through to him, even to hold a conversation. He rejected all offers of kindness or help. In fact, any overtures made by the staff would send him into a rage. So you see, we do have some idea of the life you had with him.'

'I did try to be a good wife, Doctor.' Ellen was once more near to tears. 'God knows I did my best, but nothing I did was right.'

'You did more than I would 'ave done,' Molly was moved to say. 'I wouldn't have put up with Nobby Clarke for fifteen minutes, let alone fifteen years.'

'Well all that is in the past now, and you must make a new life for yourself and your children.' Dr Jefferson leaned his elbows on the desk. 'Do you want to see your husband?'

Ellen turned to Molly. 'What shall I do, Molly?'

'You'll have to see him, otherwise yer'd never live with yerself,' Molly said. 'I'll come with yer.'

'I'll get the nurse to take you.' The doctor pushed his chair back and stood up. 'You will see a great difference in your husband, so be prepared.' He smiled as he held his hand out. 'I will no doubt see you again in the near future but, in the meantime, if you want any help or information, please don't hesitate to contact me.'

Outside, the male nurse was leaning against the wall facing the door, but he jumped to attention when Dr Jefferson appeared. 'Kindly take Mrs Clarke to see her husband, and stay with her until she's ready to leave.' He patted Ellen's arm as she passed and then smiled at Molly. 'You can stay with her.' There was a message in his eyes that was as clear as if he had spoken the words aloud. Ellen was going to need someone to lean on.

Once again they were following the nurse down the corridor, Molly's hand gripping Ellen's elbow. 'It won't be long now, sunshine.'

But even Molly was shocked into silence when they approached the iron bed with rails on both sides. There's been some mistake, she thought, that's never Nobby Clarke! The man lying in the bed was just a bag of bones with eyes sunken deep in his head. His skin had a grey tinge to it, and what little hair he had was pure white.

Molly glanced at the nurse standing on the opposite side of the bed, and he seemed to be reading her mind because he nodded before saying, 'Your husband probably won't recognize you, Mrs Clarke.'

Ellen gasped in horror before putting a hand over her mouth. She had prepared herself for a shock, but nothing could have prepared her for this. And when the wizened face on the pillow turned colourless, vacant eyes on her, she couldn't keep the tears back, and turned to find Molly's open arms ready to embrace her.

'He didn't deserve this, Molly,' Ellen cried, a picture of the old Nobby in her mind as she remembered him . . . tall, well built and with a mop of dark hair. 'No matter how bad he was, he didn't deserve this.'

Molly patted her back as she would have a baby's. 'No, he didn't,' she said soothingly. 'But I think the doctor is right, this is what Nobby wants. And if it is, who are we to judge? Since the day he walked in front of that tramcar he hasn't really been living, just existing.'

The nurse moved quickly towards the bed, his action causing the two women to jump apart. 'What is it?' Molly asked, fearing the worst.

'Mr Clarke seems to be trying to say something.' The man was looking at the figure in the bed with surprise on his face. 'He hasn't spoken for weeks, but look – what's he trying to say?'

Ellen hung back, afraid that even at death's door Nobby would still have the power to hurt her. 'You go an' see, Molly.'

'No, sunshine, you go.' Molly moved behind her and pushed her towards the bed. Then she whispered in her ear, 'Look at him, Ellen, for God's sake. If yer don't, yer'll regret it for the rest of yer life.'

Ellen had to force herself to look down at the skeletal face, knowing it would haunt her for ever. 'Hello, Nobby.'

The colourless lips moved several times, then as soft as a leaf touching the ground, they heard the name 'Corker'.

As though the effort had been too much, Nobby closed his eyes. Ellen, gripping the safety rail, turned wide eyes on Molly.

'Did yer hear that? He said "Corker"!'

'I know, I heard him.' Molly bent to look between the bars of the rail. 'Quick, he's trying to say somethin' else.'

Ellen's heart filled with compassion when she glanced down at the man who had been her husband for fifteen years. They'd been bad years, but they were in the past now and best forgotten. And looking at him now she was filled with pity. 'Yes, Nobby?'

'Corker.' Nobby ran his tongue over lips dry and cracked. 'Good . . . for . . . you . . . and . . . the . . . children.' Then the effort proved too much and his eyes closed as his head fell sideways.

'Oh, my God!' Molly gasped, looking across at the nurse. 'Has he gone?'

The nurse shook his head. 'He's like this all the time, drifting in and out of sleep. Those are the first words he's uttered in God knows how long, and they must have drained him of what little strength he had.' He made a movement with his head. 'I think you should leave now, he won't waken again for some time.'

But Ellen didn't move. She knew her husband was close to death and this would be the last time she would see him alive. She felt no love for him – he'd killed that many years ago. But she did feel pity and forgiveness, and she wanted him to know that all the anger and hatred she had harboured was now gone. So, standing on tiptoe, she reached across the bar and touched his face. Stroking it gently, she said, 'I'm goin' now, Nobby. I'll tell the kids you were askin' about them and send them your love. Ta-ra, and God bless.'

Molly couldn't stop the tears and they rolled down her face unchecked. She never thought the day would come when she'd feel sorry for Nobby Clarke, but you would have to be made of stone not to feel pity for him now. She brushed at the tears with the back of her hand, watching the moving scene through a blur. Ellen, always quiet and timid, wouldn't say boo to a goose, was now showing a strength of character that filled Molly with admiration. She wondered whether, if she'd been in her neighbour's shoes, she would have been able to handle the delicate situation with the same dignity and compassion.

'Come on, Molly, it's time to go.' Ellen linked her arm through Molly's and they followed the nurse out of the small ward. No tears flowed from her eyes now: she felt a peace and contentment she hadn't felt for a very long time. On his deathbed, Nobby had set her free. And no matter what the future held in store for her, she would always remember and be grateful to him for that.

They were sitting on the bus on the way home when Molly asked, 'Are yer goin' to tell the kids?'

'I don't know.' Ellen was staring out of the window, but she wasn't seeing the houses or trees that flashed by – she had other things on her mind. 'I've been trying to think what's best for them. They never talk about their dad, he's just a bad memory to them and I don't want to rake the whole thing up again an' upset them.'

'Nobby won't last long by the looks of things, an' yer'll have to tell them when he dies.'

'Will I?' Ellen seemed to have grown in confidence over the last few hours, and was more in control of herself. 'I could leave it for a few years until they were older and more able to understand. Seeing Nobby today took away all the bad feelings I had about him. What he said, you know, about Corker an' me, well it shows he had some good in him in the end. But that would be hard to explain to young kids who never got a kind word from him.' She sighed a deep sigh. 'I'm all mixed up, I don't know what to do for the best.'

'Sleep on it, sunshine,' Molly advised. 'Give it plenty of thought an' then do what yer think is best. Or yer could leave it until Corker comes home an' see what he thinks. He should be due in soon, shouldn't he?'

'Next week, I think. But tellin' the kids is not the only thing I've got to worry about, Molly. What am I goin' to do when Nobby dies? I haven't got any insurance policies an' I haven't got any money to bury him.'

'I don't know anythin' about things like that, Ellen, so I can't help yer. Yer should have asked the doctor while we were there.'

'He would have thought I was a right one to ask a question like that when me husband isn't even dead! Anyway, I didn't even think of it when we were in his office 'cos I wasn't expectin' Nobby to be as bad as he is.'

Molly patted her hand. 'Don't you be lyin' awake all night worrying because it won't get yer anywhere. There's not a thing yer can do, so put it out of yer head until Corker comes home.'

'Funny him sayin' that about Corker, wasn't it? I mean, how did he know?'

'I can only guess that he put two an' two together,' Molly told her. 'He knew yer courted the big man when yer were younger, and Corker went with yer a few times to visit him in hospital, so I suppose it wasn't hard for him to figure out. Anyway, what he said has certainly made a difference in you, it's stickin' out a mile! So like yer said, he turned out good in the end. And that's when it mattered.'

'I won't say anythin' to the kids, not yet, anyway.' Ellen had made up her mind to do what she thought was best. 'I'll just take things one day at a time and see how it goes.' She covered the hands Molly had clasped on her knee. 'You won't say anythin', will yer, Molly?'

'We'll have to tell Nellie 'cos she's bound to ask, an' I'll tell Jack. But apart from them I won't tell a soul. I'll keep it to meself until yer tell me otherwise.'

Nellie was standing on her doorstep leaning against the jamb with her arms folded across her tummy, watching Ruthie playing skipping with Bella. 'She's been as good as gold, girl, no trouble at all. I gave her a cup of tea an' a jam buttie and said she could play out till you came home.'

'Thanks, Nellie, ye're a pal.'

Nellie screwed up her eyes, waiting for them to tell her what the hospital had wanted Ellen for, but when nothing was forthcoming, she got impatient. 'Well, how did yez get on?'

After a nod from Ellen, Molly quickly gave her neighbour all the news while keeping an eye on Ruthie in case she dashed across the street and heard what was being said. It was a very brief account, she didn't repeat every word, but even the bare details were enough to have Nellie shaking her head and sending her chins wobbling all ways. 'The poor bugger! Who'd have thought Nobby Clarke would end up like that?'

'Ay, well, none of us know how we're goin' to end up, sunshine. If we did, we'd probably stick our head in the gas oven.' Molly turned to Ellen, her head cocked and concern in her eyes. 'Are yer feeling all right?'

'I'm fine thanks, Molly. I was hopin' to get back to the shop in time to give Tony a hand cleaning up, but it's too late now, he's probably finished.'

'It won't do him no harm for once, he managed on his own before he took you on.' Molly gave Ellen a gentle push. 'Go in an' see to the kids' dinner.'

'OK, an' thanks, Molly, for everything.' It was only a few yards to Ellen's front door and she was inserting the key in the lock when she looked back. 'Yer won't forget what I asked yer, will yer?'

'For cryin' out loud, Ellen, me memory's still in good workin' order, even if the rest of me isn't. Of course I won't forget.'

Ellen gave a weak smile. 'Ta-ra Molly, ta-ra, Nellie.'

'Funny,' Nellie said, leaning back against the door jamb and looking ready for a good chin-wag, 'she doesn't seem that upset. I would 'ave expected her to be a nervous wreck.'

'She surprised me today, I can tell yer. She was in a terrible state at first, but once Nobby had spoken, she changed completely. I couldn't have handled the situation as well as she did, she was a real hero.'

'How d'yer mean, girl?'

'I can't tell yer now, sunshine, I'll have to get in an' see to the dinner. But when yer come down in the mornin' for yer cup of tea, I'll fill yer in on everythin' that happened.' Molly rubbed her hands together to get her circulation back. There was a bitterly cold wind blowing and she was chilled to the marrow. 'In the meantime, not a word to anyone, d'yer hear? Ellen doesn't want the children to find out, not yet, anyway.'

'Not even my feller?'

'Not even your feller, Nellie – promise?'

Nellie tutted. 'My feller doesn't even talk to me, I've got to prise every word out of him, so he's not likely to repeat anything.'

'Nellie McDonough, if yer don't promise to keep yer trap shut I'll never tell yer another thing in confidence.'

'Ooh, yer don't half drive a hard bargain, girl. Ye're as tough as that stewing steak I got last week which I would have taken back if we hadn't eaten it.' When Molly didn't smile, Nellie knew her neighbour had more weighty things on her mind. What they were she would find out tomorrow. 'But yer are me mate, so I'll do as yer say an' keep me trap shut.'

'I'd better get in and see to the fire an' then sort out what we're havin' for dinner. It'll have to be somethin' easy because I haven't got time to make a proper meal.'

'They're havin' beans an' chips, girl, whether they like it or not. I've peeled an' chipped yer spuds, opened two tins of beans an' got yer chip pan ready on the stove.' Nellie bent forward to stare into Molly's face. 'An' yer don't have to worry about yer fire, I banked it up with slack when yer went out and I've been in twice since. It's roaring up the chimney as we speak.'

'Oh, you lovely, lovely, woman!' Molly almost pulled her friend off the step when she reached up to clasp her chubby face and plant a noisy kiss on it. 'A pal in a million you are, Nellie McDonough!'

'I keep tellin' yer that, but yer won't believe me! I go through life helping other people, never thinkin' about meself, but do I get any credit for it? Do I hell!'

'Yer'll get paid back when yer get to heaven, sunshine. That's where yer'll get yer just deserts.' The thought of a warm fire was drawing Molly towards her own home and hearth. 'I'll see yer in the mornin', sunshine.' She reached her front door and called across to Ruthie, 'Come in now, sweetheart, it's too dark and cold to play out. Give Bella her rope back and say goodnight.'

'Hey, girl!'

Molly turned to see Nellie standing on the pavement. 'What is it now, for heaven's sake?'

'I've been thinkin' about what yer said, girl, an' it's got me worried. If I get me just deserts when I die, I won't be goin' up there, I'll be goin' down below.'

'Listen to me, Nellie McDonough, yer won't get away from me that easy. I have every intention of goin' to heaven an' I'm takin' you with me.'

'Oh, that's a load off me mind, girl! I wouldn't 'ave slept a wink tonight, thinkin' about it.'

Molly stepped into the hall, waited for Ruthie to pass, then closed the door. She hadn't been able to see her friend's face because it was too dark, but in her mind she could see the plump face creased in a smile of mischief. And when she opened the living-room door and felt the warmth hit her, she mentally kissed that face again.

Molly drew the blackout curtains before putting the light on. 'Hang yer coat up, sunshine, and put yer slippers on.' She bent to kiss a rosy cheek. 'Get one of yer books out and sit by the fire while I put the kettle on.'

'What are we havin' for tea, Mam?' Ruthie was on her knees in front of the sideboard searching for a colouring-book. 'I'm starvin'.'

'Chips an' beans,' Molly called back. 'Your favourite.' She had the kettle in her hand but made no move to turn on the tap. For Ellen's sake she'd put on an act today, forcing herself to be calm and matter-of-fact, as though she hadn't been affected by what she'd seen. But in the quietness of her tiny kitchen she allowed her true feelings to surface. The picture in her head of Nobby Clarke as he lay in that bed would stay with her for ever. She just couldn't block it from her mind. There was no flesh on him, he was just like a sack of bones. More like a skeleton lying in the bed than a man. If she hadn't seen his lips move, heard with her own ears what he had said, she would have sworn he was dead. He would be better off dead, and she said a silent prayer for God to take him.

Molly put the kettle down on the draining board and turned on the tap. Bending over the sink, she put her hand under the running water and splashed it over her face. The shock of the freezing cold water had her gripping the edge of the sink and gasping for breath.

'Mam, have yer seen me red crayon?' Ruthie came into the kitchen with her book open at the page she was colouring. 'I've looked in the drawers an' I can't find it.'

'Look under the sideboard, I haven't brushed under there today 'cos I had to go out.'

'Where have yer been?' Inquisitive eyes peered from beneath the thick blonde fringe. 'I asked Auntie Nellie but she said she didn't know where yer'd gone.'

Good for Nellie, Molly thought. 'I had to go on a message with Mrs Clarke. It wasn't anythin' important and would be of no interest to a little girl like you.'

Ruthie held the book up for her mother to see. 'Haven't I done that good, Mam? See how I've painted the tree brown an' green, and the flowers in the garden yellow? When I find me red crayon I'm goin' to paint the cottage door red.'

'Well if yer make a good job of it I'll let yer paint our front door, it could do with it.'

Ruthie giggled. 'Yer can't paint a front door with crayon.'

'I don't know, yer've made a good job of yer bedroom walls. They're covered in crayon marks, all colours of the rainbow.'

Ruthie decided it was time to leave. 'I'll go an' look under the sideboard.'

Molly grinned as she struck a match and lit the gas under the chip pan. Crafty little article that one, knew when to make a hasty retreat. There wasn't time for a cup of tea now, Jill would be in any minute. And when it was chip night, she cooked their dinners as they came in. Her chip pan wasn't big enough to do sufficient for the whole family in one go. Tommy could eat a whole panful all to himself. Thank goodness potatoes weren't on ration – they'd starve if they were.

'Put the tablecloth on for us, sunshine.' Molly walked into the living room to see Ruthie standing on the fender reaching up to the mantelpiece, her gymslip just inches from the flickering flames. 'Get down off there, you little faggot! D'yer want to burn yerself to death?' Fear of what could have happened made Molly angry. 'Ye're eight years of age, yer should 'ave more sense. I've a good mind to give yer a good hiding to teach you a lesson.'

'What's she done?'

Molly spun around to see Jill standing in the doorway. 'Ooh, yer gave me such a fright, I nearly jumped out of me skin. I didn't hear yer comin' in, sunshine, I was too busy shouting at this stupid article. Standin' on the fender she was, her gymslip touching the fire. She could 'ave been burned.'

'That was a silly thing to do, wasn't it, Ruthie? Frightening our mam like that?' Jill slipped her coat off and pulled the scarf from around her neck. 'Why don't you say you're sorry?'

'I'm sorry, Mam.'

When two tear-filled eyes met hers, Molly's anger evaporated. She scooped up her youngest child in her arms and held her close. 'Yer gave me such a fright, sunshine, I had visions of yer goin' up in flames.' She rocked her back and forth, her hand stroking the blonde hair. 'I'm sorry I shouted at yer, but yer've got to promise me yer won't do it again. Just think what might have happened if I hadn't come in when I did, and yer gymslip had caught fire! Doesn't bear thinkin' about.'

'I won't do it no more, Mam, I promise.'

'OK, we'll forget about it now.' Molly gave her a kiss before setting her down. 'Now be a good girl and set the table for us while I see to Jill's dinner.'

'What about my dinner?' Ruthie was penitent but her rumbling tummy reminded her she was also very hungry. 'I'm starvin'!'

'I'll do your chips with Jill's, so don't start gettin' yer knickers in a twist.' Molly winked at Jill as she made her way to the kitchen. 'I won't be long, sunshine, you get yerself a warm by the fire while ye're waitin'.'

They were in the middle of their dinner when Doreen came in, bringing a cold draught with her. Her cheeks, whipped by the blustery wind, were a rosy red and her blue eyes were alive with excitement. 'I met the postman this mornin', Mam, and he had three letters for me from Phil.'

'Oh, that's good, sunshine!' Molly was pleased for her daughter, who had only received a brief note from Phil before he was shipped out. Every day for the past weeks she had waited in eager anticipation, and each day she'd been disappointed. 'Does he say where he is?'

Doreen shook her head. 'They're not allowed to. But he told me it would be either France, Holland or Belgium, and he'd start his letter with the first letter of the country he was in. So I know he's in France.'

'Go 'way! Ay, you two would make good spies, you would.'

Doreen came back from hanging her coat up looking very pleased with herself. 'It was Phil who thought it up, not me.'

'If ye're not supposed to know where he is, how can yer write back to him?'

'The address he's put on his letters isn't in France, it's just BEF and some numbers. One of the girls at work says BEF stands for British Expeditionary Forces, and all the letters go to some army headquarters where they're sorted out by the numbers and sent on.'

'I don't know,' Molly sighed as she got up to go and see to Doreen's dinner, 'what's the world coming to? All this because of one little jumped-up crackpot dictator who should have been drowned at birth.'

'How is Phil?' Jill asked.

'He's fine, but he'd rather be back home.' Doreen wasn't going to tell anyone about the words of love in the letters, that was private and not to be shared.

It was while she was having her dinner that Doreen delivered her second piece of news. 'Mam, I'm goin' after another job.'

Molly had been leaning on the table, her face cupped in her hands, but she straightened up at the news, a look of surprise on her face. 'What d'yer mean, you're goin' after another job? I thought yer liked workin' at Johnson's.'

'I do, but the money's lousy! A couple of the girls have left and they're on much better money where they're workin' now. One of them is in a factory where they make barrage balloons and she earns over a pound a week more than she did at Johnson's.'

'That's funny,' Jill said, 'I've been seriously thinking of looking for another job myself!'

Molly's jaw dropped. This was all getting too much. 'What's wrong with the pair of yer? Yer might swap jobs an' then be sorry afterwards! Better the devil yer know than the devil yer don't.'

'Mam, for an extra pound a week I wouldn't care whether I liked the job or not!' Doreen speared a chip and bit half before going on to say, 'Me and Maureen are goin' down to the Labour Exchange tomorrow in our dinner hour, yer have to have a card from them to go for an interview.'

'Got it all figured out, haven't yer?' Molly shook her head and turned to Jill. 'And what have you got in mind, sunshine? You've got a good job where yer are, and the money's good.'

'I know, but I'm not doing much for the war effort, am I? I thought I'd apply to the ROF in Kirkby, I've heard they're taking office staff on.'

'I dunno,' Molly mumbled, 'what with the BEF and now the ruddy ROF, I'm all mixed up. What's the ROF when it's out?'

Jill giggled. 'It stands for Royal Ordnance Factory. It's where they make ammunition.'

'Oh, my God! Ye're not goin' to work where there's gunpowder, are yer? Yer might get yerself blown up!'

'Don't be daft, Mam, it's as safe as houses! Anyway, I'd be applying for an office job, so I wouldn't be working with what you call "gunpowder".'

Molly was lost for words. She couldn't stop them doing what they wanted, they were getting too old for that. Doreen was seventeen in April and Jill eighteen in May, not kids any more.

But while Molly was lost for words, Ruthie wasn't. She'd been listening carefully, a calculating gleam in her eye. 'If yer get an extra pound a week, our Doreen, yer'll be able to give me an extra penny a week pocket money! And you, our Jill!'

There was a smile on Molly's face as she sighed. At least someone was happy with what she'd heard. The crafty little beggar always had her eye to business.

Chapter Eighteen

'You go and sit in yer chair by the fire, sweetheart.' Bridie stacked the three dirty dinner plates and placed the knives and forks on top. Forever watchful of her husband, she thought he looked tired. 'There's only a few pots and pans, me and Rosie will have them done in no time at all.'

'That we will, Uncle Bob!' Rosie beamed at him. Over the months she'd lived with them, she'd grown to love them dearly and shared Bridie's concern for her husband. 'Sure we'll be that quick the pans won't even know they've been washed until they're back in the cupboard.'

As Bob watched her follow his wife into the kitchen, he tried to remember what their lives had been like without her. Oh, they had plenty of things to interest them, what with Molly coming round nearly every day and the grandchildren visiting them regularly. But it wasn't the same as having someone to live with them as part of the family. Particularly when that someone was never without a smile on her face or a joke on her lips. She had made such a difference to their lives. Always bright and cheerful, she gave them something to look forward to each day. She reminded Bob of Molly, a good storyteller who could find humour in an ordinary, commonplace incident that most people would forget two minutes after it happened. Every customer she sold a pair of shoes to was worth imitating in words and actions. When you were doubled up with laughter it didn't matter that she was stretching the truth to amuse them, that the woman trying on a pair of court shoes didn't have legs shaped like milk bottles and most certainly didn't stutter.

Bob moved from the table to his favourite chair, but before sitting down he selected a book from the shelf running the width of the recess at the side of the fireplace. There was a cupboard on top where Bridie kept her best linen and china, that had been there from when the house was built, but Bob had put the shelf up himself a few years ago to house his collection of books on steam trains. They had been his hobby since he was a young boy, and his father used to take him train-spotting to the Exchange station or Lime Street. They'd spend hours writing down names and numbers whilst enjoying the noise of the bustling stations, the shuddering of the engines as they pulled up alongside the platform, the chattering of the passengers as they alighted, and the smell and hiss of steam as it bellowed from the chimneys. And to this day they still held a magic for him.

Turning the pages, Bob's mind went back to his childhood. The memories were so clear it seemed as if it were yesterday . . . in fact he imagined he could still hear the noise, still smell the steam. And to add to the excitement, if his father had a few coppers to spare they would go to the Kardomah café, and over a cup of tea and a toasted teacake they would discuss the new numbers and names they had gathered to add to their collection.

'Uncle Bob!' Rosie planted herself on the end of the couch, next to Bob's chair. 'Tell me about the trains.'

Bob smiled. 'That would take a lifetime, lass, it's not somethin' yer can learn in a few minutes. And you have to have the feel for them.'

The grin on the bonny face widened. 'Well now, aren't I thinkin' that I could very quickly get the feeling?'

'But why?' Bob's eyebrows rose. 'It's not a hobby for a young girl, you'd soon be bored stiff.'

'Sure aren't I bored stiff listening to Tommy an' Ginger

talkin' about them? When I do get the chance to be with them, which isn't often, all I hear is trains and football. And although me mammy always says yer should never think ill of anyone, I'm pretty sure they do it on purpose to make me look stupid. At least Tommy does – it wouldn't be fair to put any blame on Ginger.'

There was a half-smile on Bridie's face as she gathered the four corners of the tablecloth and shook it over the hearth. Her eyes were on Rosie as she folded it neatly back along its creases. 'So all this knowledge ye're after is just to impress Tommy?'

'Not to impress him, Auntie Bridget, just so's I don't have to sit there lookin' like an eejit.' Rosie's clear laugh rang out. 'Sure if I wanted to impress Tommy I'm thinkin' I'd have to do cartwheels all the way down the street holdin' a glass of water in me mouth. And he'd not even be satisfied then, so he wouldn't, unless I did it without spillin' a wee drop of the water.'

Bridie and Bob exchanged smiles. They were used to Rosie's childlike honesty by now. There was no eyelash-fluttering or simpering with her – if she thought it, she said it. And she'd made no bones about having set her cap at poor unsuspecting Tommy.

'Lass, you'd never learn enough about trains to impress Tommy,' Bob told her gently. 'He knows more about them than I do.'

'Now me mammy always says that if yer don't try, then yer don't deserve to get.' Rosie wasn't going to be put off. 'So tell me about the train on that page yer have open.'

Bob looked down until he'd managed to wipe the smile from his face. By the time she'd learned enough about this particular train, her infatuation for his grandson would have faded and she'd probably be married to another bloke! Still, if that was what she wanted! He held the book towards her. 'This particular locomotive is the oldest in this country, and probably in the entire world. See underneath the picture – it gives yer all the particulars.' His finger pointed to the words as he read them aloud. 'Wantage Tramway 0-4-OWT No. 5 Shannon. It was built in 1857 and is still in use today. It says a lot more, but if yer try to remember too much, yer'll forget the lot.'

'Well, did you ever!' Rosie's head wagged from side to side. 'Eighteen fifty-seven, did yer say? Sure I wasn't even a gleam in me mammy's eye at that time.'

Bridie spluttered. Where on earth did she get all these sayings from? 'Rosie, that's about eighty-three years ago! Your grandmother wasn't even a gleam in her mother's eye.'

'Ye're right, Auntie Bridget, so y'are.' Wide blue eyes studied the train and the writing beneath it. 'Sure that's an awful lot, I'll never remember it all, not in a million years.'

'A little each night, sweetheart, that's the way to do it. Just keep repeating in yer mind the name, number and when it was built. When yer know that by heart, yer can take more on board . . . like who gave her the name, when it was and which line she services.'

'Isn't there an easier one, Uncle Bob?'

'I've got books full of them, lass, but if yer want to impress Tommy, that's the one to do it with. Its name is magic to every train buff in the country.'

Rosie took the book from him and buried her head in it. 'I'll read it a few times until me brain's taken it in.' She looked up, and with a smile that would melt a heart of stone, told him, 'When I've enough knowledge of trains to keep up with Tommy an' Ginger, yer can tell me the names of all the players at Liverpool Football Club, and what positions they play in.' When she saw Bob's brows nearly touch his hairline she began to giggle. 'Yer see, Uncle Bob, I've got to be one step ahead of Tommy 'cos he's as crafty as a leprechaun, so he is. Yer can bet yer life that if he finds out I know a little about his beloved steam trains, he'll switch to football.'

Bridie had a hard job trying to look serious. 'But he's not goin' to get the better of you, is he, me darlin'?'

'That he's not, Auntie Bridget! I'll not have it said that Tommy Bennett ever got the better of Rosie O'Grady!'

'But a girl should never run after a boy, sweetheart,' Bridie warned. 'He won't think anythin' of yer if yer do, an' that's the truth of it.'

'Oh, I won't be running after him, Auntie Bridget, that wouldn't be ladylike.' Again that disarming smile. 'I'll just be walking quick enough to stop him gettin' away from me.'

As she walked to the Bennetts' house, Rosie was repeating over and over in her mind *Wantage Tramway 0-4-OWT No. 5 Shannon, built in 1857*. She was so deep in concentration as she turned the corner by Maisie's shop, that she didn't see the figure looming towards her until they collided and she was sent sprawling on the pavement. It was pitch dark and she couldn't make out who the figure was until she heard the gruff voice.

'I'm sorry, but yer weren't looking where yer were goin'.'

'And neither were you, Tommy Bennett!' Rosie tried to scramble to her feet but a sharp pain in her left ankle made her cry out. 'I can't get up, I've hurt me ankle.'

'Oh, it's you, I might have known.' Tommy sounded disgusted. 'Here, give me yer hand an' I'll pull yer up.'

Rosie couldn't see his face, but the tone of his voice told her he certainly wasn't acting out of chivalry. She held out her hand and waited until she felt his fingers grip it, then she allowed herself to be pulled to her feet. But the second her left foot touched the ground she moaned in pain. 'I can't put me foot down, it hurts.'

'God'strewth! Ye're nothin' but a flamin' nuisance, Rosie O'Grady!'

'If I'm a flamin' nuisance then you're a ruddy menace! Yer knock me over, make me hurt me foot so I can't walk, then put the blame on me! You are certainly no gentleman, Tommy Bennett, an' that's the truth of it! An' if that's not bad enough, yer sent me handbag flyin' an' I can't even see where it is!'

'Wiggle yer foot, it's probably only a pulled muscle. I'll see if I can find yer bag.' Feeling a right fool, and cursing Rosie to all eternity, Tommy scraped his foot along the ground until he came into contact with a solid object. He picked it up and held it out. 'Here's yer bag, an' yer haven't lost anythin' 'cos the clasp is still shut.'

Rosie took the bag without a word. She didn't see why she should thank him when it was his fault the bag was on the ground in the first place! She wanted to walk away with her head in the air, show him what she thought of him, but when she put her weight on her left foot she couldn't stop the cry of pain. 'It's no good – I can't walk.'

'Holy sufferin' ducks!' Tommy was exasperated. Trust her! But he couldn't just walk away and leave her, his mam would kill him. 'D'yer want to go back home, or to our house?'

'Your house is nearer. Sure it'll probably be all right in a little while.'

'Then take my arm an' yer can hop on one foot.'

And so Rosie linked Tommy's arm for the first time. But she was in pain and didn't appreciate it. Tommy's pain was mental, and he certainly didn't appreciate being in such close proximity to the girl who always rubbed him up the wrong way. I mean, look what she'd done now! If it had been any other girl he'd knocked over, she wouldn't have hurt herself. But this one had to, just to be different.

Molly opened the door and peered into the darkness. When her eyes became accustomed, she gaped when she saw the pair arm in arm. 'In the name of God, when did you two start courtin'?'

'It's not funny, Mam, she fell an' hurt her foot.'

'Will yer not be tellin' lies, Tommy Bennett! I didn't fall, I was knocked over!'

'Come in, come in, an' let's have a look.'

'I can't put me foot down, Auntie Molly, it hurts too much.'

'Lift her over the step, Tommy, don't stand there like a gormless idiot.' There was a grin on Molly's face as she held the door wide. Her son must be livid about this.

'She can hop up,' Tommy growled. 'Or you come down an' take her other arm and we can lift her between us.'

Molly pushed him aside. 'Get out of the way, ye're as much use as a bucket with a hole in the bottom.'

Molly put her arm around Rosie's waist and lifted her over the step. 'There yer are, sunshine.'

'I'll see yer later, Mam.' Tommy made to walk away. 'Don't wait up for me, I've got me key.'

'Oh, no you don't!' Molly pulled him back using some force. 'You get inside until we see what's wrong with Rosie.'

While Rosie related what had happened, Tommy stood by the sideboard moving from one foot to the other. He should be at Ginger's by now, his friend would wonder what had happened to him. Trust *her* to spoil the one night he wasn't working overtime. And just listen to the way she was gabbling on . . . what a pity it wasn't her jaw she'd hurt!

Molly went down on her knees and lifted Rosie's leg. The ankle was beginning to swell and she touched the puffiness gently. 'Does that hurt, sunshine?'

'No. It only hurts when I put me foot down on the floor.'

'The best thing yer can do is go home and get me ma to put a cold compress on it, otherwise it'll be like a balloon tomorrow and yer won't be able to go to work. I'd come with yer, but as yer can see I'm on me own. Uncle Jack felt like a pint, and God knows he deserves it, the hours he's puttin' in at work. Our Doreen's gone to Maureen's and Jill's up at Steve's. I daren't go out an' leave Ruthie in bed in case she wakes up.'

At that moment there was a knock on the door and Molly

smiled with relief. 'This is probably Jill and Steve now. They said they might come back for a game of cards.' She struggled to her feet, glaring at Tommy. 'Open the door, yer daft nit!'

'It's Uncle Corker, Mam!'

'Well I never! Jack only goes for a pint every Preston Guild, an' he has to pick tonight an' miss all the excitement.'

Corker lifted Molly off her feet and swung her round. 'How's my favourite girl?'

'All the better for seeing you.' Molly smiled down at the weather-beaten, hairy face. 'Now put me down, yer daft ha'p'orth, and tell me when yer got home.'

'A couple of hours ago. I had somethin' to eat with me ma, then came down to Ellen's.' Corker's expression told Molly he'd been hoping to find her and Jack alone. He winked before turning a smiling face to Rosie. 'An' how's me little Irish colleen, then? Still as pretty as ever, I see.'

'Her and Tommy have had a difference of opinion.' Molly pointed to the girl's ankle as she explained. 'I've told her to get home an' put a cold compress on it. The trouble is, she can't put her foot on the floor 'cos it's too painful.'

'Well now, that's no problem – we'll have yer home in no time.' Corker's roar of laughter filled the room. 'I'd carry yer in me arms, me darlin', but if we bumped into any of the neighbours they might get the wrong idea and send for the police, sayin' I'm abducting yer.' He bent his huge frame until their faces were on a level. 'With Tommy one side of yer an' me the other, we'll make a chair with our hands and carry yer home.'

'Ah, heck!' Tommy growled. 'I'm goin' to Ginger's!'

'Yer mean yer *were* goin' to Ginger's, before yer knocked Rosie down.' Molly shot him daggers. 'And when yer've got her safely home, yer can still go to yer mate's.'

Molly put her arm around Rosie's waist and helped her hop along the hall. She heard Tommy behind, saying, 'She looks like Hop-along Cassidy.'

'If yer look in the mirror, sunshine,' Molly called back, 'yer'll see his horse.'

Corker was chuckling as he and Tommy laced the fingers of each other's hands. 'When are you two gettin' married?'

'Sure I'd not be marrying him, Uncle Corker,' Rosie said. 'He's altogether too rude, so he is.'

'Chance would be a fine thing!' Tommy had fire in his voice. 'I wouldn't touch yer with a bargepole.'

When Rosie sat on the makeshift chair and Corker told her to put an arm across each of their shoulders, Molly folded her arms across her tummy and pressed hard to keep the laughter at bay. She'd wait until she got back inside before enjoying the humour of the situation. Their Tommy must be really hating this, she thought. But he did ask for it – he was like a bear with a sore head whenever Rosie was around.

'I'll be back in twenty minutes,' Corker called. 'Have the kettle on the boil.'

'Well?' Molly asked, closing the door behind Corker. 'Did she get home all right?'

'She's gettin' fussed over like a baby and loving every minute of it. Yer ma and da are running around like scalded hens, tearing a sheet into strips to make a cold compress, putting a cushion on the stool for Rosie to rest her leg on, an' making her a cup of hot sweet tea to settle her tummy after the shock.' Corker leaned back on the couch and laid his peaked sailor's cap at the side of him. 'She'll be as right as rain by tomorrow.'

'Is our Tommy still there?'

'Are you joking?' Corker dropped his head back and let out a hearty chuckle. 'He couldn't get out quick enough!'

'I don't know what it is, but he can't stand the sight of Rosie. He's never been like this with anyone else.'

Corker winked knowingly. 'I wouldn't be puttin' all the blame on Tommy, me darlin'. He's young, and not used to the wiles of you women. And for all Rosie's tender years, I have the impression she can be a mischievous little minx when the mood takes her.' He let out a loud guffaw. 'Nellie would have appreciated her acting when Tommy gave yer ma a kiss and made a bolt for the door. Rosie called him back, but he wasn't havin' any; just shouted to ask what she wanted. And as sweet as honey she said, "I forgive yer, Tommy, even though I'm in agony."'

Molly shook with laughter. 'What would yer do with them?'

'I think ye're goin' to have an interesting few years with the pair of them, an' I hope to be around to see how it ends up.'

They heard the key in the front door and Molly said, 'This will be my feller. I knocked at Nellie's after yer'd gone and asked Steve to nip down to the pub and tell Jack yer were here.'

Corker rose from the couch to shake Jack's hand. 'I'd have come down an' had a pint with yer, but I told Ellen I wouldn't be long.'

Molly briefly told Jack what had happened, then went to the kitchen to make a pot of tea. She could hear the two men laughing and knew Corker was filling in the parts she'd left out. They got on really well, the big man and her husband. They were good mates, and had a lot of respect for each other.

'What d'yer think about Nobby?' Molly asked, setting the tea tray on the table. 'I got the shock of me life.'

'Ay, it's a sad business all round.' Corker took the cup from her and placed it on the floor between his feet. 'I've never had any time for Nobby Clarke, as yer well know, but I'm grateful to him for settin' Ellen's mind at rest. We haven't been able to discuss it at length because the kids were in and out, but from what she told me, and by her whole attitude, I know she's more at ease with herself than she's ever been.'

'It's over a week since we were there, I never thought he'd last that long. Every day I've been expecting Ellen to get word to say he's gone.' Molly sipped on the piping-hot tea. 'I'll tell yer what, Corker, I take me hat off to Ellen. She's got more guts than I ever gave her credit for. I only went along to give her some support, and for a while she really did need it. But when it came to the crunch, she handled it far better than I could have done. To tell yer the truth, I was bawling me eyes out while she was as composed as anything, makin' her peace with Nobby.'

'We're going to see him tomorrow.'

'You are!' Molly quickly recovered from her surprise. 'I'm glad about that, Corker. I haven't been able to get his face out of me mind, and God knows, he probably won't even know ye're there. But no one, no matter how bad they've been, should die thinking there isn't a soul in the world who cares.'

Jack leaned forward, his face serious. 'Molly's right. At least yer can go through life knowin' yer did the decent thing.'

'We're not going until the afternoon because Ellen won't take a full day off. So if we're not back in time for the kids comin' home from school, will yer keep an eye to them, Molly, please? I know Phoebe is old enough and capable to see they come to no harm, but I'd feel better if I knew they had someone to turn to if need be.'

'Of course I'll keep an eye on them. There'll be a warm fire ready for them to come in to, and a hot cup of tea. And if by any chance you're really late gettin' home, I'll send down to the chippy for somethin' for them to eat.'

'Thanks, Molly, ye're a pal.'

'You're welcome, Corker. After all, what are mates for?'

It was the same nurse as the week before, and as he locked the door behind them Ellen asked, 'How is he?'

'Very low, Mrs Clarke. We rang the phone number you left

with us and they said they would see you got the message, but you must already have been on your way here.'

The nurse was looking up at Corker, thinking he'd never seen such a big man in all his life. And with that thick moustache and beard, he looked as though he'd stepped out of the story-book the nurse read to his son every night. Standing beside him, her elbow cupped possessively in a massive hand, Ellen looked like a doll. The nurse could contain his curiosity no longer. 'Are you a member of the family, sir?'

'In a manner of speaking.'

When Corker didn't volunteer any more information, the nurse had no other option but to say, 'Follow me, please.' After all, it would be a foolhardy person who asked this giant too many questions.

They were met at the ward door by Dr Jefferson. 'Ah, Mrs Clarke, I was just about to ask if you had been notified.' He looked up at Corker, his reaction not too different from the nurse's. What a fine-looking man! I wonder what the connection is? 'You are . . . ?'

'James Corkhill, a friend of Mrs Clarke's.' Corker met the doctor's eyes. 'Does my being here bother you?'

'Not at all! I'm glad Mrs Clarke is not alone. I've just been to see her husband, and I'm sorry to say his life is ebbing fast and I expect the end any minute.'

Corker placed his arm across Ellen's shoulders. 'We'd like to see him.'

'Yes, of course.'

When they reached the bed, Ellen stepped away from Corker's arm and leaned over the bars. *Oh dear God,* she prayed, *help me to be brave.* She forced herself to stretch out a hand and stroke the face that was now just bones with skin stretched across. 'Nobby,' she said softly, 'it's me, Ellen.' The lashes flickered but the eyes didn't open. She looked across the bed at the doctor, her eyes questioning as she mouthed the words, 'Can he hear me?'

'He's unconscious, Mrs Clarke, and opinions are divided on whether a person in that condition can hear. I believe not, but there are those who would believe otherwise.'

Ellen moved her hand to stroke the wisps of white hair. 'God bless, Nobby, from me and the children.'

Corker watched, feeling more helpless than he ever had in his life. He had seen many heart-rending sights during his years at sea. In places such as India he'd seen people dying of starvation and disease, lying at the side of the road. And beggars with bodies so deformed you had to look away as you threw them a few coppers. But the pity he'd felt for them was nothing to what he was feeling now.

'Mrs Clarke, would you leave the ward, please?' The nurse appeared from nowhere as the doctor moved towards the bed. 'Wait outside, I'll be with you shortly.'

Corker led Ellen away. 'I think he's gone, love.'

'I hope so, Corker, for his sake.'

They stood in the corridor for five minutes before the doctor joined them. 'Your husband has passed away, Mrs Clarke.'

Ellen squared her thin shoulders. 'I'm glad I got here in time. And I believe Nobby knew, I believe he could hear me.'

'Perhaps you're right, Mrs Clarke. Now, do you want to see your husband again when the nurse has attended to him?'

Ellen shook her head. 'No thank you, Doctor. But I would like you to tell me what happens now.'

'Then come along to my office and I'll organize a cup of tea for yourself and Mr Corkhill.'

'It's a good job Corker's home, isn't it, girl?' Nellie's head went to the left, her chins to the right. ''Cos if he hadn't come home, she wouldn't have been there at the end.'

'No, there is that to it.' Molly pushed her finger along the chenille cloth, making a ridge. 'Ellen's upset that Nobby's got to go in a pauper's grave, but there was nothing else for it! She hasn't got a family grave he could be buried in, no insurance and no money! So the hospital are seein' to all the arrangements an' Ellen and Corker will be goin' to the funeral.'

'How can Corker go? How long's he home for?'

'The funeral's on Monday, and he joins his ship again on Wednesday.'

'We could have a whip-round an' buy a wreath for him, yer know, girl. Can't have the man gettin' buried without even a single flower.'

'It'll have to be a whip-round between the two of us, sunshine, 'cos none of the neighbours are bein' told. Corker agrees with Ellen that it's best to wait until the kids are a bit older an' don't hate their dad so much.'

'Poor little buggers, yer can't blame them. They had a lousy life with him. No food in their bellies, no clothes on their backs, no fire in the grate and their hair walkin' with fleas because Ellen had no money for soap.' Suddenly a grin creased Nellie's face. 'Ay, girl, d'yer remember when Nobby had your Tommy by the throat and was nearly choking him to death because he said he'd kicked a ball through their window? D'yer remember that?'

Molly didn't answer right away, thinking it wasn't respectful to speak ill of a man who had just died. Then she decided it wasn't disrespectful to tell the truth. 'Second-best fight of me life, that, so I'll never forget it! I was frightened at first 'cos I really thought he was goin' to kill our Tommy. Then I got mad, an' when you told me to put me arm across his neck and press hard so he couldn't breathe, I did it with relish. Then after you'd got his hands off our Tommy's neck an' he fell to the ground, I felt like givin' him a good kick. I know yer shouldn't say such things of the dead, but yer've got to be honest, haven't yer? There were quite a few times I wanted to give Nobby Clarke a kick, particularly when I saw the state of

Ellen the mornings after he'd given her a goin'-over and her face, neck and arms were black and blue.'

'Ay, girl, yer said that was the second-best fight of yer life – what was yer first?'

'Oh, you know what the best fight was . . . you were there! I'm not daft enough to get in a fight when I haven't got you with me, sunshine, I wasn't born yesterday, yer know! You remember, it was the night the Bradleys started a fight up at the top end and the whole street was out. You did yer famous balancing act with Mrs Bradley on top of yer head.'

'Oh ay, yeah! Ay, that was a good night, wasn't it?' Nellie's bosom bounced up and down on the table as she shook with mirth. 'She was hanging on to the back of Jack's neck, nearly throttling him, an' you got hold of her legs and lifted her up backwards, while I got me head underneath! Yeah, that was certainly the best fight we've ever 'ad. When yer come to think of it, life's been pretty dull since the Bradleys did a flit. We haven't had a fight with anyone for ages! We'll be gettin' rusty if we're not careful!'

'Nellie, there's a flamin' *big* fight goin' on! Has nobody told yer yet that there's a ruddy war on?'

'Thank God today's over.' Ellen sank into the chair, her mind and body weary. Phoebe and Dorothy, her two eldest children, had just gone up to bed and at last she was alone with Corker and they could talk without fear of being overheard. 'I've been terrified of slipping up in front of the kids.'

'Well it's all over now and you can put it behind yer.' Corker patted the empty space next to him on the couch. 'Come and sit here, love.'

Ellen sat next to him and leaned her head on his shoulder. 'It wasn't as bad as I expected, Nobby being buried in a pauper's grave. It was a grave just like any other, and there was a priest there to say a few prayers which I was glad about.'

'I was worried too, thinking it would be cold and heartless, with only you and me there. So I was pleased when I saw Dr Jefferson and the nurse turn up, it was good of them.' Corker wound a strand of her hair around his finger. 'And the grave won't look bare with our wreath, the one from Molly and Nellie and the flowers the hospital staff sent. So Nobby had as good a send-off as anyone.'

'Except his children weren't there.'

'I know, love, but we did talk it through and I think it's best this way. After all, they're only kids and would be all confused about their feelings for him. When they're older and the scars have had time to heal, they might find it in their heart to forgive him, as you have.'

Ellen moved away from him so she could look into his face. 'Ay, what about lettin' the solicitor know? He doesn't have to go ahead now with trying for a divorce.'

'I've been thinkin' about that, but I haven't had time to go into town to see him. I'll have to go tomorrow because I'm due back on the ship early Wednesday morning.' Corker gently put his huge hand on the side of Ellen's face and pressed it to his breast. 'There's nothing to stop us gettin' married now, love. And you don't have to worry about being seen out with me. Oh, I've watched yer face every time we've walked down the street together, yer looked that guilty anyone would think yer'd robbed a bank!'

'Well you know what neighbours can be like when they've got somethin' to gossip about. They'd never believe there's been nothing between us, no one would.'

'I've told yer before, don't worry about what the neighbours think. While they're talking about us, they're leavin' someone else alone. We're the ones that count, you an' me, an' we know we've done nothing to be ashamed of.' Corker put a finger under her chin and lifted her face. 'Mind you, you can take the credit for that. I'm not as good-livin' as you, love, an' if it had been up to me, I'd have had my wicked way with yer long before now.'

'Corker, yer'll not be havin' yer wicked way with me until we're married, and that won't be for some time. Until we've told the children, an' the neighbours, that Nobby's dead, there can be no wedding bells for us.'

Corker sighed. 'Ye're a stickler for doin' what's right, aren't yer, me darlin'? But I love yer all the more for it.'

It had been weeks since Ellen smiled, but she did so now. 'Perhaps yer'd be better off lookin' for a flighty piece for yerself? Someone who is more generous with her favours?'

'You're the only one for me, love, always have been. I've waited twenty years – another year won't kill me.' Corker put his hands on her shoulders and turned her to face him. 'But I can't wait another year for a kiss, so how about it?'

Ellen cupped his dear face. 'Yer've been so good to me, Corker, and I do know how lucky I am to have you. You have my love and my heart, and I ask you to be patient with me a little longer.' She pursed her lips and moved towards him. 'I do love you, my gentle giant.'

Chapter Nineteen

Her head cocked to one side, Nellie gazed across the table at her friend. 'Ay, girl, d'yer know ye're gettin' quite a lot of white hairs in yer head?'

'Considerin' all the worry, it's a wonder I'm not snow-white!' Molly said. 'What with one thing an' another, it's enough to send yer to an early grave.'

Nellie lifted her massive bosom and laid it on the table so she could lean forward in comfort. 'Ay, ay, girl, don't be so ruddy miserable! What worries have you got that we haven't all got?'

'Knowin' everybody's in the same boat doesn't make it any easier when ye're traipsing round every day looking for something to make a decent meal with! Coupons for this, coupons for that, it's enough to drive yer round the twist.'

'Oh, it's not that bad, for cryin' out loud! We're not starvin', are we?' Nellie chortled. 'It wouldn't do me no harm if we were. In six months I'd have a figure like Jean Harlow.'

Molly grinned. 'In six months? You're bein' a bit optimistic, aren't yer, sunshine? You could live a couple of years without food with the fat you've got! Jean Harlow indeed!'

Happy to see her mate smiling, Nellie laced her fingers and rested her chin on them. 'A good laugh does yer as much good as a pan of scouse, girl!'

'Ay, an' those ruddy air-raid sirens are as good as a dose of Andrews' Liver Salts!'

'But we haven't had no real air-raids, have we, girl? Only

planes goin' over. My feller said they're rec . . . recog . . . recognition planes, come to spy out the lie of the land.'

'The word is reconnaissance, but I know what yer mean. Still, we're not to know that when the siren goes, are we? For all we know they might start droppin' bombs on us an' that's what yer've got to think about. We're told to treat every alarm as a real one, and run to one of the shelters. We'd look well, standin' in the street lookin' up at the planes, when one of them started droppin' bombs.'

'I wouldn't let yer come to no harm, girl,' Nellie said, her face wearing a serious expression. 'If I saw a bomb comin' down towards you, I'd catch it in me arms.'

Molly's vivid imagination went to work. 'Nellie, if you an' me saw a bomb comin' towards us, we'd run like the ruddy clappers to the nearest shelter. I can just see us pushin' each other out of the way to get there first. Best mates or not, it would be a case of survival of the fittest.'

'Yeah, ye're right there, girl.' The chair began to creak under Nellie. 'I'll have to start carryin' a clean pair of knickers with me all the time, just in case I 'ave an accident with fright.'

'Trust you to think of that!'

'Well, I was remembering what they used to say in the Girl Guides; always be prepared.'

'I never knew you were in the Guides.'

'Didn't yer, girl?'

'No! All these years an' yer've never mentioned being a Guide!'

'I had my reasons.'

'What reasons?'

The creaking of the chair became louder. 'Because I was never in the Girl Guides.'

'Nellie McDonough, ye're the biggest liar on God's earth!'

'Ah, that's goin' a bit far, that is, girl! I'll admit to bein' the biggest liar in this street, but the whole world? Never!' Content now that her friend was in a happier frame of mind than when she'd arrived, Nellie pointed to the teapot. 'Is there another cuppa in there?'

Molly put her hand under the knitted cosy. 'It's not very hot.'

'I don't care as long as it's wet and warm.'

As Molly poured the tea her brow furrowed. 'How come it's my house every mornin' for yer elevenses? Tea's on ration, yer know, we should share.'

'Yer'd be makin' yerself a cuppa at this time, wouldn't yer?' Nellie asked. 'Yer only need the same amount of tea for two as yer do for one.'

'Well why don't I come up to yours? You'd be makin' yerself one, wouldn't yer?'

Nellie shook her head, her chins going in all directions. 'No girl, I wouldn't.'

'Yer wouldn't? Why not?'

''Cos I go up to me mate's every morning for elevenses.'

Molly put the teapot back on its stand before letting her laughter erupt. 'Nellie McDonough, ye're as crazy as a coot!'

'That I may be, girl, but seein' as it's your tea I'm drinkin', then it just goes to show that bein' crazy doesn't mean ye're stupid.'

Just to get her own back, Molly said, 'Ye're not gettin' any sugar 'cos we're runnin' short.'

'Oh, are yer, girl? D'yer want me to lend yer some? Yer can pay me back when yer get yer ration.'

'No thanks, I can do without sugar in me tea, it doesn't bother me.' Molly leaned forward, her eyes narrowed. 'Ye're not suggestin' by any chance that I should borrow sugar off you so yer can put it in that cup of tea?'

'The thought had crossed me mind, girl, but I can see by yer physog that yer don't take kindly to the idea, so I'll drink it as it is an' suffer in silence.' Nellie shifted her position, causing

Molly to pray the chair would stand up to it. 'Ay, did yer tell Jack what happened yesterday, about us joinin' that queue at the fish shop?'

Molly grinned. 'Yeah, we didn't half have a good laugh.'

'I had to exaggerate when I told my feller, 'cos yer know he's not blessed with much humour.' Nellie folded her arms and sat back. 'I did get a laugh out of him, though. I told him we were walkin' round the shops when someone shouted that the fish shop had fish in. Instead of twelve people in the queue, I told George there were about thirty. I said we stood for half an hour, and when we got to the counter all the shopkeeper was selling was fish heads.' Nellie shook with the pleasure of remembering her husband's face. 'He thought it was hilarious, doubled up he was, until I told him I'd bought half a dozen fish heads and we were havin' them for tea tonight . . . eyes an' all.'

'Yer didn't!'

'I ruddy well did! An' d'yer know what, girl? If I never move from this chair, I swear this is God's honest truth – the silly sod believed me!'

Molly pressed her hands into her sides. 'Nellie, don't say any more, I've got a stitch in me side.'

'At least yer've got a smile on yer face,' Nellie said. 'When I came in yer had a gob on yer like a wet week! I thought to meself, blimey, a cup of tea made with two tea leaves, no biscuits and lookin' at a face that would curdle the flamin' milk!'

'I know, sunshine, but I can't help worryin'. It's not just being short of food that's made me like that, it's everything. Wonderin' how young Phil is over in France, your Steve likely to get his callin'-up papers any day, an' every time the flamin' air-raid siren goes I worry meself sick about me ma and da.'

'Well let's get all yer worries in pro . . . pre . . . oh, what's the ruddy word I'm lookin' for?'

'Perspective, Nellie.'

'That's it, girl! Now, first off is Phil. There's nothin' goin' on in France, so he's safe. Next is our Steve, an' it could be a long time before he gets called up because he's on war work. That leaves yer ma an' da. The air-raid shelter is right at the top of their street, only a stone's throw. They'd be settled in there, all safe and sound, long before we could get there. So yer see, girl, although there may come a time to worry, it's not here yet.'

Molly took a deep breath. 'I know, so let's talk about somethin' nice, eh? It's our Tommy's sixteenth birthday on Friday, so I'm havin' a little do for him on Saturday. I'm not askin' the usual gang – Maisie, Alec, Ellen or Doreen's mates from work, because of the eats. But we can have a couple of drinks an' a singsong. Naturally, you an' George are invited.'

'I was goin' to ask yer what he'd like as a present. How about a pair of warm gloves?'

'I think our Jill's buying him gloves, an' me an' Jack are gettin' him a tie to go with his new clothes, an' cufflinks.' Molly was thoughtful for a moment. 'A pair of socks would be a good bet, Nellie, he's always moanin' about not havin' enough.'

'That's settled then: I'll give him two pair of socks, a birthday card an' a smackin' big kiss.' Nellie's grin was cheeky. 'Is Rosie bein' invited to his party?'

'I could hardly leave her out, could I? Not when me ma and da are comin'. Anyway, she'd come without bein' invited. There's hardly a night passes when she doesn't come round.'

'I wonder if she'll buy him a pressie?'

'Ooh, don't mention it, Nellie! I dread to think what he'd do with it if she did. Ever since that night he knocked her over he's been worse with her than he was before.'

'I can't understand him,' Nellie said. 'I think she's a lovely girl.'

'Well, yer know what they say, sunshine – there's only a thin line between love and hate.'

'Is that one of Rosie's mammy's sayings?'

'No, it's one of mine, an' I just made it up.' Molly pulled her tongue out. 'So there!'

'Are the men workin' late again, Auntie Molly?'

'I'm afraid so, Rosie.' Molly smiled at the young girl, who was turning into quite a beauty. It was hard to imagine her as the same girl who, when she first saw her, was dressed like an old woman. These days, with the help of Doreen's dressmaking skills and Jill's talent for hairstyles and make-up, Rosie was always well turned out. She had lost some weight and looked very attractive in her modern stylish dresses. 'Tommy doesn't mind 'cos he likes a few bob in his pocket, an' he's young enough to stand the long hours. It's yer uncle Jack that worries me, he's always tired out.'

'Sure 'tis far too much, so it is. Don't I get tired standin' on me feet all day an' I'm only fifteen and eleven months?'

Molly chuckled. 'Don't forget the eleven months, will yer?'

'I'll not be forgettin' them, that I won't! In fact, I'm fifteen years, eleven months and five days.' Rosie glanced towards the kitchen. 'Are yer all on yer own, Auntie Molly?'

'Yes, sunshine, I'm all on me lonesome. Ruthie's in bed, and Jill an' Doreen have both gone out.' Molly cocked an ear. 'Here's the men now – I'll get their dinners.'

Tommy dashed in ahead of his father, his eyes sparkling with excitement. 'Mam, we went outside the factory when the air-raid siren went, an' we saw three German planes. They were flyin' that low we could see the pilots and all the markings on them.' He turned to Jack for confirmation. 'Isn't that right, Dad?'

Jack nodded. 'It was an unbelievable sight. They were cruising along as though the sky belonged to them an' they had all the time in the world.' He grinned. 'That is until three of our planes swooped up behind them, then they roared off, ducking and diving with our lads on their tails, closing in on them.'

Molly stood with a plate of dinner in each hand. 'Where's yer manners? Have yer not noticed we've got a visitor?'

Jack turned with a smile on his face. 'Hello, Rosie, love.'

Tommy gave her a brief glance, muttering something unintelligible under his breath. It could have been a greeting or a farewell.

Molly tutted before asking, 'Well, what happened then?'

Jack shrugged his shoulders. 'I dunno, they were out of sight in no time, making for the sea.'

'Would our lads shoot them down, Dad?' Tommy asked. 'They wouldn't just let them get away, would they?'

'You know as much as I do, son, but I can't see them shooting them down over a built-up area. Just think of the damage it would cause, an' the civilian casualties.'

'Here, sit down an' get yer dinners.' Molly set the plates down. 'You were takin' a chance, standin' there watching them, weren't yer?'

'We were on our way to the air-raid shelter, as the siren had just started, but when we saw what was goin' on nobody moved. It was like sittin' in the pictures watching a film with goodies and baddies in.' Jack picked up his knife and fork. 'The blokes from the factory were shouting swear-words at the German planes and shaking their fists, then as soon as our lads came along there was clapping an' cheering. It was a sight I wouldn't have missed. An' I'll tell yer what, love, there wasn't a man watching who wouldn't have liked to have had a go themselves.'

'Those bloody Germans have got some nerve, haven't they?' Molly pulled out a chair and sat down. 'Fancy flyin' over in broad daylight!'

'They've got to come in daylight, Mam, to take photographs,' Tommy said through a mouthful of potato. 'I bet they've got photographs which pinpoint the exact position of the docks an' other places.'

'Yer mean so they can come back an' bomb them?' Molly asked, her heart beating faster. 'One of these days they'll just drop their bombs in broad daylight an' get it over with.'

'Those planes today weren't bombers,' Jack said. 'They were light fighter planes. The Germans aren't likely to send bombers over during the daytime because they're heavier and much slower, an easy target for our fighter planes and ack-ack guns.'

'There's a bloke at work got a book with pictures in of all the German planes, an' he said there'd be two guns on those fighters we saw today.' Tommy was as tall and broad as his father and would pass for eighteen any day. But in his head he was still a young lad. 'I'm goin' to save up and buy meself a book so I can learn all the different makes and models, an' I'll know which are our planes an' which are the Germans.'

'Have yer gone off steam trains, then, Tommy?' Rosie asked.

Her question was met with a look of disdain. 'No I haven't, soft girl. I can have two interests, can't I?'

Jack cut in before any more insults could be thrown. 'Yer'd have a problem pronouncing the names of the German planes, son, I can't get me tongue around them.'

'I'll soon learn,' Tommy said with the confidence of youth. 'Won't take me long to pick it up.'

Rosie had no intention of sitting there and being left out. 'It's yer birthday on Friday, Tommy.'

'Go 'way!' Tommy rolled his eyes at the ceiling. 'Thanks for tellin' me, I wouldn't have known.'

Molly gave him a kick under the table and he grimaced. 'What was that for?'

'Don't let him bother yer, Auntie Molly,' Rosie said coolly. 'He doesn't bother me. As me mammy says, an ignorant person is more to be pitied than laughed at.'

Jack roared with laughter. 'Why don't yer put the white flag up and surrender, son?'

'Oh, I'd not be wantin' him to do that, Uncle Jack!' Rosie's lovely face beamed. 'Sure I'd hate to see a fine figure of a man like Tommy carrying a white flag, so I would!'

A knock on the door kept Tommy's reply on the tip of his tongue. 'This'll be Ginger.'

Tommy's mate was a few inches shorter than him, was slighter in build, had a mop of red hair and a face full of freckles. His redeeming feature was the set of strong white teeth he showed when he smiled. 'Hello, Mr and Mrs Bennett! Hiya, Rosie!'

'Hello, Ginger, it's glad I am to see yer.' Rosie stood up and reached for the coat she'd laid over the arm of the couch. 'I'd not like yer to think I'm leaving because of you, Ginger, but I'm on edge in case there's an air-raid warning. Auntie Bridget promised they'd go straight up to the shelter but I'd feel easier in me mind if I was there to make sure.'

Tommy's conscience began to prick at the mention of his beloved nan and grandad. 'Yer'll make sure they're safe, won't yer?'

There were danger signals in Rosie's wide, deep blue eyes. 'What d'yer think, Tommy Bennett? That I'd run like hell to save me own skin an' leave them to get on with it?'

Molly lifted a hand before her son could answer. 'Hang on a minute! I don't care if you two fight because I think it's funny. But in this case I want to see a fair fight.' She pointed a finger at Tommy. 'I was round at me ma's today, and at the bottom of the stairs there's a bolstercase filled with two blankets and some cushions. When I asked me ma if she was doin' a moonlight flit, she told me Rosie had got it ready in case she wasn't home when the sirens went. She made me ma promise to take it with her every time she went to the shelter, so if the raid lasted a long time they would be warm and comfortable.'

Tommy had the grace to blush. 'Aw, cut it out, Mam! *I* didn't say Rosie would run off an' leave them, she said that herself!'

Rosie adopted a haughty air, even though she was glowing inside. For the first time he'd actually spoken her name! But she wasn't going to let him off so easy. 'Ginger, while yer friend's eatin' his dinner, would yer like to walk me home? It's not that I'm afraid of the dark, but sure wouldn't it be my luck to meet another eejit and get knocked down?'

Ginger couldn't believe his luck. His friend might be blind to Rosie's charms, but he certainly wasn't. He glanced at Tommy and shrugged his shoulders. 'I'll be back by the time yer've washed.'

Molly chuckled silently as she walked down the hall to see them out. Oh, Tommy, my son, she thought, you don't stand an earthly. She'll get the better of you every time.

Chapter Twenty

'Happy birthday, Tommy!' Nellie held out her present. 'That's for you, and in return I want a kiss.'

'Thanks, Auntie Nellie!' Tommy duly obliged with a noisy smacker. 'I've got lots of presents, more than I've ever 'ad.'

'Ah, well, sweet sixteen an' never been kissed, eh? Or have yer?'

Tommy's face turned the colour of beetroot. 'Auntie Nellie, I wouldn't tell you if I had.'

'Go on, I won't snitch on yer.'

'All right, I've kissed over a hundred girls.' Tommy placed her present on the sideboard with the other unopened gifts. 'Are yer happy now, or shall I make it two hundred?'

Miss Clegg was the next to arrive, brought across by Doreen. She handed over a small wrapped parcel and received a kiss in return. 'I see you haven't opened any of your presents yet, Tommy.'

'No, Miss Clegg, I'll open them when everyone's here. I've never had so many in all me life . . . even at Christmas.'

Ruthie watched the pile of gifts growing, envy in her eyes. She sidled up to him and pulled on his jacket. 'Can I help yer open them, Tommy?'

'Uh-uh! I'm not openin' them until Ginger an' Malcolm are here, so scram.'

Ruthie thought about kicking him on his shin for being so mean, but then she craftily decided she might be cutting her nose to spite her face if she did. After all, one of those parcels might have sweets in, so she'd do well to be on her best behaviour.

Molly was in the kitchen buttering bread for the sardine sandwiches Jill and Doreen were making, while Steve leaned against the sink. 'Your Tommy looks like the cat that got the cream.'

'I should think so, too!' Molly said. 'I'd be lookin' like that if I'd got so many pressies.'

Jack poked his head round the door. 'Yer ma and da have arrived, with Rosie.'

Molly laid down the knife. 'Steve, you can carry on doin' this while I see to the visitors.' She wiped her hands down the front of her pinny and stood just inside the living-room door, enjoying the happy scene.

'Happy birthday, sweetheart.' After she'd handed her present over, Bridie stood on tiptoe to cup her grandson's face. 'Sure, sixteen is an important birthday, so it is, an' I hope yer enjoy it and have a year full of happiness.'

Tommy put his arms around the slim waist and held her tight. 'Thank you, Nan.' Before kissing her, he whispered in her ear, 'I love you.'

'And I love you,' she whispered back, 'more than yer'll ever know.'

Bob was next in line, and as he shook his grandson's hand there was pride on his face and a tear in his eye. 'All the best, son.'

'Thanks, Grandad.' Tommy could feel his throat tighten as his love for his grandparents threatened to overwhelm him. He coughed to clear his throat, reminding himself that men of sixteen don't cry. 'An' thanks for me pressie.'

Bob smiled and moved aside to let Rosie near. 'Happy birthday, Tommy.' She handed him a parcel. 'I hope you like it.'

'Thanks,' Tommy said gruffly, placing it with the other gifts on the sideboard. 'I'm waitin' for me mates to come before I open them.'

Rosie saw Molly standing by the door. 'Can I give yer a hand, Auntie Molly?'

'No thanks, sunshine, everything's under control. But yer can answer that knock on the door for us, if yer don't mind.'

Rosie was careful to switch the hall light out before opening the door. 'Come in, Ginger, so I can put the light on and see what we're saying.'

'This is Malcolm, he works with Tommy.'

Rosie looked up at the tall, well-built, black-haired young man. 'Hello.'

Malcolm held out his hand, smiling. 'I know who you are, I've heard all about you.' He held on to her hand. 'But they didn't tell me how pretty you are. How about a kiss?'

Oh, he thinks a lot of himself, this one, Rosie thought. He's not bad-looking but he's not a patch on Tommy. She pulled at her hand but he held it in a tight grip. 'Will yer please give me me hand back?'

Tommy had come into the hall when he heard his friend's voice and was in time to hear the exchange. Trust Malcolm to start his antics as soon as he sets foot in the door! He'd been in two minds whether to ask his workmate, because he was noted for being a flirt and thought he was God's gift to women. He even chatted up the married women at work who were old enough to be his mother! But surely he could behave himself for once instead of starting as soon as he got his nose in the door. And with Rosie, too! But she'd put the big-head in his place and take him down a peg or two.

Rosie gave Tommy a dark look as she walked past him with her head in the air. 'Take your friends' coats and hang them up.'

As Tommy's eyes followed her, he asked himself why he only ever had problems when she was around. She must be a jinx!

'Ay, she's a tasty bit of stuff,' Malcolm said as he slid his arms out of his coat. 'I wouldn't mind getting to know her better.'

'I wouldn't chance me luck if I were you.' Tommy would have liked to have torn a strip off his workmate, but this was hardly the time or the place. 'She could chew you up and spit you out without turning a hair.'

'Yeah,' Ginger agreed, 'yer won't get anywhere with Rosie.'

This sounded like a dare to Malcolm, and he was determined to prove them wrong. After all, his reputation was at stake. 'I'll bet yez a tanner that before the night's over, I'll have her eatin' out of me hand.'

Tommy hesitated. He didn't really know Rosie well enough to say what she'd do. She might well be flattered by Malcolm's attention and end up putty in his hands, leaving him a tanner out of pocket. Then Tommy mentally shook his head. No, she might be a nuisance and a pain in the neck, but she wasn't daft enough to fall for this oaf's load of baloney. 'You're on,' he said, 'a tanner it is.'

Malcolm smoothed his Brylcreemed hair, put on his Clark Gable smile and entered the fray. He was shaking hands with the more mature guests when he saw Jill and Doreen come through from the kitchen and his eyes nearly popped out of his head. Blimey, he thought, we've got three smashers here! Then he saw Steve, tall, dark and handsome, follow the girls and his hopes were dashed. He was wondering which one of the blondes with the film-star looks belonged to him, when Steve put his arm around Jill's waist and pulled her close. Well, Malcolm consoled himself, that still left two pretty, unattached girls. All was not yet lost.

'Come on, son, open yer presents,' Molly said. 'I can't wait to see what yer've got.'

Rosie waited patiently while Tommy unwrapped each present, bypassing hers in what seemed like a deliberate move. Ties, socks, gloves, carpet slippers, hankies and cufflinks.

Each present was greeted with oohs and aahs, much to the delight of Tommy who held each one up for inspection. Then came the moment when there was only Rosie's left to open. He tore the paper off, looked at the picture on the front of the book and let out a loud 'Yippee!' His face agog, he turned the pages. 'This is just what I wanted! Oh, the gear!'

Rosie let out a long, silent sigh. At last she'd done something that pleased him. She didn't expect him to single her out to thank, not when so many people had given him presents, but the delight on his face was satisfaction enough. Her present was definitely his favourite.

Malcolm was looking for a way to get near Rosie, but she had planted herself firmly between Bridie and Bob on the couch and the expression on her face said she was staying put. So until the opportunity arose, he decided to while away the time by turning his charm on Doreen. It was with amusement that Doreen listened to Malcolm bragging about his dancing skills. She'd had him taped from the minute she'd set eyes on him. With his plastered hair, false smile and affected man-of-the-world air of nonchalance, he really fancied himself as a heartbreaker. As he rambled on about his prowess on the dance floor, Doreen's eye caught the two photographs standing on the mantelpiece. They'd been taken at Jerome's in London Road, when Phil was home on his first leave and they'd gone into town with Jill and Steve. They'd ordered three copies of the photographs so Nellie and Molly could have one each, and Molly had been so proud of her daughters and their boyfriends she'd had them framed and given them pride of place over the fireplace.

Doreen reached up and took down the one of her and Phil. 'This is my boyfriend, an' if yer think you can dance, yer want to see him.'

Fighting back his disappointment, Malcolm feigned interest. 'It's a good photograph. Where is he tonight?'

'Somewhere overseas.' Satisfied that she'd put a damper

on his interest, Doreen put the photograph back. 'He's in the army.'

'Oh.' Malcolm started to move away. It was no good wasting his time on someone who was spoken for. 'I'd better go over to Tommy; after all, it is his party.'

Tommy and Ginger were bent over the sideboard, turning the pages of the new book. But even though his head was filled with the pictures of the different German aircraft, Tommy still managed to keep tabs on Malcolm. If his workmate caused any trouble he'd clock him one. But when he saw Doreen giving him a polite brush-off, he knew he needn't concern himself over her. And as for Jill, if Malcolm was soft enough to try and chat her up, he'd be asking for trouble because Steve would punch him so hard he wouldn't know what hit him.

'Don't forget yer owe me a tanner.' Tommy couldn't help the hint of sarcasm in his voice. 'Yer've no need to pay me tonight, I'll wait until next pay day.'

'I wouldn't bank on it,' Malcolm said. 'The night's only young.' He let his eyes wander round the room, thinking this wasn't his idea of a party. 'It will liven up, won't it?'

Tommy grinned. 'Just wait until the drink starts to take effect.'

'Yeah,' Ginger chortled, 'keep yer eyes on Mrs McDonough, she's the one who starts the fun.'

'Is she the big fat one?'

Tommy counted to ten. Keeping his voice even, he said, 'The big fat one, as you call her, happens to be my auntie Nellie, an' I think she's a smashin' woman, so just watch it.'

Ginger looked from one to the other. He'd never seen Tommy lose his temper before and hoped it wasn't going to come to fisticuffs. Mind you, Malcolm was so vain he would rub anyone up the wrong way. And he was out of order, what he said about Mrs McDonough. Like Tommy said, she was a smashing woman and the world would be a happier place if more people were like her. Always the life and soul of a party, she was.

Then, as if on cue, Nellie's raucous laughter filled the room. 'Did yer hear that, girl? I offered to sing a song an' my feller wants to know how much I'll take to keep me mouth shut.'

'Nellie, we'd all have a whip-round to pay yer not to sing! I've told yer, the hooters on the ships in the Mersey have more tune to them than you have.'

'Charming, that is!' Nellie put on her woebegone face. 'Well if someone else sings, I'm goin' to hum along with them whether yez like it or not. If a ruddy bee can hum, then so can I.'

'Sure, Auntie Bridget will give us a song, won't you?' Rosie pulled on Bridie's arm. 'Aren't yer singin' all the time at home?'

'No sweetheart.' Bridie tugged her arm free. 'Perhaps a bit later.'

'Oh, come on, Ma,' Molly coaxed. 'Someone's got to start the ball rollin' an' you're the only one with a decent voice.'

'Oh, no I'm not!' Bridie smiled. 'Rosie has a beautiful voice.'

'Then we'll sing a duet, that's what we'll do.' Rosie jumped up and reached for Bridie's hands. 'Yer'll have to stand, Auntie Bridget, 'cos I can't sing sittin' down.'

Reluctantly, Bridie allowed herself to be pulled up. 'Just the one song, that's all.' Then she whispered in Rosie's ear and before they began to sing, they joined hands.

> 'I'll take you home again, Kathleen, across the ocean wide and wild,
> To where your heart has ever been, since first you were my bonny bride.'

Bridie had a sweet clear voice, but Rosie's was stronger and filled the room. After a while Bridie stopped singing, and, wiping a tear from her eye, listened to the song that she loved so much but which always reminded her of home and made her sad.

And Bridie wasn't the only one affected. The haunting words, sung in a voice as clear as a bell, were playing on everyone's heartstrings.

'And when the fields are fresh and green, I will take you to your home, Kathleen.' Rosie finished on a high note, unaware that everyone listening had a lump in their throat and a tear in their eye.

'That was lovely, sweetheart.' Bridie kissed a pink cheek. 'Thank you so much.'

There was a round of applause and even Tommy was shouting for an encore. But Nellie didn't like feeling sad at a party, so after she'd sniffed hard and wiped the back of her hand across her nose, she said, 'Can't we have somethin' lively? I don't want to spend the night cryin' in me beer.'

Steve put his hand on his mam's shoulder and showed his dimples when he grinned down at her. 'Mam, ye're not drinkin' beer.'

'I know I'm not, soft lad! But if I was, then I'd be cryin' into it.'

'Is it somethin' lively yer want, then, Auntie Nellie?' Rosie grinned. 'Sure don't I know the very thing to liven yer all up? But yer'll have to move yer legs out of the way 'cos I can't sing this without me feet tapping, and that's the truth of it.'

When a space had been cleared in front of the fireplace, Rosie straightened her shoulders and stood as stiff as a ramrod. Under her breath she counted 'One, two, three,' then began to sing.

'Have yer heard of Phil the fluter from the town of
Ballymuck
Times were getting harder – the man was nearly broke.'

Rosie's legs and feet moved rapidly as she performed an Irish jig in time with her singing. The steps were intricate and fast-moving, but her feet and voice never faltered. And when Bridie started to clap, everyone in the room joined in. Even Malcolm dropped his pose to clap and stamp his feet. What a girl! He couldn't let this one get away.

The dancing stopped and Rosie held her arms wide as the song came to an end. 'Oh, hadn't we the gaiety . . . at Phil the fluter's ball.' The rafters rang with cheers and applause.

'Oh, sunshine, that was absolutely marvellous,' Molly said. 'How the hell yer managed it I'll never know 'cos I was breathin' for yer.'

'The sweat's pourin' off me, an' I was only watchin'!' Nellie wiped a hand across her forehead. 'Now, can I do me party piece?'

Molly groaned. 'Oh, no, Nellie, please?'

Jack leaned forward, resting his elbows on his knees. He winked at Molly. 'Have yer got any cotton wool, love, to shove in me ears?'

'Ay, we'll have less of that off you, Jack Bennett!' There was a stiff expression on Nellie's chubby face. 'At least I'm willin' to have a go, which is more than can be said for you, or my feller.'

'Go on, Mam,' Tommy egged. 'Let Auntie Nellie sing.'

There was a roar of approval from Steve, Jill, Doreen and Ginger. 'Yeah, let her have a go.'

Nellie tilted her head back and looked down her nose at Molly. 'Yer see, girl, I'm in great demand. The trouble with you is, yer taste is in yer backside.'

'I wish me ears were in me backside, then I wouldn't have to listen to yer.' Molly pretended to sigh. 'OK, go on, get it over with.'

Nellie left her chair and elbowed Rosie to one side. 'Make way for the main attraction, girl! Don't yer know I'm top of the bill? An' like all the best singers, I like to stand when I'm performing.' She placed the palm of one hand over the other and held them in front of her mountainous bosom. 'Now can we have a bit of hush please, 'cos the least noise will spoil me concentration.' She nodded her head knowingly at Molly. 'When Joseph Locke sings, yer can hear a pin drop.'

'Nellie, with the best will in the world, Joseph Locke you ain't! Now will yer get on with it before the people in the gallery start throwing squashed tomatoes at yer?'

'Ooh, hark at her! Don't cry, girl, there's no need to get out of yer pram, I'll pick yer dummy up!' After pulling tongues at her friend, Nellie put her hand to her mouth and coughed softly. Then she fluttered her eyelashes, gazed at the ceiling and opened her mouth.

'Auntie Mary, had a canary, up the leg of her drawers . . .'

George leapt from the chair, his hand leading the way to cover his wife's mouth. 'That's enough, Nellie, behave yerself.'

Nellie pulled away from him. 'Spoilsport!' She flicked an imaginary speck off her dress. 'The trouble with you is, yer've got no appreciation of good music.' Her chubby face creased as she smiled sweetly. 'Seein' as me husband didn't like my previous song, I'll sing yer me speciality.'

George pulled a face before sitting down and holding his head in his hands. 'God help us.'

Nellie couldn't start for laughing. After all, she knew what was coming. Then, getting her feelings firmly under control, she placed a hand on each of her ample hips and struck up a pose.

'Oh, Frankie and Johnny were sweethearts, oh, lordy how
they did love,
They swore to be true to each other, just as true as the
stars above,

He was her man, he wouldn't do her wrong.
Now Frankie went down to the corner, to get her a bucket of beer,
She said, Mr Bartender, has my lovin' Johnny been here?
He is my man, he wouldn't do me wrong.'

With her wide hips swaying and mimicking the sultry voice of Mae West, Nellie cut such a comical figure everyone in the room was in stitches. Even George had his hankie out wiping the tears from his eyes. And Nellie was thoroughly enjoying her moment of fame. She winked at Molly before changing her stance and her voice to become the bartender.

'I don't want to cause yer no trouble, don't want to tell yer no lie,
But I saw yer lover about an hour ago, makin' love to Nellie Bligh,
He is your man, but he was doin' yer wrong.'

Nellie didn't have the nipped-in waist of the famous Mae West – in fact Nellie didn't have a waist at all! But her swaying hips, the sultry voice and the trademark curling lip were spot on. To all those people crowded into the tiny living room of the two-up two-down terrace house, it was as good as sitting in the best specks at the Liverpool Empire.

She finished to thunderous, rafter-raising applause and foot-stamping, and she loved it. With her hand on her tummy, she bowed to the four corners of the room, giving a delighted Miss Clegg a special wink. Then she held up her hand for silence. 'Now for my grand finale.'

George was wiping his red-rimmed eyes when Nellie swayed towards him in slow motion. With her hands on her hips and her eyes narrowed, she spoke out of the side of her mouth. 'Why don't yer come up and see me sometime, big boy?'

'Behave yerself, Nellie.' George could appreciate his wife when he was one of the crowd, but not when she put him in the spotlight.

'D'yer know what?' Nellie stood in front of him, shaking her head. 'I bet if Mae West herself walked in, yer wouldn't turn a ruddy hair!'

'Take no notice of him, sunshine, we all thought yer were great.' Molly rubbed her aching ribs. 'Yer best performance to date, I'd say. We'll see yer name up in lights yet.'

'Yeah, an' when I've made it big I'll remember who me best mates are, so watch it. When me name's up outside a big London theatre in flashing bulbs, only me very best friends will get complimentary tickets to come and see me.'

'Nellie, there's no lights flashin' anywhere these days, so why don't yer settle for the Metropole in Stanley Road? It's only tuppence on the tram from here.' Molly pursed her lips. 'Trouble is, yer can't get rotten eggs for love nor money, so we'd have nowt to throw at yer.'

Never lost for an answer, Nellie jerked her thumb at Jack. 'Yer can throw your feller at me! They say a change is as good as a rest. An' I might find out the secret of that smile yer sometimes have on yer face first thing in the morning. I've often wondered about that smile, girl! Perhaps Jack knows somethin' my feller doesn't.'

Molly noticed Ruthie sitting cross-legged on the floor, her eyes watching and her ears listening. If Nellie wasn't shut up now, as sure as eggs she'd come out with something that shouldn't be said in front of the young ones. 'Now there's a lull in the proceedings, I think we'll have somethin' to eat.' Molly pushed herself up from her chair. 'Then our Ruthie can go to bed: it's way past her bedtime.'

'Shall I give yer a hand, Auntie Molly?' Rosie was still standing in front of the fireplace. 'As me mammy always says, many hands make light work.'

'Your mammy doesn't know my back kitchen, sunshine!

Get three people in there an' yer can't move.' Molly gave her a smile. 'Thanks for the offer, but Jill an' Doreen have got everythin' organized.'

Miss Clegg was deep in conversation with Bridie and Bob, and Steve was listening to his father and Jack exchanging views on the worsening situation in Europe. This left Rosie on her own, and gave Malcolm the opportunity he'd been waiting for. 'Have yer tanner ready,' he said with a smirk before sauntering over to Rosie.

'I really enjoyed yer singin' and dancing.'

'Thank you!' Rosie said with a smile. 'Sure it's kind of yer to say so, and I'm pleased yer got pleasure out of it.'

Ginger prodded Tommy in the ribs. 'Yer shouldn't leave Rosie on her own with that smarmy so-and-so.'

'She seems to be enjoyin' his company, she's got a smile on her face,' Tommy said. 'Anyway, she's got a tongue in her head, she can tell him to scram if she wants to.'

'I'm surprised at her, I thought she had more sense than to fall for his patter.' He suddenly straightened up. 'She's certainly not smilin' now, Tommy! In fact she doesn't look very happy at all.'

Tommy looked over to see Rosie looking red in the face and not in a happy frame of mind. If it was up to him he'd let her get on with it. She usually said what she thought and to hell with the consequences, so why was she putting up with Malcolm's shenanigans?

Tommy sighed. If his workmate upset Rosie he'd get it in the neck off his nan, so he'd better see what was going on. He walked up and stood behind Malcolm, just close enough to hear what was being said.

'Go on, change yer mind,' Malcolm said. 'We can go to the pictures one night an' I'll show yer a good time.'

Behind his back, Tommy was shaking his head and mouthing, 'Say no!'

'It's kind of yer to ask, Malcolm, and I'd not like yer to

think I didn't appreciate it.' Rosie's eyes never flickered. 'But yer see, I already have a boyfriend.'

Malcolm was taken aback. 'Tommy never said yer had a boyfriend!' Then he smiled. 'You're pullin' me leg.'

'Now why would I be doin' a thing like that?' Rosie didn't return his smile. 'Tommy Bennett doesn't know yet that I've got a boyfriend, and I'll not be tellin' him until I'm good and ready.'

Tommy walked back to Ginger. 'She's put him in his place – I'll be gettin' me tanner off him.' But he was puzzled. She had sounded dead serious about having a boyfriend, but how could she when she was round here every night making a nuisance of herself? Perhaps it was someone she'd met at work and hadn't told his nan yet. Yeah, that was probably it. Anyway, it had nowt to do with him, she was free to do as she chose. One thing Tommy was sure of, when Malcolm went out of that door tonight he'd never get back in again. He wasn't to be trusted where women were concerned. Not that Rosie was a woman, but to be fair, with her birthday in three weeks, she was as near to being a woman as he was a man.

'What yer thinkin' about, Tommy?' Ginger asked. 'Yer looked as though yer were miles away.'

'I was just thinkin' that girls don't grow up as quick as men. I mean, at sixteen they still behave like little girls, always wantin' their own way. Real childish they are, and bossy into the bargain.'

'Your Jill and Doreen aren't like that,' Ginger said. 'I think they're very sensible for their ages.'

'Oh, yeah, they are! I didn't mean them, I was thinkin' of the queer one.' Tommy nodded to where Rosie was once again seated between Bridie and Bob. 'She's dead childish and a real bossy-boots if ever there was one.'

'I don't agree with yer,' Ginger said. 'I like Rosie.'

'Ay, well, you always were a bit daft in the head.' Tommy punched his best mate on the shoulder.

'Ay, out!' Ginger gave him a dig. 'Here's Clark Gable. D'yer think yer'll get yer tanner off him?'

'I'm sure of it!' Tommy laughed. 'I'll threaten to tell all his workmates that he didn't cop off if he doesn't. That should do the trick.'

Chapter Twenty-One

It was a lovely sunny afternoon in May. The sky was a clear blue, dotted with fluffy white clouds floating like balls of cotton wool. Molly and Nellie, arms linked, were on their way back from the shops when the air-raid warning sounded.

'Oh, no, not again!' Molly wailed, as she began to quicken her step. 'If it's another false alarm, I'll spit.'

'They can sod off, girl, 'cos I'm not goin' to the shelter,' Nellie panted. 'It's takin' me all me time to breathe now, I'm sweatin' cobs! I'll never make it that far.'

'Ye're comin' if I've got to carry yer,' Molly said. 'I know we've never had a proper air raid, with bombs and that, but yer never know the minute an' I'm not takin' any chances.'

Nellie stopped in her tracks, her chubby face creased in a grin. 'If ye're goin' to carry me, girl, then I'll come with pleasure. Yer might not be able to get yer arms around me, so yer'd be best givin' me a piggyback.'

'Nellie, will yer get a move on! I'll just open me front door and we'll throw our shoppin' in the hall.'

'You run on, girl, I haven't got the breath to hurry.'

'I'm not leavin' yer, so get that into yer head. Here, give me yer basket an' I'll put it in our hall. We won't hurry to the shelter, just walk at a nice steady pace an' yer'll be all right.'

Molly hurried ahead with the two baskets, and after opening her front door she set them down in the hall. She waited for her friend to catch up and held out her arm. 'Stick yer leg in, sunshine, and we'll take it nice an' easy.'

They were halfway up the street when the all-clear siren sounded. 'Well what would that give yer?' Molly whistled through clenched teeth. 'Sometimes I think they only do it to keep us on our toes. Anyway, let's get back and have a nice sit-down an' a cup of tea. We'll go to your house for a change, seein' as it's nearest.'

Nellie gave her a sly look. 'But yer've put me shoppin' in your 'ouse, so we may as well kill two birds with one stone. Be daft to come to mine and then 'ave to go to yours. No point in wearin' out me shoe leather.'

'Ye're a crafty article, Nellie McDonough,' Molly said. 'But I'll catch yer out one of these days.'

'Yer'll have to be up with the larks to do that, girl! Still, don't let me stop yer from trying.'

Later, sitting at Molly's table, Nellie tilted her head. 'Did yer know that one in number sixteen has got herself a job?'

'No, I haven't heard nothing.'

'Yeah, I believe she's got a job in Reece's.'

'Who's looking after her kids, then? They're young to be left on their own when they come home from school.'

'I haven't found out that much yet, she only started this week.'

'She probably needs the money.' Molly curled her hands around the cup. 'Her husband was one of the first to be called up, him bein' in the Territorials. Army pay's not very much, so she's probably feelin' the pinch.'

'I can't say I like her,' Nellie said. 'She's a fly turn if ever there was one. Never has much to say to the women in the street, but always a smile an' a word for the men.'

'Some women are like that.' Molly pulled a face. 'Can't see a man without goin' all coy and fluttering their eyelashes. She probably doesn't know she's doin' it. An' at least she hasn't run off with anyone's husband.'

'My feller avoids her like the plague,' Nellie grinned. 'She frightens the life out of him, he thinks she's after his body.'

'Oh, she's not that bad! At least she keeps her house and kids neat and tidy.' Molly was silent for a while. Then she said, 'It's funny yer should bring her up 'cos when I saw her daughter, Sheila, yesterday, I was surprised how big she'd grown. She must be about nine now, an' it seems no time since she was a baby in a pram. Just shows how quickly time flies over.'

'Ye're right there, girl! I was only thinkin' about that last night, lying in bed.' Nellie's chubby cheeks moved upwards. 'Now there's proof that time's passing us by. At one time I wouldn't be lying in bed thinking, I'd be too busy being otherwise engaged. But my feller's too tired these days to rise to the occasion, if yer follow me meaning. It's a pity, 'cos I'm never too tired for a bit of you-know-what.'

'Yer've got a one-track mind, Nellie McDonough!' Molly grinned. 'The older yer get, the worse yer are.'

'I could get a bloody sight worse if someone would give me the chance! I've told George, if he doesn't pull his socks up I'll be takin' me passion elsewhere.'

'What did George say to that?'

Nellie chuckled. 'Said he'd give me the address of one of the blokes he works with.'

'Everything slows down when yer get to our age, sunshine! The men are not so young any more, an' they're both workin' all the hours God sends.'

'I bet your Jack hasn't slowed down as much as my George! I can tell you're not frustrated in the love stakes 'cos every Monday mornin' ye're walking around with a grin on yer face.'

Molly leaned across the table. 'Before yer ask, Nellie, the answer is no, you cannot borrow my husband.'

'Ye're a real meanie, you are, girl! I share everythin' I've got with you, 'cos that's what best mates do.'

'Well, that beats the band, that does!' Molly rested her back on the chair. 'When have you done any sharing? Two weeks ago, when it was our Doreen's seventeenth birthday, it just so happened that your Lily's birthday was just a few days after. Did you have a party for your Lily? Did you heckers like! No point in havin' two parties, yer said, we'll all come to Doreen's! So once again muggins here was left with all the work an' the worry.'

'Ay, well, yer see, girl, I'm not as good at givin' parties as you are. An' my house isn't as posh as yours, either! That's why I've decided to let you have the party next week for Jill and Steve. Yer haven't forgotten it's their birthdays, have yer, girl? Yer see, I wouldn't want to let me son down.'

Molly slowly shook her head. 'I must want me ruddy bumps feelin'! I fall for it every time!' She tried to look indignant but couldn't keep the humour from her voice. 'Seein' as your son will soon be my son-in-law, I wouldn't dream of lettin' him down.'

'An' as your Jill will one day be my daughter-in-law, I wouldn't dream of lettin' her down.'

'What are yer goin' to do, then?' Molly asked.

'How d'yer mean, girl, what am I goin' to do?'

'Yer just said yer wouldn't dream of lettin' Jill down, so what is it ye're goin' to do so as not to let her down?'

Nellie leaned her elbows on the table and cupped her chin on a podgy hand. Her eyes squinting, she gazed at Molly for a few seconds. Then she said, 'Yer've lost me, girl! I haven't a ruddy clue what ye're on about! What yer've just said is all double Dutch to me.'

'Well, I'll pretend it's Ruthie I'm talking to an' I'll speak slowly, OK?' Molly waited for her friend to nod. 'You are not going to let Jill down, are you?'

Nellie's chins did a dance as she shook her head. 'No, I certainly am not!'

'So what are you goin' to do to make sure you don't let her down?'

Nellie's face brightened. 'I've got it now, girl! I know what ye're on about!'

Molly pinched her nose and prayed for patience. 'Then tell me what you are going to do.'

'That's easy, that is!' Nellie looked very pleased with herself. 'I'm goin' to make sure you give her a good party so she won't feel let down.'

'Making sure I don't let her down is hardly the same thing as you not lettin' her down, is it? I mean, it's no hardship to you, yer don't even have to get off yer flamin' backside!'

Nellie pulled on her bottom lip. 'Sometimes I wonder whether Steve is doin' the right thing in marryin' your Jill. Oh, it's not that I've got anythin' against Jill, I love her to bits. It's you I'm worried about, girl, an' that temper of yours.'

Molly began to chuckle. 'D'yer realize, sunshine, that we've sat here for half an hour talkin', and said precisely nothing? It takes some doin', that does.'

'It's passed the time away, girl, if nothin' else. An' we—'

A loud rat-tat on the knocker stopped Nellie in mid-sentence. 'Are yer expectin' visitors, girl?'

'It'll be Tucker, I'd almost forgotten about him.' Molly reached into the drawer for her purse. 'Do you want to see him, or shall I tell him to throw a bag in your coal place?'

'I'll come an' see what the coal's like.' Nellie heaved herself off the chair. 'If it's anything like last week's he can keep it, 'cos it was all slate.'

Molly spoke over her shoulder as she walked down the hall. 'If he's got one, I'm gettin' a bag of nutty slack.'

But the coalman didn't wait for Molly to give her order; he was too full of nervous excitement. 'Have yer got yer wireless on, Molly?'

Molly shook her head. 'No, why?'

'The Germans have started. They're bombing airfields in Holland and Belgium.'

Molly felt her heart skip a beat. 'Is it on the wireless now?'

Tucker shrugged his shoulders. 'I think it was a news bulletin. I just happened to be in the dairy when it came on.' He looked angry. 'I wondered when the buggers would start. They've been too quiet for my liking.'

Molly felt herself being pushed down the step as Nellie faced Tucker. 'Isn't anyone fightin' back? Surely they've got some aeroplanes in those countries?'

'The announcer on the wireless said they don't have all the details yet, news was just coming through.' Tucker ran the back of his hand across a brow black with coal dust. 'From the sound of it, it was a surprise raid, catching everyone on the hop. Dozens of German bomber planes were involved, and if there was no opposition, yer can bet yer sweet life those airfields will have been razed to the ground.' He shook his head sadly. 'Yer've got to hand it to Hitler, he knows exactly how to cripple a country. Put the airfields out of action an' no planes can take off or land.'

'It might not be that bad,' Molly said, hopefully. 'I mean, someone must have tried to stop them. They wouldn't just stand there watchin' without puttin' up some sort of fight, surely?'

'I just don't know,' Tucker sighed. 'I don't think two little countries like Holland and Belgium stand an earthly against the Germans. It's like putting your Ruthie up against Corker!'

Molly began to rub the side of her nose, a habit she had when she was worried or upset. 'The wireless is not goin' on until my Jack comes home. I'm not sittin' on me own listenin' to bad news an' worryin' meself sick.'

'I'll sit with yer, girl!' Nellie said, for once a serious expression on her face as she thought of Steve. So far he'd been exempt from call-up because of his job, but if the war started in earnest they'd be bound to call up all the young ones. Already factories were employing older people and women to take over from the men who were being conscripted. 'I'd like to know proper what's goin' on.'

'I'm not puttin' the wireless on, Nellie, so if yer want to hear the news yer can do it in yer own house.' Molly opened her purse and took out a ten-shilling note. 'Throw us a bag of nutty slack in, Tucker, please.'

The coalman whistled to his horse who was standing a few houses away. 'What about you, Nellie?'

'If the coal's anythin' like last week, yer can stick it where Paddy stuck his nuts. It was a waste of money, all ruddy slate.'

When Tucker smiled, white teeth gleamed in his black face. 'One thing about you, Nellie, yer don't pull any punches, do yer?'

'Not when I'm ruddy well forkin' out for it, no!'

'It's good-quality coal I've got, an' I'll advise yer to take it, Nellie, 'cos I can't promise havin' any at all next week . . . good, bad or indifferent!'

Molly held out her hand. 'Can I have me change, Tucker, so I can go in an' get some work done? What with goin' to the shops, then sittin' jangling with me mate for over an hour, I haven't done a tap in the house.'

Nellie shook her head. 'Sucker for punishment, yer are, girl! Always lookin' for ruddy work!' She turned her eyes on Tucker. 'Her house is like a new pin, but I'll bet yer a pound to a pinch of snuff she'll be at it all afternoon. She'll either have a mop in her hand, a scrubbin' brush or a duster.'

Molly grinned. 'It'll be a scrubbin' brush, sunshine, so I can take me temper out on the kitchen floor. And when I'm wringing me floor cloth out, I'll pretend it's Hitler's flamin' neck!'

'Can I come an' watch yer, girl? Just watchin' yer would tire me out and when I go to bed tonight I'll be able to sleep instead of tossin' and turnin'.'

Oh, lord, thought Molly, she's going to talk about the lack

of activity in their bedroom . . . in front of Tucker, too! I'd better get away from here quick, before she starts. I don't know where to put me face sometimes, the things she comes out with.

Molly put the change in her purse and smiled at Tucker before turning to her friend. 'I'm goin' in now, sunshine, an' I don't want to see yer face again until tonight . . . OK?'

'Charmin', that is!' Nellie screwed up her face. 'So if I put me wireless on an' there's some news, yer don't want me to come an' tell yer?'

'No!' Molly stepped into her hall. 'I'll see yer next week, Tucker. Ta-ra for now.'

She was about to close the door when Nellie called, 'OK, if that's the way yer want it! I won't knock on your ruddy door this afternoon even if I hear the war's over . . . so there!'

Apart from the newsreader's voice and the occasional spark from the fire, there was complete silence in the room as the whole family gathered around the wireless set. Afraid to speak in case they missed something, the expressions on their faces told of the horror, disbelief and anger they felt. Listening to the reports of the bombing of the airfields in Holland and Belgium, Jack could hardly contain himself.

Only now were the true facts emerging, of the extent of the damage caused by the dozens of German planes which had razed the airfields, making it impossible for aircraft to take off or land. So unexpected were the raids, the Dutch and Belgian pilots were caught off their guard, and the planes standing on the airfields were bombed to smithereens. At the same time as the bombing raids were taking place, German airborne troops landed in Belgium and captured a bridge over the Albert Canal, giving them access to the sea.

'Well,' said Jack, reaching for his packet of Woodbines, 'the war's started in earnest now, that's for sure! Those two countries won't be able to hold out for long, that's a nap, so pretty soon Hitler can add them to the list of countries he's already taken over.' He struck a match, drew on his cigarette, then flicked the spent match into the grate. 'He's a bastard and a half, that man.'

Doreen leaned forward, her forehead creased in a frown. 'Dad, is that anywhere near where Phil is?'

'No, love, Phil's in France. As far as I know, we've no troops in Holland or Belgium.'

Doreen didn't draw any comfort from his words. She missed Phil and wished he was home, but until now the war had been merely an inconvenience, she'd never dreamt he could be in danger. 'Well, won't Hitler start on France if the other countries give up?'

Steve was sitting next to Jill, holding her hand. His insides were turning over, knowing that what had happened today was only the start. But he could see the worry on Doreen's face and didn't want to add to it. He gave her a dimpled grin, saying, 'France is bigger than Holland and Belgium put together, soft girl.' He wasn't quite sure whether that was true, but if a little lie eased the worry, it was worth it. 'An' they're better prepared. They've got the Maginot line, and experts say nothing or no one could get past that.'

Molly could see Jack's nerves were on edge. He wouldn't say what was on his mind for fear of upsetting her or the girls. He wouldn't worry about Tommy so much, because the war was something that meant excitement to his son. Almost like the cowboys and Indians films he used to love so much. In the Saturday matinée Lone Ranger series, the film always ended at an exciting bit, like when the Ranger was shot off his horse and they had to wait till the following week to find out what happened to him. He never got killed, the popular cowboy, he was always there the next week riding into danger again to help an underdog. So real men being killed with real bullets was something that Tommy couldn't visualize.

'Steve?' Jack threw his cigarette-end into the fire. 'D'yer

think yer dad would fancy a pint? We'd only have time for one, it's gettin' near closing time.'

'Yeah, he'll probably be glad of a pint! D'yer want me to go an' ask him?'

'I'll come with you.' Jill stood up, pulling on Steve's hand. She was frightened the time wasn't far off when he'd be called up, and she wanted to spend as much time as she could with him. Time on their own, where he could hold her close and tell her how much he loved her. 'We can go for a little walk after we've called at yours, get a bit of fresh air.'

'I'll come out with yer.' Tommy stood up. 'May as well go up to Ginger's for an hour.'

'Don't be too late, son,' Molly said. 'The number of hours you're working, yer need to get as much sleep as yer can.'

Tommy dropped a kiss on her forehead. 'I'll be back before me dad, don't worry.'

Tommy was reaching for the brass knocker on his friend's house when the wail of the air-raid siren filled the night. It was the first time the alarm had sounded at night and it gave Tommy a start, bringing his hand down to his side. His first thought was for his mother, but then he remembered his dad would still be at home and he'd see the family got to the shelter safely. They were probably getting Ruthie out of bed right this minute. But what about his nan and grandad? He knew they sought shelter every time the warning sounded, but up till now the alarms had been during the day – this was the first one they'd ever had at night. Tommy hesitated. Rosie was there, she'd see his grandparents were all right. But then their faces came into his mind, and fear for their safety had him moving quickly away from Ginger's house. What if his grandad had another heart attack with the fright? Rosie couldn't cope with that on her own.

Doors were opening and people were spilling out on to the street as Tommy quickly covered the ground. Eyes were turned towards the sky, looking for the sight and sound of enemy planes. If it hadn't been for the news of the German raids on Holland and Belgium that same day, most of the folk wouldn't have stirred from their beds or their fireplaces. But the war had been brought closer to home and a warning wasn't to be ignored. So children, still half asleep, were being carried or pulled along in the direction of the underground shelter. Better to be safe than sorry.

Rosie opened the door to Tommy's knock. 'Oh, 'tis yerself.' For once there was no smile of welcome, no lighting up of the deep blue eyes. 'We're almost ready, then we're going up to the shelter.'

'I just came to see if me nan and grandad are all right,' Tommy said gruffly, following her down the hall. 'Thought they might need a hand.'

Bridie was slipping her arms into her coat. 'Hello, Tommy, sweetheart! Sure, what a performance this is! Twice in one day, no less.'

Bob greeted him with a smile. 'That shelter is becoming like a second home. But we're lucky, thank God, it's only at the top of the road.'

'We'd have been out by now,' Bridie told him, 'but we were undressed, ready for bed.'

Rosie was fussing over Bridie, making sure all the buttons on her coat were fastened. 'I told you to go as you were, with yer coat over yer nightdress, but yer wouldn't have it. No one would have taken a blind bit of notice of yer, but sure it's a proud woman yer are, Auntie Bridget, and that's the truth of it.'

Tommy could feel his irritation growing. Anyone would think it was her nan and grandad, and that this was her home! A little voice in his head told him he was being unreasonable, but he silenced it. Rosie O'Grady was a thorn in his flesh and always would be.

After making sure Bob's scarf was folded across his chest

and his coat collar was turned up, Rosie cast her eyes on Tommy. 'Seein' as ye're a fine strong man, Tommy Bennett, yer can carry the bundle that's at the bottom of the stairs. An' yer can give an arm to Uncle Bob while I see to Auntie Bridget.'

Tommy opened his mouth to ask her just who she thought she was ordering around, but he closed it quickly. There was no point in upsetting his grandparents, not when they both looked so tired and frail.

The shelter was quite full, and it was Rosie who pushed her way to the far end in search of a space on one of the wooden benches built into the side walls for Bridie and Bob to sit. Tommy thought she was wasting her time because all the benches were occupied, but he'd reckoned without Rosie's determination. 'Can I ask yer if yer'd be kind enough to move along a bit, please. Sure, there's enough room for another two people on there, so there is.'

There was some low grumbling and mumbling as people moved closer together, but with Rosie smiling down at them with a purposeful expression on her face, no one refused.

'There yer are, Auntie Bridget, sit yerself down. Come on, Uncle Bob, there's room enough for you.' Rosie waited until they were settled, then turned to Tommy and held out her hand. 'The bag, please?'

Tommy watched her plumping the cushions before putting them behind Bridie and Bob so they didn't have to lean back on the cold concrete. And as she was tucking a blanket around their knees, he had to admit to a sneaking admiration for her. He'd never have had the nerve to make those people move, and never in a million years would he have thought of bringing blankets and cushions to keep them warm and comfortable. She was still a pain in the neck, and a bossy-boots into the bargain, but she did have some good points.

Rosie was kneeling down in front of Bob, rubbing one of his hands between her own. 'Are yer feeling all right, Uncle Bob?'

'I'm fine, lass, thank you. Just a bit tired, that's all.'

As Bridie kept a watchful eye on her husband, she asked herself how she could follow the doctor's orders and keep this stress from him. If it was in her power she would move heaven and earth for the man she adored, but she had no control over the blasted air-raid siren.

Tommy knelt down next to Rosie. 'It won't be long now, Grandad, yer'll soon be tucked up nice and warm in bed.'

They heard Nellie's voice before they saw her. 'Here they are, girl! Your Tommy's with them.'

Molly was yawning as she came towards them. 'Some life this is, isn't it?' She eyed her parents anxiously. 'I knew yer'd be here, 'cos I knocked on yer door as we were passing.'

'Where's Jack and the children?' Bridie asked. 'They're all here, I hope?'

'Yeah, they're down by the entrance with Nellie's gang. It was our Tommy I was worried about, but I see he's safe and sound. I thought you were goin' to Ginger's, son?'

'I was on me way there when the siren went, so I walked round to me nan's to see if they needed a hand.'

'Ay, Bridie, ye're lucky to 'ave a seat, aren't yer?' Nellie grinned. 'Or have yez been here since this afternoon?'

'Rosie got them the seats.' The words were out before Tommy could stop them. He blushed from the neck upwards. 'She made all the people move up to make room for them.'

'Good on yer, girl!' Nellie's tummy started to shake. 'D'yer think yer can shift a whole bench, so I can sit down?'

'Ah, 'tis a young bit of a thing yer are, Auntie Nellie,' Rosie beamed. 'Ye're well able to stand.'

Tommy was still kneeling, and his face was on a level with hers when he turned. And it suddenly hit him between the eyes . . . she really was very pretty! He was both surprised and annoyed at the discovery. OK, so she was pretty! It was when she opened her mouth that she spoiled things!

It was ten past twelve when the all-clear went. They'd heard planes going over, but that was all. And as Jack said, they were probably our own planes.

Tommy took the blanket from Bob's knees and folded it up. He passed it to Rosie to put in the bag before reaching for the cushion. It was then he noticed his grandad swaying as though he didn't have enough energy to stand. 'I'll come back with yer an' see to me grandad,' he said. 'An' I'll carry the bag.'

Molly had also noticed the drooping of her father's shoulders and the lines etched on his face. 'Shall I come with yer? Jack can see to Ruthie and put her back to bed.'

'No, lass, we'll be all right,' Bridie said. 'You've got to be up early to see to all the breakfasts, so you need a few hours' sleep. There's no rush for us, we can have an extra hour in bed.'

Tommy touched his mother's arm. 'I'll see they're all right, Mam. I won't leave until they're settled down.'

Molly's eyes were tender as she smiled and touched his cheek. 'Ye're a good son, an' I love the bones of yer.' She kissed her mam and dad, then hugged Rosie. 'I'll get back and sort my lot out, but I'll slip round in the mornin' to see if yer need anything.'

Rosie took charge when Molly and Nellie had left. 'Sit down for a few minutes until the crowds have gone. Sure, I'll not be havin' yer pushed and shoved, an' that's the top and bottom of it.'

When there were only a few stragglers left, they made their way out of the shelter into the fresh night air. 'That's good,' Bob said, 'I always feel as though I'm suffocating in that blasted concrete monstrosity.'

Tommy could hear his grandad's laboured breathing and kept to a snail's pace. 'You two go on ahead, we'll catch you up.'

Rosie, walking in front with Bridie, turned her head. 'Sure there's no need to rush, we'll all walk together.'

As soon as they got in the house, Rosie took command. 'Now off to bed, the pair of yer! Ye're almost asleep on yer feet! By the time yer've undressed I'll be up with a cup of cocoa and a hot-water bottle to warm yer feet on.'

Tommy knelt down to undo his grandad's shoelaces. 'She's a right little bossy-boots, isn't she?'

Bob slipped his shoes off and eased his feet into the carpet slippers Tommy had lifted from their place inside the fender. 'I'm a lucky man, son, to have two beautiful women waiting on me. What more could any man ask for?' He stood up and reached for his wife's hand. 'I think we're both ready for bed. I can't wait to get me head down.'

Tommy followed them out of the room and watched them climb the stairs. He felt sad when he saw Bob pulling himself up by the banister, as though mounting every step was an effort. He would have given him a hand, but he knew it would dent the old man's pride. They were too old to have to put up with this, and if there'd been a German handy, Tommy would have willingly throttled him. 'Goodnight and God bless, Nan and Grandad. Sleep tight and mind the fleas don't bite!'

Rosie came up behind him. 'Don't go yet, Tommy, I want to have a word with yer. I'll not keep yer long, the kettle's been on the hob since we went out so it won't take two shakes for the water to boil.'

Tommy sat in his grandad's chair. He heard Rosie rattling around in the kitchen, then watched her hurry through with a steaming cup in each hand and a hot-water bottle under her arm. He wondered what she wanted to talk to him about, because they had no shared interests, nothing in common. Anyway, whatever it was she'd better make it snappy because he had to be up early for work.

He was still pondering when Rosie came back into the room. 'They're sitting up in bed having their drink, and then they'll be fast asleep in no time.'

'What d'yer want to talk to me about?' Tommy asked. He

was so embarrassed at being alone with her, his words were abrupt. 'I haven't got all night yer know, I've got to leave for work before half-seven.'

'Hasn't everyone got a job to go to?' Rosie said with spirit. 'Sure, is it always yerself yer think about, Tommy Bennett? Have yer no thoughts for anyone else?'

'Look, I'm not sittin' arguing with yer at this time of night. Whatever it is, spit it out.'

'I've a good mind to tell yer to be on yer way, Tommy Bennett! Such a bad-tempered person yer are! If it weren't for Auntie Bridget and Uncle Bob, I'd be showin' yer the door, so I would.'

'What have me nan and grandad got to do with it? There's nothin' wrong with them, is there?'

Rosie took a deep breath and sat in the chair facing him. 'They're altogether too old to be runnin' up and down to the shelter, it'll be the death of them, so it will. An' I worry about them when I'm at work. Uncle Bob isn't well enough to have all this upset.'

Tommy nodded. 'I know, but what can we do about it? It isn't safe for them to stay here in case we start havin' proper raids.'

'I was wondering how to go about getting them one of those shelters that yer have in the house. One of the girls I work with was tellin' me her grandma has one. They're like a table and yer can sit underneath them when there's a raid on. Me friend said they're very strong and as safe as houses.'

Tommy gazed around the room. 'Me nan wouldn't like her room upset, yer know how house-proud she is.'

'If the Germans start dropping bombs, which is more important? A nice house, or a safe house?' Rosie leaned forward, her brow furrowed. 'Tommy, I know yer think I'm an eejit, without a brain in me head, but just for once can yer not be putting aside yer feelings for me and think about those two old people upstairs? I see more of them than you do, and

I'm tellin' yer that while Auntie Bridget is fit and well for her age, Uncle Bob certainly isn't. If we could get them a shelter for here it would be a godsend, and it would put my mind at rest, so it would.' She pushed a lock of hair from her eyes. 'Would yer have a word with Auntie Molly for me? See if she can find out how to go about getting one?'

'I'll have a word with me mam in the mornin' before I go to work, and ask her to make some inquiries.' The idea of something that would keep his grandparents safe was taking hold in Tommy's mind. And with it came the urgency to act quickly. It was no use waiting until the bombs started dropping, it would be too late then. 'What do they call these shelters, d'yer know?'

'I think me friend said they were Anderson shelters.' Rosie stood up, rubbing her knuckles over eyes so tired she could barely keep them open. 'Yer can go now, Tommy. I've shared me worry with yer and I feel easier in me mind. I've been goin' to mention it to yer mam a few times, but didn't want to worry her. But after what's happened today, I couldn't keep me fears to meself any longer.'

Tommy stood up, feeling awkward . . . all arms and legs. 'I'll tell me mam to start asking around tomorrow. If yer come to ours tomorrow night, she can let yer know how she got on.'

'I might be round tomorrow night, and I might not,' Rosie said. 'It depends upon the lie of the land.'

Crimson with embarrassment, Tommy walked towards the door. 'I'll see yer, then, Rosie. Goodnight.'

Rosie made no move to show him out. 'Goodnight, Tommy. Close the door quietly behind yer in case the old folk are asleep.'

Chapter Twenty-Two

Nellie was in a flap when she came down for her morning cup of tea. 'I've only gone and ruined the blasted dinner, haven't I, girl! I put the pan on a low light at seven o'clock and thought I'd leave it to cook slowly for a couple of hours.' She pulled a chair from under the table and sat down heavily, much to the disgust of the chair which creaked in protest. 'Then, like the silly sod I am, I forgot about the ruddy thing! At least I didn't forget it, not when I was goin' out. But I thought I'd only be gone five minutes, yer see. It was when I was out I forgot about it, an' now the backside is burned out of the pan and the dinner's ruined.'

'Nellie, will yer calm down so I can keep up with yer?' Molly put the teapot on its stand and covered it with the knitted cosy. 'Yer put yer dinner on at seven, right?'

'That's right, girl! I know full well it was seven because George put the wireless on an' they said the time.' She wiped the back of her hand across her brow. 'An' them fellers on the wireless are never wrong, are they, girl?'

'Nellie, before we go through the whole rigmarole properly, just tell me what the feller on the wireless has got to do with the backside bein' burned out of your pan?'

Nellie's eyes disappeared when she frowned. Picking at her bottom lip, she said, 'I'm not blamin' him for me pan bein' burned! I never said that, girl, I never said it was his fault.'

'No, you never did!' Molly spoke with infinite patience. 'I just wondered where he came into it.'

'Well, he was the one who said it was seven o'clock!'

Molly took the tea cosy off and stirred the tea with a spoon. The ration of tea they were allowed didn't run to making a nice strong cup, so they had to leave it to brew for longer in the pot. She put the lid back on, laid the spoon in her saucer, then cast her eyes on Nellie. 'If yer've burned yer dinner, it doesn't really make much difference whether yer put it on the stove at seven, half-seven or eight o'clock! Right?'

'All right, girl, there's no need to get on yer high horse! It's my flamin' dinner that's ruined, not yours!'

'That's the first bit of information I can understand! It can't be my flamin' dinner, 'cos I haven't got it on yet!' Molly couldn't hold it in any longer and her shoulders began to shake with laughter. 'Ooh, yer should see your face, Nellie, it's a picture, it really is!'

'I'm glad you can see the funny side of it, girl, 'cos I'm blowed if I can! Then again, it's not your dinner that's ruined, is it? My family will be comin' home from work to fresh air sandwiches, an' they won't be very happy about that!' Nellie had to direct her temper at something, so she pointed to the teapot. 'That ruddy tea will be stiff by the time we get it. I'll be takin' me custom elsewhere if yer don't buck yer ideas up, Mrs Bennett. I wouldn't have to wait this long in Reece's or the Kardomah.'

As Molly poured the tea, she said, 'Without any larking about, sunshine, how did yer manage to burn yer dinner?'

'Oh, it was quite easy, really! All I had to do was go out for an hour and forget about it!' Nellie clicked her tongue on the roof of her mouth. 'Yer don't half ask some daft questions, girl, honest! Anyone would think I'd done it on purpose!'

'I might ask daft questions, but you do daft things! Fancy goin' out and forgettin' yer'd left the pan on!' Molly handed a cup over. 'Where were yer for an hour, anyway? Yer know ye're not supposed to go anywhere without me.'

'Well seein' as yer forgot to put me lead on, I took advantage of me freedom and went all the way up to the corner shop on me own. Wasn't that daring of me, girl?' Nellie bit hard on the inside of her cheek to keep the smile away, but it didn't work. Then the smile turned into a hearty chuckle. 'Yer'll die laughin' when yer get an earful of this! I only went up to Maisie's for an Oxo cube to put in me stew, and when I came back an hour later it was to find I didn't need the ruddy Oxo because I had no flamin' stew to put it in!'

Tears of laughter rolled down Molly's face. Thank God for her mate! No matter what the situation, Nellie could get a laugh out of it. And Molly had been in need of a laugh after yesterday. What with the bad news about the war, having to go to the shelter until after midnight, then listening to their Tommy this morning asking about getting a shelter for her parents because they were too old to be rushing out every time the siren went. It was enough to give anyone the gripes.

'What in the name of God took you an hour to get one fiddling little Oxo cube? I know Maisie can be busy in the mornings, but I've never waited an hour to be served.'

'Well, yer know what it's like when yer start talkin', yer forget all about time. Mrs Greenfield came in, then Vera Marshall and Barney's wife . . . we had a right old natter.'

'Yer mean a right old gossip, don't yer?' Molly wagged a finger. 'I hope George and the children don't mind listening to a bit of gossip instead of gettin' a dinner.'

'Oh, they'll get a dinner, I'll think of something.'

'Such as?' Molly raised her brows. 'Yer've no meat coupons left.'

There was a crafty look in Nellie's eyes. 'What are you havin' for dinner, girl?'

'Yer know what we're havin', yer were with me when I bought the mince. I'm makin' a mince and onion pie.'

Nellie licked her lips. 'Ooh, ye're makin' me mouth water, girl! Yer don't half make tasty pies.'

'Don't be tryin' to get round me, sunshine, 'cos I only got

three quarters of mince.' Molly tilted her head to one side. 'Can't yer save any of yer stew?'

'No,' Nellie said, her chins quivering to emphasize her words. 'It was all burned on the bottom, stuck to the ruddy pan. I scraped the top part off and put it in another pan, thinkin' it would be all right if I added some water and an onion, but when I tasted it, yeuch, it was terrible. If I served it up to George he'd throw it at me.'

As she gazed at her friend, Molly remembered the times when they'd been so skint they couldn't afford meat, so they'd made blind stew and shared it between the two families. They'd shared everything in those dark days, even a loaf of bread, a cup of sugar or a shovelful of coal. And they'd shared their heartaches and their laughter.

'I've got some carrots and turnip in, so I'll split the mince in half and make two pans of stew. With onion and barley in, they won't notice the lack of meat.'

'No! I was only kiddin', girl! I wouldn't let yer do that!' Nellie's mouth drooped at the corners. 'I'll get down to the shops and see what I can scrounge.'

Molly's mind was ticking over. 'I've got a tin of stewed steak, I can make yer a pie with that.'

'But yer said yer were keepin' that tin of stew in case of an emergency!'

'Nellie McDonough, you are an emergency!'

'Ye're right there, girl! I'm a walking bloody disaster if ever there was one.' Nellie looked considerably brighter. 'I'll take yer up on that offer, save me scroungin' round the shops. But I'll pay yer back as soon as I can get me hands on a tin of stewed steak.' She folded her arms and leaned them on the table. 'I don't know about you, girl, but I feel dead tired. We didn't get to bed until one o'clock an' I'm gettin' too old for these late nights. I think I'll write to Hitler and ask him to confine his activities to Saturday nights, so we can have a lie-in the next day.'

'Talkin' about last night, and Hitler, have you ever heard of Anderson shelters, Nellie?'

'Yeah, of course I have! Elsie in the next street's got one. Big ugly things they are, but I believe they'll stand up to anythin'.'

Molly explained about Rosie's fear for Bridie and Bob. 'She's right, too, God love her. Me da looked all-in last night, he wouldn't stand up to many more nights like that.'

'Elsie got hers because of her mother. The old lady's about eighty an' crippled with arthritis . . . takes her all her time to walk.' Now that the problem of her dinner had been sorted out, Nellie wanted to do Molly a favour in return. 'I'll take yer round to Elsie's, if yer like. She wouldn't mind yer takin' a gander at it, an' she'd be able to tell yer how to go about gettin' one.'

'She'll think I've got a cheek,' Molly said. 'I don't really know the woman. I've probably only spoken a dozen words to her in me life.'

'Oh, Elsie won't mind! She'll be only too glad to help!'

It would be a good idea to see one before setting the wheels in motion, Molly thought. Then she'd know what she was talking about when she mentioned it to her mother. 'Could we go now? I'll be too busy this afternoon, makin' the pies. I've got to make one for Miss Clegg, don't forget.'

'I'm ready when you are, girl, an' there's no time like the present. Yer know Rosie's always comin' out with her mammy's sayings? Well I've got one that suits this particular occasion. "Never leave till tomorrow what yer can do today".'

Molly chuckled as she pushed her chair back. 'I don't think the feller that thought that saying up meant if yer were goin' to burn yer dinner, don't leave it until tomorrow, burn it today.'

Nellie tutted. 'I don't suppose I'll hear the end of that, will I? The least thing, an' yer'll be throwing it up at me.'

'No I won't, sunshine.' Molly put a finger to her mouth. 'My lips are sealed.'

'Still like yer job, do yer, Maureen?' Molly asked as she watched Doreen combing her friend's hair in front of the mirror. 'No regrets about leaving Johnson's?'

'I missed it at first, 'cos although the wages were lousy it was a good firm to work for. But we're earning nearly twice as much now, with overtime.' Her pretty face broke into a smile, showing strong white teeth. 'Anyway, where we are now means we won't get called up for the forces.' She caught Doreen's eye in the mirror. 'Did yer tell yer mam that Sammy and Mike have got their papers?'

'Go 'way!' Molly didn't wait for Doreen to reply. 'When was this?'

'Sammy came round to ours last night – the calling-up papers were waitin' for him when he got home from work.'

'I dunno,' Molly sighed, shaking her head. 'I don't know what the world's coming to! Young lads being taken from their homes just because of one greedy man! If I could get me hands on him I'd knock the livin' daylights out of him. At least, I'd hold him while Nellie knocked the daylights out of him.'

'I'd help yer, Mam!' Doreen slipped the comb into her bag. 'If it wasn't for him, Phil would be home and he'd be comin' dancing with us.'

'Which dance are yer goin' to?'

'Orrell Park ballroom. I'm lookin' forward to it, as well, it seems ages since we shook a leg. I don't mind workin' so much overtime because of the extra money, but yer know what they say, "All work and no play makes Jack a dull boy".'

'Are Sammy an' Mike going?' Molly asked.

'Yeah, I told Sammy about it last night when he called an' he said they'd go along.' Maureen's pretty face looked sad. 'We'll miss them when they go away.'

'Yer will!' Molly agreed. 'They've been good mates.'

Doreen came back from collecting her coat. 'I've got a key, Mam, so yer needn't wait up for me.'

'Don't forget what I've told yer, d'yer hear? If the siren goes, find the nearest shelter.'

'OK, Mam, keep yer hair on! I'm not daft enough to keep on dancin' if there's an air raid.'

'I'll make sure she does as she's told, Mrs B.,' Maureen said. 'I had to promise me mam the same thing.'

Molly watched them heading for the door, their dancing shoes tucked under their arms. 'Enjoy yerselves, and remember me to Sammy and Mike. Tell them to come an' see us before they go.'

'Will do! Ta-ra, Mam!'

'For heaven's sake keep yer voice down or yer'll wake Ruthie! And close the door quietly behind yer.'

Tommy was dying to ask if his mother had made any inquiries about an Anderson shelter, but he didn't want to bring Rosie's name into it in case they thought he was going soft on her. Heaven forbid that should ever happen! But when he was halfway through his dinner and she'd made no mention of it, he couldn't contain himself any longer. After all, it was his nan and grandad he was worried about, not Rosie. 'Did yer find out anythin', Mam? You know, about the shelter?'

'Oh, yer mean the one Rosie wanted yer to ask me about?' Molly chuckled silently when the blush rose from his neck to cover his face. She hadn't failed to notice he'd mentioned her name this morning without the usual sarcasm that went with it. 'Yeah, I've not only found out how to go about getting one, I've actually seen one!'

Jack's fork stopped halfway to his mouth. 'Go 'way! How did yer do that, love?'

'Yer might know . . . through Nellie! There's not much goes on around here that me mate doesn't know about, I can tell yer. As soon as I mentioned it to her, she said she knew a woman in the next street who's got one, and she had me round there to see it before yer could blink.'

'What are they like, Mam?' Tommy asked. 'Would it be suitable for me nan and grandad?'

Molly sucked air in through her teeth. 'Great big ugly things they are. They're made of iron or something, and they take up nearly the whole room! I went to me ma's after I'd seen it, but I never mentioned it to her. If I'd taken her to see it, she'd have pooh-poohed the idea without givin' herself time to think about it properly. I thought it might be better if it was just brought up in conversation, casual like. At least she'd have time to think about the advantages of having one, before seeing how big and ugly they are.'

'They can't be that big, love, or they wouldn't be able to get them in the houses,' Jack said. 'These doors are not that wide.'

'They don't bring them in ready-made, they make them up in the room. The top is just like a tabletop, only bigger and made of iron, and it's got thick iron legs and some sort of wire mesh on two of the sides.' Molly shuddered. 'Me ma would have a duck egg if she had to have one in her room, yer know how finicky she is.'

'I said that to Rosie last night.' Tommy could have bitten his tongue off, but the words had left his lips before he'd had time to think. And now he'd started, he may as well finish. 'An' she asked me whether it was better to have a nice house, or a safe one.'

Jack grinned. 'She's not just a pretty face, is our Rosie! She's got her head screwed on the right way.'

'Yeah, she's a sensible girl,' Molly agreed. 'Me ma and da would be lost without her. And think of all the worry she saves me! I'd be out of me mind if they were on their own with things the way they are.'

'Well in my opinion, for what it's worth, I think one of

those shelters would be a godsend for yer ma and da,' Jack said. 'To hell with what the room looks like – there's a ruddy war on!'

Molly drummed her fingers on the table, her blue eyes thoughtful. 'I've been goin' over things in me head, and there's others beside my ma and da who could do with something in the house so they'd be safe. Miss Clegg, for one. She sits under the stairs as soon as the siren goes, but that wouldn't be a ha'p'orth of good if a bomb dropped. And what about Corker's mam? I looked for her in the shelter last night, but there was no sign. Which means she was on her own in the house.'

'Yer've got a point there, love,' Jack said. 'They're both too old and frail to be rushin' out at midnight, and yer can't expect them to.' He pushed his empty plate away. 'Are they givin' these Anderson shelters out? Can anyone get them?'

'According to Elsie in the next street, they're givin' them to priority cases first. She said we'd have no trouble gettin' one for me ma and da, and the same would apply to Miss Clegg and Mrs Corkhill.'

'So what have yer got in mind, Mam?' Tommy speared the last piece of pastry. Ever since he was a small child he always saved the best bit till last. 'Are yer goin' to ask me nan?'

'I'm goin' to have to be crafty about it, son. If I ask her right out, I know what her answer will be. But if I just happen to mention that Miss Clegg is getting one, and the advantages of it, then it will give her something to think about. She'll come round in the end because she dotes on me da, and anything that will keep him safe she'll go for.'

Jack moved over to his armchair, his packet of cigarettes in his hand. 'Have you had a word with Miss Clegg and Mrs Corkhill?'

'I haven't seen Corker's mam yet, but I mentioned it to Miss Clegg when I took her dinner over. She was all for it! Thought it was a marvellous idea!'

'So the first part of yer plan has met with success.' Jack watched the smoke from his cigarette as it spiralled its way to the ceiling. 'One down, two to go, eh?'

'Ellen said Corker's due home in a couple of days, so I'll leave it to him to talk to his mam. And I'm goin' to get Rosie to help me with me ma and da. If she drops a few words here and there, all casual like, it might just sink in and prepare the ground, so to speak.'

There was a twinkle in Jack's deep brown eyes. 'An' you say that Nellie's the crafty one.'

'Ay, well, with bein' with her so much it's only natural a bit of it would rub off on me.' Molly chuckled. 'I've got a long way to go before I catch up with her, though! I tell yer, she's the craftiest person on two legs.'

It was on the tip of Molly's tongue to tell them about Nellie's dinner and give them a laugh, but she reminded herself of the promise she'd made Nellie. But she was right about her mate being crafty . . . as cute as a cartload of monkeys she was! It was a foregone conclusion that George wouldn't be told about the disaster with the dinner, and it was a pound to a penny she'd have had the nerve to tell him she'd baked the pie herself!

Molly picked up the dirty plates and headed for the kitchen. 'I'll use the water in the kettle to wash these, then put more on for our tea.'

There was a smile on her face as she put the plug in the sink and turned the tap on. Nellie was a caution all right, there was no doubt about that! But who'd have her any different? They'd had a damn good laugh today, and no harm was done. Except, of course, Molly was minus a tin of stewed steak.

Three days later, on the fourteenth of May, news came that after a heavily sustained air attack by dozens of German planes, the city of Rotterdam had been captured. The effect of the grim news could be seen on the faces of those old enough to understand the implications. In every home and workplace across the country the question on everyone's lips was how long could a small country like Holland hold out? And people were angry. Why, they asked, were we so unprepared, our forces so ill equipped they couldn't halt the Germans? Instead of appeasing the maniac in the beginning, why hadn't we foreseen what could happen, and strengthened the might of our forces?

Jack had his own very strong views on the subject. 'He's been testing us over the last year, taking a little bit here and a little bit there. And like bloody fools, our lot have only rapped his knuckles and told him not to be a naughty boy. Honestly, it makes my blood boil! Anyone with half an eye could see what was coming, but not those down in London. Oh, no, they preferred to believe every promise the little sod made! Talk about act soft an' I'll buy yer a coalyard, isn't in it.'

'They were doin' what they thought best, Jack,' Molly said. 'Trying to avoid another war.'

'Ay, well they're not the ones who'll have to pay for their mistakes, are they? It's the young lads who'll have to pay. And when they start bombing us, which they will do, we'll all have to pay.' Jack could see the worry lines on Molly's face, and tried to control his anger. What good would it do to put the fear of God into her and the children?

'I'm worried about Phil,' Doreen said. 'I hope he's not sent where there's any fighting.'

'France is a bigger country than Holland, love, and they're much more prepared. It's said they've got defence lines that will stop any army.'

Jill was picking nervously at her fingernails. 'I hope you're right, Dad! If it gets any worse, they're bound to call Steve up.'

'If I was eighteen, I'd join up,' Tommy said, his voice gruff. 'I'd love to have a go at those Germans.'

'Over my dead body yer'd join up!' Molly cried. 'I'm

praying to God the war will be over before you're eighteen.' She pushed her chair back so sharply it almost toppled over. 'I'm goin' round to me ma's for half an hour to tell her Miss Clegg has had a visitor and she's getting an Anderson shelter next week. It'll give me ma somethin' to think about, might gee her up a bit.' She glanced from Jill to Doreen. 'Are you two goin' out?'

'I'm not,' Doreen answered, 'it's too late, and anyway I'm having an early night – I'm dead tired.'

'Steve's working until nine,' Jill said, 'then he'll be down.'

Tommy grinned. 'Before yer give me the third degree, Mam, I'll fill yer in with me intended movements. I was goin' to Ginger's, but I've changed me mind. It's a few days since I saw me nan and grandad, so I'll walk that far with you.'

As Molly got her coat from the hall-stand she gave a silent chuckle. Who did Tommy think he was kidding? It would seem her son was having a change of heart about young Rosie.

'I won't be long, love,' Molly said, slipping her arms into her coat. 'I'll be back before yer've finished reading the *Echo*.' She stooped to plant a kiss on Jack's forehead before jerking her head at Tommy. 'Come along, sunshine, it's a long time since I had a male escort.'

When Rosie answered the door to their knock her face lit up. 'Hello, Auntie Molly! Sure it's glad I am to see yer.' She gave Molly a hug and a kiss, then glanced briefly at Tommy. 'And good evening to you.'

Ho, ho, thought Molly, rubbing her nose to hide a smile. It would appear that Tommy wasn't the only one having a change of heart. Rosie's greeting had been far from welcoming and held none of the usual enthusiasm she displayed when she set eyes on Tommy. In fact it would be fair to say his appearance had been met with a very cool reception to say the least!

Bridie switched the wireless off when she saw who the visitors were. 'Well now, this is a pleasant surprise, so it is.'

Molly dropped a kiss on to the silver-grey head. 'I felt like a breath of fresh air.' She turned to her da and put a hand on each of the wooden arms of his fireside chair before bending down to kiss him. 'Tommy was comin' round, so I thought I'd give him the pleasure of my company.' She managed to keep the smile on her face when their eyes met, even though she was saddened by the weariness on his lined face. 'It's not often me big son walks out with me, he thinks he's too big now to be seen with his mother.'

'Oh, he's big all right, I'll grant yer that!' Rosie said loftily, her nose pointing to the ceiling. 'But he's not too big to take his mother's coat and hang it up for her.'

'Oh, God,' Tommy groaned, blushing furiously. 'I bet she's goin' to come out with one of her mammy's sayings now.'

'Oh, I could be doin' that all right, Tommy Bennett! Sure hasn't me mammy got more sayings than she knows what to do with?' Rosie tapped a finger on her chin. 'Let's see now. How about a nice short one? Like "Manners maketh the man"?'

'One of these days I'll throttle you, Rosie O'Grady, just you wait and see.'

'Tut, tut, what a temper yer have, Tommy Bennett!' Rosie became all efficient. 'You take Auntie Molly's coat while I put the kettle on.'

Molly slipped off her coat and handed it to Tommy. 'I'll give yer a hand, sunshine!' She followed Rosie into the kitchen and turned on the tap to drown out their conversation. 'Did yer manage to have a word with me ma, Rosie?'

'Sure I have that, Auntie Molly! I've mentioned it a few times, but whether it's sunk in is another matter. I can't get a yea or nay out of her. Uncle Bob showed more interest, so perhaps it's him we should be working on.'

'I'll bring it up while we're having our tea.' Molly folded her arms and leaned against the sink. 'Have you and our Tommy had a falling-out? Yer didn't seem that happy to see him.'

Rosie glanced towards the door then put a finger to her lips before saying in a low voice, 'I'm changing me tactics, Auntie Molly. Now I wouldn't want yer to be telling him, even if he is your son.'

'I won't breathe a word, sunshine.' Molly was dying to laugh at the serious expression on the pretty face. 'I cross my heart and hope to die.'

'It was Auntie Bridget's idea, so it was. She said if a girl chases after a boy he doesn't think anything of her for it. Pretend ye're not interested and play hard to get, she told me, and if he thinks anythin' of yer, he'll come running.'

'She's right, sunshine!' Molly grinned. 'Me ma is always right.'

'So that's what I'm doing . . . playing hard to get. If there's any running to be done, it won't be done by me.'

'Quite right, too! But I'll just ask yer to bear in mind that our Tommy is only sixteen an' knows nothing about girls. He's never had a girlfriend, so make allowances for him.'

'Sure, haven't I been doing that, Auntie Molly? But I'm only sixteen meself, yet the minute I clapped eyes on Tommy I knew he was the boy for me.'

'Well I hope it works out for yer, sunshine, 'cos I think ye're a little smasher.'

'I thank yer kindly, Auntie Molly.' Rosie beamed. 'But it's not you I want to marry, it's yer son.'

Chapter Twenty-Three

Molly gave a cry of surprise when she opened the door to see Ellen and Corker standing on her step. 'Corker! Well, you dark horse, Ellen Clarke! Fancy, never a dickie bird out of yer when yer called in on yer way home from work!'

'I didn't know he was home!' Ellen said. 'I got the shock of me life when he turned up as bold as brass an hour ago.'

'Well don't stand there, come on in!' Molly waited until they passed, closed the front door and hurried ahead of them, apologizing. 'Yer'll have to excuse the place, Jack and Tommy have not long got in from work and they're having their dinner.'

Jack's pleasure at seeing his friend was evident on his smiling face. His knife and fork clattered to the plate as he jumped to his feet. 'Corker! It's good to see yer.' He shook the big man's hand up and down. 'Yer've been on me mind the last day or two, 'cos I know yer boat calls at Rotterdam sometimes and I've been worrying in case yer were in port there when the Germans bombed the city.'

'We were lucky, Jack, we got away just in time.' Corker took Ellen's arm and led her to the couch. He waited until she was seated, then sat beside her. 'We finished unloading, turned around and were about half an hour out at sea when it started. We could hear the planes, the sky seemed to be full of them, and we heard the explosions. And I don't mind admitting that I stood at the rails and I prayed like I'd never prayed before, in thanks to God. If we'd still been in dock when the raid started I wouldn't be here now.' He felt Ellen shiver beside him and placed a hand over hers. 'Don't be gettin' yerself all upset, love, 'cos I'm here, and all in one piece.'

'And could yer see the explosions from where yer were?' Tommy asked, his eyes wide. 'I'd have thought yer were too far away.'

'We could hear and see the planes, we could hear the explosions and we could see the fires start and grow until the flames reached the sky. The whole of Rotterdam seemed to be on fire, and I felt like crying for the people who had been given no warning. Innocent civilians, men, women and children, who had never asked for a war and had never done anyone any harm. If only they'd been given an hour's notice, so they could get themselves to places of safety . . . but Hitler doesn't show any mercy. He doesn't care who or how many he kills, young or old. Just bomb them into submission so they can't fight back.'

'The bastards!' Jack glanced at Molly. 'I'm sorry, love, but I can't think of another word to describe Hitler.'

'What about evil, cruel, murderer?' It was Ellen who spoke. She was beside herself with an anger she'd never known before. An anger brought out by the realization that she'd very nearly lost the gentle giant she'd grown to love so much. And the knowledge that she'd never know a moment's peace every time he put out to sea. 'He wants lockin' up and the key throwing away.'

'What d'yer think about the situation in Holland, Corker?' Jack asked. 'Can they hold out against Hitler?'

'I doubt it.' Corker's eyes sent a message across to Jack. He didn't want to say too much in front of the women. 'Anyway, the pub will be closing in half an hour and I'm dying for a good old English pint of bitter. How about you, Jack, d'yer fancy a pint?'

'Of course he does!' Molly said quickly. 'His life is all bed and work, so it'll do him good to get out for a bit. Ellen can sit an' keep me company.'

Corker glanced sideways. 'Is that all right with you, love?'

'Need you ask?' Ellen said. 'Me an' Molly can have a good old natter. She can fill me in on all the gossip.'

Molly grinned. 'I'll go and get her, shall I?'

Ellen looked puzzled. 'Get who?'

'Nellie of course! She *is* all the gossip! In fact, I don't know why Jack bothers to buy the *Echo* every night when Nellie only lives a few doors away.'

Corker's chuckle was hearty. 'The whole world is in a helluva state, all topsy-turvy. But one thing never changes, thank God, and that's Molly's and Nellie's fine sense of humour. It borders on the ridiculous sometimes, and yer have to be mad to understand it, but it'll keep us going if nothing else will.'

'If Nellie was here, she'd be asking yer if that was a compliment or an insult.'

Corker set his cap at a jaunty angle and his white teeth gleamed through the mass of hair on his face. 'It's a compliment, Molly, me darlin'.'

'Oh, well, I'll let yer off the hook.' Molly watched Jack struggle into his coat. 'Have yer got enough money on yer, love?'

'Yeah, I won't need much. We'll only have time to buy a round each.'

Corker winked at Tommy, who was standing beside Jack. 'Ye're as tall as yer old man, son! Another year, an' yer'll be catching up with me.'

Tommy's chest swelled with pride. 'Another year an' ten months an' I'll be comin to the pub with yer.'

'Oh, God, he's puttin' years on me!' Jack laughed. 'Come on, Corker, before the towels go up.'

'I'll walk out with yer,' Tommy said. 'I may as well go up and knock on Ginger's door.'

'Take a key with yer,' Molly said, 'in case yer dad and I want to go to bed.'

'No, I don't need to. I'll be back well before our Jill and Doreen are in.'

Tommy leant against the wall of Ginger's house. It was a warm evening, too nice to be inside. And anyway, unless they sat on the stairs, there was nowhere they could talk in private. 'Which pictures are we goin' to on Saturday?'

'I dunno! Abbott and Costello are on at the Astoria, Cary Grant at the Atlas and James Cagney at the Carlton in Orrell Park. I don't mind which one we go to.'

'It's your turn to pick,' Tommy said, 'I had my go last week.'

'We'll go to the Carlton then.' Ginger scraped his shoe on the pavement, trying to pluck up the courage to say what he'd been rehearsing all day. 'If I ask yer somethin', yer won't bite me head off, will yer?'

'I don't think I'd fancy bitin' your head off, no matter what yer asked me. What is it, anyway?'

'Er . . . do . . . er . . . do you like Rosie?'

Tommy straightened up. 'How d'yer mean, do I like Rosie? She's all right I suppose. The only thing wrong with her is she's a girl! What are yer askin' me such a daft question for?'

'I just wanted to know if yer liked her. I mean, you know, have yer got yer eye on her?'

'What!' Tommy exploded. 'Got me eye on Rosie O'Grady! Yer wouldn't be havin' me on by any chance, would yer?'

Ginger was glad it was dusk; he'd never have had the nerve in broad daylight. 'I was only wonderin'. I mean, if yer liked her, I'd leave the coast clear for yer.'

'Yer've lost me, Ginger, I don't know what ye're on about! What d'yer want to leave the coast clear for me for?'

'That's only if yer had yer eye on her!' Ginger was finding this far harder than he'd thought it would be. 'But seein' as yer haven't, then I don't need to bother.'

'D'yer know what?' Tommy said. 'Yer sound just like me

auntie Nellie! But when she goes all around the houses to tell yer somethin' it's always funny, an' at least yer get a laugh. Why don't yer just come right out and say what's on yer mind?'

Ginger began to kick the front step, his nerves shot to pieces. But he'd come this far: he might as well carry on. 'I was thinkin' of askin' Rosie if she'd come to the pictures one night.'

'Yer what! Yer mean – with you an' me? Not on your life, mate!'

The speed of Ginger's kicks increased. His big toe was beginning to throb, and if he wasn't careful he'd have no toecap left on his shoe. But in for a penny, in for a pound. 'I didn't mean with you, I meant just her and me.'

Tommy was flabbergasted. He and Ginger had been best mates since the day they'd started school, and he never thought the day would come when a girl came between them. And trust that girl to be Rosie O'Grady! He was momentarily lost for words. Then he blurted out the first thing that came into his head. 'Me nan would never let her go out with yer, not just the two of yer.'

The kicking stopped as Ginger got his dander up. 'Why not with me? What's wrong with me? I'm as good as anybody else!'

'I never said there was anythin' wrong with yer! I just think me nan will say she's too young to be goin' out with a boy, that's all!'

'I'll never know if I don't ask, will I?' Ginger said with spirit. 'I can't see how yer nan can object to me takin' Rosie to the pictures, we could go to first house an' be home early.'

'Oh, please yerself, but don't say I didn't warn yer.' Tommy was experiencing a feeling of jealousy, but he couldn't make out who he was jealous of. 'It would serve yer right if she said yes, 'cos she'd talk the ears off yer.'

'Yer don't mind me askin' her, then?' Ginger had taken a

shine to Rosie, but he didn't want to fall out with his friend over her. 'It wouldn't make any difference to us – we could still go out together on a Saturday night, like we always do.'

'Suit yerself,' said Tommy, feeling very piqued. 'But don't say I didn't tell yer. An hour with her an' yer'd have a headache for a week.'

'Yer haven't got a cob on, have yer?' Ginger asked. 'I mean, we're not goin' to fall out over it?'

'No, why should we?' Tommy stretched to his full height. 'I think yer need yer brains testing, but there's no accounting for taste. Anyway, I'm off home. I told me mam I'd only be an hour. I'll see yer, Ginger, ta-ra for now.'

'Ta-ra, Tommy.' Ginger was feeling sick as he watched his friend walk away. He only hoped Rosie didn't turn him down, 'cos he'd look a right nit if she did.

'Have the boys been all right?' Ellen asked when she came back from Molly's with Corker. 'They haven't been givin' yer a hard time, have they?'

'No, there hasn't been a peep out of them.' Phoebe was thirteen and blossoming into a nice-looking girl. She was very sensible for her age and could be relied on to do her share of the housework and looking after the other three children when Ellen was at work. 'They've been good, haven't they, our Dorothy?'

'Yeah!' Dorothy had her arms around Corker's waist, smiling up into his face. She was two years younger than her sister, a happy child with a sunny disposition. She was usually in bed by eight o'clock, but when Corker was home she was allowed to stay up late to keep Phoebe company. 'Will yer come down early tomorrow night, Uncle Corker, before Peter an' Gordon go to bed, an' read us a story?'

'I'll do that with pleasure, me darlin'.' Corker stroked her short, straight, mousy-coloured hair. 'I'll tell yer one yer haven't heard before, about three men stranded on a desert island.'

Dorothy turned shining hazel eyes on her mother. 'Did yer hear that, Mam? Ooh, I can't wait!'

Ellen smiled. What a difference Corker had made to the lives of her children. He'd given them the love and safety that their own father never had. 'Up to bed now, and when you're asleep the time will go quicker. Kiss Uncle Corker goodnight, then poppy off.'

The girls were happy as they went up the stairs. They couldn't wait for tomorrow night.

'D'yer want a cup of tea?' Ellen asked. 'Or have yer had enough liquid for one night?'

'I've had enough, love.' Corker patted the space beside him on the couch. 'Come and sit down. This is the first time we've been on our own for ages.'

Ellen sat down and rested her head on his shoulder. 'It's good to have yer home.'

He slipped an arm across her shoulders and pulled her to him. 'I've been thinking while I've been away, love, and I think it's time we brought everything out in the open.'

'But we said we'd leave it for a year or two, until the children were older.'

'I know what we said, love, but things have changed drastically since then. Time is too precious to waste. We don't know what's going to happen from one day to the next, so let's make the most of the time we've got together. I need you, Ellen, and I want you to marry me. Every time I go away I want to know you'll be here waiting for me when I get back – as my wife. And I want to hear the kids calling me Dad, not Uncle Corker.'

'There's nothing they'd like better,' Ellen said, reaching up to touch the hand on her shoulder. 'An' I suppose I don't mind telling them, or the neighbours for that matter, that Nobby's dead. But have yer thought about your mother? You can't leave her in that house on her own, not at her age. An' we couldn't have her here because with only the two bedrooms, we're crowded as it is.'

'I know there's problems, love, I've gone over them dozens of times in me head. But if you'll help me, we can overcome them.' Corker gave a deep sigh. 'I wouldn't leave me ma, I love her too much for that. She's been a good mother, the best there is, and I'm all she's got in the world.' He gripped Ellen's shoulders and turned her to face him. 'I know it's a lot to ask, but until the war's over and we can look for a bigger house, will yer let me share me time between here an' me ma's house when I'm home on leave?'

Ellen drank in every feature of the beloved, weather-worn face. 'I love you, Corker, an' I'll be content with the time yer can spend with me an' the kids. I'll take you on any terms.'

Corker breathed out a sigh of relief. 'When I come down tomorrow night we'll tell the kids, eh? Then we'll tell Molly, an' she'll pass the news on to the neighbours, save you gettin' embarrassed.' He pulled her towards him and held her tight. 'Yer don't know how happy yer've made me, I feel like a young lad again.'

'I'm only worried about how yer ma will take it,' Ellen said, her head pressed close to his chest. 'I hope she won't be upset, you takin' on a ready-made family.'

'It'll come as no surprise to her, love, she's not daft. I think she saw the way the wind was blowing a long time ago.'

Ellen pushed him away so she could look into his face. 'Where do we go from here?'

'I've only got three days' leave, so we can't get married until I come home again. We can get a special licence and get married at Brougham Terrace . . . unless yer want a church wedding?'

Ellen shook her head. 'Brougham Terrace will suit me fine. I haven't got the money to be buyin' fancy clothes.'

Corker felt light-headed with relief. 'I wouldn't care if yer turned up wearing a sack. But there's one thing I would like: I'd like us to spend our wedding night in a hotel.'

Ellen's eyes widened in apprehension. 'I've never been in a hotel in me life, Corker! I'd feel out of place!'

'I'm not thinkin' of takin' yer to the Adelphi, love!' Corker laughed at the expression on her face. 'There's a few little hotels in Mount Pleasant, one of those would be ideal.'

Ellen wasn't keen on the idea, but she could sense his excitement and didn't want to put a damper on it. Besides, she had to admit she'd feel awkward with the kids, if they simply came home. 'OK, you win. I'll ask Jill to sleep here that night, save me worrying about leaving Phoebe in charge. But don't always expect to get yer own way, Jimmy Corkhill, or yer'll be in for a disappointment.'

Corker chuckled. 'I can see I'm goin' to have me hands full with you! Yer can be a real little spitfire when yer want.'

Corker's happiness was overshadowed the next day with the news that Holland had capitulated. He'd been expecting it, but it still came as a shock. In his mind it spelled disaster for Britain and her allies, but he kept his fears to himself. Ellen didn't understand much about the strategy of war; wouldn't know one country from another if you showed her a map. And she'd come in from work with such a smile on her face, he wasn't going to wipe it away by discussing bad news.

He'd eaten with his mother, so he sat quietly with his thoughts until Ellen and the children had finished their meal and the dishes were washed. Then he gathered the children round him. They were expecting a fairy story, and were surprised when he held out his hand to their mam and said, 'Come and sit next to me, love, and we'll tell them together.'

Slowly, and with great understanding and compassion, he explained about their father dying. There was no reaction to that news, no cries of surprise or sadness . . . nothing. The children didn't even look at each other, they kept their eyes glued to his face. He paused for a while, then went on: 'I have loved your mam for a long time, and now I love every one of you. So how do you feel about me and yer mam gettin' married, and you having me for a dad?'

As Ellen was to tell Molly later, she thought the roof was going to come down with all the shouting and cheering. All four of them tried to get close to Uncle Corker – or Sinbad, as they used to call him. Kisses were rained on his face, even by the two boys, Peter and Gordon. They'd have a dad they could be proud of, and be the envy of every kid in the neighbourhood.

'I think you've got yer answer,' Ellen said, her new-found happiness making her look like a young girl. The young girl Corker had fallen in love with all those years ago.

Ginger was in a quandary. How could he ask Rosie for a date when the only time he ever saw her was at Tommy's house? And it was no good asking his friend to help – he'd be told to take a running jump. He thought about calling on her, but quickly discarded that idea. I mean, what would he say if Mrs Jackson opened the door? He'd die on the spot! No, he'd have to try and bump into her accidentally on purpose. She came round to the Bennetts' most nights, so he'd lie in wait for her. So it was that Ginger, on cue, walked out of the entry just as Rosie turned the corner. He'd been hanging around for half an hour, but she wasn't to know that.

'Hiya, Rosie!'

Rosie turned, a ready smile on her face. 'Hello, Ginger! Off out, are yer?'

'I'm goin' to the corner shop for some ciggies for me dad,' Ginger lied. 'It's a nice night, isn't it?'

'Ay, it is that, Ginger! It's a pity the people in the world aren't as nice as the weather.'

'Oh, yer mean about Holland havin' to give in? Yeah, things look bad, don't they?'

'They do indeed.' They were outside the corner shop and Rosie went to walk on. 'I'll see yer, Ginger!'

'Wait a minute, Rosie, I want to ask yer somethin'.'

Rosie turned back. 'Yes, what is it, Ginger?'

Beetroot was pale in comparison to the colour of Ginger's freckled face. His bottle was gone, and it was only the sight of Rosie's pretty face that stopped him running away. 'Would, er, would yer like to come to the pictures with us one night?'

Rosie was taken aback. 'Yer mean with you and Tommy?'

'No, just with me. We could go to the first house and I'd get yer home early.'

'Oh, Ginger, I thank yer kindly, that I do! But yer see, I have a boyfriend an' I don't think he'd be keen on me goin' out with another boy.'

Ginger's mouth gaped. 'Yer've got a boyfriend?'

'I have that, Ginger! And very nice he is, too!'

'Oh, well, it was worth a try.' Ginger tried to sound cocky as his thoughts raced on a fast track. Did Tommy know she had a boyfriend, and hadn't let on? If he did, it was a lousy trick. 'If Tommy's in, will yer ask him to slip up to ours for five minutes? There's somethin' I want to ask him.'

'Sure I'll do that, all right, Ginger. Goodnight to yer.'

There was a smile on Rosie's face as she walked down to the Bennetts' house. That should give Tommy something to think about. Auntie Bridget would be proud of her.

The object of her affections was just finishing his tea. She greeted everyone, and then, as though it was an afterthought, she passed Ginger's message on.

A frown creased Tommy's face. 'Did he say what he wanted me for?'

'He did not! An' sure, I wasn't interested enough to ask him.'

Molly winked across at Jack. She had informed him about Rosie's change of tactics and now he was seeing it in action.

'I'll go up an' see what he wants.' Tommy was intrigued. If Ginger had asked her for a date, she wasn't giving anything away.

Ginger was waiting for Tommy to pass the window, and he dashed down the hall and had the door open in a flash. Stepping into the street, he squared up to his friend. 'You're a fine one, you are!'

'What have I done?'

'Yer let me make a fool of meself, that's what yer've done! Yer must 'ave known Rosie had a boyfriend, yet yer didn't say a word. I felt a right ruddy fool!'

'Ginger, yer don't need my help to make a fool of yerself, ye're quite capable of doin' that on yer own. I warned yer not to ask her, but yer wouldn't listen!'

'I wouldn't have done if I'd known she already had a boyfriend.' Ginger was still smarting. 'An' you *must* 'ave known.'

'How the hell would I know?' Tommy was feeling a bit guilty, the memory of his birthday party coming back to him, but he was getting his temper up too. He hadn't done a thing wrong but was getting the blame! And wouldn't you know, once again Rosie O'Grady was the cause of it! 'I don't know what she gets up to, an' I don't ruddy well care! She might have ten boyfriends for all I know . . . so what?'

'I can't believe that if she's got a boyfriend, you an' yer mam wouldn't know about it! She must talk about him, where they go, what his name is.' Ginger was becoming deflated. Either his mate was a ruddy good actor or he was telling the truth. 'I mean, someone must have seen him, unless he's the Invisible Man.'

All the things Ginger was saying, Tommy was thinking. It was queer when you came to think about it. No one in the family had mentioned it, not even his nan, and if anyone knew, she would! Yet this was the second time Rosie had turned down a date saying she already had a boyfriend. Seemed a bit fishy when you thought about it. But whichever way it went, it was no skin off his nose. It wasn't his worry, and he certainly wouldn't lose any sleep over it.

'Look, Ginger, just leave me out of it, all right? Yer got yer eye wiped, it was yer own doing, and that's all there is to it.' Tommy had had enough. 'Uncle Corker's comin' to ours, so I'd better get back. I'll see yer Saturday, if not before. OK?'

'Yeah, OK, Tommy.' Ginger punched his friend on the arm. 'We'll go to the Carlton, like we said. Ta-ra.'

Chapter Twenty-Four

'You're late today! The kettle's been boiled about three times.' Molly closed the door after her friend. 'What kept yer?'

'The ruddy wireless, that's what kept me.' Nellie's turban had slid down to her eyebrows, and she pushed it back impatiently as she waddled down the hall and into the living room. Pulling a chair from beneath the table she sat down heavily. 'The news is not half bad, yer know, girl. Those ruddy Germans are just pushing ahead all over the place.'

'I know,' Molly said, shaking her head. 'Jack had the wireless on while he was havin' his breakfast, an' his face was like thunder. Yer should have heard the names he was callin' Hitler. And poor Mr Chamberlain didn't come off much better; he got the blame for everything. Jack called him all the weak so-and-so's under the sun.'

'Jack's right, girl, my George said last year that Chamberlain wasn't the man for the job.'

'He wasn't a bad man, though, Nellie, an' I felt sorry for him. His only mistake was trusting Hitler when he shouldn't have done.'

'Well we've got Mr Churchill now, thank God. He's a different kettle of fish, and no one will pull the wool over his eyes.' Nellie jerked her head towards the kitchen. 'Where's that cuppa, girl? Me mouth's as dry as sawdust.'

Molly waited until she had poured the tea before asking, 'What did it say on the wireless?'

'I can't remember it all, yer know what big words those

fellers use. An' they speak as though they've got a mouthful of plums. But from what I could gather, the German forces have pushed forward and reached the sea. Now what sea that is, I haven't a clue. But from the sound of it our troops, with some French and Belgian, are trapped and ready to retreat. Now how they can retreat if they're trapped, is somethin' else I don't understand. But yer know me, I'm as thick as two short planks and probably didn't hear what he said proper.'

'Oh, dear God! I hope Phil's all right! Did they say whether any soldiers had been killed?'

Nellie had no intention of being the bearer of any more bad news, so she shook her head. 'I couldn't tell yer, girl, me heart was in me mouth an' I missed half of what he said.'

'What a flamin' life!' Molly felt a knot of fear in her tummy. 'I slipped over to see Miss Clegg earlier, and she'd been listenin' to the wireless an' all. She's in a terrible state over Phil, worryin' herself sick. If anythin' happened to him it would be the end of her. Our Doreen went to sit with her last night, and when she came back yer could see she'd been crying.'

'I might have got it wrong, girl, so why don't yer put the wireless on an' we can listen while we're havin' our tea?'

Molly shook her head vigorously. 'Nellie, I'm not puttin' it on until my Jack comes in. I feel bad enough as it is, with me tummy all wound up and me head splittin'.'

'Then let's change the subject, eh, girl? Forget about the war for a while an' talk about somethin' nice.'

'Can you think of anythin' nice, 'cos I can't!'

'Well we can talk about Ellen an' Corker gettin' married,' Nellie said. 'I still can't believe it, I never thought it would come off.'

'Oh, I did! I never expected it to be quite so soon, mind you, but it comes as no surprise.' Molly refilled the cups and stood the pot back on its stand. 'I'm made up for them, they both deserve a bit of happiness.'

'Oh, I'm not sayin' they don't, girl, an' I'm made up for them too! But with Corker sayin' he's still goin' to be staying with his ma, he's goin' to have his work cut out. He can't be in two places at the same time, unless he chops himself in half.' A grin crossed Nellie's face. 'Mind you, he'd make two men, would Corker.'

'They'll manage all right,' Molly said. 'With Ellen at work all day, he can spend that time with his ma.'

'The way I heard it, girl, he intends sleepin' at home! I mean, if he does that, how are they goin' to . . . er . . . going to . . . oh, you know what I'm gettin' at!'

Molly looked all innocent. 'I don't know what ye're gettin' at, sunshine, so spell it out for me.'

Nellie tutted, her chins quivering. 'Playin' silly beggars, are yer? Right, well I'll tell yer. When a man an' a woman get married, they go to bed together to conta . . . consam . . . oh, what's the ruddy word I'm lookin' for? It's on the end of me tongue but I can't get it out.'

'The word is consummate, Nellie.'

'That's it, I knew it all the time!' Nellie folded her arms and pushed her bosom up. 'Well now, how are they goin' to do what you've just said, you know, that big word?'

Good, Molly thought. Here's my chance to pull her leg and get my own back on her. So, feeling pleased with herself and keeping a straight face, she said, 'What usually happens, Nellie, is that the woman lies on the bed looking all innocent and coy, and the man gets on top of her.'

Nellie banged her fist on the table. 'Oh, God, girl, I remember now! D'yer know it's been that long I'd forgotten?' She leaned forward, her face eager. 'I'm all ears, so remind me what happens next.'

Molly tutted. Once again the tables had been turned on her. 'If your George could hear you now, he'd be ashamed of yer.'

'But don't yer see it's for his sake I'm askin' yer! You remind me how it's done, an' I'll remind him! See, yer'd be doin' us both a great big favour.'

'Nellie McDonough, the older yer get, the worse yer get! Honest, yer'd make a saint blush, you would.'

'You're no saint, girl, so I don't know why you're blushin', 'cos there's only you an' me here! An' I'm not goin' to tell anyone what yer said about the woman lying on the bed an' the man gettin' on top. Only George, of course, I've got to tell him.'

'You'll do no such thing, Nellie McDonough, or I'll break yer ruddy neck for yer! He'll think I'm sex-mad!'

'Nah, he wouldn't think that! He might see yer in a new light and start lookin' sideways at yer, but that's all. He's harmless, is George . . . too bloody harmless for my liking.'

'Nellie, can we change the subject, please? How we ever got from Ellen and Corker gettin' married to your George lookin' sideways at me, I'll never know!'

'OK, girl, I think I've milked that for all it's worth now, anyway! So we'll talk about somethin' that won't make yer blush. Are yer buyin' a new coat for the weddin'?'

Molly shook her head. 'Not likely! We won't need a coat in the middle of summer!'

'It's not the middle of summer yet, it's only spring!'

'Nellie, don't start that again, for God's sake! It's not far off the end of May now, so by the time Corker gets back off his next trip it'll be summer . . . OK?'

'All right, don't lose yer rag!' Nellie pulled a comical face. 'I only asked if yer were buying a new coat.'

'And I said no! I've asked our Doreen to run me a dress up, and she's making Jill and Ruthie one.'

'I couldn't go in a dress, not with my figure. Once around me, twice around the gasworks.'

'There's nothing wrong with yer figure,' Molly said. She wasn't having anyone running Nellie down . . . not even Nellie herself! 'I bet our Doreen could make yer a dress, and she could do yer a little jacket to go with it. Yer'd look proper posh.'

'D'yer mean a jacket of the same material?' Nellie was beginning to show interest. 'That would look nice, girl! If Doreen could do it, I'd be over the moon. A little jacket would hide me biggest problem . . . or should I say problems, seein' as how I've got two of them?'

'Of course she—' Molly broke off at the sound of the front knocker. 'I wonder who this is?'

'Probably the rag-and-bone man again,' Nellie shouted after her. 'Tell him not to bother knockin' at ours 'cos the only rags I possess are on me flamin' back.'

'Oh dear!' Molly's hand went to her mouth, immediately thinking the worst when she saw Ruthie with Miss Devereux, a teacher at the school. 'What's wrong?'

'It's nothing to worry about, Mrs Bennett.' The teacher had her arm across the girl's shoulders. 'Ruth fell in the playground and has cut her leg.'

It was then Molly noticed the bandage. 'Has she been to the hospital? Is it bad?'

'No, it's badly grazed and there are a few small cuts, but nothing serious. I have cleaned it up as best I can, but there are small stones in the playground and I thought it best to bring her home so you could clean it properly and put some antiseptic cream on.'

Molly opened the door wide. 'Will you come in, Miss Devereux?'

'No, I'll have to get back to my class.' The teacher put a hand under Ruthie's chin and smiled down into her face. 'I hope you feel well enough to come to school tomorrow, young lady.'

Ruthie's lip quivered. 'Yes, Miss.'

'Thanks for bringin' her home, I appreciate it.' Molly held out her hand and her daughter gripped it. Like a wounded soldier she hobbled up the step and limped down the hall, hanging on to the wall for support. 'She's goin' to lap this up,' Molly said, laughing. 'She'll have us all running around after her.'

'It must be sore,' Miss Devereux said, preparing to depart, 'so perhaps a bit of pampering won't go amiss.'

'Thanks once again.' Molly waved before closing the door and hurrying down the hall. 'Now, what's all this, then?'

'Mam, it bledded all over the playground.'

'There's no such word as bledded, sunshine,' Molly said.

'No, yer mam's right,' Nellie added her twopenny's-worth. 'Yer should 'ave said bleeded.'

Molly spun round expecting to see a grin on her friend's face, but no, Nellie was dead serious. She'd said 'bleeded', and as far as she was concerned, bleeded was right! Still, now wasn't the time to be giving her lessons in grammar.

'Let's have a look-see.' Molly knelt down and began to unwind the bandage. She was as gentle as she could be, but still Ruthie whimpered as she gripped the arms of the chair. 'All right, sunshine, that's enough now! If anyone heard they'd think I was killin' yer.'

'It's stuck to me leg, Mam! Don't pull any more please, it hurts.'

Nellie, sitting sideways in her chair, watched with interest. 'Get a bowl of warm water, girl, an' give it a good soaking. It'll come off easy then.'

'That's a good idea.' Molly scrambled to her feet. 'Pass her one of those biscuits, Nellie, while I'm gettin' the bowl.'

The bandage proved to be very stubborn. Molly soaked it with water but it refused to be parted from the girl's knee. The trouble was, she didn't want to hurt her daughter and was too gentle. Nellie watched in silence for a while, then decided desperate measures were needed. In one quick movement she pushed Molly aside, and pointing upwards, said to Ruthie, 'Ooh, look at that big spider crawling across the ceiling!' As soon as the girl looked up Nellie gave one good pull and the bandage was off. 'There now, all over an' done with.'

Molly waited for screams of protest, but there wasn't a peep out of Ruthie. It had all happened so quickly she hadn't felt a thing.

'My, you did come a cropper, didn't yer?' Molly's maternal instincts came to the fore when she saw how deep and angry-looking the graze was. 'You poor thing, it must be sore.'

'It is, Mam!' All it needed was a little sympathy to bring on the tears. 'It hurts terrible.'

'How did yer come to fall over?' Molly asked. 'Were yer fighting?'

'No, we were only playin' leap-frog. It was my turn to bend down an' Sally Moffatt didn't jump proper and she sent me flying.'

'Well I'll clean it up for yer, put some ointment and a fresh bandage on, then yer can lie on the couch an' put yer leg up.' Molly gave her a big hug. 'How about that, eh?'

Ruthie nodded. Her lips were still trembling but she was beginning to see the advantages of being an invalid. If she played her cards right, she could be off school for the rest of the week.

'I'll have to run to the corner shop, I've no bandage or ointment in,' Molly said. 'But Auntie Nellie will sit with yer till I come back.'

'Yeah, I'll keep yer amused, darlin',' Nellie grinned. 'I'll tell yer a story about what happened to me when I was a little girl and I was playin' leap-frog with me mates.'

Molly stopped on her way to the door and turned. 'I hope ye're goin' to behave yerself, Nellie McDonough, an' think before yer speak. Don't be lettin' yer tongue run away with yer.'

Nellie's eyes rolled. 'Yer don't trust me, do yer, girl? Anyone would think I was a bit soft in the head.' She flung her arm out. 'On yer way, missus, an' go an' teach yer mother how to milk ducks.'

Ruthie frowned. 'I didn't know yer could milk ducks, Auntie Nellie.'

'Ay, well yer see, sweetheart, there's a lot of things yer don't know that yer auntie Nellie could teach yer.' Nellie jerked her head at Molly. 'Go on, scarper!'

'Stick to tellin' her about Cinderella, Nellie, an' leave the facts of life to me,' Molly warned. 'One word out of place, an' so help me I'll flatten yer.'

'It would take a steamroller to flatten me, girl, an' I don't know anyone yer can borrow one of them off.' Nellie turned wide eyes on Ruthie. 'D'you know anyone that's got a steamroller to lend yer mam?'

Ruthie tittered, forgetting for the moment that she was supposed to be in pain. 'Oh, you are funny, Auntie Nellie.'

Molly was grinning as she hastened down the hall. They say you can't keep a good man down; well in this case it was a woman. No one could keep Helen Theresa McDonough down . . . not even ruddy Hitler!

Molly looked up in surprise when Jack and Tommy walked in. 'You're early, I was just sayin' to the girls that yer wouldn't be home for another hour!'

'We finished at seven,' Jack said, pulling a face. 'I'm fed up looking at the place, I seem to spend all me life there. I told our Tommy he could work on if he wanted, but I think he's had a bellyful himself.'

Tommy nodded in agreement. 'I like the extra money, but it's no joke working twelve or thirteen hours a day.'

'If I'd known, I'd have let Ruthie stay up to see yer . . . she wanted to.' Molly related the events leading up to her daughter being escorted home from school. 'Talk about a wounded soldier!'

Jack looked concerned. 'It's not serious, is it?'

It was Doreen who answered, 'No, she's makin' out it's worse than it is, isn't she, our Jill?'

'I'm afraid so,' Jill said. 'She knows me mam's a soft touch.'

'Ay, well, I was just as soft with you when yer were her age.' Molly went into the kitchen and reached for a towel to take the plates off the pans of boiling water. 'An' it's not often she makes a fuss, she's not a cry-baby.'

'I don't feel hungry,' Jack said when his dinner was put in front of him. 'I've no appetite.'

'I've cooked it, sunshine, so you're goin' to eat it whether yer like it or not!' Molly pointed a finger at him. 'Food is too scarce to waste, so get it down yer.'

Jack pulled a face but obediently picked up his knife and fork. 'I'll eat what I can.'

'Dad.' Jill leaned her elbows on the table. 'I was just telling me mam that I've got the job I applied for in the ROF. I start in the wages office two weeks on Monday.'

'Good for you!' Jack smiled. 'What with our Doreen making barrage balloons, you in the munitions and me an' Tommy on war work, no one can say this family isn't helping the war effort.'

'It's not enough though, is it, Dad?' Doreen said. 'Everybody at work's talking about the way Hitler's got all our blokes on the run. I'm just prayin' that Phil's not near where the fightin' is.'

'From what the bloke in the shop said when I called in for me *Echo*, no one is certain what's going on.' This wasn't quite true, but Jack didn't see any point in worrying his daughter unless it was absolutely necessary. And, please God, it wouldn't come to that. 'It'll be a few days before we get the full picture.'

'But Hitler has got our fellers on the run, hasn't he?' Doreen wasn't to be put off. 'I mean, that's true, isn't it?'

'I'm afraid so, love. But it could be just a temporary hitch, until our lot get their wind back. But although it leaves a bad taste in me mouth to say it, 'cos I hate their guts, I've got to admit that the men commanding the German army have planned it well. They've outwitted and outflanked us at every turn. They're better equipped than our lads and there's a damn sight more of them.'

Molly looked at Doreen's downcast face. 'Don't you worry, sunshine, the tide will turn, you'll see. Hitler might be gettin' things his way at the moment, but it won't last. They'll never beat us, not in a million years.'

Doreen sighed. 'I hope ye're right, but I haven't had a letter from Phil for nearly a week now and I can't help worrying.'

'You often go a week without hearing from him, then yer get a bundle of letters all in one go! Look on the bright side, an' don't be thinkin' the worst. An' if ye're goin' over to Miss Clegg's, don't go with a miserable face, try an' cheer her up.'

'OK.' Doreen gave another sigh. 'I'll go and sit with her for an hour, pass the time away.' She turned to her sister. 'D'yer feel like comin' with me, Jill, or are yer seein' Steve?'

'Yeah, I'm going up there now.' Jill felt deeply for her sister. She knew how afraid she'd be if she was in her shoes. 'He was working until eight o'clock, so he'll be home by now.'

After the two girls had left the house together, Molly eyed Tommy. 'Are you goin' out, son?'

'I might go up to Ginger's.' He pushed a potato round his plate, trying to find the right words to ask a question without appearing too interested. 'Did I tell yer Ginger's asked Rosie for a date?'

'Go 'way! Well, I never thought Ginger would have the nerve.' Molly chuckled. 'And what did our Rosie have to say to that?'

'She turned him down . . . said she already had a boy-friend.'

'Ah, he got knocked back, eh?' Molly could see Ginger's

freckled face in her mind and she thought the whole idea was hilarious. 'Still, it happens to us all some time in our lives. He'll live to tell the tale.'

Tommy waited for her to volunteer some more information about the mysterious boyfriend, but Molly's lips stayed firmly sealed. So Tommy had to swallow his pride and ask, 'She told Malcolm the same thing, but I've never heard of no boyfriend, have you?'

'I think she's mentioned that there's a boy she fancies, but that's all I know.' Molly would have liked to have told him he was the boy in question, just to see the look on his face. 'Ask her yerself when yer see her.'

'Nah, I'm not that interested, just curious.' Tommy pushed his chair back and picked up his plate to carry to the kitchen. 'I bet Ginger felt a right nit, though.'

'He'll get a lot of knock-backs before he's much older,' Molly said. 'And you as well – just wait until you fancy a girl an' she turns yer down, then yer'll know how he felt. Because you fancy a girl doesn't mean she's got to fancy you.'

'Oh, I'm signing the pledge until I'm about twenty,' Tommy said, with all the experience of a sixteen-year-old who had yet to have his first kiss. 'Girls are nothin' but a nuisance, always chattering about stupid things, and they're bossy into the bargain.'

Jack had been listening with a grin on his face. 'You won't always feel like that, son, believe me. Yer'll meet a girl one of these days who's the right one for you, an' yer won't know what's hit yer.'

'Well it won't happen before I'm at least twenty, I'll make sure of that.' Tommy glanced at the clock on the mantelpiece and saw it was nearly a quarter to nine. 'I'll go and see if Ginger feels like a walk, but I'll be back for ten and have an early night.'

'It's a nice night for a walk,' Molly said. Then as her son

reached the door, she called, 'Yer never know yer luck, son, you and Ginger might get a click.'

As Tommy closed the door behind him, he thought, There's no chance of that! Ginger might be daft about girls, but I'm not. Still, it was queer about this boyfriend of Rosie's. She never went anywhere to meet a boy, so how come? Sounded right odd to him.

Tommy was strolling up the street whistling, his shoulders hunched and his hands in his trouser pockets. His mam was right, it was a lovely evening. He took a deep breath, drinking in the fresh air. It made a pleasant change from the noise and the smell on the shop floor. Then he saw a familiar figure walking towards him, and without giving it any thought, he took his hands from his pockets, straightened his shoulders and adopted a jaunty swagger. This was the time to do as his mam said and ask her outright. Well, perhaps not outright, but in a roundabout way he'd get it out of her. 'Hiya, Rosie!'

'Oh, it's yerself, is it?' Rosie was looking very pretty in a light-coloured floral dress, with a cardigan draped across her shoulders. Her rich dark hair curled about her face and shoulders and there was a smile in her vivid blue eyes. 'I didn't think yer'd be home from work yet.'

'We finished early. It's gettin' too much, working late every night an' all day Saturday.'

'Sure yer must get fed up, I can understand that, so I can.' Rosie's ruby-red lips parted in a smile. 'As me mammy says, "All work and no play, makes Jack a dull boy." So you go out and get a bit of enjoyment, Tommy, you're only young once.' She made to walk on. 'I'll be off now, so I'll bid yer goodnight.'

'Just a minute!' Without thinking, Tommy laid a hand on her arm to detain her, then when he realized what he was doing he withdrew it quickly.

'I hope yer weren't annoyed that Ginger asked yer for a date?'

'Indeed I wasn't! Not at all, at all. I took it as a compliment an' think it was very gentlemanly of Ginger to ask me. An' if I wasn't spoken for I'd have gladly gone to the pictures with him.'

Tommy stood his ground. He'd find out about this boyfriend if it was the last thing he did. Not that he was worried or interested, he was just curious. 'He said yer turned him down 'cos yer've got a boyfriend.'

'I declined his offer, yes,' Rosie agreed, 'but I take kindly to him making it.'

'Who is this boyfriend?' There, she couldn't avoid it now. 'Funny I've never heard of yer goin' out with anyone.'

'Is there any reason why yer should? Sure, I don't have to tell you what I do, Tommy Bennett, or who I do it with.'

'Well, have you or have you not got a boyfriend?'

'Why d'yer want to know?'

Tommy was flummoxed. She was answering his question with one of her own! 'Er, so I can tell Ginger.'

'I've already told him, so I have, Tommy Bennett. Is it a liar yer think I am?'

'No! I'm just curious, that's all! I mean, what's his name, where does he work and what does he look like? It seems funny to me that no one has ever set eyes on him.'

Rosie looked down at his feet then worked her way up until her eyes met his. 'D'yer want to know all these things so yer can tell Ginger? Or is it yerself that's being nosy?'

The question caught Tommy on the hop. 'Er – so I can tell Ginger. I've got a feeling he thinks yer only made the boy up 'cos yer didn't want to go out with him.'

Rosie tilted her head and surveyed him with a critical eye. 'Mmm! I'd say he's about your height,' she tapped a finger on her chin. 'Yes, I'd say that, all right. And funny enough, his name's Tommy as well. In fact he's quite like you to look at, but, praise be, he doesn't always have a scowl on his face like you.'

Tommy narrowed his eyes. He had a feeling he was being taken for a ride.

'Tell us where he works, then?'

'I'll do no such thing, Tommy Bennett! How would you like it if I asked you all these questions about your girlfriend?'

Tommy's lip curled. 'I haven't got no girlfriend.'

Rosie chuckled. 'Oh ay, Tommy, and the band played believe me if yer like!' She straightened the cardigan on her shoulders and began to walk away. 'We'll call it quits, then, Tommy, shall we? You haven't got a girlfriend an' I haven't got a boyfriend.'

Tommy stared after her. 'But I haven't got a girl!'

'Whatever you say, Tommy,' Rosie smiled over her shoulder. 'Whatever you say.'

Tommy felt like kicking himself. My God, she'd made a right fool of him and he was still no wiser than he was half an hour ago! As he turned in the direction of his friend's house there was one thing certain in his mind. He wasn't going to repeat to Ginger one word of what had been said. The high and mighty Rosie O'Grady wasn't going to make a laughing-stock of him! And whoever the poor bloke was she was going out with, well, he felt sorry for him.

Meanwhile, Rosie stood outside the Bennetts' house waiting for someone to answer her knock. There was a smile of satisfaction on her pretty face as she recalled the conversation. She'd given Tommy something to think about all right, but wasn't he slow on the uptake? Still, as her mammy would say, patience is a virtue. And she could be patient, all right, so she could . . . as long as he didn't take too long about it.

Ellen came down from seeing the two boys to bed, and sank into a chair for a well-earned break. She looked forward to this time of the day, when she could put her feet up for half an hour before seeing to the clothes that had been in steep since the night before. She'd rinse them out and then put them through the mangle before hanging them out on the line. That was the beauty of nice weather, there was no need to have wet clothes hanging everywhere.

She reached over to the couch for the *Echo*, smiling at the two girls who were having a last game of Ludo before being packed off to bed. 'Don't start another game after that one, Phoebe,' she warned. 'It's late as it is.'

'OK, Mam.' Phoebe flicked the red counter and it found its way straight into the eggcup. She slapped her sister on the back, a happy smile on her face. 'That's two games I've won, our Dorothy, to your one.'

'I'll get me own back tomorrow night,' Dorothy promised. 'Yer've just been lucky.'

'Pack the board away, girls, and get undressed.' Ellen laid the paper down. She was worried enough about Corker without reading the bad news that filled the papers these days. 'Rinse yer hands and face before yer go up to bed.'

'Mam?' Phoebe threw the counters in the box and put the lid on. 'D'yer mind if I ask yer somethin'? Yer won't get mad at me, will yer?'

'It's not very often I get mad with yer, is it?' Ellen smiled. They were four good kids, she couldn't ask for better. 'What is it yer want to ask me?'

'Did me dad really say he wanted yer to marry Uncle Corker?'

Ellen looked shocked. This was the first time any of the children had mentioned their father. 'What made you ask that?'

'Well, me an' Dorothy heard you an' Uncle Corker talkin', and that's what we thought yer said.'

'Yes, when yer dad was very ill, he said he thought Uncle Corker would be good for me and for you.'

Phoebe bit on her bottom lip while Dorothy sat wide-eyed. 'I know I shouldn't say it, Mam, but we didn't like me dad. He wasn't nice to us, always hittin' us and shoutin' at us even though we hadn't done nothing wrong.'

'Yes, I know that, love. I didn't like him myself at times because he was mean and cruel. But when he was sick, he changed.' Ellen chose her words carefully, knowing that what she said could affect her children's lives for a long time. She didn't want them to go through life hating their father. 'He knew he hadn't been a good husband or father, and was sorry. He wanted us all to be happy, and he knew we would be with Uncle Corker. That's why he said what he did.'

'If he'd stayed bad, he wouldn't have said that, would he, Mam?' Dorothy said. 'He must have turned good before he died.'

'Yes, love, he did.'

'An' he must have found out he really loved us, mustn't he?'

'Yes, he did.' Ellen felt tears pricking her eyes, but they were tears of relief. The children would remember their father, not with love, no – he had never given them any reason to love him – but at least when they thought of him now it wouldn't be with hatred.

'I'm glad he turned out good, Mam,' Phoebe said, 'but we love Uncle Corker, and we're lookin' forward to him being our dad.'

'Yes, I know, love.' Ellen's smile was tearful. It was funny the way children could cope with things better than adults. But this little talk had cleared the air, and her mind. 'An' I love Uncle Corker, too, very much.'

Chapter Twenty-Five

Molly pulled the key out of the lock and stepped into Miss Clegg's hall. She stood still for a while, her head cocked, until she heard a sound that had her scurrying to the living room. There she saw the old lady rocking in her chair, her hands covering her face as sobs shook her frail body.

'Ah, come on, sunshine, don't take on so.' Molly knelt down at the side of the chair and put her arm across the thin shoulders. 'Yer'll make yerself ill if yer carry on like this.'

'I can't help it, Molly,' Victoria sobbed. 'I keep thinking that something terrible has happened to Phil.'

'There now.' Molly held her close, wishing she could reassure the old lady that everything would be all right. But how could she when the whole country was in a state of shock at the news coming through from Europe? The German army was advancing on all fronts and the Allied forces were being pushed backwards, towards the sea. According to the latest news bulletin, there were thousands of them stranded on the beaches at Dunkirk with no protection from the waves of German aircraft dropping their deadly bombs. Molly felt like crying herself when she thought of those lads being killed and maimed without any chance of fighting back, and it was only her anger that kept her tears in check. Like everyone she spoke to, she was asking herself how it could have happened. Someone, somewhere, had a lot to answer for.

'Come on, sunshine, dry yer eyes, there's a good girl.' Molly struggled to her feet. 'We don't want Phil comin' home to find you unwell, do we?'

'Molly, d'yer think he will come home?' Victoria dabbed at her red-rimmed eyes. 'If I could, I'd give my life for his.'

'Ay, yer can cut that talk out for a start! I know things are bad an' I'm as worried as you are, but we've got to keep going! There's thousands of women with husbands and boyfriends over there, but they've got to carry on, otherwise we might as well hold up our hands, surrender an' let Hitler win!' Molly's anger was rising as she spoke. 'An' I'll tell yer this, Victoria, I for one am not about to let that happen. I'll take a bloody gun meself before I let that swine win.' She managed to smile as she added, 'I'll take Nellie with me, of course.'

The tears had ceased now, and Victoria nodded in agreement. 'You're right, Molly, we can't let him beat us.'

Molly stroked the sparse white hair. 'That's the spirit, sunshine! You, me an' Nellie, we'd take the Germans on an' lick the pants off them.'

'A fat lot of good I'd be, I'm useless, good for nothing.'

'Oh dear, we are feeling sorry for ourselves today, aren't we?' Molly bent to wag a finger in her face. 'Snap out of it, sunshine, an' don't be burying Phil when he's not dead. D'yer hear? He's not dead!' Molly knew she had to be cruel to be kind. 'If everyone gave up hope, who would make the guns an' ammunition for our boys to fight with, eh? And they'll fight back, oh yes, they'll fight back all right. And next time it'll be the Germans on the run, take it from me.'

Victoria gave a weak smile. Molly's fighting talk had done the trick. She would worry again when she was on her own; she couldn't help it. But, like her neighbour said, she had to believe that Phil wasn't dead. 'Would you stick the kettle on for a cuppa, Molly, please?'

Molly was talking to herself as she hurried across the cobbled street.

'I didn't intend stayin' that long, but I couldn't just leave her, not the state she was in.' She glanced at the house three doors away as she slipped the key in the lock. 'Nellie will be here any minute for her elevenses an' I'll have to drink another ruddy cup of tea, even if it kills me.'

She walked through the living room to the kitchen, filled the kettle and set it on a high light on the gas stove. 'No wonder the old lady's feelin' the way she does, she's got nothing to occupy her mind. Sittin' there all on her lonesome the whole day long, it's understandable she gets down in the dumps.'

Molly was setting the tray when there was a bang on the front window that had the glass rattling in the frame. 'Why the hell she can't use the knocker like everyone else is beyond me.' She threw open the front door. 'One of these days, Nellie McDonough, yer'll put that ruddy window in! An' if yer do, yer'll flamin' well pay for it!'

'I only rapped with me knuckle, girl, gentle like.' Nellie smiled into Molly's face as she passed. 'I can't help it if I've got knuckles like a navvy.'

'Why can't yer use the knocker?'

Nellie pulled out her usual chair and plonked herself down. 'I knock on the window so yer'll know it's me.'

'Nellie, yer come every morning at the same time, so who else would I think it was?'

'Someone yer owed money to, like the club woman. Now if she knocked on the door, an' yer wanted to give her a miss, yer wouldn't know it was her at the door, would yer? An' yer'd be caught out.'

'If I wanted to miss the club woman, sunshine, I'd have the good manners to tell her to her face.' Molly tapped a finger on the side of her nose. 'Not like someone I know who hides in the kitchen until she thinks the coast is clear.'

'Hey, you just watch it, girl, that's defur . . . er . . . defin . . .' Nellie scratched her head, thought for a minute, then said, 'That's a lie, that is.'

Molly spluttered at the look on her friend's face. 'Nellie, were yer trying to say defamation of character?'

Nellie rested her elbow on the table and cupped her chin in one of her chubby hands. 'I could have yer up in court for that, yer know.'

'Have me for what?'

'What you've just said.'

'No you couldn't 'cos it's the truth.'

Nellie's body began to shake. 'I know it's the truth, you know it's the truth, but the club woman doesn't, so she could take yer to court.'

'On what grounds?'

'Calling her a liar!'

'I didn't—' Molly broke off. Rubbing a fist across her forehead she counted to ten, telling herself not to encourage her friend because she'd keep it up until the cows came home. 'I'll brew the tea.'

'I've got some scandal for yer,' Nellie called out to the kitchen. 'It'll make yer hair curl.'

'That would be handy,' Molly said, placing the tray on the table. 'It would save me gettin' a perm for the wedding.'

'I'll wait until yer've poured the tea, then we can do to her what you've just done to me.'

'What have I just done to you?' Molly asked.

Nellie screwed her face up. 'If I get it wrong, girl, an' yer laugh at me, I'll flatten yer. I think it was defamation of character. The only difference is, we were actin' daft. What I'm goin' to tell yer isn't funny.'

Molly poured out the tea quicker than she'd ever done. She didn't know where Nellie got her news from, but she was never wrong. 'Right, I'm all ears.'

'I've got a bit of good news, so I'll give yer that first.' When she folded her arms, Nellie's bosom was pushed out to form a shelf. 'Our Lily's got a feller.'

'Oh, go 'way! Since when?'

'Well I don't rightly know how long she's known him, 'cos she can be very deep sometimes, can our Lily. But she brought him in last night after they'd been to the flicks.'

'And?' Molly arched her brows. 'What's the verdict?'

'He seems a nice enough bloke, but yer can't really tell until yer've known someone a while, can yer? He was very nervous at first, I felt sorry for him. Then George mentioned football, found out the lad was a Liverpool supporter an' they got on like a house on fire.'

'Your Lily is very sensible for a seventeen-year-old, she wouldn't take up with anyone that wasn't decent.' A slow smile spread across Molly's face. 'Those big hats we're goin' to buy, we'll get our money's worth out of them all right. There's quite a few weddings on the horizon.'

'Ye're not gettin' dolled up for Corker's wedding, are yer?' Nellie looked concerned. 'I'm goin' to be strapped for cash, what with a new dress an' shoes, an' a present into the bargain.'

'No, they're getting married in a register office so there's no need to get dolled up.' Molly felt sentimental as her mind went back over the years. 'D'yer remember, Nellie, the day we sat here an' said when your Steve married our Jill we'd buy the biggest hats we could find? Well I'm sticking to what I said then. The day our Jill walks down the aisle with your Steve, I'll be wearin' the biggest, poshest hat that Blackler's have got.'

'Ay, I can remember that day, girl! You said yer were goin' to buy one as big as a cartwheel, an' because I couldn't think of anythin' bigger than a cartwheel, I asked if I could stand under yours.' Nellie sniffed and wiped a stray tear from her eye. 'They'd fallen out at the time, remember? But you were certain they'd get back together, that's why yer mentioned the big 'at.'

'And I was right, as per usual. If ever a couple were made for each other, it's Jill and Steve.' Molly reached for Nellie's empty cup. 'Anyway, we've got off the subject of defamation of character. Who are yer goin' to defame?'

Nellie's mouth gaped for a second. 'Ay, girl, yer don't half know some big words, don't yer? Proper bloody encic . . . encec . . . oh, God, here I go again, what's the word?'

'Encyclopaedia, Nellie, but yer could have said dictionary.' Molly hissed through her clenched teeth. 'For heaven's sake, will yer get on with whatever yer've got to tell me?'

'Oh, all right, keep yer ruddy hair on! It's about that fly turn in number sixteen.'

'Oh, not her again, Nellie! Yer've really got it in for that woman an' I'm blowed if I know why. She's never done you no harm.'

'Chance would be a fine thing, girl, 'cos I steer well clear of her.' Nellie laid her elbows flat on the table and fixed her gaze on Molly. 'Have I, or have I not, always said she was a brazen hussy?'

'Ever since she moved into the street,' Molly said. 'But I don't know why 'cos she's never done nothing wrong.'

'Until now.' When Nellie nodded slowly, her chins moved up and down in slow motion. 'Until now.'

'Oh dear, what's she done to upset yer now?'

'I'm not upset, girl, I'm blazin' mad . . . spitting feathers if yer must know.' Nellie's nostrils flared. 'She's got herself a fancy man.'

'Come off it, sunshine! Yer've been listening to too much gossip, that's your trouble.'

'I've been listening to gossip for weeks, girl, but I never said a dickie bird to yer 'cos I knew yer'd blow yer top. But this time it isn't gossip 'cos I saw it with me own eyes.' When Molly remained silent, Nellie went on. 'I saw her take him into their house last night. My feller fancied a bag of chips so I went down to the chippy. And who was I walkin' behind on me way back? The bold one, that's who, an' her fancy man.'

Molly looked shocked. 'She wouldn't have the nerve to take

a man into that house with the kids there. Perhaps it was her brother, or a cousin or something.'

'If it was her brother, then all I can say is he's a very loving brother 'cos he had his arm round her an' was kissing her.' Nellie huffed. 'I don't know, you must go round with yer eyes an' ears closed. She's been the talk of the street for weeks, an' last night isn't the first time she's been seen takin' a man in the house.'

Molly cast her eyes down. 'I can't believe it! Her husband's out in the Middle East somewhere, surely she wouldn't cheat on him?'

'You can believe it, girl, 'cos there's worse to come,' Nellie said. 'I was talkin' to Mrs Pearson who lives next door to her, an' she told me that when her husband was goin' out at half-five yesterday morning, who should come out of the next door but the bold laddo himself. Mrs Pearson was seeing her husband out, he's on the six to two shift, and she said the bloke never said hello, kiss me arse or anythin', just legged it hell for leather down the street.'

Molly was convinced now that what Nellie was saying was true. 'It's not only her husband she's cheatin' on, she's lettin' the children down as well. They shouldn't have to see that sort of carry-on, it's not fair on them.'

'She's takin' a chance, girl, that's all I can say. I mean, the war won't last for ever, an' when her husband comes home there'll be plenty of wagging tongues to tell him what she's been up to.' Nellie banged an open palm on the table. 'I told yer all along she was hot stuff, but yer wouldn't have it. You might be good with big words, girl, but I'm good at reading people. And I've had her tabbed since the word go. Her husband might have kept her satisfied in bed when he was home, but now he's thousands of miles away she'll make do with anybody. As long as they've got a pair of trousers on, she'll go to bed with them.'

Molly's face was a picture of dejection. 'I dunno, it's not

twelve o'clock yet an' I've heard enough sadness to last me a lifetime. First the news on the wireless . . . all bad. Tryin' to cheer our Doreen up before she went to work . . . without success. Comforting Miss Clegg when I felt like bawlin' me own eyes out. An' now you tell me that the wife of one of our soldiers is cheatin' on him.'

'Be fair, girl, I did give yer some good news.' When Molly looked puzzled, Nellie reminded her. 'Our Lily's got herself a feller.'

'With the best will in the world, Nellie, you can hardly say that compensates for all the bad news.'

'I dunno about that.' Nellie knew it was time to go home and get some work done, but she didn't want to leave her friend feeling down in the dumps. 'Yer see, I thought our Lily was goin' to be left on the shelf.'

Molly gasped in surprise. 'What! Left on the shelf! Nellie, your Lily is only seventeen years of age!'

'I was married at eighteen, girl! Mind you, I proposed to George. And the fact that I had his arm up his back at the time might have had somethin' to do with him accepting . . . he was too bloody frightened to do anything else.'

Molly was smiling widely now and Nellie was satisfied. 'I'll see yer later, girl . . . ta-ra.'

Tommy was chewing so hard on the inside of his cheek he could taste blood in his mouth. But he had to do something to stop himself from crying. He was a man now, and grown men don't cry.

He glanced sideways to where Doreen and her friend Maureen had their arms around each other, sobbing, and his mam and Jill were holding hands as tears rolled down their faces. They were listening to the voice coming from the wireless, telling of the armada of small ships that had braved the German bombers to cross the Channel to rescue the British soldiers, who were stranded on the beaches at

Dunkirk. Even the announcer's voice broke with emotion as he told of the bravery of the men who had risked their lives in any vessel that would sail on water . . . from the smallest fishing boats to yachts. And they'd brought hundreds of soldiers back, landing them on the coast and returning to Dunkirk to help the others. The risk was great, and some of the heroes had paid with their lives, but they were prepared to take that risk. Only the sea separated them from the stranded soldiers, and they just couldn't stand by and do nothing.

'Thank God for them,' Jack said, lighting yet another cigarette. 'At least our soldiers will know somebody cares about them. Every one of those men is a hero, 'cos what they did took some guts.'

Molly wiped the back of a hand across her eyes. 'Some of them lost their lives.'

'Ay, I know, love, there'll be plenty of families grieving tonight. But they saved a lot of our boys, and the families can take comfort from that and be proud of them.' He shook his head in disbelief. 'It must have been some sight, all those hundreds of little boats setting off across the Channel not knowing what they would find, or if they'd ever come back.'

Doreen was sobbing into Maureen's shoulder. 'They brought some wounded soldiers home – I wonder if Phil is one of them?'

'Please God he's safe and sound,' Molly said. 'We should know in a couple of days. He's put Miss Clegg down as next of kin, so she'll be the one to be informed.' In her mind Molly was praying to God that Phil was alive and not one of the hundreds of bodies lying on thc beaches. 'Why don't you an' Mo go over and sit with her for a while? But wash yer face first so she won't know yer've been crying.'

After the two girls had left and Jill had gone upstairs to change, Tommy said, 'They weren't half brave, those men, were they, Dad?'

'When your country or countrymen are at risk, son, then

that's when patriotism shows. When there's no war on, yer never think about whether yer love yer country or not, but when anybody threatens it, then yer realize what it means to yer.' Jack knew Molly was watching, but his nerves were at breaking-point so he chanced her anger and lit another cigarette. 'I don't think there's many men in this country, no matter how old they are, who, given the chance, wouldn't have joined the men on those boats. I know I would.'

'Yer dad's right, son,' Molly said. 'War's a terrible thing, but it don't half bring out the best in people. I remember the last war, and how everyone stuck together through thick and thin and helped each other.'

'If the war's still on when I'm eighteen, Mam, I'm definitely goin' to join up.'

'Over my dead body!' Molly flared. 'You ain't going anywhere, sunshine, so get that into yer head.'

'Will you two stop arguing?' Jack said. 'Time to get the boxing gloves out when he's eighteen.'

'Ay, ye're right, love, there's more important things to worry about.' Molly brushed a stray hair from her eyes. 'I hope to God Phil's all right. How long d'yer think it'll be before we hear anything?'

'You heard what the man on the wireless said, it'll be a few weeks before they know anything for certain. Don't forget, the evacuation is still going on. It's goin' to be some job finding out who's dead, who's missing and who's alive. An' it's not only our lads, there were soldiers from France and Belgium fightin' alongside of them.' He sighed as he watched the smoke from his cigarette waft up to the ceiling. 'It's a right bloody mess an' someone's got to take responsibility for our lads being stranded on open beaches . . . easy targets for the blasted Germans to just pick them off at leisure. I'm so flaming mad I could strangle Hitler with me bare hands and get a great deal of pleasure from it.'

Molly stood up and smoothed down the skirt of her dress.

'I feel more like flying, but I must get some ironing done; our Ruthie's got no clean knickers.' She stopped near the kitchen door and turned her head. 'I know you two heathens never say a prayer, but I'm asking yez both to pray tonight that Phil comes home. And yer can say another one for all the other lads out there.'

It was three days later when a hammering on the front door had Molly flying down the hall, wiping her hands on her pinny as she went.

Maisie from the corner shop was standing outside, and from the look on her face Molly knew she'd brought news. 'What is it, Maisie?'

'Phil's in a hospital down south.' The words poured from Maisie's mouth. 'He rang up himself and told me to tell Miss Clegg and yourselves that he's been wounded, but ye're not to worry.'

Molly blessed herself as she looked up to the sky. 'Oh, thank you God, thank you.' Then she asked, 'Did he say how bad his wounds are, or what they are?'

Maisie shook her head. 'He didn't have time to say much. He just wanted you all to know he's all right.'

'How did he sound?'

'Molly, the line was crackling and there was a lot of noise at his end, so it was hard to tell how he sounded. But he said Miss Clegg and Doreen will be getting a letter from him in a few days.'

'D'yer know, Maisie, I feel as though a ton weight has been lifted from me shoulders.' Molly let out a deep breath. 'I've had a headache for days worrying about him, and our Doreen's a nervous wreck. Oh, thank God for that, me mind's easier already.' She glanced across the street. 'Have yer told Miss Clegg yet?'

'No, I thought you'd like to be the one to do that.'

'Maisie, ye're a real pal. They say a friend in need is a friend indeed, well that's what you are. And right now, with the good news yer've just brought, I could kiss yer.'

Maisie feigned horror. 'Oh, not that, Molly! Anything but that!'

'Get away before I clout yer one! Turning me kisses down, it's enough to give me an inferiority complex.' Molly felt light with relief. She was so happy she wanted to sing and dance for joy. 'You go back to weighin' yer spuds and I'll nip across and tell Miss Clegg. Ooh, I can't wait to see her face.'

'I'll see yer then, Molly, ta-ra for now.'

'Thanks a million, Maisie, yer've taken a load off me mind.' Molly glanced back down the hall. She'd been in the middle of peeling potatoes when Maisie had knocked, but they could wait, there was plenty of time to do them before dinner. She patted the pocket in her pinny to make sure she had Miss Clegg's key, then pulled her front door to and ran across the street.

There was a surprised look on Victoria's face when Molly walked in. 'I didn't expect you back so soon.' Then she saw the excitement in Molly's eyes and her hand went to her throat. 'You've had news?'

'Yes, sunshine, we've had news.' Molly drew a dining chair up so she could sit next to the old lady. 'Maisie's just been down to say Phil rang.'

'He rang?' Her voice was choked with emotion. 'Where is he? Is he all right?'

Molly held her hand and quickly told her all there was to tell. 'You'll be hearing from him in a day or two, but he wanted you to know he's safe and back in Blighty.'

'But you said he's been wounded!'

'Ay, come on now!' Molly stroked the thin, veined hand. 'Last week yer had him dead and buried! He's alive, Victoria, an' he phoned himself, so his injuries can't be so bad.'

'You're right, Molly, I should be thanking God he's home

safe.' Her eyes shining with tears, she smiled. 'I just want to see his face, I've missed him so much.'

'Of course yer have, sunshine, we all have. Just wait till our Doreen gets home, she'll be over the moon.'

'She's a good girl, Molly, she's been a tower of strength to me.'

'Yeah, she's surprised me, I can tell yer. She used to be a proper cheeky little madam, but she's more understanding now, more grown-up.' Molly stood up and pushed the chair back in place. 'I'll get off, Victoria, 'cos I want to finish preparing the dinner before I give Nellie a knock. You know what me mate's like, once she starts talking there's no stoppin' her.'

Victoria grinned. 'I'd say you were a well-matched pair, Molly.'

Molly smiled back. 'In other words, I talk too much as well.' She arched her eyebrows. 'I know what I'll do! I'll give her a knock now an' she can sit in ours while I do the spuds. That's what they call killing two birds with one stone.'

For the first time in weeks, Victoria laughed aloud. 'I would hardly call Nellie a bird.'

'Oh, I would! She's a talking parrot! In fact, according to you, we're a pair of talking parrots! I'm goin' to tell her what yer said and give her a laugh.' Molly bent to kiss the old lady's cheek. 'I'll be over later with yer dinner and, if I were you, I'd try and get a bit of shut-eye.'

'I'm too excited to sleep, Molly, my brain is working overtime.'

'Well at least yer've got something nice to think about, better than all the worryin' yer've been doing lately. Anyway, I'll see yer later.'

Jack could feel the charged atmosphere as soon as he walked in the room. He made no attempt to take his donkey jacket off, but stood by the table glancing from one smiling face to the other. He was about to ask what was going on when Doreen rushed up to him and flung her arms around his neck. 'Phil's all right, Dad! He's in a hospital somewhere down south.'

Jack disentangled her arms, holding them so he could look into her face. 'You've heard from him?'

Doreen nodded, her eyes blurred by tears. 'He rang the corner shop and asked Maisie to pass the message on.'

Tommy squeezed past his father. 'Ay, that's the gear, our Doreen!'

'That's putting it mildly, son,' Jack said, his face beaming. 'It's bloody marvellous! By, that's the best news I've had for God knows how long.'

Molly didn't want to spoil their happiness, but it was too early to get carried away. She'd been giving it a lot of thought since the first wave of relief and happiness had passed, and worry was beginning to niggle again. After all, they didn't know how serious Phil's injuries were. 'He's been wounded, Jack, but didn't give Maisie any details.'

'But he rang himself, didn't he?' Doreen said. 'So he can't be badly wounded.'

Jack met Molly's eyes before saying, 'We'll just have to wait and see, love. The main thing is, he's alive and back in England.'

'He's writing to me an' Miss Clegg – we should get a letter in a couple of days.'

'So you'll have all the answers then.' Jack slipped his coat off and gave it to Tommy to hang on the hall-stand. 'With a bit of luck we should be seeing him soon.'

'Ooh, I can't wait.' Doreen put her arms around her waist and hugged herself. 'It's been ages.'

'Now yer've seen yer dad and Tommy, go over and see Miss Clegg,' Molly said. 'She'll be on pins waiting for yer.'

They waited until they heard the front door close, then Jill said, 'He can't be badly injured, Mam, or he wouldn't have been able to phone up himself.'

'It's no good guessing, sunshine, we'll just have to bide our time until he writes. But he's alive, and for that we must be thankful.' Molly went into the kitchen to get the two dinners keeping warm on top of pans, and when she carried them through she said, 'I'll slip over to me ma's and let them know. They've been worried, so it'll put their minds at rest.'

'I'll go for yer, Mam, there's no need for you to go out,' Tommy said, his eyes on his plate. 'I don't mind going, a bit of fresh air will do me good.'

Molly winked at Jack. Tommy seemed to have taken a liking for fresh air these last few days; he was always walking round to his nan's. 'That's good of yer, son, it'll save me legs.'

Tommy ate his dinner with gusto and had cleared his plate before Jack was halfway through his. 'I enjoyed that, Mam!' He patted his tummy. 'I'm full up now, a walk will do me good.'

'Off yer pop, then, son, I'll take yer plate out.' Molly watched her son combing his hair in front of the mirror and her chest swelled with pride. He was a handsome lad, no doubt about that. 'Tell me ma I'll be round in the morning.'

Satisfied he looked respectable, Tommy said, 'I'll see yer later, then. I won't be late.'

Molly waited until he was halfway down the hall, then she bawled, 'Oh, an' give my love to Rosie!'

'And mine!' Jill shouted.

Tommy could feel his face burning as he pulled the door behind him. He'd have to stop this blushing lark, he was getting too old for it. He should be able to take a joke without going the colour of a postbox. They were only pulling his leg, hinting it was Rosie he was really going to see, not his nan and grandad. It wasn't true of course, and he should just laugh it off instead of getting himself in a twist. It wasn't his fault that Rosie lived with his grandparents. He went round there to see them, not their lodger. Not that he had anything against Rosie – she was all right when you got to know her. Her only fault was being a girl.

Chapter Twenty-Six

It was three nail-biting days before Doreen received a letter from Phil. And when it came it was so brief, just the one page, her heart sank. He merely wrote that he'd been injured in his right leg and had been operated on. He was confined to bed, but as the hospital was overcrowded he was hoping to be transferred to another hospital nearer home. He didn't say what or how bad his wounds were – none of the things she wanted to know. He sent his regards to everyone, hoped to see them soon, and that was about it. Except for the bottom line that said he loved her very much. That was the one thing that kept back her tears of disappointment.

Molly studied her daughter's face as she reread the letter for the third time and sensed she wasn't too happy with the contents. 'Don't keep us in suspense, sunshine, tell us what Phil's got to say.'

Doreen folded the bottom of the letter over and ran a finger over the crease. The last line that said he loved her wasn't for anyone's eyes but her own. 'He doesn't say very much.' She passed the letter over. 'Don't you dare read the bit I've turned over, that's private.'

'If he says he still loves yer, then yer should be happy, not sittin' there with a face as long as a wet week.' Molly grunted before holding the letter near to her eyes. 'Ay, if he gets transferred to a hospital in Liverpool, wouldn't that be great? We'd all be able to visit him.'

'His letter doesn't tell us much, though, does it, Mam?'

'What the hell d'yer expect? The lad's lying in hospital after an operation, you're lucky you got a letter at all!'

'Can I see it, Mam?' Jill turned to her sister. 'You don't mind, do you, Doreen?'

'Be my guest!' Doreen chewed on her bottom lip. 'Did Miss Clegg show yer the one she got?'

Molly nodded. 'Before yer ask, he only told her the same as he told you. He even told her he loved her, but he didn't put it the way he put it to you.'

'You sneaked!' Doreen said in a high voice. 'Oh, you, Mam, yer sneaked!'

Molly smiled. 'I didn't, sunshine, but I didn't need to, did I? Yer've just given the game away.'

Ruthie had been sitting quietly on the couch, her eyes wide and her ears taking in every word. 'Can I read it, our Doreen? Phil likes me, he wouldn't mind if yer let me have a look.'

Doreen rolled her eyes. 'I think I'll nail it to the front door an' then the whole street can have a read.' But her heart was lighter now her mother had explained that Phil would have difficulty writing and she was lucky to get a letter at all. She should have thought of that herself instead of being so selfish. 'Come and sit next to me,' she beckoned her kid sister over. 'I'll read it to yer.'

'Yer've no need to,' Ruthie said, tossing her head. 'I'm not a baby, I can read joined-up writing.'

'You read it then, but I'm keeping hold of it, I don't trust yer.' Doreen looked across at her mother. 'If I write to him tonight, will yer post the letter first thing in the mornin'? I could post it meself on me way to work, but I haven't got a stamp.'

'The corner shop will have one,' Molly said. 'If yer catch the first post he might get the letter the day after.'

'Shall I go to the shop for yer, our Doreen?' Ruthie's offer was sincere but there was a bit of craftiness behind it. Who knows, she might get a halfpenny for going.

'Is it all right if she goes, Mam?' Doreen asked. 'It's still broad daylight out.'

Molly nodded, knowing full well why her youngest daughter was so keen to run the message. 'But right there and back, mind, no playing out.'

Doreen fished in her purse and brought out a threepenny joey. 'Yer can get yerself some sweets, but bring me the change back.'

Ruthie was off the chair and out of the house like a streak of greased lightning, bringing a smile to Molly's face. 'She's a cute article, that one. She can wrap circles around the lot of us.'

'I'll write him a nice long letter to cheer him up.' Doreen's eyes were dreamy. 'I'll tell him I can't wait for him to come home and we can go dancing to Barlow's Lane.'

Molly had been straightening the mat in front of the fireplace; now she spun around. 'Have yer lost the run of yer senses? He's been wounded in his leg, had an operation, an' you're going to say yer can't wait to go dancing with him? A bit insensitive, don't yer think?'

Doreen gazed at her mother, realization dawning. 'Yer mean . . . yer mean he might not be able to dance again?'

'How the hell would I know? But dancing should be the last thing on yer flaming mind! The lad's alive and he's coming back to Liverpool soon, so count yer blessings an' stop worrying about ruddy dancing.' Molly huffed. 'If it turns out he can't dance again, will yer be givin' him his marching orders?'

'Of course not!' Doreen felt ashamed of herself. She was so excited at the prospect of seeing Phil again she wasn't thinking straight. 'I don't care if we never go dancing again, Mam, as long as he's all right. It's a good job I mentioned it to yer, otherwise I'd have been stupid enough to talk about Barlow's Lane in me letter.' She gave a half-grin. 'Someone bang me head for me.'

'I shouldn't have taken off on yer like that,' Molly said,

'but yer've got to be prepared, in case Phil's injuries are serious. That's all I was trying to do, sunshine, prepare yer for whatever's in store.'

'I know yer were, Mam, and you were being sensible while I was being stupid. I'll write him a nice letter and try and cheer him up.'

'That's the spirit! An' don't forget to tell him we're all looking forward to seein' him again. Yer can tell him about Uncle Corker and Auntie Ellen getting married, that's a good bit of news.'

'And don't forget to tell him you're making our dresses,' Jill chipped in. 'Even Auntie Nellie's.'

'That should put a smile on his face.' Molly laughed. 'Tell him she asked yer if yer could make tents, an' if yer couldn't, could yer pinch a barrage balloon from where yer work.'

It was Friday night and the room was filled with laughter. Nellie had come down for the fitting of the dress Doreen was making and the things she was saying had them all in stitches. There was no side to Nellie, not a trace of vanity, and her jokes were at her own expense.

'Why haven't yer got a full-length mirror so I can admire meself?' she asked, standing on tiptoe in front of the mirror over the mantelpiece. 'I can only see me ruddy neck in that thing.'

Jack got to his feet, chortling. 'I'll take it down and lean it against the wall, then yer can see every inch of yerself.'

Nellie pretended to glare. 'Ay, Jack Bennett, don't you be gettin' sarky with me! Every inch of mine is worth six of anyone else's, so put that in yer pipe an' smoke it.'

'I think yer've got yer sums wrong, Nellie,' Molly said. 'You've got six inches to every one we've got.'

Nellie screwed her eyes up. 'Is that right, girl? In that case I'm better off than any of yer.'

'I'm not sayin' anything, Nellie McDonough, 'cos yer've

got one of yer funny half-hours on.' Molly watched Jack struggle with the heavy looking-glass as his eyes sought the best place to stand it. 'Hang on a minute, love, and I'll move one of the dining chairs. If yer stand it against that wall at an angle, and Nellie stands well back, she'll be able to see herself full-length.'

Nellie inspected herself from every angle and was delighted. The dress was in navy blue with a small white leaf pattern. And Doreen had done a good job on it; it fitted her perfectly. 'By the stripes, girl, yer've done me proud, I look like a ruddy film star.'

'I'm glad you like it, Auntie Nellie.' Doreen, like the rest of the family, loved the big, cuddly woman. The dress had been the devil of a job to make, Nellie's measurements being practically double her own, and there'd been times she thought she'd never get a perfect fit. But she had, and she was proud of herself. 'I've cut the jacket out, but I'll have to tack it before I can try it on yer.'

'It looks lovely on you, Auntie Nellie,' Jill said. 'You'll outshine everyone at the wedding.'

Steve, sitting next to Jill and holding her hand, smiled widely, his dimples deepening. 'Yer look a cracker, Mam! It suits yer better than any dress yer've ever had. In fact, yer can keep it for when me and Jill get married.'

'Not on yer ruddy life!' Nellie jerked a thumb at Molly. 'Me mate here is gettin' dressed to the nines for your wedding, big picture hat, high-heeled shoes, the lot! So I'm not goin' to be the poor relation, she's not goin' one better than me! I'll be dressed like the flamin' Queen of Sheba for your wedding, son, just you wait an' see.'

The room erupted with laughter and Nellie gazed around with a puzzled look on her face. 'What 'ave I said that's so funny?'

Jack, his hand pressing at the pain in his side, looked over at Molly. 'Will you tell her, or shall I?'

'You tell her, love, I'm too busy enjoyin' meself.'

'Nellie,' Jack tried to keep his face straight, 'the Queen of Sheba didn't wear a dress.'

Nellie gaped. 'She didn't! Well, the dirty little faggot! Fancy goin' around with no dress on, an' her a queen! Didn't nobody tell her she couldn't go around bare-arsed? Her bein' a queen, like?'

'Nellie, she didn't go around bare . . . erm . . . she didn't go around with no clothes on.' Molly knew her friend was having them all on, but she wasn't going to spoil her fun. God knows, they could all do with a laugh to offset the horrors that were happening in the world. 'She wore one of those flimsy things, like Cleopatra did when we saw her in that picture.'

'Go 'way!' Nellie shook her head as though in disbelief before turning to Doreen. 'Ay, girl, d'yer think yer could make me one of them flimsy things for the wedding?'

Steve was used to his mother; she was always funny. But she was never as funny as when she was with Auntie Molly. They had the same sense of humour and their jokes seemed to bounce off each other. 'Mam, I don't mind yer lookin' like Cleopatra for Uncle Corker's wedding, but me and Jill will settle for something less . . . less . . . what word shall I use?'

Molly chuckled, 'How about outrageous?'

'That's it, Mrs B., yer've hit the nail on the head.' Steve squeezed Jill's hand, thinking how lucky they were with their families. In fact the Bennetts and the McDonoughs were one big happy family.

Nellie surveyed herself once more. 'All I need now is a pair of gloves to set the outfit off. What d'yer say, girl?'

'Yeah, I need to get gloves as well.'

'Well how about goin' to Paddy's Market tomorrow?' Nellie asked. 'We could pick up a pair cheap there.'

'It'll have to be in the afternoon, Nellie, with Jack working in the morning. Say about two o'clock.'

Nellie nodded before giving a last twirl in front of the

mirror. She smiled in satisfaction, then made her way to the kitchen. 'I'd better get undressed in here.' They heard her laughter before she shouted, 'If Jack saw me in me birthday suit he'd bring his dinner back. An' we can't have that, can we, girl? Not after you slaving over a hot stove all day.'

'They're the largest size gloves we've got in navy blue,' the market-stall man said, trying hard to keep his patience after Nellie had tried unsuccessfully to squeeze her chubby hands into every pair of navy gloves he had. 'I'm afraid I can't help you.'

Nellie looked so down in the mouth Molly felt sorry for her. She'd been lucky finding a pair to match the beige dress she'd had made, but then her hands weren't as big as Nellie's. Then Molly had an inspiration.

'White gloves would look nice, Nellie, they'd set off the white pattern on the dress.'

'Ay, that's an idea, girl!' Nellie brightened up. 'Have yer got a bigger pair in white?' she asked the man.

The stallholder groaned inwardly. She'd separated every pair of navy gloves on his stall – now she was going to start on the white! 'I doubt it. Yer've just got big hands, missus, it's not my fault.'

'It's not my fault either!' Nellie's voice rose. 'I can't help the way God made me. An' I'm flaming well sure that He wouldn't make anyone that couldn't get a pair of gloves to fit them!'

Molly was rummaging in the pile of gloves that was now topsy-turvy. She brought out three pairs of white gloves. 'Try these on, Nellie.'

The second pair Nellie tried were in a soft, brushed cotton, and although she had to struggle, she finally got them on. They were too tight and very uncomfortable, but what the hell – she'd only be wearing them for half an hour. 'How much are they?'

'Yer can have them for a tanner.' The stallholder would have given her them for nothing, just to get shut of her. But she'd been such a ruddy nuisance he might as well try and get something for his trouble. 'An' that's cheap at twice the price.'

Nellie beamed. 'I'll take them.' She pulled at the ends of each of the fingers but the material was stuck to her flesh and the glove wouldn't move. She tried the other hand; same thing. 'Oh, come on, yer stupid things!'

Molly could see the stallholder was fast losing his patience and customers were waiting. 'Give us yer purse, Nellie, and I'll pay the man.'

Nellie was still wearing the gloves as they pushed their way through the crowds. 'I look a right ruddy nit with me old coat on, a turban on me head and snow-white gloves on me hands!'

'Wait till we get outside, we're gettin' crushed to death in here.' Molly cupped her friend's elbow and steered her into the street. 'Now, take it easy an' don't be gettin' all hot and bothered.'

But Nellie was hot and bothered. And as she pulled at the end of each finger in turn, all she succeeded in doing was stretching the material until it appeared she had two-inch-long nails. 'I give up,' she snorted, 'I'll have to cut the blasted things off when I get home.'

'Just hold yer horses, sunshine, an' don't be losing yer rag.' Molly took hold of one of her friend's hands. 'Let's see if we can do it this way.' Starting at the wrist, Molly eased the material over Nellie's palm. 'I'll hold the glove, you pull yer thumb out.'

Two minutes later Nellie was standing with the creased gloves in her hand and sweat running down her cheeks. 'Phew! Honest to God, I thought I'd be sleepin' in them tonight. The best thing I can do is throw them away, I wouldn't go through that again for a big clock.'

'Nellie, if yer hadn't got yerself so het up, yer wouldn't have had to go through that! Yer've got no patience an' go at everything like the ruddy clappers.'

A smile lit up the flushed face. 'That's what my feller says in bed at night!'

'I dunno what I'm goin' to do with you,' Molly tutted. Then she burst out laughing. 'How come that no matter what we're talking about, we always end up in your bedroom?'

'Because that's where me mind always is, girl! I can't help it if I've got a passionate nature, can I?'

'You could keep it to yerself,' Molly said, linking her arm. 'How about callin' to see how Denis and his mam are?'

'That's a good idea, I could do with a cup of tea, me throat's parched.'

Nellie's hip brushed Molly's as she waddled from side to side. 'As long as we're 'ome in time to make something to eat for my lot . . . hungry buggers they are.'

The front door was wide open at the Latimers' house, so Molly called down the hall, 'Anybody home?'

'Well, what a pleasant surprise! Denis was only talking about you last night, said it was ages since we'd seen you.' Monica Latimer stood aside and beckoned them in. 'He'll go mad when he knows he's missed you, he's taken the children to the matinée. But I'm really pleased to see you.'

'Well we couldn't go to the market without calling,' Molly said over her shoulder as she walked down the hall. 'We often think about yer.' She stood inside the door of the living room and her face showed surprise when she saw a man sitting on the couch with Deborah, the baby, on his lap. 'Oh, yer've got a visitor, Monica, we won't stay.'

'Don't be silly.' Monica pushed her forward. 'James isn't a visitor, he's a friend.'

Molly smiled a greeting but felt like an intruder. Nellie on the other hand had no qualms. 'Hiya, James, nice to meet yer.'

As soon as James smiled, Molly relaxed. He had a mop of thick dark hair, hazel eyes and a strong, square jaw. He would have been handsome but for his nose, which was on the big side. But his eyes were warm and friendly and Molly quickly decided she liked him.

'I've heard such a lot about you two, it's a pleasure to meet you in person,' James said, as Deborah clambered from his lap and made a beeline for Nellie. 'Denis has a very high opinion of you, he says you're his fairy godmothers.'

'Some fairy I am, eh, James?' Nellie chuckled as she swept the little girl up in her arms. 'More like a flamin' elephant! We've just been to the market an' d'yer know what? I couldn't even get a pair of gloves to fit me!'

'You did in the end,' Molly said. 'If yer had a little more patience we wouldn't have had to spend an hour at the ruddy stall.' She turned to Monica. 'This one separated every pair of gloves on the stall, the poor man was nearly tearing his hair out.'

'He didn't have no hair,' Nellie laughed, 'the poor feller was as bald as a billiard ball. At least he was when we left, I can't remember whether he had any hair when we first got there.'

Molly gasped. 'Nellie, the man had a full head of hair!'

'Did he hell's like!' Nellie was tickling Deborah's tummy and the little girl's squeals of delight filled the room. 'Yer want to get yer eyes seen to, girl, I think yer need glasses.'

'There's nothing wrong with—' Molly stopped in mid-sentence and closed her eyes. Would she never learn to recognize when her friend was pulling her leg? She opened her eyes just in time to see Nellie giving James and Monica a broad wink. 'Ay, I saw that, clever clogs!'

Deborah, at nineteen months, was getting too heavy for Nellie, so she put the girl back on James's lap before grinning at Molly. 'Yer might know every big word in the dictionary, girl, but yer still don't know when someone's havin' yer on.'

James was thoroughly enjoying the exchange. 'Denis told

ne about you two, but I thought he was exaggerating. Are ou always like this?'

'It's not me!' Nellie said. 'I'm perfectly normal when I'm ot with me mate here, it's her what eggs me on. She'd argue ith Our Lord, she would.'

Before Molly could reply, Monica stepped in. 'When you wo have finished sparring, will you sit down and I'll make a up of tea.'

'D'yer know, Monica,' Nellie said as she pulled a chair om under the table, 'I thought yer'd never ask.'

'I haven't had the chance to open my mouth!' Monica rinned, finding herself in the same position as Molly often id – being wound up by Nellie. 'You are both crazy.'

'Did yer hear that, James?' Nellie rested her elbows on the able. 'Some friends I've got, eh? Me best mate says I'm a liar n' Monica says I'm two sheets to the wind!'

'They both mean it in the nicest possible way,' James said, smile covering his face. 'I think you and your friend make good comedy act.'

'Me friend's name is Molly, an' I'm Nellie, so now yer now. Tell me, do you always get yer full title, James? If er lived round our way yer'd get Jimmy whether yer liked or not.'

'Nellie, for heaven's sake, don't be so personal!' Molly said. Leave the poor man alone.'

'I don't mind,' James said. 'If you want to call me Jimmy, hat's fine by me, but I usually get me full title, as you call it.'

Nellie fell silent. She was dying to know what he was oing in Monica's house but didn't know how to go about nding out. She thought for a while as she listened to Monica pottering about in the kitchen, then she decided he only way to find out was to ask. 'Are you a relation of Monica's? Brother, cousin?'

'Nellie, you're goin' too far!' Molly felt uncomfortable. Leave him alone and don't be so nosy.'

'It's all right, Molly.' Monica appeared at the kitchen door 'James is a friend, a good friend. He worked with my husban and I've known him a long time.'

'Does that satisfy your curiosity,' James asked in a kindl way, 'or is there anything else you'd like to know?'

'Yeah, there's stacks more I'd like to know!' Nellie laid he palms flat on the table before meeting his eyes. 'I'm not bein nosy just for the sake of it, but because me an' Molly ar interested in Monica and the children; we care about them.

'I know, I've heard how good you've been to them.' Jame pulled on an ear lobe as he looked at Monica. When sh nodded, he went on, 'My wife died in childbirth ten year ago. The baby was stillborn. So I live on my own and believ me, it's a lonely life.'

Molly's heart went out to him. 'That's very sad. And I can imagine it is very lonely for yer. Have you no othe children?'

James shook his head. 'It would have been our first, and when I lost my wife and the baby, I was devastated.'

'Oh, yer would be!' Nellie said, her eyes brimming with tears of sympathy. 'Fate certainly dealt you a cruel blow.'

'For years I went around with anger and hatred in my heart,' James said. 'I kept asking myself why it should happen to me. But time is a great healer. You don't forget – no, you never forget, but the wounds heal.'

'You're a good man, James, I can see that,' Nellie said. 'A kind man and a good man.'

James smiled at her, then at Molly. 'What is it about you two? I set eyes on you for the first time about twenty minutes ago, yet I've told you more than I've ever told anyone, except Monica.'

'Well, ye're both in the same boat, aren't yer?' Molly said. 'Yer've both lost someone yer loved, so yer know what the pain and suffering is like.'

Monica sat down. 'You will get your cup of tea, Nellie,

promise. But first I'd like to clear the air. I hadn't seen ımes since my husband died, until about four months ago. bumped into him at the shops and we talked for a while. He 'as buying his food in to last him for a week, and he told me e does his own cooking and cleaning. I invited him round for cup of tea, and we've been friends ever since. And it's made ıch a difference to both our lives, we no longer feel lost and lone. We've even been to the pictures together a couple of mes, leaving Denis to mind the children.' She waved her rm around the room. 'As you can see, the place has been ecorated since you were last here, all thanks to James.'

'I noticed yer'd gone all posh, but I didn't like sayıg anythin'.' Molly looked around at the pictures hanging n bright walls that had been bare the last time they'd alled, and the ornaments on the mantelpiece and sideoard. 'It looks really nice, yer've done a good job on it, ımes.'

'It was a pleasure to do, gave me something to fill me time ı. It was only by chance I met Monica, but it was a chance ıeeting that changed my life. She's allowed me into her home ɔr which I'm grateful, and the children accept me and treat ıe like one of the family. Before, I had nothing to interest ıe, nothing to look forward to except an empty house full of ıemories.'

Monica rose from her seat. 'I'd better make the tea or Nellie 'ill have me guts for garters.'

Valking down the street arm in arm, Nellie said, 'Yer know, irl, I feel really happy for Monica an' the kids. He's a nashing feller, a real gentleman.'

'And what a difference he's made to the house,' Molly said. Remember the first time we went? It looked poverty-stricken. Now it's as good as yours an' mine.'

'I wonder if anythin' will come of it?' Nellie said.

'I hope so,' Molly answered. 'They're a nice couple and they deserve a bit of happiness after what they've been through. I hasn't half cheered me up, I'm glad we went.'

'I hope they get married.' Nellie nodded her head vigorously, setting her chins bouncing. 'They're both young, an it must be a long time since they—' Nellie gave a cry. 'Wha did yer pinch me arm for?'

'Because I had a feeling we were heading in the directio of the bedroom.'

Chapter Twenty-Seven

'Yer don't know what's goin' to happen next, do yer, girl? Talk about don't blink or yer'll miss it, isn't in it!' There was no smile on Nellie's chubby face as she sat opposite Molly for their elevenses. In fact, smiles and jokes had been in very short supply for weeks now as the two friends, like everyone else up and down the country, were left reeling from the shocks that had come thick and fast in a very short time. First came the surrender of Holland, then the horror of the evacuation of Dunkirk, where many British soldiers lost their lives. Belgium was the next to surrender, and now France had capitulated. The country was stunned. For so long it had been called the phoney war as so little was happening: now they were unprepared for the success of the German army in capturing one country after another with an ease and speed that left people gasping. 'There's only us now,' Nellie went on, putting her cup back in its saucer. 'Just us against Hitler an' the whole of ruddy Europe! Mind you, if he starts his shenanigans with us we'll soon show him what for.'

'We're lucky we've got the sea all around us, Nellie, he wouldn't find us a walk-over, not like the other countries.' Molly sighed. 'I find it hard to believe that it's really happened. All the talk there was about that Maginot line that France had . . . they said no one would ever get through that. They were probably right, too, that's why Hitler didn't even try – he just went round the ruddy thing! He out-smarted the lot of them, but wouldn't yer think the French, or one of our lot, would have had the brains to think of that?'

'I've given up tryin' to figure any of it out, girl.' Nellie's chins wobbled in agreement. 'But there's one thing that's really got me flummoxed. I'll never understand it if I live to be a hundred.'

'What's that, sunshine?'

'Well, d'yer know when the French declared Paris an open city? I couldn't make head nor tail of it, so I asked my feller. An' he said it was to stop the Germans from bombing it. Now I ask yer, if there's a ruddy war on, how can yer say I don't want yer to bomb that so I'm makin' it an open city? Sounds ridiculous to me. I mean, why can't we say to Hitler that we're making Liverpool an open city, so keep yer hands off!'

Molly smiled at her friend's logic. 'I don't know much more than you do, sunshine, but I don't think it means what you think it means. According to Jack, the French were prepared to hand Paris over to the Germans to *save* it from being bombed, like Rotterdam was.'

'Well I never heard anythin' like it in all me born days.' Nellie's face was flushed with temper. 'Yer mean they just handed it to him on a plate, never even put up a fight?'

'Yer can't blame the ordinary French people for it, Nellie, 'cos they didn't have the option. It's the government that makes the decisions, just like ours does. We don't get asked what we want, do we? When one of our lads gets his calling-up papers, he can't say "Oh, I'm sorry, but I really don't want to join the army." He gets a rifle stuck in his hand and he goes where he's sent, like it or lump it.'

'I've got a feelin' in me bones that our Steve will be gettin' his call-up papers soon.' A shiver ran through Nellie's body. 'They'll be conscripting all the young ones, reserved occupation or not.'

Molly had been harbouring the same fear for a while, but she didn't want to upset her friend by voicing it. 'Nobody nows from day to day what's going to happen, sunshine, 'e can only hope for the best. But don't forget there's a ›t worse off than us. Look at all the foreign lads walking round Liverpool looking lost. Yer've only got to walk down Church Street or Lord Street and yer'll pass every nationality nder the sun. French, Dutch, Belgian – you name them an' e've got them here. Poor buggers, can't get back to their ountries and haven't a clue what's happened to their families. o we should be counting our blessings, sunshine, 'cos there's illions would swap places with us if they had the chance.'

'Yeah, what ye're sayin' is true, girl.' Nellie smiled as she ised an arm from the table to give her wrist a resounding ap. 'That's for bein' a moanin' Minnie, Nellie McDonough, behave yerself.'

'How's your Lily gettin' on with that feller?' Molly asked, hanging the conversation to something a bit brighter. 'Is she ill courting?'

'Yer mean Paul? Yeah, he's round nearly every night.' ellie started to chuckle and her whole body shook. 'I'm oin' to leave it for a few months, then if they're still ourtin' I'll ask him if his intentions are honourable.' Her yes screwed up tight, she took a couple of deep breaths to em her laughter, then she said, 'If he says his intentions owards my daughter are serious, I'm goin' to tell him they'll ave to get married around the same time as Jill and Steve.' he noted the surprised expression on Molly's face and went n quickly, 'If that's too soon, I'll give them until your Doreen nd Phil tie the knot. That way, we can use the same hats r all the weddings. We can't waste good money, now can e, girl? It doesn't grow on ruddy trees . . . not around here, nyway, seein' as how we haven't got any trees.'

Molly shook her head. 'Nellie McDonough, you can move om one subject to another quicker than anyone I know. In vo minutes we've gone from Hitler to your Lily getting arried! She's only known the lad five minutes an' yer've got them married off already! If he hears yer talking like tha he'll be showin' a clean pair of heels.'

'He better hadn't, not if he knows what's good for him When Nellie's head went down, her turban slipped forwar to cover her eyes. Pushing it back, she said, 'I've welcome that lad into the family with open arms, waited on him han an' foot and kept a tight rein on me tongue so as not to pu him off. Not one swear-word has left me lips, I haven't tol one dirty joke in front of him, and I'm not havin' all that effor wasted just to have him turn tail and run.'

Molly's imagination was working overtime. 'I can see hin legging it down the street with you in hot pursuit, waving rolling pin in the air.'

'Make it a shotgun, girl, it sounds more dramatic. But i hasn't been easy for me bein' polite all the time, yer knov what my mouth is like, I've no control over it sometimes But I've been like a ruddy angel in front of Paul, honest t God I have.'

Molly smiled. 'A real paragon of virtue, eh, sunshine?'

Nellie frowned. 'What does that mean, girl? Are yer praisin me or insulting me?'

'Praising you, sunshine.'

Nellie pursed her lips and nodded. 'That's all right, then. She folded her arms and hitched up her massive bosom. 'D'ye know, I feel a whole lot better after that little laugh,' she said 'We've been dead bloody miserable lately.'

'Well there hasn't been much to laugh about, has there? I'l be glad when Phil's transferred to a hospital near here, so we can see for ourselves how bad his injuries are. He's very cagey about it in his letters to Doreen and Miss Clegg, and so they think he can't be that bad. But I'm not so sure. If it wasn't anything serious they wouldn't keep him in hospital, they'd have sent him home by now.'

Nellie placed her palms flat on the table and pushed hersel up from the chair. 'Ay, I'm on me way before we start gettin' ll miserable again. Yer can worry until the cows come home, ;irl, but it won't alter anything. So just look on the bright ide.' She waddled towards the door. 'I'll see yer later.'

'Yeah, OK, sunshine.' Molly picked up the two cups. 'I'll ;ive yer a knock when I'm ready to go to the shops.'

Tommy was leaning against the wall by Ginger's front door, iis hands in his trouser pockets. 'Which flicks are we goin' o tomorrow night?'

'I wouldn't mind goin' to the Broadway to see James Cagney and Pat O'Brien in that gangster film.' Ginger's reckled face split into a grin. 'It's always a crackin' picture vhen them two are in it.'

'Yeah, OK, that's all right by me.' Tommy straightened ıp and took his hands from his pockets. Trying to sound asual, he asked, 'Why don't yer ask Rosie if she'd like to ome with us?'

Ginger stepped back, shaking his head. 'Not on yer life! I've ried that once and she turned me down – I'm not stickin' me ieck out again.'

'But yer wouldn't be askin' her to go out with yer on yer ›wn, I'd be with yer! She'll come if the three of us are going.' Tommy lifted his leg and brushed an imaginary speck off his hoe. 'Or don't yer fancy her any more?'

'I fancy her all right, but I don't fancy bein' told no again. Why don't you ask her, she'd probably say yes if you asked.'

'You're the one that fancies her, not me! I only suggested t because I thought if she came out with the two of us, then ou could ask her out one night on her own. I was trying to lo yer a favour.' Tommy hadn't been expecting his friend to efuse, and was at a loss. 'I'll come round with yer if yer ike, for a bit of moral support, but you've got to do the sking.'

Ginger tilted his head and narrowed his eyes. 'You must hink I'm tuppence short of a shilling! You won't ask her yerself 'cos yer haven't got the nerve, so yer want soft lad here to do it.'

'I'm not frightened to ask her! If the day ever comes that I'm afraid of Rosie O'Grady, then I'll eat me flamin' hat!' Tommy squared his shoulders and threw out his chest. 'She's only a flippin' girl!'

'I bet yer any money yer wouldn't have the nerve to ask her.' Ginger threw down the challenge. 'A tanner says yer haven't got the bottle.'

Tommy turned his head from one side to the other, as though somewhere in that silent street lay the solution to his problem. If he refused to pick up Ginger's dare, he'd never live it down. 'OK, let's go.'

'Oh, no,' Ginger said, 'you're the one who's not afraid of her, the big he-man, so it should be easy for yer.' He leant against the wall, a smirk on his face. 'I'll wait here for yer.'

'Ye're like a flippin' big soft kid, you are,' Tommy spluttered. 'All this because I wanted to do yer a favour.'

'Well if yer ask her, an' she says yes, then yer'll have done me a favour, won't yer? And yer'll have won a tanner into the bargain.'

Doing his best to look nonchalant, even though his heart was thudding and he was calling himself all the stupid beggars under the sun for getting himself into this mess, Tommy sauntered away. 'I'll be back in fifteen minutes, so have me tanner ready.'

Rosie opened the door to Tommy's knock. 'Oh, it's yerself, is it? Come on in.'

Tommy's voice, when he could find it, was low and gruff. 'I won't come in, Rosie, I just came round to ask if yer'd like to come to the pictures tomorrow night with me and Ginger.'

Rosie moved to the edge of the top step and met his eyes. 'Is it Ginger who wants me to come but doesn't have the nerve to ask me himself?'

'Er, well, er, no, we'd both like yer to come.' Tommy was hoping the evening dusk would hide his blush. This wasn't vorking out as he'd planned. He was wishing now he'd kept ıis trap shut. 'Yer don't have to if yer don't want to.'

'Sure don't I know that, Tommy Bennett? I'd not be doing ınythin' I didn't want to, and that's the truth of it.' The dusk hat was hiding Tommy's embarrassment also hid the gleam n Rosie's eyes. 'But before I give yer me answer, I'd like to now what brought on this generous offer. Was it Ginger's dea, or yours?'

'I told yer, it was both of us!' Tommy moved uncomfortably rom one foot to the other. 'Look, you obviously don't want to ome, so let's just skip it, eh?'

'Now I haven't said I don't want to go out with you so don't e putting words into me mouth.' Rosie folded her arms and eant against the door jamb. 'So the invitation is from you,' he hesitated just for a second, then added, 'and Ginger?'

'I said that, didn't I?' Tommy was wishing he'd given Ginger the tanner stake money instead of going through this. Hurry up, Rosie, it's late an' I'm up early in the morning.'

Rosie didn't answer right away: she stood tapping a finger n her chin as though giving the invitation some deep thought. Then she smiled and nodded. 'I'll be delighted to come with ou, Tommy, so what time will you and Ginger call for me?'

Oh lord, Tommy groaned inwardly. He could visualize miles and nudges from his nan and grandad, and just wait ıntil the family found out – he'd get his leg pulled soft. But here was no going back on it now, not unless he wanted to nake a laughing-stock of himself. 'We'll pick yer up about even o'clock,' he said grudgingly, 'so will yer be ready, 'cos ve're going to the Broadway.'

'I'll be ready, Tommy.' Rosie put her hand on the door atch. 'Goodnight to yer.' And without further ado she shut he door in his face and skipped down the hall, eager to let Auntie Bridget and Uncle Bob know of the latest development n her plan to snare their grandson.

* * *

Rosie sat in the picture house between Tommy and Ginger. They had insisted on paying for her ticket, putting threepence each towards it. She looked very pretty in a short-sleeved, pale blue dress with a scoop neckline, a nipped-in waist and a flared skirt. Her black hair had been brushed until it shone, and the mass of curls bounced around her face and shoulders when she turned her head to speak to one or the other. When the lights dimmed for the start of the big picture, Tommy caught a movement out of the corner of his eye and nearly gasped aloud when Ginger produced a small box of Cadbury's chocolates from his pocket and placed them on Rosie's lap. Well, the sly beggar, Tommy thought, feeling a pang of jealousy for the second time in his young life. He didn't know it was jealousy of course, he thought it was anger against Ginger for being so underhand. Fancy him doing that without telling him! He'd have gone halves with him to buy it if he'd let on, then it wouldn't have looked as though he was too mean to buy her sweets.

'Oh, thank you Ginger, that's very kind of yer, so it is.' Rosie smiled at Ginger before holding the box towards Tommy. 'See, Tommy, isn't Ginger thoughtful?'

Right at that moment Tommy was wishing he had his fingers round his mate's neck. Fancy showing him up like that, the creep! 'I'll get them next time,' he growled.

Tommy usually enjoyed tough gangster films, but he was too busy watching Ginger to take much notice of what was going on on the screen. Just let him try and hold her hand, he thought, and I'll knock his flipping block off. Stupid nit, he's acting like a lovesick kid. Never once did Tommy question his own feelings. As far as he was concerned he was only protecting Rosie, like his nan would expect him to.

At one point in the film, James Cagney, playing the baddie as usual, pointed a gun at Pat O'Brien's head and brought forth a gasp of horror from Rosie. She covered her face with her hands and cried, 'Ooh, he's a terrible man, so he is! Sure

I'll be having nightmares if I watch any more. Let me know when it's over.'

Tommy was about to tell her not to be daft, it was only a film, but Ginger got there before him. Patting her hand, his voice full of concern, he said, 'Don't worry, I know how it ends. Cagney doesn't shoot him 'cos they've been pals since they were kids together. I'll tell yer when this bit's over.'

Tommy leaned forward to glare at his mate, and if looks could kill Ginger would have been the one to drop down dead and not Pat O'Brien. But Ginger was oblivious to the scowl – he was too busy watching Rosie. And it was at that precise moment that Tommy allowed the truth to enter his mind and it hit him like a sledgehammer. He was jealous! He wasn't trying to do Ginger a favour – he was just using his mate as an excuse to get closer to Rosie! Well, from now on it was every man for himself. Ginger wasn't his mate, he was his rival.

If Tommy's gaze had lingered on Rosie and not Ginger, he might have seen the bright eyes peeping between her fingers. She was enjoying every minute of this. The more restless Tommy became, the happier she was. She didn't care whether James Cagney killed Pat O'Brien or not! At least she would care if it was real: Pat O'Brien seemed like a good, kindly Irishman and she certainly wouldn't wish him any harm. But what was happening on the screen was only make-believe. What was happening in the sixpenny seats in that darkened cinema was real life, and she was relishing every second of it.

The two boys hardly spoke a word to each other on the way home. Rosie chatted to both of them, favouring them equally. And when they stepped on the tram it was silently agreed that they would sit upstairs on the long back seat so neither lad had the advantage of sitting next to Rosie.

Their antics when they alighted from the tram would have

kept Molly and Nellie laughing for weeks. They walked up the street, one either side of Rosie, until they came to the crossroads where she would turn off for home. Ginger had been hoping Tommy would leave them when they passed his house, but no, he was still with them when they reached the turning. 'I'll see Rosie home,' Ginger said, 'you needn't bother.'

'Oh, it's no bother to me.' Tommy stood his ground while Rosie looked from one to the other, trying hard not to laugh. She knew what she wanted all right, but she wasn't going to take sides, not tonight anyway. If Tommy wanted her, it wouldn't do him any harm to have to put up a bit of a fight. 'You buzz off, I'll see she gets home safe.'

Ginger shook his head, equally emphatic in his determination. 'We'll both walk her home. It's not late, and we can have a lie-in tomorrow.'

So the three of them set off, the two lads glowering at each other while Rosie, the little minx, walked with a spring in her step. Her cup of happiness was indeed overflowing.

When Doreen arrived home from work on the Monday night it was to find her mother pacing the floor. Her heart skipped a beat and she knew a moment of fear until she recognized the expression on her mam's face was one of excitement and pleasure. 'Good news, Mam?'

'I'll say!' Molly was grinning from ear to ear. 'It's been quite a day for good news, I can tell yer. But I won't keep you in suspense, so we'll start with yours. Phil's been transferred to Walton Hospital.'

Doreen sat down on the nearest chair, her face white. 'When and how did yer find out?'

'He rang Maisie, said you could go in any time tomorrow morning after ten o'clock. It'll mean yer takin' time off work, but they shouldn't mind under the circumstances.'

'I don't care whether they mind or not!' Doreen didn't know

if she felt like crying or laughing with happiness. 'I'll turn in for two hours and knock off about ten.'

Jill's pretty face was lit up with a smile – she was delighted for her sister. 'It'll be lovely to see Phil again, won't it?'

'You can say that again, our kid!' Doreen hugged herself. 'It's been such a long time, I can't wait to see him.' Then she remembered how vague Phil had been about his injuries and a shadow flitted across her face. 'Mam, will yer come to the hospital with me? I'd be frightened to go on me own for the first time. Just this once, Mam?'

'Of course I'll come with yer, sunshine! I can't wait to see Phil meself, and Miss Clegg will be waiting for news of him. She's like a cat with two tails at the moment.'

'Tell Doreen the rest of the news, Mam,' Jill said. 'It all seems to be happening at once.'

Molly bent down in front of Doreen and smiled into her face. 'Uncle Corker's home. Him and Ellen are getting married on Saturday.'

Doreen's mouth gaped. 'On Saturday?'

Molly nodded. 'Yep! Not much time to prepare, but yer know Uncle Corker, he takes everythin' in his stride. He's got two weeks' shore leave, so after the wedding they'll have a full week to settle down.'

'Are they having a reception after the wedding, Mam?' Jill asked.

'No, there's too many people to ask an' it would cost too much. As Corker said, they can put the money to better use. But we can't let them get married without some sort of party, so I've offered to have one here.'

'But what about food?' Doreen asked. 'With all the rationing it won't be much of a party.'

'I've been told to leave all that to Corker,' Molly said. 'He's wangled quite a lot of stuff from the ship, so we should be all right. An' he's got mates everywhere he can cadge off. If I know Corker, we won't go short of anything.' She met

Doreen's eyes. 'He's asked me to tell Phil that he wants him at his wedding. He said he wants all his friends around him an' he considers Phil one of his friends.'

Tears welled in Doreen's eyes. 'But we don't know what's wrong with Phil, he might not be able to come.'

'Don't start crying before you're hurt, sunshine! Let's wait an' see what tomorrow brings, eh? Things might work out better than you think, please God.'

When Doreen stepped off the bus outside Walton Hospital, her mother was waiting for her outside the gates. They linked arms and set off up the long path. 'I'm shakin' like a leaf, Mam.'

'I know, sunshine, me own tummy feels as though there's thousands of butterflies flying around in it. But keep a stiff upper lip and a smile on yer face. No matter what's wrong with Phil, don't let him see you're worried. Don't forget – no matter what, he's still the same Phil inside.'

Doreen waited in the hall of the hospital while Molly went to the reception area to ask for information. When she came back, she said, 'Come on, let's see if I can remember what the woman told me. She gave me so many turn lefts, turn rights, I couldn't keep up with her. But I know he's on a ward on the first floor, so we'll make our way up the stairs and if we get lost we've got tongues in our heads, we can always stop and ask someone.'

They were walking down a corridor on the first floor, peering into each ward, when Doreen grabbed her mother's arm. 'Mam, look, there's Phil, standing by the door of that ward.' She came to a halt, overcome with fear. 'Oh Mam, he's on crutches.'

'Doreen, yer knew he was on crutches, the lad told yer himself!' Molly drew in breath through clenched teeth. 'Now you just pull yerself together, my girl, for God's sake! If you start crying an' upset him, then so help me I'll wring yer ruddy neck for yer.' She shook her daughter's hand from her arm. 'Now go and give him the biggest kiss yer've ever given him. Let him see how glad yer are to see him.'

'Oh, Mam, yer'll never know how glad I am to see him.' Doreen took to her heels and ran towards the tall, blond man who looked as handsome as when she'd last seen him, even though he was wearing a dressing gown instead of a soldier's uniform. Her arms were outstretched, ready to hug him, but she pulled up sharp a yard from him. 'Oh Phil, it's so good to see yer.' She pointed to the crutches. 'How can I kiss you?'

'With care.' Phil had been dreading this moment. Would Doreen still love him when she knew there was a chance he'd never walk properly again? He dropped his gaze to his right leg which was bent at the knee to keep his foot off the floor. 'The old leg's taken a bit of a battering.'

'It's not your leg I want to kiss, yer daft thing.' Doreen stood on tiptoe and kissed him gently on the lips. 'That will have to do to be going on with.'

'Hey, is this a private conversation or can anyone join in?' Molly came up behind her daughter and smiled at the lad she hoped would one day be a member of her family. 'Phil, sunshine, it's so good to see yer.'

'And you, Mrs B.' Phil smiled. 'Looking forward to this day is the only thing that's kept me going.'

Molly kept the smile firmly on her face to hide the sadness that now weighed on her heart. From a distance he didn't seem to have changed at all, but get close and it was a different story. He wasn't the happy, bright-eyed boy who'd gone off to war. His face was lined, and his smile didn't reach his eyes. This lad's suffering from more than leg wounds, Molly told herself as she asked, 'Can we go anywhere to sit down? Me feet are killing me.'

Phil's eyes went to the door of the ward. 'There's only my bed, if yer don't mind sitting by that. But I've got to warn yer, some of the lads in there have been very badly injured and it might upset yer.'

'Upset me?' Molly's voice rose. 'Soldiers are injured fightin' to protect me and mine, and you think it might upset me? Come on, sunshine, I thought yer knew me better than that.'

Phil was about to tell them to go ahead, but changed his mind. Better to let Doreen see things as they really were. Grimacing with the pain from his injured leg, and also the soreness under his arms caused by the crutches, he moved slowly into the ward and stopped at the second bed on the right. 'There's only one chair, I'm afraid, but you could borrow another from one of the other beds.'

'Where will you sit?' Molly asked. 'You're the invalid, we're only visitors.'

'I'll sit on the edge of the bed, it's more comfortable for me.' Phil handed one of his crutches to Doreen, lowered himself down, then passed her the other. 'Just stand them by the wall, love.'

'You have the chair, Doreen, while I have a chat with a couple of the lads.' Molly grinned. 'See how thoughtful I am, leavin' you two love birds alone? If Nellie was here I'd use a big word like diplomacy, but seein' as she's not, I won't bother.'

This time the smile reached Phil's eyes. 'How is Mrs McDonough?'

'Her usual modest self. She's looking forward to seeing you, everyone in the street is. Especially a little old lady called Victoria Clegg. She's so eager I think she must have a crush on yer. But yer'll see them all on Saturday, God willing.'

'On Saturday?' Phil looked stunned. 'They're not all coming in here on Saturday, are they?'

Molly shook her head as she moved away. 'I'll leave our Doreen to tell yer all about it.'

As soon as her mother left the bedside, Doreen leaned

forward and took one of Phil's hands between hers. 'Now we're on our own, tell me what's bothering yer. An' don't say there isn't anythin' because I know there is.'

Phil didn't answer her question, but asked one of his own. 'What did yer mam mean about Saturday?'

'Uh-uh!' Doreen squeezed his hand. 'You answer my question then I'll fill yer in with all the news from the street.'

His eyes lowered, Phil told her he had been hit by shrapnel at Dunkirk and part of his leg was shattered. The doctors were confident they would be able to remove most of the shrapnel and would try to rebuild his leg. But they wouldn't commit themselves to how successful they'd be. 'So you see,' he said, still reluctant to meet her eyes, 'I don't know how much of a cripple I'll be.'

'Phil, look at me, please?' Doreen begged. 'I'm sorry about your leg, I really am. If you're in pain, I'm sorry, if you end up a cripple, I'll be sorry. But it's you I'm sorry for, not meself! I don't care how or what you are, as long as you love me.'

Hope flared in Phil's eyes as he raised his head. 'You mean you really don't mind? You still love me?'

'Love you? I'm crazy about yer, Phil Bradley, have been since the minute I clapped eyes on yer. And if yer don't tell me soon that you still love me, I'll scream the ward down.'

When Molly approached the bed twenty minutes later she found the young couple holding hands and gazing into each other's eyes. 'Everything in the garden rosy, is it?' she asked, thinking of the two poor lads she'd just been speaking to. One had very bad facial injuries, the sight of which had torn her heart. The other had caught it in the arm and shoulder. Neither of them were Liverpool lads, and they wouldn't be getting many visitors. So she'd promised faithfully to visit them and bring a friend with her to cheer them up. 'What d'yer think of Ellen and Corker gettin' wed, eh, Phil? It'll be knees up and jars out on Saturday night.'

Phil was laughing now. The shadow of doubt had been

lifted and he was feeling light-headed with relief. 'I'd love to be there, but I don't see how I can.'

'You don't have to worry about a thing, sunshine, it's all goin' to be sorted out for yer. Corker's comin' tomorrow to see the doctor, and he's so determined you'll be at his wedding, yer can bet yer life yer'll be there, even if he has to carry yer. All being well, Steve and Tommy are coming to pick you up in a taxi and will bring you back safe and sound when you feel you've had enough.'

Once again Phil's eyes were downcast. 'I'll need a wheel-chair.'

'If yer need a wheelchair, sunshine, then a ruddy wheelchair yer'll have, believe me!' Molly nodded for emphasis. 'Corker will see to that! We're not havin' a wedding without you there, and that's the top and bottom of it.'

Doreen nodded her agreement. 'Yer've got to come to see me in me new dress. It's no good me gettin' all dolled up if you're not there to see me.'

'It would be marvellous to see all the old crowd again.' Phil's voice was thick with emotion. 'I think about them a lot.'

'Well it's only a few more days, so be patient.' Molly gave him a broad wink. 'I'll be in to see yer before then, an' I'll bring Nellie. She's better than any dose of medicine, she'll cheer the lads up.'

Molly gazed around the ward; they were the only visitors and she felt so sorry for the other patients. But come what may, she would keep her promise to come and see them. 'I'll wait in the corridor for yer, Doreen, but don't be too long 'cos yer've got to get back to work. See how many kisses yer can get in in five minutes, OK? An' you take care of yerself, Phil, and keep your chin up. Ta-ra for now.'

With a last look around the ward, Molly walked to the corridor. I'll never moan again, she told herself, not after what I've seen today.

Chapter Twenty-Eight

Saturday dawned bright and clear, not a cloud in the sky. And as the day progressed the sky became more blue, and the narrow street of two-up two-down houses basked in brilliant sunshine. It was a perfect day for a wedding, and Molly said she couldn't make up her mind whether her eyes were dazzled by the sun or the radiance of Corker's smile.

The taxi came at a quarter past one to take the bride and groom to Brougham Terrace register office. Only Molly and Jack accompanied them, to act as witnesses. It was the way Ellen wanted it; no frills and no fuss. And as Corker said, he didn't care if they got married in a coal yard as long as the marriage was official.

The short, impersonal service was conducted by a man wearing a sombre suit and a matching expression on his face. He spoke in a monotonous voice that would have suited a funeral more than a wedding. Even when he pronounced them man and wife, there wasn't a flicker of a smile on his lips. But his demeanour didn't dampen Corker's enthusiasm or his happiness. He placed his huge hands on Ellen's waist, lifted her up as though she were a doll and kissed her soundly on her lips before saying, 'Welcome to my life, Mrs Corkhill.'

Molly wiped a tear from her eye. The man was the size of a bear but as gentle as a lamb.

Walking down the steps of the building, Ellen breathed a sigh of relief. 'Thank goodness that's over, me knees are knockin'.'

'Well yer won't have to go through it again, love.' Corker saw a taxi coming down West Derby Road and stepped into the gutter to flag it down. 'And yer'll soon be back home with all yer family and friends.'

But even Corker wasn't prepared for the welcome awaiting them. All the neighbours were out lining the street on both sides, and they rushed forward when the taxi stopped to shower the newly-weds with confetti. Ellen was startled at first, then emotion brought a lump to her throat. She'd never had the chance to get to know her neighbours when Nobby was at home because nobody liked him. He was a drunkard, always fighting and using foul language, so the neighbours steered clear of him and his family. The only real friend Ellen had in the street during those dark days was Molly, who knew of the terrible life she led. But although the neighbours didn't bother with her, they weren't soft – they knew how she suffered a life of violence and drudgery. And now they were wishing her and Corker all the luck in the world.

Dozens of hands were shaken and kisses bestowed on bride and groom before they could escape into the safety of Molly's house, where family and friends were waiting.

Ellen's fragile composure crumpled when she saw her four children. They were waiting in the hall for their mam and their new dad. Phoebe, Dorothy, Peter and Gordon, all dressed in their new clothes and barely able to contain their excitement. Corker gave a roar of happiness and gathered all four in his arms. 'Hello, me darlings! You're me family now.'

'Uncle Corker,' came the muffled voice of Gordon, the youngest, 'can we call yer Dad now?'

'Go on, yer daft ha'p'orth,' Phoebe said, feeling all grown-up in her new dress and with her long hair tied back with a ribbon, 'yer've just called him Uncle Corker!'

'Well I 'ad to ask, didn't I?'

Corker released them and dropped to his haunches. 'From

now on I am yer dad, an' if anyone says otherwise, give them a fourpenny one from me.'

Molly and Jack had been left standing in the street, and now Molly bawled, 'Ay, come 'ed, let's get in!'

There was a loud cheer as Corker and Ellen entered the crowded room and a surge forward until Corker waved them back. Putting a protective arm across Ellen's shoulders he asked, 'Can we have a bit of hush for a minute, please?' He spied his mother sitting in Jack's chair and pushed Ellen towards her. 'Come on, Ma, give yer son an' yer new daughter-in-law a kiss.'

Tears were streaming down the old lady's face as she struggled to her feet. She took Ellen in her arms and kissed her. 'You look after my son, d'yer hear? He might be the size of a mountain, but he's still my baby.'

There was a loud roar of laughter and Nellie shouted, 'Some baby he is, Mrs Corkhill, unless yer mean a baby elephant.'

Corker was looking round until his eyes lighted on the person he was looking for. Phil was sitting in a wheelchair near the window, the fireguard strategically placed at the side of him to prevent anyone accidentally bumping into his injured leg. 'Come on, Mrs Corkhill, let's welcome home the wounded soldier.'

For the first time in many long months, Phil was at peace with himself. There had been times on that beach at Dunkirk when he thought he'd never see his friends again. Now he was amongst them, he felt he was well and truly home. Doreen was standing beside him, looking very pretty and very proud. He leaned forward to shake the hand of the man he held in such great esteem. 'Congratulations to both of you. May you have a long an' happy marriage.'

Miss Clegg, Bridie and Bob were the next for special treatment, then it turned into a free-for-all, with everyone wanting to add their good wishes. It was half an hour before Molly could restore order. The room was crowded, even though the table had once again been moved up to Nellie's to give more space. 'Yer'll have to spread out,' she said, 'some of yez in the kitchen, the others on the stairs.'

'Hang on a minute!' Nellie, resplendent in her new dress and matching jacket, wasn't about to take second place. It might be Molly's house but Nellie was, after all, one of the hostesses. She hadn't got herself all dolled up like a dog's dinner, suffering agony through the night trying to sleep with dinky curlers in her hair, just to be relegated. 'All the eats are in Ellen's house. The two houses are open, so yer can come an' go as yer please.' She gave a curt nod to Molly and pulled a face that was as expressive as if she'd stuck her tongue out. 'There's plenty to eat an' drink, but don't make pigs of yerselves. And we don't want no rowdiness 'cos don't forget we run respectable houses.'

Molly chuckled before waving her hand to take in all the people watching with interest. 'Folks, in case yer haven't recognized this fine specimen of womanhood, it's me mate, Nellie. Now as you all know, Nellie is usually very quiet and modest, but today she's agreed to come out of her shell and give me a hand. So as my second in command, she'll expect yer to obey her orders. If yer don't, she'll flatten yer.'

'Oh no, girl!' Nellie feigned innocence. 'I won't be hittin' anyone today, not with me glad rags on. I mean, what if I drew blood an' it went all over me new clothes?' Nellie's chins did a quickstep. 'No, any troublemakers will have to answer to my feller. An' yez all know what a terrible temper George has got when he gets his dander up, so don't say yer weren't warned.'

Ruthie was pulling on her mother's skirt. 'Mam, can't I go over for Bella?'

'I'm sorry, sunshine, but the house is bursting at the seams now! She can come over later when all the young ones are going next door. Will that suit yer?'

Ruthie nodded. 'I'll go over an' tell her.'

Steve had his arm around Jill's waist and was steering her towards the door. 'Come on, let's sit on the stairs.'

But his mother had heard and she grabbed his arm. 'Instead of sittin' whispering sweet nothings in each other's ears, why don't yer make yerselves useful? Go next door an' help dish out the eats an' the drinks.'

'Sure, I can make meself useful as well, so I can,' said Rosie. She was perched on the arm of the couch where Bridie and Bob were sitting with Miss Clegg. 'If they come in the front door, I can hand them a plate and a serviette all right. They can fill their plates and go out the back door.'

Corker turned at the sound of the lovely Irish lilt. 'Sweet Rosie O'Grady, prettier than ever. Sure yer'd steal the heart of any man, so yer would. But tell me, has any boy stolen your heart while I've been sailing the seven seas?'

A beaming smile lighting up her beautiful face, Rosie tapped the side of her nose. 'Now that would be telling, Uncle Corker, an' Rosie O'Grady isn't a girl to tell tales.'

Tommy, standing near, felt that familiar pang of jealousy again. Every time he saw her it was the same. He'd tried to create an opportunity to ask her to go out with him, but she didn't give him an opening. She was very offhand with him these days, never passing him any compliments like she used to.

Pretending he didn't care one way or the other, Tommy said to Steve, 'I'll give yer a hand if yer like.'

He was halfway down the hall when the nudges and winks began. There wasn't a soul in the room who didn't know of Rosie's ploy. In fact the only person who wasn't in the know was the lad himself.

The table was laden with food. Molly and Nellie had stayed up until the early hours making trifles and jellies, and they'd been up at the crack of dawn making the sandwiches with the help of the girls. Corker had supplied all the food, including sausage rolls and meat pies which came with the goodwill of a friend who happened to know someone with a bakery. And he'd supplied the barrel of beer and bottles of port and sherry. Molly had been astonished at the sight of it all, and had remarked to Nellie that 'it isn't what yer know, it's who yer know'. To which Nellie had replied, 'Ask no questions, girl, an' yer'll be told no lies.'

'Doesn't the table look grand, indeed?' Rosie said, her eyes wide. 'Sure it's a shame to spoil it, so it is.'

Tommy sidled up to her. 'Yeah, me mam an' Auntie Nellie have done a good job, it looks great.'

Jill gave her brother a dig in the ribs. 'Ay, me and our Doreen did our share.'

Steve grinned. 'If we're all bragging, I may as well add that our Lily gave a hand with the sarnies an' I helped carry the drink.'

Rosie turned a cool eye on Tommy. 'And can I ask what you were doing, Tommy Bennett, while all this to-do was goin' on?'

'I helped Steve carry the drink,' Tommy said, feeling gawky under her gaze, all awkward limbs. 'And then we went to pick Phil up from the hospital.'

Rosie nodded as though satisfied. 'I'll fold the serviettes and you can put them in between the plates. And don't you be dropping any now, 'cos some of them are Auntie Bridget's and she wouldn't be at all happy if any got broken.'

Tommy felt it was time to stick up for himself. 'I think yer forget, Rosie O'Grady, that your auntie Bridget happens to be my nan.'

'Sure I'm not forgettin' that at all.' Rosie folded a paper serviette and handed it to him. 'Isn't the dear woman always singing yer praises?'

They heard a sound in the hallway and Steve said, 'Here's our first customers. You see to the food, Jill, and I'll pour the drinks out.'

The four of them burst out laughing when their first customers turned out to be Ruthie, dragging a very frightened-looking Bella behind her. 'Me mam said it was all right,' Ruthie sounded defiant, 'so can we have somethin' to eat, please?'

'Ruthie, I bet me mam never said anything of the sort,' Jill said, trying to look stern. 'I think you're telling fibs.'

Her sister scowled. 'She would 'ave said it was all right if I could 'ave got near her, but there's that many people in the 'ouse I couldn't even get in the door.'

'Give them plates, Rosie,' Jill said, 'but not the best ones.'

'I'll 'ave two of those,' Ruthie pointed to the trifles, then moved her finger to the stand the jellies were on, 'an' two of those.'

'Don't be greedy, you'll have one of each and some sandwiches.' Jill began to fill the two plates held out to her. 'And you can sit on Mrs Clarke's stairs and eat them.'

Ruthie took the plate before sticking her tongue out. 'She's not Mrs Clarke any more, so there! She's Mrs Corkhill now.'

'Oh dear, I forgot,' Jill said. 'Stupid of me really, 'cos if she was still Mrs Clarke we wouldn't be standing here now.'

And they weren't left standing for long when the trickle of guests began. Doreen and her friend Maureen were the first of the grown-ups, and they filled an extra plate for Phil. After that the foursome were kept on the go, with Tommy taking over the giving-out of the plates while Rosie helped Jill serve the food and Steve was kept busy filling glasses.

It was a happy occasion and everyone was in a cheerful party mood. Especially Tommy. He was like a pup with two tails being able to stand so near Rosie, and he felt a thrill of excitement every time their hands touched accidentally. Lately he'd found himself being drawn towards her, but couldn't have said why. But now he was seeing things he'd never noticed before, and he was captivated by her. The black, finely arched eyebrows that he would swear had never seen a pair of tweezers. The complexion that was flawless, no spots or pimples to mar it. Deep blue eyes that twinkled when she smiled and a tinkling laugh that brought a smile to everyone's face. Why hadn't he seen all these things before? Why were the very things that used to irritate him now drawing him to her, as though a spell had been cast over his heart?

There was a lull as the long queue came to an end and Steve took the opportunity to give Jill a hug and steal a kiss. And the special look that passed between them wasn't lost on Tommy. He gazed at them with envy, wondering how it would feel if Rosie looked at him that way. He was so wrapped up in his thoughts he didn't see Nellie waiting for him to hand a plate over. 'Come on, Tommy! Me tummy's rumbling with ruddy hunger!'

'Sorry, Auntie Nellie, I was miles away.'

'Now don't be shoutin' at him, Auntie Nellie,' Rosie said. 'Sure hasn't he been a grand help to us?' She bestowed upon Tommy a smile that was both coy and teasing, sending his mind whirling, his pulses racing and his tummy doing somersaults.

After Nellie had filled her plate, she ran an eye over the table. 'Not much left now, is there? Why don't yer pile the stuff on to a couple of plates and let any latecomers help themselves? Yer've done very well, the four of yer, so clear the table an' come next door and join the party.'

'We were waiting for the plates to come back so we can wash them,' Jill told her. 'Better get them out of the way and done with.'

'An' I can't just walk away and leave all the drink here, Mam,' Steve said, patting the top of the barrel. 'All the kids in the street would be in, helping themselves.'

Nellie demolished a sausage roll in one mouthful. 'I'll tell yer what,' she said, wiping the back of a hand across her lips. 'I'll get two of the men to carry all the drink next door.

That's where it should be now, anyway! We can't have the men coming in here every time they want a pint, it would be a waste of drinkin' time.'

'You do that, Auntie Nellie,' Rosie said, sliding the remains of a plate of ham sandwiches on to a half-empty plate of cheese ones. 'Jill and Steve can go now, I'll wait for the dirty plates and wash them.'

'I'll stay and help,' Tommy said, for once not caring that his blush reached his forehead. 'We'll do it between us.'

Nellie quickly lowered her eyes. Keep that mouth of yours closed, girl, she told herself. The lad's embarrassed enough without you taking the mickey out of him. 'I'll go an' get it sorted out.' She ran her fingers over her now empty plate and gathered in the crumbs to pop in her mouth. 'It'll take Corker an' Jack to carry that barrel, so I'll send them in.'

Steve didn't wait for his mother's back to disappear before he was around the table and holding Jill tight. 'Mmm, I love you that much, Jill Bennett, I could eat yer.'

'Behave yourself,' Jill laughed nervously, 'we've got an audience.'

'Oh, Rosie and Tommy don't mind.' Steve nuzzled her neck. 'Tommy might pick up a few hints.'

'And what makes you think Tommy needs hints?' Rosie was quick to defend him. 'Sure, I'll bet he's got a few girlfriends of his own on the quiet.'

Tommy opened his mouth, had second thoughts, and closed it again. If he said he had girlfriends then Rosie would chase him if he asked for a date, and if he said he hadn't then Steve would have the last laugh. This was one situation where it was better to say nowt.

Corker and Jack arrived, made two journeys with the drink, and within ten minutes Rosie and Tommy were on their own. Both were ill at ease, so Rosie made a suggestion. 'Tommy, why don't you go next door and collect the empty plates? The sooner they're washed an' out of the way, the sooner we can join the party.'

Tommy gazed into the deep blue eyes and could feel goose-pimples running down his spine. Her cherry-red lips were parted and with a certainty he'd never known before, he knew he wanted his first ever kiss to be with Rosie O'Grady.

They heard footsteps running along the hall and Phoebe and Dorothy came in, their faces aglow. 'Me dad said you two are to go next door.' The pride Phoebe felt at having Corker for a father was written all over her face. 'Our Gordon an' Peter are collectin' the dirty dishes an' me and Dorothy are goin' to wash them.'

'Would yer not be wanting me to give yer a hand?' Rosie asked. 'It's a lot of washing.'

'Uh-uh!' Dorothy smiled. If she'd been asked to wash a mountain of dirty dishes it couldn't diminish the warmth in her heart. 'Me dad said ye're to go now.'

'Well, partner,' Rosie smiled at Tommy, 'we'd better obey orders.'

Tommy was disappointed when the girls put in an appearance: he'd been hoping for some time alone with Rosie so he could pluck up the courage to ask her for a date. But when she called him 'partner', his disappointment turned to joy.

However, his joy was to be short-lived. For as soon as they set foot in the Bennetts' house Rosie left him without a word and went to sit beside Bridie and Bob. The room was alive with chatter and laughter, and with Corker and Jack replenishing the glasses as soon as they were empty, it wasn't long before the party was in full swing.

'Shall I give yez a song?' Nellie moved to the centre of the room. 'I don't mind bein' first turn.'

'Can you leave it for a while, sunshine?' Molly chuckled. 'Say for a couple of hours, when we're all pie-eyed.'

Nellie put a hand where she thought her heart was. 'Honest, girl, yer've cut me to the quick. Here I am, prepared to give my all to stop the party from bein' a flop, and all I get in return is insults.' Her hand went to her forehead now, in a Greta Garbo pose. 'I want to be alone to nurse my wounds.'

Amid hoots of laughter, Molly shouted, 'Nellie McDonough, you are incorrigible.'

Nellie's hand dropped and her eyes narrowed. 'What did you say I am, Molly Bennett?'

'I said, sunshine, that you are incorrigible.'

Nellie's eyes darted around the faces until she spotted George. 'Hey, George, did yer hear what she called me?'

George nodded. 'Yeah, I heard.'

'Well, what are yer goin' to do about it?'

'Why should I do anythin' about it?'

Nellie placed her hands on her ample hips and huffed. 'Are yer a man or a mouse, George McDonough? You're supposed to protect yer wife, not sit there an' let her be insulted.'

It took will-power, but George kept a straight face. 'Who insulted yer, light of my life?'

'This one here!' Nellie jerked a thumb at Molly. 'You heard what she called me.'

'I heard what Molly called yer, but I didn't hear her insult yer. Mind you, I might have heard wrong, so tell me what she said.'

'She said I was incon . . . incom . . . incot . . .' Nellie scratched her head and looked at Molly. 'What did yer say I was, girl?'

'Incorrigible.'

'That's it,' Nellie grinned, 'ye're proper clever with words, you are, girl.' She turned her head and addressed George. 'Is that an insult, or not?'

George shook his head. 'In your case, I'd say it was a compliment.'

Nellie beamed. 'Oh well, that's all right, then. An' for paying me a compliment, Mrs Bennett, I agree not to sing until you're all legless. How about that, eh?'

While the room rang with laughter, Corker noticed that Phil's smile was cut short, to be replaced by a grimace of pain. Not wanting to draw attention, Corker picked up his glass and casually made his way over to the wheelchair. 'Are yer feelin' all right, son? Not tired, are yer?'

Doreen was sitting on the floor at the side of Phil's chair and he now handed her his empty glass. 'Get us a drink of water, love.' He waited until she was out of earshot before answering the big man. 'I had an injection for the pain before I left the hospital, but it's wearing off now and the pain's getting worse.'

'D'yer want us to see about gettin' yer back to the hospital? Me and Jack will take yer.'

'I don't want to go yet, Mr Corkhill, it's so good to be back with all me friends – I'd like to stick it out for another half-hour.'

'I bet Miss Clegg was glad to see yer.'

'That's putting it mildly,' Phil said. 'The boys took me over there first for half an hour and I got more kisses in that short time than I've had in me whole life. And in between the kisses she kept apologizing for that big table shelter she's got in the room.'

Corker laughed. 'She's not the only one who's complaining; me ma and Bridie have done nothing but curse the things. But I'm grateful to Molly for getting them, even if they are a nuisance, 'cos I think they'll have cause to be glad of them when things start hotting up.'

When Phil winced and gripped the arms of the chair, Corker leaned down and said quietly, 'Look, son, there'll be other days – don't push yer luck on yer first day out. There's a taxi coming at nine o'clock, we'll take you back to the hospital then. Me and the wife are going to a small hotel in Mount Pleasant for the night.' The big man grinned and stroked his beard. 'Doesn't that sound good, me an' the wife? It's taken me over twenty years, son, but I made it in the end. And you will, too, I promise yer that. I know yer've had a bad time, I've spoken to some of the lads that were at Dunkirk, but things will get better; just be patient.' He leaned closer to whisper, 'An' yer couldn't get a prettier or nicer girl than Doreen, nor a better family than the Bennetts, they're the salt of the earth. They'll see yer right.'

'I know, I'm very lucky.' Phil smiled when Doreen appeared at his side with a glass of water. 'Mr Corkhill's been tellin' me how lucky I am to have landed a pretty girl like you.'

Doreen smiled and winked. 'I'm the lucky one, Uncle Corker, landing a handsome brute like Phil.'

Ellen turned in her seat to nudge Corker's arm. 'A bit of quiet, please, for the singer.'

Rosie was standing in front of the fireplace, her eyes dancing and a glow lighting up her face. 'This is a special request from Uncle Bob for me auntie Bridie.' She glanced at the couple who had treated her like a daughter since the day she'd arrived from Ireland, and whom she had grown to love dearly. She saw them joining hands and when she began to sing, the emotion she felt came through in her voice.

'I wandered today to the hills, Maggie,
to watch the scene below,
The hills and that creaking old mill, Maggie,
where we used to love, long ago.
The green grass is gone from the hills, Maggie,
where once the da-a-aisies sprung,
But to me you're as fair as you were, Maggie,
when you and I were young.'

There was complete silence as Rosie's clear voice filled the room. And when Molly saw her mother wiping a tear from her eye, she reached for her own hankie. Doreen was gripping Phil's hand, Steve held Jill close, and even the usually undemonstrative George had his arm across Nellie's shoulders as she sniffed and wiped the back of her hand across her nose.

'That was bloody marvellous,' George said, as the thunderous applause died down. 'I've always said that was the best song ever written, and when it's sung by someone with a voice like Rosie's, well, I don't think yer can beat it.'

'I won't beat it,' Corker said, putting his glass down and wiping traces of beer from his moustache, 'but I'll sing a little song especially for our lovely Irish colleen.'

Ellen grabbed his arm. 'Corker, yer can't sing!'

'Love,' he bent to kiss her lips and she flushed with embarrassment, 'I know I'm no Al Jolson, but I'll do me best.'

The big man smoothed his moustache and beard. 'It won't upset me if any of yer want to cover yer ears.' He crossed to where Rosie was standing with a look of delight on her face. 'This is just for you.'

After a cough to clear his throat, Corker began to sing. And to everyone's amazement, his voice wasn't bad at all.

'My wild Irish Rose,
the sweetest flower that grows.
You may search everywhere, but there's none can compare,
with my wild – Irish – Rose.'

After the first verse Bridie joined in, followed by Bob and Molly. And within seconds the rafters were ringing as every single person in the room added their voices. Even Tommy, who didn't know the words, watched his mother's lips and sang with gusto. What did it matter if he was a word or two behind everyone else, when he was enjoying it?

And through it all, Rosie's dancing eyes and laughing face gave meaning to the song.

Ellen was dreading taking leave of her friends. She knew she'd get her leg pulled soft about spending the night in a hotel, and the thought terrified her. She'd slipped home a few times with Corker to make sure the children were all right, and on their last visit they'd said their goodbyes, so she had that part behind her. Now she waited with trepidation for the arrival of the taxi. But much to her relief her fears proved to be groundless, as Phil was the centre of attention, taking everyone's mind off the newly-weds.

His wheelchair was pushed to the side of the taxi and instead of the trouble Steve and Tommy had had getting him out of the chair and into the taxi when they'd brought him home, it proved to be a doddle for Corker. The big man lifted him up in his arms as though he were a mere boy, and placed him with infinite care on the back seat. The wheelchair was folded and placed in the space next to the driver, and the engine roared into life. Then they were returning the waves of their friends and blowing kisses. And so Ellen and Corker started their married life, and Phil returned to the hospital filled with hope that very soon he'd be back home for good.

'Well,' said Molly as the taxi disappeared from view, 'it's been a day and a half today, that's for sure.'

'You sure said a mouthful, girl!' Nellie tucked her arm into her friend's and squeezed. 'I've got a feelin' in me water that we won't have another day like it for a long time. Still, we'll have something nice to look back on.'

Miss Clegg was waiting inside the living-room door. 'You don't mind if I go, do you, Molly? It's been a long day and I'm tired.'

'Of course I don't mind, sunshine! Our Doreen will take yer across an' see ye're safely tucked up in bed.'

'We'll be on our way too, lass,' Bob said, helping Bridie to her feet. 'Old age is creeping up on us, we can't keep up with the young ones like we used to.'

Tommy's face fell. If his grandparents went, so would Rosie. 'Ah, ray, Grandad! It's only half past nine!'

'There's no need to break the party up just because we old

fogeys can't stand the pace,' Bridie said. 'You carry on an' enjoy yourselves, you're only young once.'

Rosie looked disappointed but went to the hall-stand for the coats. When she came back Bridie said, 'There's no need for you to come with us, sweetheart, you stay and enjoy yourself.'

Molly had been quick to note the look on her son's face and she stepped in to help the course of true love. 'You won't have to walk home on yer own, Rosie, our Tommy will take yer.'

'Sure I must be goin' a bit deaf,' Rosie said as she helped Bridie on with her coat. 'I didn't hear Tommy offer.'

Feeling all eyes on him, Tommy said gruffly, 'I'll walk yer home.'

But that wasn't good enough for Rosie. 'Oh, I wouldn't dream of putting yer out, Tommy Bennett! If it's too much trouble then sure, yer don't have to bother.'

'I've said I'll walk yer home, so I'll walk yer home.'

Rosie turned her head so he couldn't see the mischief in her eyes. 'Only if yer really want to, Tommy Bennett.'

'All right then, I want to!'

Nellie leaned closer to Molly. 'Thank God for that! He's too bloody slow to catch cold, is your Tommy. I was just about to give him a kick up the backside.'

Molly put a finger to her lips. 'Shut up an' listen.'

There was no gloating in the smile Rosie bestowed on Tommy, just genuine pleasure. 'Thank yer kindly, Tommy! Sure I'll be happy to let you walk me home, so I will.'

'Don't stay too late, though, sweetheart,' Bridie said. 'It's early Mass in the morning.'

'Sure I'll not be that long after yer, Auntie Bridget. I can hear the sandman calling me already, and it wouldn't do for me to fall asleep and leave poor Tommy to carry me home.'

'It wouldn't be very ladylike to have to be carried home.' Bob kissed her cheek as he passed her on his way to the door.

He turned to wink at Tommy before adding, 'But I think my grandson would be up to the task.'

After moving some of the furniture back into place and clearing away empty glasses, the few people left at the party were too tired to do anything but sit and discuss the events of a day that had been long but well worth while in every respect. Doreen listened and feigned interest, but her heart wasn't in it. So after a while she pleaded tiredness and made her way upstairs, intending to lie on her bed and think of Phil. But sleep came quickly and soon she was lost in a dream where he was holding her in his arms whispering words of love. And next door, where her sister undressed in the darkness, quietly so as not to wake Phoebe or Dorothy, Jill's mind was filled with her own tender thoughts. Steve had managed to get her on her own in the kitchen and she could still feel his arms around her and hear his vow to love her until the end of time.

Rosie was ready to take her leave. 'I'll gladly wash these few glasses for yer, Auntie Molly, before I go.'

Tommy was on his feet, eager to be away. He'd rehearsed what he wanted to say so many times, he was word-perfect. But if she didn't hurry up, he'd lose his nerve.

Molly got to her feet, stretched her arms and yawned. 'No thanks, sunshine, me and Nellie will see to them. I'll see yer to the door.'

'I'll come with yer.' Nellie smoothed the front of her jacket. 'Get a bit of fresh air in me lungs. Me throat's sore with all the singin'.'

Jack chuckled. 'Singing, Nellie? Is that what it was?'

Nellie jerked her head at George. 'Sort him out, will yer?'

Her husband nodded. 'Right away, my pet, right away. Shall I give him a fourpenny one, or shall I strangle him?'

'Whichever is the quietest and the cleanest, 'cos we don't want no mess on me mate's floor.' With that, Nellie hotfooted it down the hall to join Molly at the door. 'Goodnight you two! An' no goin' down the entry, Tommy Bennett, keep to the straight an' narrow, d'yer hear?'

Molly gave her a sharp dig in the ribs. 'For once in yer life, Nellie McDonough, behave yerself and keep yer mind out of the midden.'

'Oh, don't be so bloody miserable, girl, it's only a joke!' Nellie curved a hand round her mouth and bawled, 'Don't do anythin' I wouldn't do!'

Tommy turned his head and called back, 'That gives us a pretty wide scope, Auntie Nellie, 'cos there's not much you wouldn't do.'

Nellie dropped her hand in surprise. 'Well, the cheeky beggar!'

Molly giggled. 'You asked for that, sunshine! My son is growing up and learning fast.'

'Well I hope he doesn't grow up as strait-laced as you, girl, 'cos one in the family is enough.' Nellie gave a low howl of pleasure and slapped an open palm on her forehead. 'I've got just the word for you, girl! It's the only word with more than four letters in that I've ever been able to remember an' I've been waitin' ages for the opportunity to use it. Parsimonious, that's what you are!' Nellie folded her arms, pleased with herself for getting the word right first time.

'Yer cheeky thing!' Molly cried. 'I'm not tight with me money!'

'Who mentioned money?' Nellie sounded surprised. 'I never said yer were tight with money.'

'Parsimonious means a miser, a skinflint.'

'Go 'way! Trust me to get it wrong! Well, it serves me right for bein' so cocky with me best mate.'

'The word yer should have used was *sancti*monious, an' I'm not that, either! Anyway, get in, Nellie, before I clock yer one.' Molly pushed her friend backwards down the hall. 'I'll buy yer a ruddy dictionary for yer next birthday.'

'A fat lot of good that would be! Yer've got to know how to spell a ruddy word before yer can flaming well look it up in a dictionary!'

Tommy heard his mother slam the front door and grinned. 'Me mam and auntie Nellie are a treat when they get going. There's never a dull moment when they're around.'

''Tis lucky yer are with yer family and friends, Tommy,' Rosie said. 'I love every one of them.'

Tommy moved closer, narrowing the distance between them. As they turned the corner of the street, he watched the way Rosie's arm was swinging and moved his in the opposite direction. Pretty soon their hands collided and he was quick to grab hers and held on tight. He was expecting some opposition and when none came he found the courage to ask, 'Will yer come to the pictures with me one night, Rosie?'

'Yer mean with you and Ginger?'

'No, just you an' me.' They were nearing his nan's house now and Tommy was glad to see the place in darkness. He loved his grandparents dearly, but this was one time he didn't want them to put in an appearance. 'Will yer come?'

Rosie had withdrawn her hand and was rummaging in her bag for her front door key. 'Are yer asking if yer can walk out with me, Tommy Bennett? Be my boyfriend?'

Tommy coughed. 'Yes.'

'Then yer'll have to do it proper. Yer can call tomorrow and ask me auntie Bridget for her approval and me uncle Bob for his permission.'

'But they're me nan and grandad!' Tommy croaked. 'I can't ask them, I'd look a right fool!'

'Me mammy always says that if yer want a thing bad enough, then yer should be prepared to fight for it.' Rosie slipped the key in the lock before looking over her shoulder. 'If I'm not worth suffering a little bit of embarrassment for, then yer can't think much of me.'

Tommy kicked the pavement with the toe of his shoe. 'I think it's daft that yer can't make up yer own mind whether yer want to go out with me or not, but I'll come and see me nan tomorrow if it makes yer happy.'

'Oh, I made up me mind a long time ago, Tommy, and the truth of it is I do want to be your girlfriend. And seeing as I have no secrets from me auntie Bridget and me uncle Bob, they know all about it. Sure 'tis over the moon they'll be, all right.' Rosie pushed the door open. 'I'll see yer tomorrow, Tommy.'

'Rosie?'

'Yes, Tommy?'

Tommy screwed his eyes up tight. If he didn't ask, he knew he wouldn't sleep tonight. 'Will yer give us a kiss?'

Rosie turned, and without saying a word she closed her eyes, tipped her head back and puckered her lips.

Tommy looked down on the upturned face and wished he knew what to do. How did you go about kissing a girl? *Just get on with it*, came the answer. Put your lips on hers, just like Clark Gable or Tyrone Power does, and see what happens.

Keeping his arms to his sides, Tommy bent his head and let his lips find Rosie's. Then a thrill of pleasure rippled through his whole body and a million stars seemed to explode in his head like fireworks. The sensation was breathtaking: he felt giddy and thought his legs were going to give out on him.

Rosie was the first to break away, leaving Tommy swaying like a drunken man. 'Goodnight to yer,' Rosie said, her voice low and husky, 'an' I still say, Tommy Bennett, that ye're the finest figure of a man I've ever met in me whole life, so yer are.'

It was the gentle closing of the front door that brought Tommy back to the present. He stood for a moment, disappointed that Rosie had gone without giving him the chance of a second kiss. Then it dawned on him that she had promised to be his girl, so tomorrow they could repeat the performance, and the day after and the day after. He punched the air with his fist and attempted a Charlie Chaplin jump. Then he thrust his hands in his pockets and walked away with a spring in his step and whistling loudly, 'Sweet Rosie O'Grady.'

Standing behind the closed door, Rosie touched her lips lightly, a wide, blissful smile on her face. Sure Tommy had been slow, right enough, there was no getting away from that! She'd had to wait a long time for him to realize what she'd known from the moment she'd set eyes on him – that they were made for each other.

But sure, hadn't it all been worth it in the end?

ES.
H.S.